D1594019

GHOSTLY PRESENTS
FOR YOU TO OPEN—

"A Foreigner's Christmas in China"—Alone and lonely in a foreign land, she was visited by a Christmas Spirit that offered her the greatest gift of all. . . .

"Upon a Midnight Dreary"—Even with the angels on his side, coming up with a real '90s kind of TV screenplay for a holiday special about the birth of Christ was going to be a challenge. . . .

"Merry Christmas, No. 30267"—Tomorrow he might find himself with the devils but tonight his own special Christmas specter would take him on a tour through time he'd never forget. . . .

These are just a few of the seasonal spirits conjured up by masters of fantasy, science fiction, and horror for your holiday entertainment in stories that will have you shivering with delight, fear, or anticipation as you await new visitations by the—

CHRISTMAS
GHOSTS

A Holiday Treasure Trove
of DAW Anthologies:

CHRISTMAS BESTIARY *Edited by Rosalind M. Greenberg and Martin H. Greenberg.* A spellbinding, all-original collection of holiday tales about such legendary creatures as selkies and sea serpents, elves and pixies, a transplanted Yeti, and a blue-nosed reindeer. Join such talents as Jennifer Roberson, Harry Turtledove, Elizabeth Ann Scarborough, Tanya Huff, Jane Yolen, and Alan Dean Foster as they deck the halls and then fill them with as wild a collection of party guests as any fantasy lover could wish for.

ALADDIN: Master of the Lamp *Edited by Mike Resnick and Martin H. Greenberg.* All new stories by such top writers as Jane Yolen, Pat Cadigan, George Alec Effinger, Judith Tarr, David Gerrold, and Katharine Kerr. Wondrous tales which either recount the adventures of Aladdin or tell the stories of other people who gain control of his magical lamp and must then try to outwit the djinn imprisoned in it to gain their wishes without paying the price.

DINOSAUR FANTASTIC *Edited by Mike Resnick and Martin H. Greenberg.* From their native Jurassic landscape to your own backyard, from their ancient mastery of the planet to modern-day curiosities trapped in an age not their own, from the earth-shaking tryannosaur to the sky-soaring pterodactyl, here are unforgettable, all-original tales, some poignant, some humorous, some offering answers to the greatest puzzle of prehistory, but all certain to capture the hearts and imaginations of dinosaur lovers of all ages.

Christmas Ghosts

EDITED BY

Mike Resnick and
Martin H. Greenberg

DAW BOOKS, INC.

DONALD A. WOLLHEIM, FOUNDER

375 Hudson Street, New York, NY 10014

ELIZABETH R. WOLLHEIM

SHEILA E. GILBERT

PUBLISHERS

DAW Book Collectors No. 933.

Supernatural Index

humca

First Printing, November 1993
1 2 3 4 5 6 7 8 9

DAW TRADEMARK REGISTERED
U.S. PAT. OFF. AND FOREIGN COUNTRIES
—MARCA REGISTRADA
HECHO EN U.S.A.

PRINTED IN THE U.S.A.

ACKNOWLEDGMENTS

Introduction © 1993 by Mike Resnick.
Hunger © 1993 by Michelle Sagara.
Merry Christmas, No. 30267 © 1993 by Frank M. Robinson.
The One That Got Away © 1993 by Mark Aronson.
Elephantoms © 1993 by Lawrence Schimel.
A Foreigner's Christmas in China © 1993 by Maureen F. McHugh.
Upon a Midnight Dreary © 1993 by Laura Resnick.
Modern Mansions © 1993 by Barbara Delaplace.
Cadenza © 1993 by Terry McGarry.
Gordian Angel © 1993 by Jack Nimersheim.
The Timbrel Sound of Darkness © 1993 by Kathe Koja and Barry N. Malzberg.
A Prophet for Chanukah © 1993 by Deborah J. Wunder.
Dumb Feast © 1993 by Mercedes Lackey.
Shades of Light and Darkness © 1993 by Josepha Sherman.
The River Lethe Is Made of Tears © 1993 by John Betancourt.
Absent Friends © 1993 by Martha Soukup.
Presentes © 1993 by Nicholas A. DiChario.
Peter's Ghost © 1993 by Marie A. Parsons.
The Case of the Skinflint's Specters © 1993 by Brian M. Thomsen.
Christmas Presence © 1993 by Kate Daniel.
The Ghost of Christmas Scams © 1993 by Lea Hernandez.
Wishbook Days © 1993 by Janni Lee Simner.
Holiday Station © 1993 by Judith Tarr.
State Road © 1993 by Alan Dormire and Robin J. Nakkula.
The Ghosts of Christmas Future © 1993 Dean Wesley Smith.
Three Wishes Before a Fire © 1993 by Kristine Kathryn Rusch.
The Ghost of Christmas Sideways © 1993 by David Gerrold.
The Bear Who Found Christmas © 1993 by Alan Rodgers.

To Carol, as always,

And to absent friends:
Lou Tabakow
Bea Mahaffey
John F. Roy
Stan Vinson

CONTENTS

I love science fiction, I know, the premise goes
which you just naturally connect these in some logical
only they can't it work that...

Take this anthology, for example, the stories
from publishers to editors was clear. Pieces of stories
about the power of Christmas Past Present and Future. The result: an anthology chock-full of tales
essentially concerning truth, and such... In front
of Christmas Past, Present, or Future... and the further they got into Christmas, the better...

Simple, right?...

Except that these writers, scientists, and editors are
dealing with...

"I'll only do it if I can write one. Third of comes
first. Sideways," replied David Gerrold, "so I should
said it just to annoy me." So I don't mind either, of
course, he did...

"I don't care about the power of Christmas," replied Deb Winters, "but I'll write about the ghost of
Christmas." "Sure, so I gave her the piece, too...

Mark Aronson's story came in... "I'm glad you let
me leave Dickens alone," he replied, "and I didn't
really interest me... of these the piece was not the
sides I didn't bring you..." "Okay, so I said... Deb-
ens story, too...

Alan Rodgers heard about the piece and called
me. "I'm working on a kind of unbearable mistletoe
that involves a ghost," he explained... "a mistletoe tale

14

INTRODUCTION

I love science fiction writers: the smaller the box in which you attempt to imprison them, the more vigorously they fight to break free.

Take this anthology, for example. The directive from publisher to editor was clear: a book of stories about the ghosts of Christmas Past, Present, and Future. The invitation from editor to writers was identical; each of them was to do a story about the ghost of Christmas Past, Present, or Future ... and the farther they got from Dickens, the better.

Simple, right?

Except that these are science fiction writers we're dealing with.

"I'll only do it if I can write 'The Ghost of Christmas Sideways,'" replied David Gerrold, who I'm sure said it just to annoy me. So I dared him to, and, of course, he did.

"I don't care about the ghosts of Christmas," replied Deb Wunder, "but I'll write about the Ghost of Chanukah." Sigh. So I gave her the go-ahead.

Mark Aronson's story came in. "I know you said to leave Dickens alone," he replied, "but I thought of a really interesting way of using the material, and besides I didn't believe you." So okay, we've got a Dickens story, too.

Alan Rodgers heard about the book and contacted me. "I'm working on a kind of unclassifiable novelette that involves a ghost," he explained; "it wouldn't take much rewriting to set it at Christmas." So all right, not all the stories have to be classifiable.

Then Brian Thomsen checked in with one of his Mouse Chandler mysteries. I gently pointed out that the last time I read a Mouse Chandler story, it was set ten thousand years in the future and halfway across the galaxy. "So what?" asked Brian with an innocent smile.

Puck Schimel handed in a 400-word vignette. I had asked for 3,000 to 6,000 words. "I know," he said, "but this was exam week at Yale, and besides, Alan told me he was coming in long."

And, of course, in every case, the stories were *good*.

I won't recite my experiences with each author, except to tell you that they're all cut from the same mold. What you hold in your hands is a collection of amazingly varied stories about what I had thought was a rather restrictive seasonal theme. Once again, my hat is off to the men and women who write imaginative literature for a living; they not only manage to please the readers, but to constantly (and pleasantly) surprise this editor.

—*Mike Resnick*

HUNGER

by Michelle Sagara

Fantasy novelist Michelle Sagara was a 1992 Campbell Award nominee.

I used to hate Christmas more than any other time of the year.

Not because of the commercialism. Hell, with my VCR and my laser disk player and my stereo sound system and car and you name it, I'm just as much a consumer as anyone else. And I didn't hate the hypocrisy of it, at least not in the later years, because I understood it. I didn't hate the religious overtones, and I'm not a religious man; I didn't hate the idiotic television specials or the hype or the gathering of the family.

I hated Christmas because every Christmas after my fifth year, I saw her.

Let me tell you about her, really briefly; it'll make the rest of it all make sense. Well, at least I hope it will.

When I was five, I went traveling with my parents. We had three weeks at Christmas—and three weeks, at least to a five-year-old, are forever. My dad didn't like snow much, and he especially didn't like to shovel it, so when we chose a place to travel, we went south. Fifty years ago and more, South America wasn't a really civilized place; hell, in many places it's pretty primitive now. But it had warm weather, and it had lots of people fussing over my dad, which made him

15

happy; it had good food, and Christmas was still celebrated.

Of course, it wasn't Christmas like here, and there wasn't any tree, and there certainly wasn't much in the way of presents—I got more than anyone else—but it was happy enough, until she came to the window of the dining room. The place we stayed, it was a big house—a friend of my dad's owned it, but I don't remember him well. It had lots of servants and lots of land, and huge rooms. I ran about in it for days; I thought I could get lost.

Well, I saw her at the windows of the house while we were eating. She was thin and scrawny, with sun-darkened skin and these wide, night eyes that seemed to open up forever. Her fingers were bony; I remember that because she lifted her hand and touched the glass as if she wanted to reach through it. I called out to her, but she was gone, and I grabbed my mother's hand and dragged her from the table to the window.

"It's nothing," my mother said, and drew me back. But I knew better.

"She's hungry," I said. "It's Christmas." As if those two words meant something, meant anything. I didn't understand the glance that my mother gave my father, but he shook his head: No.

They didn't have doorbells in that huge, old house; they had something that you banged instead, hard. So I knew it was her at the door when I heard that grand brass gong start to hum. I slipped out from under my mother and ran toward the door. Because I knew she was hungry, you see, and it was Christmas, and of course we would feed her.

The servants didn't see it that way though. Neither did our host. To them, she was just another one of the countless beggars that came at inopportune moments. And I even understand it, sometimes—you don't see me giving away all my hard-earned money to every little street urchin with a hand held out.

But whether I understand it or not doesn't matter.

Because I feel it with a five-year-old's shock and anger, after all these years. They drove her *away*. I didn't understand what she was saying, of course, because I didn't know any Spanish back then. But I know now, because I learned enough to try to speak to her later.

I'm hungry. Please. I'm hungry. Like a prayer or a litany. She had a thin, raspy voice: she coughed once or twice although it wasn't cold. I could see her ribs. I could see the manservant shove her, hard, from the open door. Well, I was five and I wasn't too smart then, so I picked up the nearest thing and started hitting him with it and hollering a lot. It was an umbrella, and a five-year-old can't damage more than pride.

And I just kept shouting, "It's Christmas! It's Christmas!" until my mother came to take me away. My father was furious. The host was embarrassed, and made a show of remonstrating the servants, who were only doing their job.

I went back to the table like a mutinous prisoner, and I was stubborn enough that I didn't eat a thing. Not that night, anyway. My mother was angry at my father, that much I remember. Dinner kind of lost its momentum that night because of the tantrum of one half-spoiled boy.

And Christmas lost its magic for that boy.

Maybe it wouldn't have, had she stayed away. Maybe the toys and the food and the lights on the trees would have sucked him right back into family comfort. Maybe Santa's lap and Santa's ear would have encouraged him to feel the exact same way he always had. I'll never know. Because in the winter of my sixth year, tucked under the covers and dreaming of Santa, I heard her tapping at my windows.

Back then, I had my own small room on the second story of our house, and when I heard the tapping at the window, well, I thought it was monsters or something. I gathered my blankets around me like a shield, yanked 'em off the bed, and then trundled, slowly, over to the window.

And I saw her standing there, with her gaunt, darkened cheeks and her wide, wide eyes. She was rapping the glass with her thin, bony fingers and she said the same words over and over again. I think I screamed, because I could see the northern stars blinking right through her, and I knew what that meant, back then.

My mother came first—she always did, moving like a quiet shadow. She asked me what was wrong, and I told her, pointing—and my mother looked at our reflection in my window and shook her head softly. You were having a nightmare, she said. Go back to sleep.

But it's her, I said. It's her, can't you see her? She's dead, Mom, and she's hungry. I don't want her to eat me.

She's not here, she's not dead. Hush. My mother held me in her arms as if she were a strong, old cradle. And I cried. Because over my mother's whispers, I could hear the voice of the hungry girl.

It didn't stop there, of course. Sometime in my teenage years, I stopped being afraid that she would eat me. Instead, I started being afraid I was mad, so I never talked about the dead, starving peasant, and my mom and dad were just as happy to let the matter drop. But she came every Christmas midnight, and stayed for a full twelve days, lingering at the window, begging me to feed her. I even left the table once and threw open the door, but all I got was snow and a gust of wind. She didn't come into the warmth.

She was there every year. Every day. She was there from the minute I went to college to the minute I graduated. She was there when I finally left home, found my wife, and settled down. It wasn't my parents she haunted although they wouldn't feed her. It was me. I even railed against the injustice of it all—*I* was the only person who'd even cared about her that night—but hunger knows no reason, and she came to me.

I have three children—little Joy, Alexander, David. Well, I guess they aren't that little anymore; fact is, they're old enough now that they don't mind being called little. I consider it a miracle that they survived their teenage years—I don't know why God invented teenagers.

But Melissa and I, we had four children. You see that black and white photo in the corner there? That baby was my last child, my little girl. She didn't see three. It's funny, you know. They talk a lot about a mother's grief and a mother's loss, but Melissa said her good-byes maybe a year or two after Mary died, and me—well, I guess I still haven't. It's because I never saw her as a teenager. It's because I can't remember the sleepless nights and the crying and the throwing up.

I just remember the way she used to come and help me work, with her big, serious eyes and her quiet, serious nod. She'd spread the newspapers from here to the kitchen, same as she saw me do with my drafting plans. I had more time with her than I had with the older kids—maybe I made more time—and I used to sit with her on weekends when Melissa did her work. Mary'd sleep in my lap. Draw imaginary faces on my cheek.

I remember what she looked like in the hospital.

But I'm losing the story, about Christmas. Let me get back to it.

Mary died when I was thirty-five. Died in the spring, in a hospital thirty miles north of here. I couldn't believe anything could grow after she died. I hated the sight of all that green. Took it as an insult. Cosmic indifference. Come winter, everything was darker, which suited me best.

We went to Mary's grave—at least I did—once a week or more. Took flowers, little things. Near Christmas, I took a wreath, because she liked to play with them. I've heard all about how people think grave-yards are a waste of space and greenery, and maybe they're right. But I know that having that site, where little Mary rested in the earth, was a boon. I'd come to it weekly like a pilgrim to a shrine, making these little offerings. Talking to her like a crazy person. You don't know what it's like, to lose a child. I hope you never know it.

That Christmas, when I was thirty-six, my regular little visitor came, as usual, at midnight. I wasn't in bed then; Melissa and I were wrapping our presents, late as always, both of us crying and trying not to look at the fireplace, where Mary's little stocking wasn't. Family things like this, they're hard. But sometimes you have to cry or go mad. Melissa's pretty good; she'd rather see me cry than go mad. Most of the time, anyway.

She knew when I heard it, of course. I went stiff and lifted my head, swiveled to look out the window. Melissa couldn't ever see the little ghost, but after she decided I wasn't completely crazy, and that she wasn't going to leave me if the worst thing about me was that I saw ghosts on Christmas, she did her best to be understanding.

The little nameless girl stared right through me, with her wide, hungry eyes. Her lips moved over the same words that she spoke every year. Not for the first time, I wondered when she'd died, and whether it was from starvation. Not for the first time, I wondered where.

But for the first time ever, I wondered if any parent have ever gone to mourn her passing or her death, the way I had with my little Mary. And for the first time, the little ghost girl stopped her endless litany and smiled at me. Smiled, translucent and desperate, standing inches above the untouched snow.

I knew what I had to do then. Wondered why I was so stupid I couldn't have thought of it before.

Melissa and I had the worst fight of our marriage on Christmas Day.

"Can't you just leave it until next year?" She'd shouted, her eyes red, but her tears held in check. "This is the first Christmas we've had to spend without—without Mary. It's the most important time for you to be with the rest of your family."

" 'Lissa," I said, because I knew she was right, but I knew I was right, too. "I've got to do this. That little ghost—"

She snorted, which was about as close to open criticism as she'd come.

"That little girl died somewhere, and I don't think her parents ever found her. She's lost, she's hungry, and she might even be trying to reach them, if they're still alive. Think about how you'd feel. How I'd feel. I have to go."

"Next year," she said, but her voice was softer. "Just wait until next year. Please."

It took me two days to find a flight down south, which meant drawing money out of the savings account. Two days' notice isn't usually enough to get any kind of decent charter. I thought we'd have another blow over that one, but Melissa was silent in a mutinous way.

I thought she'd refuse to take me to the airport, but in the end, she and the kids piled into a car, and I had to explain to my three living children why I was leaving them to go chasing after a ghost they couldn't see. Only Alexander remembers it now; the others were just a little too young or a little too distracted.

When I got onto the plane, I heard the tapping on glass that always came for each of the twelve days of Christmas. The window was a tiny oval plastic pane, and the clouds were streaking past at hundreds of miles per hour, but the little hungry girl was there, with her wide eyes and her voiceless plea. This time

I nodded and watched her face against the background of columned clouds and sunlight.

Well, to make a long story a little bit shorter, I followed her. From the moment we landed, she appeared, floating on air in the arrivals lounge. Thin, scrawny and openly ravenous, she followed me with her eyes, and I followed her with my legs. I didn't bring much in the way of luggage because I thought it'd be best to travel light, so I zipped right out of the airport on her trail.

She walked beside my car, tapping against the smoked glass, begging for food. It was hard to say who was leading who, because I knew where I was going, or at least I thought I did. In retrospect, it was lucky I had her with me, because everything had changed in the years between my five-year-old and thirty-six-year-old selves. The great old manor house that haunted my inner eye was still there—but it wasn't a house anymore, it was a small hotel and, at that, one that had seen better days. There was a paved road leading up to its doors which showed that the place had had money once, and I took the bend slowly, keeping an eye on my little companion.

After I got out of the car, explained what I wanted to four different people in two different languages, and checked into a small room, I found the little girl waiting for me by the window in the dining room. There were two elderly couples in the dining room, so it was quiet, almost austere.

That's where I first saw you, I thought. And I stood up, pushed my chair back, and walked out through the front doors. It didn't surprise me when I found her on the porch, wringing her hands dramatically and begging for food. She didn't need to be dramatic; her arms were almost skeletal, her eyes, sunken disks in the paleness of ghostly skin.

"All right," I said quietly. "Where?"

She started walking, and I started to follow her. All

the while she was chattering away. Food, please. Please, I'm so hungry. Please, feed me.

"I'm not doing this for you," I said. "You're already dead." But I didn't realize, until the words left my mouth, how true both statements were. She stopped her chattering then; left it behind as if she didn't need it anymore.

I must've looked funny, coming away from my car with a shovel and a pick-axe. If I did, no one commented, and I made a note to leave a generous tip if I wasn't interrupted or interrogated. You see, the site that she came to stand on wasn't all that far away from the grounds of the house.

"Did you die here, that night?" I asked her, in between shoveling dirt.

She said, *Feed me, please, I'm so hungry; feed me.* So I didn't ask her any more questions. I just kept upending shovels full of dirt until my back ached with the effort. You'd probably laugh if you knew how shallow the unofficial grave was, but I didn't get as much exercise as I should back then. But I found her, and this was the only Christmas miracle I can think of: The body. It was dead, all right, and it was obviously the same little girl that had plagued my nights for twelve days each year, but it hadn't decayed at all. No smell, no worms, no rot. I thanked God—and I didn't care whose. I hadn't thought much beyond finding the body.

Should've, though, because as it turns out, it was a *long* walk from the hotel to the place that the little ghost began to lead me to. This was the fourth day, and the day was definitely gone. There's really not that much in the way of light along the dirt roads, and the lamp I held didn't help—the body didn't weigh much, but it was really awkward to carry one-handed. I managed.

Funny what runs through a mind in the dark with a small girl's corpse hugged against your chest. Mostly,

I was worried that the police would appear over the horizon, see me with this young girl, and have me shot on sight. I thought I was crazy; I thought I was stupid. But I wouldn't have let go of her; this was as close a chance to peace as I was ever going to get. I kept following her and she kept leading.

And then we found it. An old farm, of sorts. Not a good farm, and not one that was meant to make a lot of money either, although I'll be the first to admit that I'm no judge of farms. There was this little light flickering in the window of the small farmhouse, and as I approached it, I realized that it was candlelight. Someone was awake.

You've never frozen solid in the middle of a dark night with a little girl's ghost nagging you and a little girl's corpse in your arms. I didn't know what to do. I mean, now that I'd found her and brought her home, I wanted to drop her body and run. But she kept on at me, asking for food with her pale thin lips and her wide eyes, and I knew by now that it meant she wasn't quite finished with me. So I did the stupid thing.

I walked up to the closed door of the little house, and I knocked as loudly as I could. After five long minutes, someone answered. She was short, little; she seemed ancient. I thought she was going to drop the candle she was holding when she saw what I was carrying; she went that funny white-green color that people go when they're in shock.

I'm sorry, I said, in my broken Spanish. *I wanted to—*

But I didn't get a chance to mangle the sentence; the little pale ghost suddenly threw herself over the threshold of the house, chattering away—chattering in a child's high, fluting burble. Saying something other than *please feed me* or *I'm so hungry.* She pressed herself tightly against the apron of the old woman.

No one in the world had ever seen the little ghost but me; she'd ruined every Christmas I'd ever had. Except this one. This one was to be the exception.

The old lady looked down at the apparition, and then she did drop the candle. I caught it before it hit the floor, but she didn't seem to notice; her arms were tightly pressed into her granddaughter's shoulders.

No, not her granddaughter.

She began to speak in rapid Spanish, and the girl replied softly, almost soothingly. Neither of them spared a word or glance at me for the better part of an hour, and all I could do was stand and stare. I wondered if Mary'd ever come back this way for me. Shook my head, to clear it—but the thought was so fierce, I've never forgotten it.

It might have been my shaking that caught their attention, either that or it was the fact that dawn seemed ready to clear away the night's ghosts. That included my little tormentor. She came to me first, and reached out softly to touch her own dead cheek. Pulled back at the last minute and shook her head.

Thank you, she said, in toneless but perfect English. *I'm not hungry anymore.* She turned to look back at the old woman who had been her mother. Said something else in Spanish.

Tears were streaming down the old woman's cheeks, and even though my Spanish was bad, I understood what she said back. Her daughter walked into the dawn and vanished like morning mist. And I stood on the porch, with my stiff arms and her daughter's body, waiting for her to say something.

I buried the body on the grounds in front of the house, and made a rough cross to mark the grave. There were other such rough graves, but I didn't ask her and she didn't volunteer. Maybe if we'd spoken the same language, we might have communicated better. But maybe not; I understood what it meant for her to rest a battered old doll against the newly turned earth; I understood what it meant when she whispered to the face of the awkward cross.

In the end, she said "Thank you," and I said,

"You're welcome." There was a lot of pain in her face, but there was a lot of peace there, too. If I could have brought her daughter back to life, I would have. But I would have brought mine back, too. Sometimes you just have to live with your limitations, no matter how much they hurt you.

I gave her all the money I had with me.

I know it's tacky, but she took it. I told her to feed the children, but I didn't ask her what she was going to do with it. I didn't care. I wanted to be back home, with my own family, before the end of Christmas.

On the fifth day, there was no sign of my hungry little ghost. On the sixth, there was nothing either. And on the seventh, while I sat on the plane, tapping my feet and wondering if Melissa had moved all of my things into the guest room, it was blissfully silent.

She met me at the airport, Melissa did. Her face had that searching look to it, and she stared at me for a long time before she hugged me. It was a good hug, a real welcome home.

"I'm free," I told her, and I meant it.

That was thirty years ago, and that was the year that Christmas became a time of peace, rather than a thing to hate or fear. I tell you about it now, because I saw her again—the little ghost girl. Only this time, when she knocked at my window, I wasn't terrified and I wasn't angry. I know what she's trying to tell me this time, though I don't know why she'd be bothered. You'll have to take care of your mother when I'm gone. Yes, she does need taking care of—just not in the obvious ways. Let her talk at you, let her talk to you.

Just like I'm doing now.

I always loved all my kids, and I know that it doesn't have to stop just because one of us is dead.

I love you.

Merry Christmas,
No. 30267

by Frank M. Robinson

Frank M. Robinson is entering his fifth decade as a major science fiction writer.

His nickname was "Scrooge" and even in the eyes of his fellow prisoners, Lyle Jaffery had no redeeming qualities whatsoever. He'd been on death row for 365 days and this night was to be the last night of his life. At five-thirty in the morning, the priest would hear his final confession and walk with him down the short hall to the room where they would strap him in a chair and attach electrodes to his shaved head and legs.

At five-thirty-five he would be a footnote in criminal history and there wasn't a man among the other inmates who didn't think that, at least in his case, justice would have been served.

Short, belligerent, and sly—the kind who never met your eyes when he talked to you, Lyle Jaffery was not a very likable man. He had a rap sheet that would have filled an entire volume of the Encyclopedia Britannica, starting when, as a youngster, he had been given a Daisy repeating BB gun for Christmas and promptly drilled out the left eye of Mrs. Krumpkin's tom cat next door. He married early, became disenchanted with marriage shortly thereafter, and on another Christmas shot his overweight, nagging wife somewhere between the turkey and the pumpkin pie.

27

It took investigators only a few hours to find the insurance policy he'd taken out on his former beloved two months before.

Lyle may not have been very smart, but he was *very* lucky and got off on a technicality. And he considered himself even luckier because he had found a profession. Ever since the gift of the Daisy, he had been overly fond of guns. As much as Lyle loved anything, he loved the smooth, operating qualities of a Beretta and the simple, functional brick form of the Uzi. He became very good at using both and there was no end to those who wanted to hire his talents.

But luck, like love, doesn't last forever. Eventually he was apprehended, convicted, and sentenced to life imprisonment. In the joint, Lyle was assigned to the machine shop where he turned out as fine a one-shot pistol as the guards had ever seen. They discovered it in his cell on still another Christmas when, in a frivolous argument over a pack of cigarettes, Lyle offed the most popular prisoner there—one Steven Marley, young scion of a wealthy family, who was serving a three-year stretch for tax fraud. He had more relatives than Madonna has bras and all of them remembered him at Christmas with boxes of goodies whose contents Steven liberally distributed among the other inmates. His absence was sorely missed.

It was a year later and all Lyle's appeals had failed and no "Save Lyle Jaffery" partisans bundled up in sweaters and watch caps had appeared outside the cold prison walls to wave their signs and shout for his freedom. Lyle huddled, half-asleep, on the end of his bunk reflecting bitterly on his life and feeling the first faint twinges of remorse. It was close to midnight and the cell block was deathly quiet.

Then Lyle jerked completely awake. Even though it was well-lit, the corridor and the cells were filling with a chill fog that had to be coming off the nearby river and the banks through which it flowed. Somewhere in the town a few miles away a church bell struck twelve while far down the corridor, Lyle suddenly heard a clanking sound and a low moaning. He shouted for a guard, but the fog muffled his voice and his cries didn't carry more than a few feet.

The clanking came closer and he shrank back against the concrete block wall, shivering beneath his blankets. Just outside his cell bars the wisps of fog swirled, then gradually coalesced into a roughly human figure of mist and dust that sparkled in the light and solidified into the unmistakable features of Steven Marley, complete with pimply face, cowlick, and the usual apprehensive look in his eyes.

"How's it going, Scrooge," the apparition chirped in Marley's irritating high-pitched voice. "Pretty cold inside here, guess the appropriation never came through for the new heating plant, huh?"

Lyle was amazed by the resemblance to the Marley he remembered and almost embarrassed by the gaping hole in the chest right over the heart. He had been proud of it before—a clean hit—but now he had second thoughts. Marley obviously hadn't come back to thank him for it.

Then he took another look. Draped around Marley's neck and waist and trailing after him down the corridor was what looked like a long iron chain tufted with spreadsheets and Rolodex cards and twined around an occasional laptop.

Lyle pointed. "What the hell's that?"

Marley gave the chain a slight shake.

"That's my penance, Lyle. Have to lug it around for Eternity. You remember, I cooked the books for Daddy's Savings and Loan. Cost the depositors millions." He shook his head. "If only I had known, I would have fixed it so Daddy took the fall." He tried to look fearsome, then gave it up, realizing he was too baby-faced to appear as anything more than petulant. "I'm not here to talk about me, Lyle. I'm here to talk about you." He looked faintly embarrassed. "I'm supposed to be the Ghost of Christmas Past."

"Wise up, stupid," Lyle growled. "Christmas is a week away."

"Technicality," Marley said breezily. He rattled his chains again. "I'm here to give you a chance to repent before you fry, Lyle."

"I ain't ashamed of anything," Lyle said sullenly.

"You never were a quick study," Marley muttered, shaking his head. "Look, enough small talk, Lyle, take my hand and we're outta here."

Marley thrust a pale hand through the bars but Lyle hesitated.

"Aren't you going to open the cell?"

"No need to—it'll be just like in *Terminator* 2. C'mon, let's go."

Lyle took his hand—it was somewhat cold and dry to the touch—and oozed through the bars. The cells and the corridor and the prison itself promptly disappeared and he found himself floating with Marley in a sea of gray.

"Down there," Marley said. "Look familiar?"

"I can't see a thing," Lyle grunted, and then a moment later, of course he could. They were floating over Evanston, Illinois, just north of Chicago. He could make out whitecaps on Lake Michigan off the Northwestern campus and then a little farther south, the home on Seward Street, close by the elevated tracks, where he'd been born and raised. It was a big brick-and-stone house with a huge backyard and an apple tree with a swing suspended from a lower limb. Blackberry bushes almost hid the fence separating the house from Mrs. Krumpkin's small bungalow on the right and the Flohr house on the left.

He used to play with the Flohr brothers, but they had the disadvantage of being bigger than he was which meant there was no way he could bully them. Instead, he'd hung out with the young van Dyke boy down the block who was usually too scared to say no to the various misadventures Lyle suggested.

Lyle had even managed it so it was Mark van Dyke who got sent to juvenile hall instead of himself after they had burglarized a poster shop.

There was a little wisp of smoke coming from the chimney of his house, almost lost in the blowing snow of an early winter. Lyle shivered, then realized in his present condition he really felt neither cold nor warmth.

"We ought to look inside," Marley said. "That's the way the scenario usually goes."

They drifted down toward the rooftop and Lyle closed his eyes as they sank through the asphalt shingles and plywood into the house below. When he opened them again, he was in a large living room that smelled of roast turkey and mincemeat and was fragrant with the odor of pine needles from the Christmas tree in the corner. The top of the tree nearly brushed the ceiling, while the bottom was swathed in an old sheet on which were piles of presents. The tree was decorated with shiny glass ornaments and chains of paper links made from brightly colored drawing paper. Lyle remembered with pride that the paper chains had been his work.

The family was sitting around the dining table finishing the meal before trooping into the living room for the distribution of the presents. His father, heavy-set and florid, with a thick head of black hair just beginning to silver at the temples. His mother, matronly and pink cheeked, with a checkered apron wrapped around her middle.

And finally, his two brothers. David, his father's favorite, at sixteen barrel chested with the build of a high school wrestler, which he was. Later, he would go to college, earn an MBA and become a VP with Bechtel. He would marry and have three kids and live happily ever after, like first sons were supposed to. He would also fall out of touch with Lyle shortly after he married. In fact, Lyle reflected bitterly, David would tell him never to show his face around his house, ever.

Nice bro, Lyle thought, aggrieved—what'd he ever do to him?

Bob was much the same story. A degree in drama from Northwestern, and now a documentary film producer. The only contact he'd had with Lyle after leaving home was an offer to make a film of his life to be shown in high schools as a warning to students who might be headed for a life of crime.

"Okay, Marley, I've seen them," Lyle grumbled. "A bunch of losers. What happens now?"

"Come off it, Lyle, they were all winners. Shows you genetics has a sense of humor." Marley pointed with a bony finger. "The boy at the end of the table. Don't you know him?"

Oh, yeah, the skinny little kid. A shock of red hair and freckles, a torn sweater and thin face smeared with gravy and flecks of cranberry sauce. There was something sly about his expression. Lyle watched while his younger self coated a piece of turkey with pepper and then surreptitiously held it below the table for the family dog, Barney, who would be sick for the rest of the evening. Now the younger Lyle turned his attention to brother David, talking to his father. When David took his hand off the plate holding his half-eaten pie, young Lyle deftly switched plates with his own now empty one.

David glanced back down at his plate, then shot a withering glance at young Lyle, all innocence while he complimented his smiling mother on the pie.

"Smart kid," Lyle said admiringly.

"You're a real dummy," Marley said sharply. "That was when your older brother first started hating you."

Lyle shrugged. "Where's it written that I had to love my brother?"

The family had finished dinner now and were sitting in the living room. His father had knelt down by the tree and had started doling out the presents. Furry slippers for his mother, a cable knit sweater for David, a pair of skis for brother Bob, a pair of pants for him. . . .

Lyle sniffed. Nothing he'd ever wanted. But Christmas had always been like that, his brothers got everything, he got the leavings. . . .

"Jesus, Lyle, turn off the tears," Marley interrupted. "This Christmas, you got exactly what you wanted."

The stack of presents dwindled and the pile of discarded wrapping paper grew to mountainous proportions. Now there was only one present left—a box that was long and thin which his father handed over to the younger Lyle with a wide smile.

"Merry Christmas, son."

The older Lyle watched with growing interest as his younger self tore off the paper and felt his own heart jump in unison with that of himself as a small boy. The Daisy repeating BB gun. Bright and shiny with a hand-carved stock, or at least one that looked like it was.

The boy ran his hands down the barrel, then held the rifle to his eye and aimed at the star on top of the tree.

"Be careful," his mother warned sharply. She'd never wanted him to have it, Lyle thought. If the old lady had had her way, he would've ended up playing with dolls. . . .

"Okay, freeze frame," Marley said. The tableau in the living room obligingly froze with young Lyle still aiming at the star. "This is where it all began."

"All what began?" the older Lyle asked suspiciously.

Marley threw up his hands. "You know what I mean, Scrooge. Do I have to remind you that in five and a half hours you'll be toast?"

The gun, Lyle thought. The beautiful gun that was the first of so many beautiful guns. . . .

"I guess they shouldn't have given me the gun," he said reluctantly.

Marley was exasperated.

"A little more contrition would help, Lyle."

Lyle hung his head. "I wish they'd never given me the gun," he whispered, with what he hoped was the proper amount of regret.

"No wishes," Marley sighed, "that's another story. But I'll see what I can do."

The tableau in the living room suddenly went soft focus and then his father was handing the younger Lyle a different box, one that was shorter and thicker and somewhat heavier.

The boy tore the paper off it and stared in wonder and pride at the A. C. Gilbert chemistry set. It was the exact present he'd been hoping for. . . .

"Okay, that should do it," Lyle yawned. "Drop me off at my apartment, Marley." His future would be different now, he was off the hook—his love affair with guns had never happened. He could hardly wait to be out and about. A six-course meal at Gordon's, the little cocktail waitress he'd been dating—

There was a blur and a brief sensation of cold. It took him one long moment to realize where he was, though the surroundings were certainly familiar enough. The concrete walls, the hard bunk, the slight noises of the other prisoners, the fog in the hallway. . . .

"You lied to me!" Lyle shouted and grabbed for the somber Marley. His hands slipped easily through the mist and fog and he sank back on his bunk, swearing. "What the hell went wrong"

Marley shrugged.

"I said it was your last chance to repent, Lyle. Repentance is good, people like repentance, especially *Him*."

"I thought if I never got the gun . . ."

Marley shook his head.

"You didn't shoot anybody, Lyle. Not this time—it's not your M.O. any more. You were right about that."

"So why the hell am I back here?" Lyle snapped.

Marley casually rearranged his sheet of fog where Lyle's hands had momentarily disturbed it.

"For poisoning your late wife. Plus quite a few others along the way." He looked sympathetic. "It probably all started with the chemistry set."

Damn, Lyle thought.

"You have to repent," Marley repeated, trying to look helpful. "And mean it."

Lyle felt surly.

"What if I don't?"

Marley said nothing, but the hands of the clock on the corridor wall suddenly started to spin around. There was a flash of darkness and Lyle was standing beside himself, watching along with Marley as the priest heard his Confession.

"This is your last chance to confess your sins, my son. What is punished in this world may be forgiven in the next."

The Lyle on the bunk snarled and the priest murmured quietly, then turned as the guard unlocked the cell door. Two more guards were waiting for Lyle in the corridor.

Lyle shivered as he watched himself stumble out into the corridor. The guards held him up all the way to the small execution room, dragging him the last few feet. His other self whimpered as they strapped him in the chair and snapped the buckles around his wrists and tightened the electrodes to his ankle and head.

"You'd better close your eyes for this part," Marley whispered.

Lyle couldn't. Out of the corner of his eye, he watched one of the guards staring at the clock and at the precise moment the hands struck five-thirty, he pulled the switch

There was arcing around the electrodes and the body in the chair struggled against the restraining straps. There was the smell of ozone and the smell of something . . . else. Cooking meat, Lyle decided after a moment. More sparking and then the body went limp in the chair, its eyes as dead and opaque as poached eggs.

Repentance, Lyle thought feverishly. Marley hadn't been kidding, that was the only way out.

"Oh, God, I repent," Lyle murmured in a low voice.

"I can't hear you," Marley said.

"I REPENT!" Lyle shouted. "I REPENT, DAMN IT!"

The scene faded and he was back in his cell, seated on his bunk once again while Marley picked at his nails and studied him for a moment.

"You have to really mean it, Lyle, or otherwise you don't stand a chance in—if you'll pardon the expression—hell. Frankly, the odds are against you. Human nature rarely changes." Marley glanced at the corridor clock. "We're running out of time—"

Lyle hung his head and whispered hoarsely, "I want another chance. Please—give me another chance. I'm . . . sorry for everything I've ever done." He meant every word of it, but then Lyle always meant every word of it at the time he said it. "The least you can do is let me see what Christmas might be like if I . . . changed."

Marley shrugged. "You've got a point. One changed future coming up."

Once again there was a brief moment of blackness and then Lyle was in a living room even larger than that in his father's house. There was a Christmas tree in the corner whose top almost touched the ceiling and a sheet wrapped around the bottom that was piled high with gifts.

"Be a little more quiet, Lyle," a nasal voice said. "You'll wake the kids."

He pinched himself. He could see Marley standing quietly in the corner but there was no other Lyle. Which made sense, the future hadn't happened yet. At least not for him.

"Did you hear me, Lyle?"

He was wrapping a doll and perversely crinkled the paper more than was necessary.

"Sure thing, dear, I'll keep it down."

He tied a ribbon around the doll's waist, then turned to see how lucky he'd been in marriage. It was hard to recognize the cute cocktail waitress with her hair in rollers and wearing a shapeless bathrobe. Unfortunately, the bathrobe couldn't quite disguise the fifty extra pounds she'd put on. And even allowing for the passage of time, she was older than he'd thought. Must've been the lights in the bar. . . .

"I think you could've gotten Johnny something more practical than a BB gun; he could've used some shirts and a sportcoat."

Her voice was petulant, whining, and a part of him realized he had been listening to that voice for at least ten years. It had the same effect on him as pulling his fingernails down a blackboard.

"His birthday's in February; I'll get him the damned clothes then."

There was an added edge to the voice: "Don't forget me dear. I could use a new coat and some shoes as well."

He walked over to put the doll under the tree, pausing at the mantle to glance at the photographs on it. A boy and a girl, both as homely as ditch water. The boy was chubby cheeked with eyes too close together and the girl was thin with stringy hair and a squinty expression on her face. They probably took after her.

The other photo was that of an older man in his office. Expensive suit, an expensive desk, costly paintings on the wall. Her father, not his, that was for sure. He looked around the living room again. Posh house, real elegance. The waitress gig must have been for kicks; he'd married into money.

And then he wondered just how *much* money.

"Dear, the children will be up any moment—you know they always get up early on Christmas morning—and you said you'd fix the lights."

Jesus Christ . . .

"What lights?"

"The tree lights, sweetie. Can't you see where the string is out?"

He had to wrestle the ladder out of the basement and by the time he got it to the living room he'd made up his mind. There were other cocktail waitresses out there, no reason why he had to be stuck with this one. He'd have to take out a policy and he might have to wait a few more months than before, but there was no way he was going to live the rest of his life saddled with her and her two brats.

And just how much *money?*

He'd completely forgotten Marley's ghost in the corner, watching with pained disapproval. He wrapped the new string of lights around the tree, then climbed up the ladder to plug it into the other string already in place.

It wasn't until he was holding the plug between his fingers and pushing it into the end of the other string that he realized the plastic plug had broken and bare wires were touching his fingers. And that he was standing in his bare feet on the iron strapping that ran down the steps of the ladder to reinforce them.

There was a blue arc and a sudden shock and he could sense himself toppling off the ladder, still holding on to the broken plug, his body jerking from the pulse of electricity that flowed through it.

He never heard his wife scream. Nor was he aware of Marley's ghost leaning over his body and shaking his head and murmuring that nobody could change his future unless he repented of the past.

And then the ghost of Steven Marley glanced at the clock on the mantle and smiled faintly.

Five-thirty, it thought with satisfaction. Right on time.

THE ONE THAT GOT AWAY

by Mark Aronson

Mark Aronson is an advertising executive who began writing and selling science fiction during the past 18 months.

I hate my job.

Ebenezer Scrooge is furiously scribbling away at a shabby writing desk in the corner of his threadbare sitting room. Every so often he cackles, and when he does, his breath—you can see his breath, for Scrooge wastes little gold on such luxuries as coal—his breath freezes the meager flame of the stumpy yellow candle he writes by. It shivers, beggared by the concentrated gloom and greed in the thousands of frozen Scroogish droplets.

I hate it.

Scrooge should not be scribbling in his sitting room or anywhere else. At this moment, by the schedule I have created, the schedule I have followed so many times before, Scrooge should be cowering under his bedclothes, vainly snatching at courage, vainly hoping that I am not real.

In a sense, of course, I suppose that I'm not entirely real. How real is a ghost, even the Ghost of Christmas Past? Yet I'm real enough to impel people to action. I have, within the limits of my job description, free will; I can do my job as I see fit. And it's not an easy job, believe me.

I can see Marley pointing at me, grinning with that hideous smile. He knows how much I dislike it when

he removes that bandage and lets his jaw drop. Oh,
sure, it's easy for him to cast stones. All he had to do
was materialize, show himself to Scrooge and mutter
and moan and set the stage for us Ghosts. A lousy
page of dialogue, that's all. And who do you suppose
wrote it? One page, one manifestation—five minutes,
tops!—and he cuts his time in purgatory by a handsome term. And now he has the gall to laugh at me.

It's humiliating. But it's not my fault. I'm really terribly overworked. Anyone examining my situation ob-
jectively would have to agree. I know it isn't simply
envy. I've thought about this a great deal and I'm sure
of it. The other Ghosts really do have it a lot easier.
Though not to hear *them* talk about it. But the facts
are the facts.

Who digs into the background of all those back-
sliders we try to haul back into the light on Christmas
Eve? *I* do. Who flits from month to month and year
to year to find psychologically perfect moments for
malefactors to relive? And perhaps to regret? *I* do.
Greed, lust, envy, sloth—the whole lot—that's what I
get to see.

It's depressing.

And I do it all by myself. It's not as if I had any
help. Not like the Ghost of Christmas Present, for
example. He's got assistants—almost 2,000 and counting, so far. And for what? All he has to do is carry
the client around the here and now and point out
the obvious.

For this he needs 2,000 assistants?

Who softened the client up? Who put the fear of
God into him? Who planted the notion, just on the
horizon of his perception, that this was real and not
just some disturbing dream to tell his therapist about
on Thursday afternoon?

And Mister Christmas-Yet-to-Come—well, give him
credit for imagination. He's the closer, after all, and
has to concoct all those inventively bleak and dreary
what-if futures. If you ask me, he's the only one of us

who has any fun. But that doesn't let him off the hook as far as I'm concerned. After all, he gets to make it all up. He doesn't have to do a lick of research. The client is handed to him, fearful and trembling—cowering, too, nine times out of ten—ready to believe, ready to do anything to avoid whatever delightfully grisly yet not inevitable future he knows he's going to see.

He doesn't even have to say anything. Gestures suffice. More than once, I've watched clients pass out cold the moment Mr. Future extends that bony hand of his out from under his robe. Why? Because they were well prepared, that's why. By me.

It's really too bad. I was rather looking forward to Scrooge's reaction at that stage. My bet was that a hard case like him would tough it out with little more than a good cringe and a couple of whimpers. Now, of course, all bets are off.

It all started off quite well. I had done my homework on Scrooge. He really is a textbook case, you know—a loner, abusive family, low self-esteem, deep-seated feelings of insecurity rooted in successive abandonments as a child. There was a wealth of choices, an embarrassment of riches, negative-role-model-wise. It should have been a cinch.

So I assembled my data, pinpointed the most poignant moments in Scrooge's past: His formative moments, all those moments which taken together plainly turned him from a potential nice guy into the grasping, unpleasant, mean—and, admittedly, highly successful—gnome of business he had become.

According to the profile, he was a sitting duck. And for a while, everything went smoothly.

The opening bit, with Marley manifesting himself on Scrooge's door knocker, was a nice touch that set up Marley's walk-on perfectly. It didn't hurt that Scrooge was under the weather, thanks to the merest touch of food poisoning arranged by yours truly. (Although considering the condition of the kitchen in that urinous tavern where Scrooge insists on dining, it's a wonder I had to do anything at all.)

So when I appeared, Scrooge was already just the tiniest bit out of control, just a little off balance. His defenses were down, and he was open to suggestion.

Please understand that in the early stages of the game, my only goal is to subtly misdirect the client's attention while engaging his imagination. I want him to gradually suspend his disbelief in the supernatural, and I have found that small steps are sure steps. It's very important to begin with something slight, something that can be explained away—nervously, perhaps, but rationally—thinking it nothing more than, say, a blot of mustard or a bit of undigested beef, as I believe Scrooge put it at the time.

Then, as the client's belief in the patently unbelievable grows (for we tend to trust the reports of our own eyes and senses), it becomes possible to take larger and larger steps, until at last we reach the flights of fancy engaged in by the Ghost of Christmas Yet to Come. But let me remind you that I am the one who does all the careful groundwork, who makes it possible for the GOCYTC to reduce the client to a state of blubbering repentance.

For which he takes full credit, by the way. Irksome. Very irksome.

The first two scenarios proceeded very smoothly, almost perfectly according to plan. I generally begin with an incident or two in the client's childhood, and Scrooge's case was no exception. For as much as a person claims to remember about childhood, seeing it again in full color—reliving it, even as an observer—is quite a shock. And as we traveled through the countryside to the dingy boarding school where Scrooge had passed much of his boyhood, we were able to smell the cider steeping in the nearby farms, feel the bite of the wind and the weakness of the winter sun.

I watched Scrooge taking all of this in and felt a

certain degree of satisfaction. He reacted with wonder and a hint of regret to see himself there, all alone and unclaimed for the Christmas holiday, filling himself with fantastic and comforting visions from the escapist literature he was fond of as a child. I saw the ghost of a smile—pardon the play on words—at the corner of his mouth, surely the first smile anyone had seen on Scrooge's face besides that reserved for business rivals who had gone down flaming in bankruptcy.

All very well and good. So on to the next scenario—same place, somewhat later in childhood. His sister Fan had arrived to bring him home at last, and it was my thought to remind him that somewhere in the ashes of his heart lay a few dim embers of human feeling.

"Always a delicate creature, whom a breath might have withered," I said. "But she had a large heart!"

"So she had," cried Scrooge. "You're right. I'll not gainsay it, Spirit. But she had a big mouth as well!"

I was startled. With my prompt, Scrooge should by all rights have been led to reflect on his poor treatment of Fan's son, his nephew, whom he would barely acknowledge in the streets of London. He should have felt a pang of guilt about the boy, which should have led him well along the path to self-examination. His response threw me off stride.

"A big mouth?"

"Yes, a big mouth," he replied waspishly. "Look at her—even then inclined toward expensive illness. For her frailty she bears no responsibility, but for her disposition . . . look at her! Dragging me to the carriage, prattling on about Father's change of heart! Did she ask me whether I cared? Did she ask me but one time whether I might rather ponder the winter solitude in the familiarity of my rooms at that school, than return to a home I barely knew? Did she consider, in her youthful zeal, that I had come to enjoy my own company, and that she might do well to keep her own counsel and leave me to keep my own?

"No, she did not, not once. And I was left with the choice of enduring her constant chatter or of rudely silencing her. And despite what you may have heard of me, Spirit, rudeness is not within my nature. It well bespeaks a man of business to cultivate an efficiency of deportment which others may interpret as rudeness; that, sir, is their concern. Mine is the conduct of my business, and I am grateful to you for illuminating one of the reasons I chose my present course."

I should have aborted the mission. I have that power. I have already told you that I can do my job as I see fit, and I can reset to zero, so to speak, if a situation begins to get out of control. It is a discretionary power I had never felt the need to exercise, and I suppose it was my own confidence in my abilities— all right, call it arrogance—that kept me from exercising it this time. That and the fact that Marley would never let me hear the end of it.

I decided that nothing further could be salvaged from this situation, and so proceeded to the next level of the game.

There we were at the warehouse of jolly Mr. Fezziwig. Once again Scrooge showed signs of recognition and perhaps even moments—very brief—of joy. Very well, I thought, if we can't use guilt, we'll go for the gusto.

In Scrooge's life, his apprenticeship at Fezziwig's was an important plateau. I was hoping that re-exposure to this early, positive role model would remind him that there is more to life than acquisition, that even a man of business—even a successful man like Fezziwig—could still find the time and wherewithal to bring joy into the hearts of his staff and associates. And this particular evening, one of Fezziwig's memorable Christmas Eve parties, was sure to provide a perfect example.

Scrooge watched with a certain hunger as Fezziwig closed his business down for the Christmas holiday—

watched as the shutters were put up, the furniture moved, the fiddle tuned, and the punchbowls filled.

As the party progressed, I felt a lightening of my own spirit (if a Spirit may be said to have a spirit). This, I was sure, would go well. This would make up for Scrooge's less than satisfactory response to my efforts thus far.

Yes, yes, I should have been more careful, more observant. I shouldn't have taken anything for granted. But I was intoxicated by the joy of the party, much as I had hoped Scrooge would be. I began to enjoy myself.

I told you at the beginning that I hate my job. You may have noticed that it isn't this part of it that I hate. Even when things are not going as well as they might, this part, the execution of the plan itself, is the part I enjoy. It's the grinding research that I hate. It's the brutal schedule, the overbooking.

Christmas comes but once a year? Is that what you're thinking? Not for me. Do you truly think that highly trained resources like the three of us devote all of our attention to a single individual on Christmas Eve? What a terrible way to run a business!

All right, it's not a business, but the same principles apply.

Any given moment can be Christmas for me. I am a Spirit. I am no longer bound by mortal rules of time. I have my list, and I check it twice, but only the naughty appear on it, never the nice. It is a nonstop job to run through the beads of time to find the last possible Christmas to redeem a client, and chase back through his past (or her past—there are, alas, far more women clients on my list than there once were) to find the proper moments to carry them back to.

And it's all last-minute work. The Folks Who Run Things up here take the concept of free will quite seriously, despite the posturings of some of their more vocal representatives on Earth. I have to wait until the last possible moment before intervening, and I confess that my would-be clients sometimes surprise me by making it back onto a decent path on their own.

But if they don't, they're mine. And that's when the tedium begins. See, time, at least the way humans experience it, has no existence of its own. Your path through time is a pattern created by the decisions you make. Try to see it the way I do: Imagine an endless plain covered with beads; make them any color you want. Your life is a string attached to a needle. In the beginning, you can pick a point on the horizon and thread yourself through the beads that lead directly to it. Nice and simple. Direct. Some people lead their lives that way, but most take detours. Each bead is a decision, and some of the decisions you make take you nearer to or farther from your original goals. Sometimes you wind up in totally unexpected places.

But as the string grows longer, your options become fewer. Where you could have picked any point on the horizon in the beginning, your scope becomes more limited as you leave whole sectors of beads—of decisions, possibilities—untouched and untouchable.

My job is to find you as you have but one chance left to make a good choice, and persuade you to take it. Think of those millions of beads, think of the fragility of the thread, think of the impossibly vast number of decisions you have made and have yet to make, and consider what my job must be like.

I doubt you would like that part of it. I know I don't. And I must even consider the possibility that this job is not a reward for a life well lived, but a punishment.

Whose servant am I really? That's a question I can't seem to get anyone to answer.

With such considerations cluttering my mind, perhaps it's no surprise that my attention wandered. Still, by my own lights, I was doing the best job I knew how to do. So I focused on the situation at hand, vowing to make up for previous errors.

In due time, the revelries in Fezziwig's warehouse

mellowed and dimmed, even as did the candles that lit the room. Fezziwig's loud good cheer echoed through the streets to accompany his departing guests, and they responded in kind with shouts of heartfelt thanks and good wishes for the coming year.

Judging this to be the perfect psychological moment, for Scrooge plainly was reliving this scene internally even as he watched it, I ventured an observation.

"A small matter," I said, "to make these silly folks so full of gratitude."

"Small!" echoed Scrooge, clearly preoccupied.

"Why! Is it not?" I asked. "He has spent but a few pounds of your mortal money: three or four, perhaps. Is that so much that he deserves this praise?"

"It isn't that," said Scrooge. "It isn't that, Spirit. Well could old Fezziwig afford to be jolly. Well could he afford such merriment, and more, much more. For the money he spent on good cheer, and, for that matter, on many less cheerful but more profitable endeavors, was not his to spend. It was money that entered through yonder doors, but never stopped to visit the pages of the ledgers kept by Dick Wilkins and me. If Fezziwig was merry, it had more to do with a second set of account books kept by him alone, never seen by and certainly never shared with the shareholders who were the foundation and lifeblood of his enterprise.

"And so I must once again thank you, Spirit, for reminding me of another early example by which I have shaped my life. Business is to me a sacred trust, and never a laughing matter. Do my practices seem overly sharp? My dealings too clever? Do I seek every possible advantage before entering into negotiations and striking a deal? Yes, yes, and yes! For as a capitalist—how nobly rings the name—I am responsible for the capital not only of my firm, but of those many individuals whose faith in my acumen gives me my bargaining power. I am as responsible to them as to myself. To cheat them would be to cheat myself—an absurdity! Let those who speak against me produce proof. There is none!

"Grasping? Greedy? Penurious? Me? Bah! Humbug! The empty words of the envious. I am a model of probity, as Fezziwig was not—a practical man of business. And those who do not like me as I am must look to their own faults for explanation."

Scrooge had drawn himself to his full height, and despite the fact that his clothing consisted of nothing more than a nightshirt and nightcap, he presented the very picture of wounded dignity.

How was I to know that happy old Fezziwig was an embezzler? It's hard enough to trek through the world-lines of my clients; how can I possibly do the same for the people they encounter?

I was in trouble; there could be no doubt of that. And I had a difficult decision to make: Continue or abort? Please understand that my ability to terminate an encounter is not absolute. If I left you with that impression, I apologize. For if I play out my last scheduled scenario, as I was about to do with Scrooge, I am forced to turn the client over to the Ghost of Christmas Present (or to one of his numberless assistants, at any rate), no matter how ill prepared he might be.

I decided to gamble on the final scenario. It was, after all, the first I had investigated, and by far the most powerful. In fact, early in the planning process, I had given serious thought to making this, Scrooge's last encounter with the one woman to whom he professed love, the only scene I would force him to relive.

Personal pride prevailed. A single scene seemed to be such a slipshod effort. Surely more material would be more convincing—if not to Scrooge, then at least to those whom I suspect are looking over my insubstantial shoulder at all times.

Doubtless—doubtless!—that single, potent moment would mellow old Scrooge as the others could not. For while there are many who survive their heart's first breaking, who can survive that same experience twice?

And so I transported us to the secluded bower where a somewhat older and world-worn Scrooge conversed with Belle, the woman with whom he had long intended to spend the rest of his life.

Belle had harsh words for Scrooge, words all the more harsh because they were uttered in sadness and gentle regret. She alluded to his singleminded pursuit of the golden idol, as she put it. How his simple love and hopeful outlook had become tainted by the pollution of business. How he had changed, how they had grown apart.

"That which promised happiness when we were one in heart, is fraught with misery now that we are two. How often and how keenly I have thought of this, I will not say. It is enough that I *have* thought of it, and can release you."

"Have I ever sought release?" asked the young Scrooge.

"In words. No. Never."

"In what, then?"

"In a changed nature; in an altered spirit; in another atmosphere of life; another Hope as its great end. In everything that made my love of any worth or value in your sight."

I observed the latter-day Scrooge most carefully during this exchange. He was riveted to the vision. His mouth twitched, as if he had played this scene over and over again from memory through the years.

"You may—the memory of what is past half makes me hope you will—have pain in this. A very, very brief time, and you will dismiss the recollection of it, gladly, as an unprofitable dream from which it happened well that you awoke. May you be happy in the life you have chosen!"

She left him; and they parted.

I turned to Scrooge, expecting, if not a tear, then

at the very least a dawning realization of all he had cast aside in reaching this point in his life.

"Spirit!" said Scrooge, "show me no more!"

I breathed a sigh of relief. It was working!

"No more!" cried Scrooge. "No more. I don't wish to see it. Show me no more! The betrayal! The final betrayal! I learned well from the treachery inflicted upon me by that woman. Why do you delight to torture me with the one moment of my life that will ever be with me?"

This was not as it should be. Despair, yes, but a despair that quickly turned to anger. My last hope was turning to dust.

"Spirit! I know not how we came to this place, but I would show you another, not far removed. Can you take us there?"

You understand, it's not as if I can change my plans at a moment's notice. Every instant I visit with a client is rigorously programmed. I can't just gad through the space-time continuum like some relativistic surfer, skimming from one event to the next. But Scrooge insisted, and as he was able to pinpoint both the time and the place, I acceded.

I was desperate, grasping at straws. I had taken my best shot, and missed. I don't know how or why it happened; I will probably never know. And now I was operating in completely unknown territory.

Following Scrooge's directions, we went back in time three weeks and across the fields to a village not far from the glade where Belle had taken final leave of Scrooge. We were in a back guest room above a comfortable inn.

"Behold!" said Scrooge with bitterness. "Behold the inconstancy of the so-called human condition. Behold the high regard accorded the love of the naive!"

I beheld. And what I beheld nailed shut the door on any hope I had of escaping my predicament. For there lay Belle in the arms of another, conversing between unabashed expressions of affection.

"And how will you tell him?" asked Belle's lover, for so he must be. "Will you be direct? Will you tell him the simple truth about us?"

Belle laughed. "Why must I tell him at all?"

"Belle . . . if we are to marry . . ."

"Silly dear! Of course I'll tell him. In my own time, in my own way. He has grown too serious; he's no fun anymore. Not as much fun as you are!"

She . . . well, never mind what she did.

"I'll have to find a way to make it sound as if it's all his fault," she continued, pondering. "I'll have to come off as the noble, injured victim who is breaking it off for their mutual benefit. Let's see . . ."

"You're terribly clever, sweet. You'll think of something."

They both laughed.

Scrooge was not laughing. He glared at me.

"It was years before I discovered her treachery, quite by accident. Years in which I pined, in which I sought desperately to find wherein I had erred to lose the love of such a one. And when the truth presented itself to me, I resolved to devote the energy of my affection to the honest pursuit of business. You cannot be betrayed by a balance sheet. And unlike love, success is always rewarded, with grudging respect at least.

"I am again in your debt, Spirit, for confirming within me the simple, honest virtues of the world of business that I have always lived by, and which I will now pursue with undiminished—indeed, strengthened!—vigor. Let us return at once to my modest home, for if, as you say, I am to have further Ghostly visitors, I must prepare to greet them.

"I confess to you, Spirit, that before you came to me and showed me this long night's wonders, I had actually considered modifying some of my principles. Contribute to charity, perhaps, or even promote that lazy clerk of mine, Cratchit. But you have showed me the value of sticking to one's credo. What worked for me will work for others. Believe in yourself! Trust no others! Up by your own bootstraps and scorn the treacherous hand offered in aid; it will come asking for recompense many times over!"

He actually grabbed my hand and shook it mightily, wishing me a Merry Christmas.

And so we returned.

And there sits Scrooge, writing in outline form the further turning points in his life, preparing for the Ghost of Christmas Present. He's having a wonderful time.

The bells are pealing, and I tremble for my own future. One thing is certain, and it is small consolation. This night, for once, I do not envy my two associates their jobs.

Perhaps it is not Scrooge who has been tested this sad Christmas Eve. Perhaps it is I who have been tested and found wanting. If so, I fervently resolve to do better. I resolve to mend my slipshod ways, to become a better Ghost of Christmas Past—as good a Ghost as this old world ever knew.

But let my lesson be yours as well. For when your turn comes—and it will—I will be far more diligent with your case than I was with Scrooge's. And this Christmas Eve, as you hear the bells toll, know that I am watching and waiting.

ELEPHANTOMS

by Lawrence Schimel

*Lawrence Schimel, though still a student at Yale, has
more than a dozen science fiction stories to his credit.*

A bright star twinkled low over Kilmajaro, calling
him north.

As he walked, he came across three elephants between the river and the road, pulling apart the skeleton of a fourth. Their action was not unusual; though
he did not know its purpose, he knew elephants would
pull apart any elephant skeleton they came across. But
the elephants themselves did not belong together—an
old bull with broken tusks, a younger bull in musth,
the dark ichor thick above his eyes, and a small calf
who looked too young to be weaned from its mother—
and for that reason he stopped to watch them.

Their skins were all the same light gray, pale as
mud baked white by the sun.

The old bull picked up a leg bone and lumbered
west into the drylands. Trees grew up around him at
every step, turning the desert green. Soon they had
grown so thick the elephant was lost to sight.

The younger bull took a rib and walked back along
the road into his village, which he had just left. It
walked past the houses of all the warriors to the house
where his wife and children were sleeping and disappeared behind the side.

The calf picked up a tusk in his trunk, and walking
backward, dragged it to the east. With each step he
grew larger, his burden easier. Soon he was able to

lift the tusk off the ground. He lifted it with his trunk and turned around, to walk proudly into the future. A man stepped out from the edge of the forest and shot him. The poacher took the tusk from his trunk, then cut off his own two tusks, which had grown large as he walked. There were no elephants left to separate his bones; his soul was forced to linger in pain, and watch as the forest was razed by men.

He looked down; the skeleton before him was still whole. The elephants had been ghosts. They could not lift the heavy bones. If the bones were not separated, this elephant, too, would become a ghost yearning for peace.

The king of the Masaai scattered the gold he carried, as he separated the elephant's bones.

When he was done, he picked up a tusk and walked in the fourth and last direction, carrying a gift of ivory and wisdom to give to the child newborn in a manger.

A FOREIGNER'S CHRISTMAS IN CHINA

Maureen F. McHugh

Maureen McHugh is the author of two science fiction novels and a handful of powerful short stories.

I don't usually drink, maybe a couple of times a year. I warn you, a couple of wine coolers, a little sleep deprivation at a convention like this, and I'll bore anyone to death. But since everybody is telling about weird experiences. . . . My one paranormal experience was in China, and it could have been a stress reaction.

Let me preface my story by stating that in my estimation the People's Republic of China is not a particularly mystical place. Granted, I came to China because I thought it would change me, would make me into something more than I had been before, but I foresaw this change to be purely an experience of character. I wanted experience to make me wise. *Not* spiritual wisdom, not the new age *Tao of Kites* and union of souls pseudo-wisdom. I wasn't looking for ancient Eastern secrets; I'm biased against most of that kind of thing anyway. And in my limited experience, mysticism and spiritualism seem more particularly debased in China than they are even in the U.S. When any of my many Chinese friends launched into a description of paranormal experiences, I got the same uncomfortable feeling I do when someone in the U.S. tells me about the time they saw a UFO. I nodded and tried to appear to take them very seriously, because they were usually confiding something they felt slightly embarrassed about, but which was very real to them, namely about miracles of kung fu and the magic psychic healing powers of people that a friend of theirs knew.

I do try to keep an open mind. For example there's a lot of herbal medicine in China, and although my preference is for antibiotics I am willing to concede that seven thousand years of pharmaceutical experience has probably discovered things that Eli Lily hasn't yet had time to research and get past the FDA. So when my translator came down with persistent diarrhea I was interested in his remedy, a kind of tea brewed out of something that the college infirmary gave him that looked more like tree bark and grass clippings than it did my estimation of controlled medication. But Xiao Wong was 5'9" and 120 odd pounds and he didn't haven't enough body mass to lose much weight or fluid, so when three days later he was still excusing himself abruptly in the middle of conversations I gave him two days' worth of little white pills out of my own horde of prescription medication, and his problem cleared up within six hours and did not manifest itself again.

So let me begin by way of apology by saying that I do not place much stock in the metaphysical.

I was the only foreigner on staff at my college. I lived in Shijiazhuang, which is a city about the size of Kansas City, located about five hours south of Beijing, in a place where two railway lines cross.

Shijiazhuang was a sere place less than 400 miles from the edge of the Gobi Desert. It was cold in the winter, hot in the summer, dusty and windy and ugly all the time.

Christmas in China is hard.

The Chinese don't celebrate Christmas, although they have heard of it the way we have heard of Chinese New Year, and they know it is a big deal. Christmas fell on a Thursday, which meant I taught British and American Culture and History. I dedicated the class day to Christmas.

So much of Christmas is the build-up. I bought gifts in Beijing; a tea set for my mother, cloisonne for friends, a tiny jade horse for my sister; but I had sent the gifts off in October. My family sent chocolate chip cookies, but there wasn't any reason to wait until the twenty-fifth to open the cookies, they'd just be more stale. My sister sent me a new white sweater; a white sweater in Shijiazhuang was so inappropriate I almost cried. By the end of a day anything I was wearing had a ring of gray dirt at the neck and cuffs. But the college decided to have a Christmas Eve party and to invite all the foreigners—there were twelve Americans and Canadians in a city of over a million—so I went and wore the sweater.

Chinese parties usually involve speeches, and then everybody has to sing a song or something. The most successful song I have ever done was "Oh Lord, Won't You Buy Me A Mercedes Benz," sung a la Janis Joplin (the only impression I can do), but that was for students. At the Christmas party there were teachers and administrators, so I sang "Silent Night" badly, but in English. Singing in English is so foreign to most Chinese that it is like watching a dancing bear, it is not that it is done well, but that it is done at all.

I was tired so I left just after the Mitchells. The Mitchells were retired, and they came to China sponsored by their church. They taught English using Bible stories, but could not openly proselytize because it is against Chinese law. Anyway, they tended to leave early, and I had yet another cold, so I left early, too. There are no streetlights, and very few lights in the windows. China is dark in the winter, and this close to Beijing it's about ten degrees colder than New York City in the winter.

I thought maybe I'd get a beer, a kind of Christmas present. I liked the local beer, and a bottle would make me sleepy. I walked out the back gate and up

Red Flag Road, watching for bicyclists coming out of the dark.

I usually bought my beer at a place made out of the carcass of a bus. Sheet metal was welded over the wheel wells and there was a narrow counter where the driver's window would be. They had bootleg electricity from an apartment building and a little refrigerator where they kept pork sausage and a bottle of beer for me. (The Chinese don't drink cold beverages, they believe it causes stomach cancer.) The electricity meant that it was dimly golden in the bus, almost the same frail light as some of the other stalls lit only by kitchen candles. Most nights the proprietor or his very pregnant wife were there until about eleven—and it wasn't a holiday for them so I assumed they'd be open—but halfway up the street I could see that the bus was dark.

I was tempted to just sit down on the road except that it was China, and China was so foreign, and I was so tired of its relentless foreignness. It was Christmas and I wanted to be home, but I was between homes, and when I left China I didn't precisely know where I was going. A cold winter night in China, standing in the street where I could see the window of my apartment and it was as dark as anything else here and I was lost.

A Chinese girl stopped and said, *"Tongshi,"* (Comrade.)

It was dark and she couldn't make out my face. She was about to ask me directions, it had happened before. *"Wo shi weiguoren,"* (I'm a foreigner,) I said and added that I didn't speak Mandarin.

"Miss," she said in English. "I have come looking for you."

A student, or a friend of a student. I was tired from my cold and I didn't want to be polite to this girl in the middle of Red Flag Road. "Yes," I said, without enthusiasm.

"You must come with me," she said.

"I'm sorry, it's very late and I have to teach tomorrow."

"No," she said. "It is Christmas, and I have come for you."

A party, I thought, feeling sick. They do that, make plans and don't tell you until the last minute, and it is rude not to go along.

"No," she said. "I am your Christmas spirit."

The beer was supposed to be my Christmas spirit. "I don't understand," I said. "That isn't clear in English. Do you mean you are going to wish me good spirits?"

"No, no. I am your Christmas spirit," she said. "Like a ghost." I could not really see her face in the dark, just a pale oval turned toward me. The rest of her was shapeless, buried under the interminable layers of sweaters and coats that we all wore. She was only as tall as my shoulder.

"Ahh," I said, as if I had a clue. "I am sorry, but it is very late and I am sure you must be going on your way, and I have a cold, I have to go to bed."

"Come with me," she said firmly and took my hand. I was going to pull away, but something happened. Something ... happened. I know I said that, I am trying to explain it, but there is a space where the thoughts should be, no exact memory, just the sense that something happened.

And then.

We were in a large unheated room full of people in coats. The people were all standing in rows, their backs to me, rows of Chinese overcoats, women with hair permed in the precise curls of those old Toni perms from the 50s and 60s (home perms had just hit China the way they did the U.S. in the 50s) and men with their hair shining a little, because in China in the winter the heat isn't on very long and no one wants to wash their hair.

Someone was murmuring.

I was standing at the back of the room, next to the

girl from the road. A blackout. A seizure of some sort. And a deep, cowardly relief, that this was serious, and it meant that I could go home. I was stunned at the enormity of my relief. A blackout, brain tumor, neurological disease—who cared. I wanted to go home, to run from being here. I realized that the tiredness I was carrying was a kind of despair.

I wondered what time it was, how far we were from my apartment, and how long it would take to get back there.

The people all murmured together, a long muttered response in unison. "It's a church," I whispered. I don't know why I said it out loud, but a person who has had a blackout has a right to be disoriented.

The girl from the road nodded. "A Catholic church."

Christmas Mass. A sad dispirited Christmas Mass. Being Catholic is a hard thing in China. I had one Catholic girl in my third year class, and she was almost mute, her voice inaudible when she answered questions, silenced by the pressure of being a Chinese girl and a Catholic.

"Christmas is a celebration," I said.

The girl from the road shrugged. What was she supposed to say? I supposed she was Catholic, too, and had brought me here thinking that being in a Catholic church would console me.

I had not been in a church in years, only went for weddings and funerals. When my father died, I went to church for the funeral and my strongest memory was of an altar boy holding a white candle. The candle tilted and wax ran onto his hand. He sucked in his breath but made no noise, because a funeral mass is a solemn thing. No altar boys in white here, plastic flowers on a makeshift altar.

I wondered how she had gotten me here during the space of my blackout, had I seemed normal? One of those multiple personalities that no one notices?

"Are you Catholic?" I whispered.

At that moment people turned and smiled and offered each other their hands to shake. I almost shut my eyes when they turned, somebody would see me, notice the foreigner, and then all of a sudden everyone would fuss.

No one offered their hand to me, no one noticed me. So strange not to be noticed, everywhere I went I was noticed. I walked down the street and people hissed to each other, *weiguoren*, "foreigner," tapping their companions to get their attention, "look, a foreigner." I caused bicycle accidents. Buses nearly hit people, the whole row at the window turning their head to watch me, in a flannel shirt and jeans and four months without a haircut, waiting to cross the street. But here in this church, no one looked at me. No one saw.

I went still, thinking that perhaps they just hadn't noticed me. I wanted them to have just not noticed me.

"I'm not Catholic," said the girl from the road, her voice normal and therefore loud among these whispering people. No one blinked. It was as if I wasn't there.

My Christmas Spirit looked at me and I willed her not to say anything.

Sick with apprehension. I was losing my mind. My Christmas Spirit had a sidelong look, a face with smooth heavy eyelids and long eyes, an ancient face. Not civilized ancient, primitive ancient. Bone-old, faintly green in the shadows under her eyes, like oxidized copper. She was waiting and expectant. Expecting something from me. Willing to wait.

I had always wanted to be invisible in China. You don't know the strain of doing everything under the public eye, of having every purchase, even my choice of toothpaste or laundry soap, discussed in front of me.

I thought I was dead. There was no explanation. And I would spend eternity like this, haunting China.

Shaken. I did not know if I would ever go home.

We stood through the mass. There was a closing

hymn, plainsong in Chinese. It took me a moment to hear it through the strangeness, but they were singing "Oh, Come All Ye Faithful." Was I brought here to reprimand me for having given up on the church? My Christmas Spirit said she wasn't Catholic, then what was she?

They filed out, looking through my Christmas Spirit and me as if we were not there. Middle-aged women in cloth coats, middle-aged women with tired eyes. Why is church a woman's thing? They didn't look saved, they looked alienated and cold and subdued. It still looked strange to see Catholics in China.

And then the little room was empty. My Christmas Spirit still looked at me. I didn't know what to say.

She shrugged again. "Come," she said, and something . . . happened.

A Chinese flat, four rooms, concrete floor, walls painted blue to waist height and then white the rest of the way. Comfortably-off people if they had four rooms. A Chinese man with an unruly shock of thick hair came out of the kitchen. He was wearing a white T-shirt despite the chill and smoking a cigarette and I knew him.

It was Liu Liming, cook for the special dining room and therefore, most of the time, only me. He was an alcoholic and a cynic, and a dealmaker, and I liked him very much. We were the same age. He spoke almost no English, I spoke pidgin Mandarin, and yet we were friends because, somehow, we were. I got his jokes, we shared a sense of irony.

But I had never been to his apartment. Never expected to. I knew a little about him—China is a place for gossip.

He stood there for a moment looking at his wife. Their son was asleep on the couch, head thrown back. He was still wearing his glasses. The little boy was four, and he had an eye that crossed inward and it made him shy. His father was hard on him, always a little angry because the boy was not a charmer, not like his father.

Liming's wife was watching television.

"Why don't you put him in bed," Liming said and I understood. Which was the other thing I always wished for, to understand what was going on around me. Be careful what you wish for. Liming wasn't aware that I was standing in his apartment and although I understood Liming better than I did most people who spoke Chinese, I had never had this easy, conversational understanding.

His wife didn't answer, pretending not to hear. She was the daughter of the president of the college and she was a shrew. He was a clever country boy who had seduced an upper class girl and expected to live happily ever after.

He made a little sound of disgust, a very faint ai-yah, and I could see in her face that she heard him but she wouldn't admit it. So he went back into the kitchen and came out with a bottle of the clear sorghum liquor the Chinese drink. It's about 120 proof and smells like fingernail polish. He poured it into a little Chinese drinking cup and tossed it back, *gang bei*, bottom's up. It was for her benefit.

She refused to look at him.

Awful little scene, I thought.

"Are you going to raise the second one like this, too?" he asked.

They had been granted permission to have a second child, because of the first boy's inward turning eye.

"Are you going to see Xiling," she said.

His best friend's wife. There were rumors about them, but most people seemed to think neither of them would really have an affair.

He looked at her with hatred. "I am going to bed."

I shook my head.

The Christmas spirit watched me.

"They don't have to live this way," I said.

She shrugged. "What should they do?"

"Divorce," I said. "It's not against the law, people in China do."

"Where will he live?" she asked. "The work unit has a waiting list for housing."

"He can rent a room," I said, "Some people do. That's not what's stopping him."

"What's stopping him?" she asked.

A thousand things. The fact that he would have to either share a single room with another unmarried man, or pay for a room. The fact that she was the reason he had a good job. That in China, divorce was the moral equivalent of bankruptcy.

"Why did you bring me here?" I asked.

"To show you his choice," she said.

And took my hand and I closed my eyes.

She took me to the girls dormitories where my students lived eight to a room, building curtains around their bunk beds to hide themselves and make themselves a little space. I saw Lizhi, a girl from the third year class who had stopped showing up. She was lying on the bed, unable to sleep. Her grades had plummeted before she left and she told me she had headaches and insomnia and she couldn't concentrate and she was sad all the time. But China doesn't treat depression. During the Cultural Revolution it was decided that depression was a sign of an unhealthy society, and mental illness shouldn't exist in a socialist country. So people like Lizhi were self-indulgent.

I had come to visit her twice in the dorm, had talked to her and held her hand, but I hadn't really done anything for her. Hadn't spent any real time on her. I had almost eighty students, and I convinced myself that she wasn't my problem, that I wasn't equipped to help her. But no one was equipped to help her and I was at least aware that talking to her would help her feel less alone.

What would happen to her? She would kill herself. She had talked about dying the last time. Or like many people who suffered from depression, she would get better, have bouts of it for the rest of her life. And unless China made antidepressant drugs available, she would live a kind of half-life, never knowing when she would be swallowed up. I could see her on her bunk, curled on her side, her eyes open, while the other girls slept. I could see the pearl of the whites of her eyes.

My Christmas Spirit stood next to me.

I understood depression, had spent some nights awake and alone. Had walked at two in the morning just to feel the movement, hoping to be tired enough to sleep when I got back, hoping maybe something would happen to me, then it wouldn't be my problem anymore, something would have happened and everything would be changed.

And I remembered getting better, I remember the moment, walking to class, when I looked up at a great beech tree whose roots grew through a stone wall and reached down to uproot the sidewalk, and saw pale new green leaves against the white wood and through the tree saw the intense blue of the sky and I realized I had not looked for beauty for over a year.

I remembered choosing at that moment to look for beauty. And I remembered that it had not happened over night, but that slowly, the world had come back to me.

When had I stopped looking again? How had I come to China? I had come to China to make something happen, the way I had gone on those 2:00 a.m. walks, hoping something monumental would happen. There are people for whom depression is an indescribable force. For someone like Lizhi, there was no choice, her depression was an illness, rooted in the chemistry of her body, as inescapable as cancer. But then there are people like me, who walk a sort of cliff and who can look into the abyss and know that it is down there, and who have to maintain their balance. I had learned how to balance, I thought.

When had I stopped trying?

"Choose," said my Christmas Spirit, standing in the black dorm room. I could see the halflit face of my Christmas Spirit in the little bit of light from the window at the end of the room, barely make out the ancient shape of her head, her heavy lidded eyes. Lizhi did not stir, did not hear, the whites of her eyes like pearls.

"I choose beauty," I said, thinking of the pale tree and the green leaves and the intense blue sky.

And something happened.

I was alone on the road outside the college. I was chilled to the bone. A person on a bicycle swerved as if I had just appeared on the road in front of him, and maybe I had.

Of course, this is just a ghost story, a travel story. I should stop now, tell you only that I finished my year in China, during which time I made many close friends, and declined the college's offer to teach another year. That I came home, and went back to writing. That I sold a novel and a couple of short stories.

But I want to say something about why I went abroad. No one goes abroad to go to something. Everybody goes abroad to flee something. One of the people I knew in Shijiazhuang was in remission for lymphatic cancer and had been for three years. He was hiding from death in China, and that year, in January, in the city of Kunming, China, 150 kilometers north of the Vietnam border, seven of us foreigners working together got him on a plane to Beijing so he could fly from there to the Mayo clinic. The things you flee find you, even in China. But that is another story.

It's old-fashioned to have morals for stories, but indulge me. I was trying to escape myself, trying to become someone else, someone wise. Maybe I had a sort of black-out on Red Flag Road, or maybe I met an old Chinese spirit. I am telling you now, I don't know. But some things you must choose. Choose a bad marriage, choose a bad life, or choose to look around you and see.

UPON A MIDNIGHT DREARY

by Laura Resnick

Laura Resnick has sold more than a dozen romance novels and some 15 science fiction stories, and was a nominee for the 1992 and 1993 Campbell Award.

Becker hunched gloomily over his computer keyboard, his mind a blank, his stomach a gurgling repository of Coke and chili dogs, his soul a sea of despair. He clutched clumps of his curly, carrot-red hair in his pale hands and turned his bespectacled gaze toward the window. Viewed from the fifteenth floor, the smog of Los Angeles seemed to hover over the city like a living thing. It swelled and undulated like some inchoate, supernatural creature preying upon the ant-sized inhabitants of the streets, sucking away their life force to nourish itself for some dark, sinister purpose, so that eventually its strength would multiply a thousandfold, whereupon it would take over the dying, decadent city and ... and ...

"Well, maybe not," Becker mumbled, reaching the end of that unpromising train of thought.

In any event, he was safe from the smog for the time being. His window didn't open, and he was unlikely to be released from the building until he completed the task at hand. And he was starting to fear he would *never* complete the task at hand.

Becker had a meeting scheduled tomorrow morning with Aaron Speller, the hotshot television producer affiliated with Paramour Pictures. Speller was expecting Becker to present him with a storyline for a

Christmas special: an action-oriented, tastefully violent, and reverently sexy retelling of the birth of Christ.

"We want it to remain true to the original," Speller had explained, "while giving it a nineties twist. The characters have got to be really gutsy, sexy people, especially the hero."

"The hero?" Becker had asked.

"Yeah. You know: Christ."

"Uh, sir, if you will recall ... Christ was a baby at the time of his birth."

"Well, we might have to change that," Speller had said absently, glancing at his Rolex. "Gotta go, kid. I'm meeting Sean and Roger for dinner to discuss a James Bond comeback."

"Really?" Becker asked.

"Yeah, but with a nineties twist. This time, James Bond is *twins*. Is that great, or what?" Speller lit a cigar as he passed by the "No Smoking" sign and concluded, "I'll see you Thursday morning, Belcher."

"That's Becker, sir," Becker said to the closing elevator doors.

That had been two days ago, and no inspiration was forthcoming. Becker remained locked in his modest office and resolutely attempted every possible remedy for writer's block. He meditated. He exercised. He screamed primally. He wrote his name seven thousand four hundred and twenty-six times. He stood on his head for ninety minutes; but even after regaining consciousness, he was still without ideas.

He didn't need the hourly phone calls of various members of Speller's senior staff, who were "just monitoring progress," to remind him that there would be serious consequences if he failed on this, the very first project for which Speller had singled him out. He would probably lose his job. Even if he didn't, he would certainly lose his parking space and his key to the restroom, two amenities without which he might as well be dead.

Hoping to banish these unpleasant thoughts, as well as to prevent them from ever becoming a reality, Becker returned to his task with renewed vigor.

"Gutsy. Sexy. Action. Nineties." He shook his head. "A fresh twist on the birth of Christ." He rolled his eyes. "Oh, God," he moaned piteously. "Please. Help me."

And lo there came a voice from on high. "Well, since you asked nicely."

"*Yah!*" Becker leapt out of his chair, crashed into his printer, and fell prostrate at the feet—so to speak—of an angel.

"Tsk, tsk. Rather clumsy, aren't you?"

He stared up at the apparition, a pale, golden-haired, bewinged young man dressed in flowing white robes. "Excuse me?"

"You look a bit peaked," said the angel. "But then, it's quite stuffy in here, isn't it? Perhaps we should open the window."

"It doesn't open," Becker croaked.

"Ah, yes. Silly of me. Progress and all that. Not like the old days."

"Who are you? How did you get in here?" Becker demanded, glancing at the closed door.

Following his gaze, the angel said shrewdly, "Oh, don't worry. It's still locked, so none of Speller's people can barge in to bother us."

"Did security let you in here in that garb?"

"It's not as if they could stop me," the angel pointed out. "But, no, I bypassed security and simply materialized here. I hope you don't think it rude of me."

Becker cleared his throat, straightened his glasses, and rose to his feet. "Who are you?" he repeated.

"I am the angel Gabriel." He added hopefully, "Maybe you've heard of me?"

"I shouldn't have eaten those chili dogs," Becker said.

"I assure you you're not dreaming."

"No, that's not what I . . ." Becker turned an unbecoming shade of chartreuse.

"Oh, dear."

"Excuse me!" Since there was no time to find the keys to the restroom and dash down the hall, Becker made use of the wastebasket.

"Good grief," Gabriel said after a noisy interval. "Being mortal really is a messy business, isn't it?"

Becker glared at him. "What are you doing here?"

"You asked for help. Remember?"

"I was thinking more in terms of a muse of fire."

"Sorry, you'll have to settle for an archangel," Gabriel said somewhat sourly.

"Give me a break."

"I assure you I am fully qualified for this sort of work." Becker's disbelieving stare spurred the angel to add huffily, "Just who do you suppose worked with De Mille all those years? He could *never* have made *The Ten Commandments* without my help."

"You worked on *The Ten Commandments*?"

"Uh-huh."

Becker's high forehead furrowed in thought. "And *Samson and Delilah*?"

"Of course."

"Hmmmm. But how can you help me put a new and fresh spin on the birth of Christ?"

Gabriel rolled his eyes heavenward. "That's so obvious it's almost embarrassing."

"Oh?" Becker's expression was a struggle between pathetic eagerness and the natural skepticism of the self-proclaimed intellectual.

"I'm going to take you to the real event, the *first* Christmas. I'm going to escort you to the past."

"Oh, yeah, right. And, like, where's Jacob Marley?" Becker quipped as skepticism won out.

Gabriel frowned. "Who?"

"I'll be visited by three ghosts, right?"

Gabriel blinked. "No. There's just me. Of course, I could bring along several cherubim if you really—"

"And they're going to show me Christmas past, present, and future," Becker sneered.

"The present and future? No, I'm sorry, that's not my field," Gabriel said with scholarly modesty. "I'm a specialist in early Christianity. I was there for all the big events, after all. Look it up if you don't believe me."

"It's not the chili dogs that are the problem," Becker mused, circling Gabriel. "It's overwork."

"Overwork? All you've done is sit here staring out the window for two and a half days."

"That's what I call working!"

"Then I know a few angels who'd love to switch jobs with you," Gabriel shot back.

"It's the Dickens special." Becker nodded emphatically.

"What?"

"Another Christmas special. That's the project Speller pulled me off of to work on this. We were supposed to put a new and fresh nineties twist on *A Christmas Carol,* to make it an action-packed extravaganza filled with gutsy, sexy characters—"

"I get the idea," Gabriel sighed.

"But I was just a junior scriptwriter on that show. So when Speller offered me this opportunity . . ." He shrugged wearily.

"Your vaulting ambition o'erleapt itself, so to speak?" Gabriel guessed.

"Something like that," Becker admitted. "And now I'm stuck alone in this little, airless room, fantasizing about smog and . . . and . . ." His voice started growing shrill. "And not answering my phone because I can't handle *another single call* from Speller's people, monitoring my progress and breathing down my neck! And now," he continued in mounting hysteria, "I'm being seduced by spectral images from the Dickens special, and I . . . I . . . I can't *stand* anymore of this! I'll crack! I'll—"

"I am *not* seducing you," Gabriel snapped. "Angels

don't do that sort of thing. Look it up. Anyhow, if I *were* going to seduce someone, it would be a pretty Canaanite girl and not some demented Hollywood scriptwriter with high blood pressure."

Becker gasped. "I have high blood pressure?" he demanded in alarm. "Are you sure?"

"Look, I haven't got all eternity. Can we get started?"

"What are we going to—"

"Stick with me, kid." One graceful, white-sleeved arm reached for Becker, and suddenly they were soaring through the centuries with an explosion of special effects that could have put Industrial Light and Magic to shame.

"Wow!" Becker cried when they finally came to rest. "That was great! Sort of like *Terminator* meets *The Abyss*."

Gabriel winced. "With such limited powers of description, how did you ever become a writer?"

Becker scowled at him and then looked around at the hilly, arid landscape. It was nearly dark, and his Ralph Lauren sweater wasn't much protection against the chilly, dust-laden wind. "Where are we? *When* are we?"

"Christmas Eve." The angel added, "Of course, no one else knows that."

Becker's eyes widened. "*The* Christmas Eve?" When Gabriel nodded, he asked, "Is that town over there Bethlehem?"

"Yes, we're just on the outskirts. And any minute now, we should bump into ... Ah! Here they are!"

Becker looked in the direction Gabriel was pointing. Sure enough, he saw two people approaching them from the north. The man was small and dark, with an incredibly bushy black beard and a long-suffering look in his eyes. He wore old leather sandals, a tan robe with fading blue stripes, and a dirty cloth around his head. He was leading a sour-faced donkey which carried on its back an enormous burden of clothes, bun-

dles, wineskins, and one extremely pregnant woman.
When the man turned to speak to the woman, the
donkey bit him.

The man hollered at the donkey, which brayed at
him. Then the man and woman began arguing back
and forth in quick, guttural phrases.

"What are they saying?" Becker asked

"Oh, of course. How silly of me," Gabriel sighed.
He waved one hand majestically, and suddenly the
people before them were speaking English.

"How much farther to the inn?" the woman demanded, her voice strident and irritable.

"Not much farther, dear," the man replied through
gritted teeth.

"You've been saying that since this morning," the
woman snapped. "I'll bet you don't even know where
we're going, do you, Joseph?"

"Of course I do, Mary, my angel," Joseph answered
evenly, though his face grew darker and he twisted the
donkey's rope with agitated hands. "That's Bethlehem
right in front of us."

"*That's* Bethlehem? You can't be serious! I am not
staying in this dumpy little rattrap of a town
overnight!"

Joseph sighed and turned away, pulling the reluctant
donkey behind him. "We have no choice, my treasure.
The Emperor Augustus has ordered that every Jewish
man report to his home town to see that his name is
added to the electoral roll."

"Only so he can figure out how many subjects he
can grind under the heel of his Roman boot, so he
can bleed them for taxes. I can't believe you're being
so spineless as to cooperate with this farce! My brother
Ezra isn't obediently trotting back to Nazareth to en-
list himself in the Roman tax rolls."

"Dear, your brother Ezra hasn't been gainfully em-
ployed since the Flood."

"That's not funny, Joseph! He's just had trouble

finding a patron, that's all. Ow! Can't you keep this damn donkey from stepping in holes?"

"I'll try, my little ray of sunshine."

"What the hell is wrong with her?" Becker asked Gabriel. "Not even my Great Aunt Prudence is as nasty as this chick."

"It's a little known fact that Mary was in her tenth month by the time they traveled to Bethlehem. She's rather uncomfortable right now. And," Gabriel added significantly, "she doesn't quite recognize the symptoms, but she started labor about an hour ago."

"Well, I suppose that's some excuse," Becker admitted. "But why is he putting up with her bitching? I thought that back then . . . er, back *now* . . . that men were men and women knew their place."

"True. But, my dear boy, Mary of Nazareth is, after all, carrying the King of Kings."

"You mean, Joseph knows?"

"Of course he knows. I told him. Don't you know *any* of the story?"

Stung by the angel's criticism, Becker said, "Of course. Uh, ah, brightly shone the moon that night . . ."

"That's the Feast of Stephen."

"Oh. Well, then, isn't there supposed to be a partridge in a pear tree somewhere around here?"

"Wrong again."

Getting flustered, Becker continued, "Anyhow, I know that when they got to the stable, there was a red-nosed reindeer waiting for them."

Gabriel shook his head sadly, causing his wings to flutter. "You are a hopeless victim of pop culture. Haven't you read your source material?"

Becker shrugged. "I tried, but it's kind of slow going, you know what I mean? So I watched a bunch of old T.V. specials instead."

"I can see I've got my work cut out for me."

"Hey, one thing I know for sure. When they get to town, they'll be told there's no room at the inn."

Now Gabriel looked uncomfortable. "Well, actually,

I'm forced to admit that even the source material isn't all that accurate."

"What?"

"Well, we had to clean up a few details for posterity," the angel said defensively.

Becker stared at him. "So what really happened at the inn?"

"Come. I'll show you."

In the blink of an eye and the flutter of a wing, Becker found himself standing before a dirty, sand-covered, low-ceilinged hovel. Mary, still perched on the donkey, was shouting at Joseph, while the reptilian-looking innkeeper watched them with unblinking eyes from the crumbling doorway.

"I will not stay in this filthy, flea-ridden hole in the ground, Joseph!"

"But, dear, it's rather late to find another—"

"You should have made reservations at the inn my father recommended!" she snapped. "But *noooo,* you had to ignore perfectly good advice and choose some rat-infested heap of rubble!"

"Darling," Joseph said tightly, "let's not antagonize the innkeeper, since we may not be able to get a room at another inn so late in the—"

"Joseph, I would sleep in a *stable* before I would sleep in this dump!"

"Think of your condition, my love. It's not good for you to get so excited," Joseph ground out sweetly.

"Are you taking the room or not?" the innkeeper asked in a bored voice.

Mary gave Joseph a look that Becker recognized immediately, since his ex-wife had used it on him often during their two-year marriage. It was a look that said, *I blame you for everything, and I'm going to make you so terribly sorry for it all.*

"Uh, I think we'll keep looking," Joseph told the innkeeper.

So Becker and Gabriel followed Mary and Joseph around Bethlehem until late that night, but none of the inns pleased Mary. One was too expensive, one was too drafty, another was too near the main thoroughfare, and yet another had too many painted women hanging out in the lobby.

"What does she want?" Becker asked Gabriel. "The Dorchester?"

"She's just nesting," Gabriel said generously.

"As picky as she is, I suppose that Nazareth must be a pretty nice place."

Gabriel was still chuckling over this naive comment when Mary's labor pains started in earnest.

"Please, you've got to let us have that room!" Joseph cried as he pleaded with an innkeeper, upon whose ancestry Mary had speculated rather insultingly a few minutes earlier.

"Sorry. It's taken," the innkeeper said with a smirk.

"But we've been standing right here, and no one else has come along," Joseph argued.

"No room at the inn, sonny."

"But my wife's about to have a baby!"

"*Mazel tov.* Good luck finding a room."

"Please in the name of mercy . . ." Joseph glanced heavenward, then confided to the innkeeper, "My wife is about to bear the Son of God, the Messiah, the Redeemer. If you help us out, I'm sure it would count in your favor on *Yom Kippur*."

"Man, what have *you* been smoking?" the innkeeper asked.

At that moment, Mary let out a scream that shook the pillars of the earth. Both men turned pale.

"All right," Joseph said, stiffening his resolve. "If you won't give us a room, my wife will have her baby right here on your doorstep. Now how would that look to the tourists, huh?"

As if to punctuate this threat, Mary screamed again, and the donkey brayed and urinated.

"Let's strike a bargain," the innkeeper suggested, rolling his eyes. "I believe the lady said something about preferring to sleep in a stable?"

"She says that everywhere we go," Joseph answered dismissively. "It's just a figure of speech."

Apparently the innkeeper didn't think so. He offered them a stall in the stable out back for half the price of a room.

"Take it or leave it," he ordered when Joseph protested.

"And that," Gabriel told Becker, "is how they wound up in the stable."

Becker thought it over and shook his head. "No, it wouldn't go over well with the prime time audience."

Gabriel started to argue, but Becker cut him off with an excited cry. "Look!" He pointed to the night sky, where a single star, directly above the stable, shone brightly in the dreary night sky. "It's the star of Bethlehem!"

"Oh, you've heard of it, have you?"

"Sarcasm doesn't become an angel, Gabriel. Of course I've heard of it. The three wise men followed it to find the Christ child so they could bring him gifts fit for a king."

Gabriel cleared his throat. "Actually . . ."

"What?"

"Well, the star was my idea."

"Really?"

"Yes, but we weren't trying to guide three wise men. No, we were trying to help the midwife get here on time from Ashdod."

"We?"

"Me and Yahweh."

"Wow. You and the Big Guy, huh?"

"Please. He doesn't like that appellation. He's sensitive about his weight problem."

"Sorry. What did you need a midwife for?"

"Honestly, Becker, sometimes I think you're as dim as that Smeller fellow you work for."

"That's *Speller*."

"This is a winter night in Judea at the end of the first century B.C. There's a woman in that stable about to give birth to the Son of God. Did you really think that we were just going to twiddle our thumbs and hope for the best? Of course not! We notified a midwife! We planned ahead! It's not our fault that ..." He swallowed and blushed.

"What happened?" Becker demanded.

"How were we to know that the midwife was dyslexic?"

"Got lost, did she?"

"Even as we speak, she's on her way to Megiddo."

"Well, easy come, easy go."

"So, we had to settle for three wise men."

"Tough break."

"We couldn't just let the event pass unnoticed," Gabriel insisted.

"Who's arguing?"

"And we tried to play up the whole aspect of the animals gathering in the stable to witness the birth of the Savior. It really didn't catch on until the Victorian era, since hardly anyone was sentimental about animals for the first eighteen centuries after Christ, but I told Yahweh I thought it would be a good long-term policy."

"So where did you find the wise men?" Becker asked, hunching his shoulders against the cold and wiping dust from the lenses of his glasses.

"The only place a wise man would be on a miserable night like this," Gabriel said.

And Becker found himself in the Roman bathhouse. "Hey, this steam is no good for my sweater," he protested. "It might shrink."

"I thought you wanted to see the wise men. This won't take long. There they are: Melchior, Gaspar, and Balthazar."

"They're so young!" Becker said in surprise. The three lean, dark-haired fellows all appeared to be around twenty years old. "Hey! Speller would like this. One of the three *young* wise men could fall in love with Mary, or maybe with some pretty female slave, and—"

"Forget it, Becker. These guys are on their way to Greece to join the gay rights movement there."

"In *Greece*?"

"Things have changed a lot in the past two thousand years," the angel explained. "Anyhow, these lads are wealthy intellectuals from the East, so they kind of fit the bill, if you see what I mean." He frowned and said, "Maybe we'd better go check on Mary."

"Must we?" Becker asked faintly.

It was cold, windy, and dusty once they were back out in the Judean night. Becker grumbled, "What about all those songs? *Silent Night* and *Away in the Manger*? I thought this was supposed to be a clear, quiet, peaceful night with bright stars and a brilliant moon."

"Ah, here we are!" Gabriel said when they found Mary in the stable. "The baby's just coming now."

"Joseph, can't you keep these lambs and goats away from me?" Mary snarled between panting breaths.

"Push, darling, *push*. Remember what the instructor in Nazareth said?"

Mary's expletives were cut off by another scream, and then the baby was born.

"Oh, gross!" Becker turned away. "I've seen delivery scenes on T.V. shows before, but I had no *idea* . . ."

"It's a boy!" Joseph cried with joy.

"Well, of course it is," Mary grunted. "We knew that."

"We shall call him Jesus," Joseph said. "That is what the angel told me to name him."

"Well, that's just tough, because the angel told *me* to call him Emmanuel."

"Emmanuel? You can't be serious," Joseph protested.

"Who saw the angel first, you lunkhead?"

"Well, perhaps the angel changed his mind after he

talked to you, because I *know* he told me to call the baby Jesus."

"You're not calling any baby of *mine* Jesus, and that's final."

"And you're not calling any baby of *mine* . . . er . . ."

Mary arched her brows. "Yes?"

"Well, he's, you know . . . *sort* of mine. I mean, I'm the one who's got to put food in his belly and clothes on his back—"

"Can't you settle this for them?" Becker asked Gabriel as the argument continued.

Gabriel watched Mary bundle up the infant. Then Joseph laid him to sleep in the manger. The angel replied. "I *did* solve it for them. Here come the wise men. Oh, and there are the shepherds I rounded up." He shook his head and added, "I'd forgotten what a rough night's work this whole event was for me."

"Jesus!" cried one of the richly garbed, wise, young men. "An angel told us of your birth, and we come bearing gifts!"

"You see?" Joseph said smugly to Mary who glared at him.

"Wow!" Becker said, eyeing the gold, frankincense, and myrrh. "How'd you get the wise lads to part with that stuff?"

"I got *you* to part with the twentieth century, didn't I? When an archangel talks, people usually do as they're told."

"Myrrh?" Mary said. *"Myrrh?"* she repeated shrilly. "That's hardly in good taste, young man."

"Myrrh was a fragrant spice used in burying the dead," Gabriel explained to Becker.

"What on earth can you be thinking of?" Mary said critically. "Why didn't you bring him a rattle or some diapers? *Myrrh!*"

"I'm sorry, It's all I could find on such short notice," the fellow apologized.

Apparently hoping to ease the tension, another of

the wise men asked, "So, are you three heading back to Nazareth in a few days, then?"

"Egypt, actually," Joseph answered.

"Egypt?" Mary cried. "When did you decide we were going to Egypt?"

"Well, this angel came and told me—"

"I am *not* going to that *filthy* country with its incestuous kings and its—"

"My love, it's the oldest, most cultured nation in—"

"And that stuff they wear on their hair! Do you honestly think I'm going to raise my baby—"

At this point, the shepherds started singing in praise of God, the donkey started braying, and the three wise men milled about in confusion while the baby cried and Joseph and Mary continued their argument.

"It's all kind of downhill from here for the next couple of decades," Gabriel admitted. "Shall we go?"

"I've seen enough," Becker said, thinking longingly of the heated bathrooms back at Paramour Pictures.

Becker's return to his office was as dramatic as his departure had been, but he arrived alone. Only a message on his wall, written in fire, gave proof that the angel Gabriel had ever been there at all: *Good luck with your meeting tomorrow!*

Becker worked through the night, and the meeting with Speller the following morning did indeed go well. Speller was thrilled with the concepts Becker presented to him.

"Oh, wow, yeah!" Speller exclaimed enthusiastically. "I especially love the part about the three *young,* handsome, wise men. The wise *lads*!" He guffawed with delight. "These are gutsy, sexy characters! And that bit in the bathhouse, with a beautiful Nubian slave girl pouring oil over their bodies—perfect!"

On the wall behind Speller, Becker saw words of fire appear: *You can't be serious.*

"But I think my favorite part," Speller continued, "is the voluptuous young midwife who gets kidnapped on her way from Ashdod by the handsome, sexy Jewish zealot who falls madly in love with her."

Kidnapped?

"Glad you like it, sir," Becker said, trying not to look at the burning wall again.

"Now, Mary needs to be reworked a bit, Belcher—"

"That's Becker, sir."

"I mean, she was the Virgin Mother, the Madonna, Our Lady of Perpetual Purity. She's got to be sweetness and light. A little human touch is nice, but you're taking it too far."

"I see what you mean, sir. Sweetness and light. Of course. I should have thought of that myself."

"Hey, kid, that's what I'm here for. Right? To inspire you!"

"Yes, sir. I don't think I could have done this without your inspiration."

Hypocrite.

Speller popped some pills and lit up a cigar, talking the whole while about how pleased he was with Becker's progress on the project. "In fact, I think you're just the man to handle my next idea."

"Sir?"

"A new two-hour special to pull up those sluggish late spring ratings: The Immaculate Conception."

Becker nodded knowingly and used his best Hollywood drawl. "In-ter-est-ing."

"We want to remain true to the original, while giving it a nineties twist," Speller continued. "And the characters have got to be really gutsy, sexy people."

"Uh, sir, if you recall . . . there was no sex involved in the Immaculate Conception; Mary was a virgin."

"Well, we may have to change that," Speller said absently, glancing at his Rolex. "Gotta go, kid. I've got a meeting with Jackie, Kate, and Farrah. We're looking into doing an *Angels* comeback."

"Funny you should say that, sir." Becker glanced at the wall.

"Only this time, the angels will travel back through

time to the court of Louis XIV, who wants them *all* to be his mistresses. Is that great, or what?"

After Speller's departure, Becker looked at the wall and murmured, "So, what do you know about the Immaculate Conception, Gabe?"

Well ... The fire stopped for a moment, and then scrawled rapidly across the wall. *I* was *there, you know*.

MODERN MANSIONS

by Barbara Delaplace

Barbara Delaplace is the author of more than 20 short stories, and was a 1992 and 1993 Campbell Award nominee.

"The worst of a modern stylish mansion is that it has no place for ghosts."
—Oliver Wendell Holmes, Sr.

Mondays are always hectic. That seems to be a given among humans—particularly my master—and, of course, that means it is hectic for me as well. I have some empathy with a young woman I saw recently, wearing a lapel-crawling active-brooch bearing the legend "Abolish Mondays." But this particular day "took the cake," if I may interject a note of slang, even before the ghost appeared in the reception room.

From the moment my master and I had entered the office suite after taking the airlift down from the penthouse, there had been a steady stream of televid calls and holofaxes blinking for attention on my desk's touch panels, and human visitors to deal with. As a Personal Servitors, Inc. Model 6251-PA (Personal Attendant) it was my job to sort the important calls and visitors from the ones my master regarded as a waste of time. (A good many of them, by his estimation.) Usually my judgment was quite accurate.

But it appeared that this time I had made an error. I had assumed that my master would be willing to meet with the representatives from a worthy cause like

---

the hospice building fund, flattered that they had sought him out. Unfortunately, programming does not cover *all* possible human behavior—in fact, I harbor suspicions that my programmers had never met a man like Jacob E. Widdoes—and I could hear him shouting, even through the bonded ceramic door.

"No, I'm *not* interested in funding some home for dying people! It's a criminal waste of money. They're going to die anyhow—what's it matter *where* they die?"

"But, Mr. Widdoes, surely you can understand our desire to make the final days of a fellow human being more comfortable? That a patient might want to end his life in more congenial, peaceful surroundings than those of a hospital, which is devoted to massive technical intervention to sustain life?" One of the visitors attempted to reason with him, which I could have explained was a mistake. When he was in this mood, my master was not responsive to reason.

"If they're dying, they can die in a hospital where they belong. In fact, they can die in the street for all I care. Who let you in here, anyway?" His voice suddenly became louder as the door jerked open and he stood there, pointing accusingly at me. "*Friday!* I *know* I told you I didn't want to have my time wasted by trivialities. Get these professional beggars out of here!"

"At once, master," I replied. "Madam, sir, if you would come with me, I will be happy to escort you to the airlift." The man and woman, both smartly clad in executive gray, filed out of the office with very mixed expressions of anger and relief. My master slammed the door after them.

"Is he always that ... touchy?" the woman asked me. I paused while attempting to frame a sympathetic response—for I thought my master's rudeness toward them was uncalled-for—yet one that would not be indiscreet. The man mistook my silence.

"Come on, Dianne, you know android servants can't say anything bad about their owners."

I felt I should correct his misapprehension. "While it is true that we are programmed to treat matters concerning our owners as confidential, I may say that I fail to understand Mr. Widdoes' opposition to your project. It seems to me a laudable initiative, and one I would willingly donate to, were artificial constructs permitted to have money."

The woman smiled at me. "I wish you were permitted, too. What did Widdoes call you? Is Friday really your name?"

"Yes, madam. After a servant famous in literature, I'm told." We reached the airlift and I passed my hand over the panel. The tell-tales blinked from red to orange to green, indicating the air cushion was now completely formed, and the safety field vanished in a sparkle of silvery force patterns. "There, the lift is ready for you."

"Well, Friday, I'm sorry I won't be getting to know you better."

"Thank you, madam. I regret it as well. However, I'll remember our meeting and derive pleasure from doing so." She smiled at me and stepped onto the air-cushion; her companion followed her. The safety field re-formed, barring access to the lift. I turned to the man. "Good-bye, sir." He nodded briefly. "Good-bye, madame."

"Good-bye, Friday," she replied, smiling again, as the cushion moved downward to the main floor. I could hear the man's voice fading away.

"Dianne, why do you bother talking to those dummies? They're just machines. . . ."

("Dummies" is a popular slang term for androids.)

The ghost was waiting in the reception room when I returned.

Initially I did not realize that he was a ghost. He merely seemed a dark-bearded human male dressed in a manner I had not seen before: he wore a long, belted, deep green robe bordered with white fur around the cuffs, neck and hem. Somewhat more unusual, his feet were bare. However, since I knew it was considered impolite to remark upon a person's appearance, I simply inquired his business.

"I'm here to discuss something of great importance with Jacob Widdoes," he said.

"Do you have an appointment, sir? Mr. Widdoes is an extremely busy man."

He relied, "No, I don't, but he'll see me."

I was doubtful, but said, "If you give me a moment, I will inquire if he is available."

He smiled. "That's not necessary, my friend. I'll just slip into his office." And before I could respond, he strode across the room—and straight through the closed door.

My programming is designed to cover a wide variety of social and business situations so that I may respond appropriately. But it had not prepared me for a sight like this. I ran an internal diagnostic, but my sensors were all working at optimal levels.

Meanwhile, it did not take long for my master to react. "*Friday!* Get this intruder out of my office this instant!"

I interpreted this as an invitation to enter the office and did so. My master was on his feet, red-faced with rage. The strange intruder, however, was sitting quite at ease in one of the chairs that furnished the room.

"Oh, no, Jacob, it won't be that easy getting rid of me. You see, I'm here on an important mission—to rehabilitate you."

"I don't care if you're here to crown me Miss Universe. I want to know how you got in through that closed door. And more important, I want you to get the hell *out* of here!"

"The answer to how I got in is easy: I'm a ghost, so doors aren't much of an obstacle. I simply walk through them. Through walls, too." The ghost winked at me.

"Garbage. There's no such thing as ghosts. How did you *really* get in here? I know the door's security shield is working—they were in here yesterday testing it. Speak up! I'm willing to pay well for new technology."

I decided to speak since my master was obviously laboring under a misapprehension. "Oh no, master, he did indeed pass through the door. I saw it myself, and my optical sensors are in perfect working order. He is what he claims to be, a discorporeal being."

"A *what*?"

"A ghost, sir," I replied.

"Ridiculous! They don't exist."

The ghost spoke again. "I'm afraid we *do* exist, Jacob. If you can't believe the evidence of your own senses, you should trust those of your attendant here. If an android can see me, I *must* exist. After all, android senses are more acute and less prone to error than mere human ones."

My master smiled grimly. "You've never owned one, that's obvious. They're incredibly finicky and break down all the time."

I would have liked to correct this statement—my downtime since I had been purchased five years before was six hours per annum for annual servicing. But it did not seem a good time to mention it. Besides, my master was speaking again.

"A holo projection, of course. I should've guessed."

The ghost replied, "No, I'm afraid not, Jacob. Run all the tests you like, but it won't change the fact of my presence here."

It appeared that my master was doing exactly that; his fingers moved over the touchpads on his desk. At last, he leaned back and rolled his eyes. "All right, you're a ghost. Get out and leave me alone."

"Ah, Jacob, that's the problem, you see. You want to be left alone, and that's not good for your soul."

"My soul? What the hell are you talking about?"

The ghost looked at him gravely. "Here it is, only

a few days before Christmas, and I see no signs that you're celebrating this time of good will toward your fellow mortals."

"Christmas? Why on earth should I celebrate an outdated religious holiday? It's just an excuse for merchants to make a bundle of credits while piously mouthing worn phrases about brotherhood and peace. Hypocrites, the lot of them."

"I'm getting the distinct impression you bear little good will toward anyone at *any* time, Jacob."

"Why should I? No one's ever borne any for *me*." My master scowled.

The ghost frowned in turn. "You think you're entitled to receive before you have to give? That's not how it works, Jacob. I fear you're in graver peril of losing your soul than I thought."

"Who cares about my soul? Assuming I have one, it's no one else's business."

The ghost sighed. "I was afraid this was going to be a long assignment."

"What do you mean, 'a long assignment'? Who sent you?"

"Since you're doubtful about the existence of your soul, I don't think you'd believe me if I told you. Why don't we just leave that question for the time being?"

"Fine with me, since I'm not going to have anything more to do with you. Friday, get rid of this idiot."

I could see that was going to pose a problem. "How, master?"

"What do you mean, how? Pick him up and carry him out if you have to. Do I have to explain every little detail?"

Of course I can't refuse a direct order, so I reached out to take the ghost's arm. And as I expected, my hand went right through him. "I am afraid I cannot, master. There is nothing for me to touch."

"Face up to it, Jacob. You can't get rid of me until I decide to leave," said the ghost. I could see my master's face turning a deeper shade of red, never a good sign. Apparently the ghost was also aware of this, for he continued, "However, I think you need time to adjust to the idea, so I'll leave you for now." And he walked out of the room. I noticed his feet floated a few centimeters off the floor.

My master glared at me. "Well, what are you waiting for?"

"Do you have any orders for me concerning our guest, sir? It appears he will be with us for some time."

"He can hang around all he wants. It doesn't make a damn bit of difference to *me*. Now get out."

"Yes, sir." I left the office.

The ghost was in the reception room. I asked, "Is there anything you require, sir? Any service I can perform for you?"

He smiled at me. "None, thank you, Friday."

"Very well, sir. If you will forgive me, I must return to my duties." My desk's touch panels were lit up to an alarming degree.

"One question before you do. I'm curious: the idea of talking to a ghost doesn't bother you? It certainly seemed to distress Jacob."

"In the course of my reading, I have learned of the existence of discorporeal beings, such as those from Beta Pisces. Why should I not speak to you?"

He sounded amused. "There's been a great deal said, over the centuries, about the benefits of having an open mind. My friend, it's a pleasure to meet someone with a *truly* open mind," and he bowed to me.

At a loss for an appropriate response, I paused, then with some hesitation nodded and replied, "Thank you, sir." He did not seem displeased with my reaction. I returned to my desk and began dealing with the waiting message traffic.

When I had finally referred or otherwise disposed of everything, I glanced up. The ghost had vanished.

I commented on the fact to my master that evening

as we floated up the airlift to the penthouse apartment. "The ghost did not stay very long, did it?"

"Ghost, my butt. I'll bet those irresponsible idiots in R & D were fooling around again."

I was puzzled. "But sir, you checked with them—I put the call through myself."

"They're b-s'ing me again. Not that it matters, I expect that sort of thing. I told them to cut it out. They got the message. Good riddance to it, whatever it was."

But my master was premature in his conclusions. The ghost was in the office when we entered the next morning. It appeared that he had been there for some time, for he was seated at my desk, and displayed in the view tank was a company file. A confidential company file—I could see the triple scarlet "C" flashing in the corner of the document. The ghost glanced up, disapproval on his face. "Not implementing the new safety regulations? Really, Jacob, this is inexcusable."

"How *dare* you invade my files!"

"Quite easily. How can you stop me? There's advantages to being a ghost, you know." The ghost looked grim. "You must put this right, Jacob. You're needlessly endangering the lives of your workers. To say nothing of breaking the law."

I shared the ghost's views; it did not make sense to me that my master would deliberately contravene legal regulations. But when I tried to discuss it with him, he would tell me to be quiet, and, of course, that ended the matter since it was a direct order. I was curious to see if the ghost would prove more effective in getting him to change his behavior.

But it did not appear promising. My master reacted as he always did, bristling with anger. "Who the hell are you to tell me how to run my business?"

The ghost spoke firmly. "You have lived in and for yourself for far too long, Jacob. It is time you came out of your shell and looked around you. And what better time for an awakening than Christmas, the time of good cheer and joy among people?"

My master snorted. "Christmas again! One day a year everyone behaves like little angels. Then they all go back to their usual lying, cheating, stealing selves. Why bother at all?"

The ghost replied, "You're wrong. Christmas doesn't live in the hearts of people of goodwill only one day a year, but every day of the year. But so what if a few only live it one day a year? Or a few days of the holiday season? You're hardly in a position to pass judgment, Jacob—you don't live it at all."

"At least I'm honest about it."

"That kind of 'honesty' doesn't merit any pride. And you've been dishonest about those safety regulations."

"I don't give a damn *what* you think!" he shouted at the ghost. "And keep your nose out of my business affairs!" He stormed into his office, slamming the door behind him.

I looked at the ghost. "I was hoping you would succeed where I failed in the matter of the safety regulations. He refuses to discuss it with me."

The ghost raised his eyebrows. "An android with a sense of moral outrage? You intrigue me, Friday."

"Oh, no, sir. But I do know what is considered ethical business practice. If nothing else, his refusal strikes me as short-sighted. It will cost money to implement the regulations, but in the long run, there will be less downtime due to injuries, fewer medical pay-outs, and so on. And it is unfair to his employees: implicit in their service to him is the trust that he will provide safe working conditions."

The ghost smiled. "You may deny it, but you certainly *sound* like an android with ethics. I don't think Jacob has any idea of how special his personal attendant truly is."

I felt a stirring of pleasure and was astonished. Personal Servitors, Inc. regards itself as one of the most advanced manufacturers of android servants, and felt it important that androids receive gratification from satisfactory performance of their duties. Thus, programming for personal attendants such as myself allows us to experience such feelings in response to our masters—and supposedly *only* our masters. Yet here I was feeling an emotional response to another being—a discorporeal being at that. Perhaps those tracks of my bubble memory were faulty? They are the most sensitive parts of our programming. Furthermore, they had seldom been accessed in my years with my master. I made a mental note to run some memory checks in the evening, after my duties were ended.

Now that I considered it, I seemed to be running a lot of diagnostics as a result of the ghost's presence.

If my master thought he could get rid of the ghost by slamming the door on him, he was sadly mistaken. The ghost would simply appear without warning and there was nothing my master could do about it. This put him in a foul temper immediately, so that he was in no mood to listen to whatever it was the ghost wished to say to him. When he reached the shouting stage, the ghost would retire from the field of battle. He always had a pleasant greeting for me, but I could not help but notice how he was looking more discouraged as the days wore on.

I was in the kitchen one evening, just removing a batch of Christmas cookies from the oven, when the ghost appeared.

"You cook, too? You're a multi-talented creation, Friday," he laughed.

"Personal attendants have a wide range of skills," I replied. "Though I do not prepare my master's meals—he uses the auto-cook for that, or he has me order a meal to be delivered."

"I notice Jacob seems to place great confidence in modern technology, judging by the way he relies on it in his household," said the ghost.

"I would have to respectfully disagree, sir," I replied. "My master often complains about how expensive the various mechanisms are, and how precise he must be in his instructions to them and to me. He has said a number of times to me that he prefers dealing with humans, who 'don't have to have to be told every little detail.' "

"Then why doesn't he employ human servants? He certainly could afford them."

"He complains that they are unreliable and cannot be counted on to show loyalty." I paused. "I believe it might have something to do with the fact that human servants would not work for him for very long."

The ghost smiled slightly. "It seems that poor Jacob is doomed to perpetual disappointment, then."

"It would seem so," I replied. The cookies had cooled enough to hold their shape, and I used a spatula to lift them off the sheet and onto a rack to cool further.

The ghost watched with interest. "I can't imagine Jacob being interested in frivolities like Christmas cookies. There's not even any decorations around the apartment."

"I did put up seasonal decorations the first Christmas I came to work for Mr. Widdoes—I thought it was the accepted thing to do. I purchased a tree and put tiny glo-globes on the branches, and glass balls. And I bought a Nativity scene and put it on the mantle, and wreaths on the windows." I paused, remembering how he'd swept the tiny manger, the shepherds and kings, to the floor in anger. "But my master informed me that it was not appropriate, and I refrained from doing it again."

The ghost looked at me with sympathy in his eyes. "I'm sorry to hear he felt that way, Friday. I can promise you, with any other master, your decorations would have been greeted with delight."

"Perhaps you are right, but it is irrelevant. My duty

is to Mr. Widdoes, and of course his wishes are paramount."

The ghost was silent as I finished transferring the cookies. The previous batch I had made were ready to be packed away, so I placed them in a gaily decorated box, then closed the lid. I added it to the other, already prepared boxes on the counter.

"Since Jacob isn't interested in cookies, who *are* you baking them for? And why?" he asked.

"I bake them for the junior staff. I fear my master pays what you might call 'bottom dollar' for some of his less-skilled employees, yet expects them to work the same extensive hours he himself does. For them, both time and money are limited resources."

"Doesn't Jacob get annoyed at the waste of your time and his resources?"

I was mildly uncomfortable, as my programmers intended me to be when I am edging close to contravening my duty parameters. "I have not told him. The cost is a very small percentage of his household budget, and I do the baking at times when he does not require my services. I regard it as a way of rewarding his staff and thus keeping them working at optimum efficiency."

The ghost gave a delighted laugh. "And how does the staff feel about the boss's personal attendant baking them Christmas goodies?"

I paused, uncomfortable again. Pleasure in performing my duties . . . perhaps those memory tracks had been faulty longer than I had permitted myself to realize. "They seemed pleased that I would take the time," I said at last.

"Friday, you're a source of constant delight to me," said the ghost.

Once again I felt a stirring of gratitude in response to his words, stronger this time than before. Perhaps I should arrange for servicing? It was not yet time for my annual check-in, but. . . .

"Thank you, sir. May I say that I enjoy your company?"

The ghost chuckled. "You certainly may."

Matters between my master and the ghost did not improve. One evening, I was in the study with Mr. Widdoes, helping him plan his schedule for the next quarter. Neither of us heard anything, but when my master glanced up, the ghost was sitting on the sofa, studying him intently.

"I've never met anyone as unrepentant as you, Jacob. What am I going to do with you?"

"Nothing," growled my master. "I'm sick of hearing about Christmas, good will, and my fellow man. I just want to be left alone so I can run my business in peace."

"So you've told me many times, Jacob. You feel money is a more worthwhile pursuit than faith."

"Damn right I do. I've never killed anyone, but millions of people have been slaughtered in the name of religion."

The ghost's expression became sad. "And so you turn your back on it. You're confusing the message itself with those who speak about the message. Not that you're the first to do so."

"And I'm quite sure I won't be the last."

"I'm quite sure you won't either, unfortunately."

My master regarded the ghost. "If you're so all-fired concerned with rehabilitating me, why don't you show me something solid that will force me to believe you? Show me Hell. Or Paradise—either will do."

"I can't do that, Jacob. I'm not permitted to compel. The mortal must choose his path of his own free will."

My master looked delighted. "*That's* all it takes? For me to make my choice?"

"Yes, Jacob, that's all."

"And you'll leave me alone if I do?"

"Yes," said the ghost, resignation in his voice.

"Then I choose to stay as I am."

"Very well, Jacob. I'll make no more attempts to influence you."

"Good. That's exactly what I wanted to hear. Now get lost." Without another word, the ghost vanished before our eyes. "At last!" my master sighed. Then he turned to me. "And you—if that thing reappears and I catch you talking to it, I'll send you to the salvage yard. Do you understand?"

"Of course, master," I replied.

But things did not end quite there.

My master had long since gone to bed and the night was still. I was in the library, reading a very old story about Christmas, when I sensed I was not alone. I looked up, and saw the ghost sitting in the chair across from me. "Hello, my friend," he said.

"Hello," I replied. "Did I misunderstand? I thought you had gone, now that my master has made his choice."

"Oh yes, I'm gone, as far as he's concerned—I won't appear to him again. But you, Friday, you're another matter. Full of surprises you are. I've been checking the household accounts," said the ghost. "Baking cookies on the sly isn't your only secret, is it?"

I cannot blush, of course, but I began to have some comprehension of what my master felt upon discovering the ghost going through his confidential business files. I did not know how to reply, for I knew at the time it was possible I was exceeding my initiative parameters.

My discomfort must have showed, for the ghost smiled at me and said gently, "Come now, what you were doing is something to be proud of, not ashamed. Anonymously sending a Christmas hamper of food to a needy mother and her young child is hardly a hanging offense."

At last I found my voice. "But I was not instructed by my master to do so."

"Let me guess. Jacob told you to 'take care of it' after deciding to fire her, correct?"

I nodded. "His reasoning seemed faulty to me. If he had allowed on-site childcare, she would not have missed the work days due to the illness of her baby."

" 'Childcare? Too damned expensive,' I imagine," the ghost said wryly.

"A short-term view, it seems to me. In the long run, the benefits—"

The ghost held up his hand. "I know, my friend, and I agree with you." He paused. "I'd say you carried out his instructions to the letter. You 'took care of it,' fully and with compassion." I felt gratification at his words, as I had before, and again wondered at my reaction. "In fact, I'd say that you understood what Christmas is truly about far better than the man you call your master. Forgive me for not noticing it sooner."

"Of course, sir," I answered. "It is entirely understandable. You could hardly be expected to expend precious time on an android servant, when your task is to redeem my master."

He frowned. "Redemption is not for me to grant. That gift belongs to the Child whose birth we celebrate. And I fear Jacob is truly in need of His mercy, for it's proved beyond my skill to reach him." Then he looked at me and smiled. "But *you*, now. . . ."

I foresaw a problem. "But, sir," I said, "From my reading I understood that in order to be redeemed, one must have a soul. I am an artificial construct." I paused, for to my surprise, I found it difficult to ask the question I knew must be asked. "Do I have a soul?"

The ghost regarded me for a long moment, then he said at last, "My friend, I don't know. I'm not the one Who judges."

Disappointment is not part of my programming, so the reaction I felt in response to his answer might have been related to the possible problem with my bubble memory. "Metaphysics is a subtle topic, one I do not fully understand," I said. "I will have to read more deeply, and perhaps that way achieve enlightenment."

"I'm not sure that more reading will help you find an answer," said the ghost. His face brightened. "Some things are best learned by living. Why not come with me? You'll have an opportunity to meet many people, some wise in the ways of mercy and compassion, some poor in spirit, some eager to right the wrongs they've seen committed, others needing but a touch to start down the path of good will—and some, like Jacob, unreachable. You'd learn much and I know you'd enjoy it."

I felt a sudden surge of longing that overwhelmed my usual programming. To have such an opportunity offered to me! To travel the world and learn as no one of my kind had ever had a chance to learn before! To fully exploit the potential designed in me! How could I refuse?

The ghost said gently, "Well, Friday? Will you be my companion?"

Companion. Not servant or attendant. An equal, not an underling.

But then my programming reasserted control. My duty was to my master. That was why I had been constructed, why I had been programmed, and why the man Jacob Widdoes had purchased me.

I looked at the Christmas ghost and finally replied, "I cannot."

The ghost looked at me a long, long time, and his expression was sad. "I'm not permitted to compel, only to offer. This is the first time I have ever regretted that stricture, Friday."

I could think of nothing to say.

He smiled, but it was not a happy smile. "One will not, one cannot. I don't know which is the greater tragedy." He paused for a moment. "I've failed in my assignment, so it is ended; and we are not allowed to linger. I must bid you farewell, my friend. I will never forget you."

"Good-bye, sir. I will not forget you either." My voice seemed unsteady for some reason; I made a note to set a firm date for servicing. Whatever the cause, obviously I was not performing at peak efficiency.

"Friday!" I turned; my master had entered the room. "I heard your voice. Have you been talking to that spook?"

I glanced back to where the ghost had stood. "It has gone, master, and will not return."

"So you were talking to yourself, were you? Make an appointment to get serviced. I won't put up with a half-crazy android."

An odd heaviness of spirit seemed to descend on me, but I responded promptly. "An excellent idea, master. I was thinking of doing exactly that—I have noticed that I do not seem to be operating at optimum levels."

He stalked away, muttering under his breath. My acute audio sensors could pick up the words, however: "Dummy!"

I was inclined to agree with him. The chance of a lifetime, and I had declined it.

I wonder if my programmers would be proud of their work?

CADENZA

by Terry McGarry

Terry McGarry was runner-up for the 1992 Gryphon Award.

The night they first heard her, the air seemed cold enough to freeze sound. It left Jeffreys Falls, a quiet town on any night, swathed in silence; crossing the parking lot of St. Mark's, Anna wondered if, were she to speak, the words would crystallize as they came out of her mouth, forming lattices as complex as snow-flakes, which would collect in drifts of thought on the hard ground.

Inside, the rest of the choir was gathered around the organ in the sanctuary. On Sunday mornings, before services, they practiced around the old upright in the undercroft, so as not to disturb early worshipers, but this was a weeknight and they had the small church building to themselves.

"I–I'm sorry I'm late," Anna mumbled, as she draped her coat over the back of a pew and grabbed a hymnal.

She was not that late, though she had hoped to be; Charles, the portly organist and choirmaster, had not even sat down at the organ yet, and he waved her apology off. "I have that music for you, Anna," he said, riffling through papers in a folder. "We can try sight reading it tonight."

Oh, well, Anna thought; not late enough.

While the other choir members chatted quietly, Anna, along with Grace and Nancy, stepped up to the

organ and listened while Charles played through the
alto solo from the "Messiah" that he had chosen for
them to do as a trio. Usually the introductions to the
hymns washed over Anna like warm water, relaxing
muscles and leaching tension away, leaving her free to
revel in the joy of singing. But not this time.

"Anna, why don't you go first—try the whole thing
through," Charles said. She looked up at him quickly,
but saw only kindliness on his face. Perhaps he wanted
to help her break the ice, get it over with as quickly
as possible.

He was still patient when, after three tries at a long
melisma in the second section, she kept running out
of breath in the same place.

"It's a long phrase," he said. "It won't be so bad
when you sing it up to speed."

She smiled shyly; inwardly, she cringed. The offer
to do a trio on Christmas Eve had been too flattering
to refuse, but even here, in the familiar, high-raftered
church, with only her choirmates listening, she was so
nervous she could barely sing. Thank goodness they
had all of Advent to rehearse. Thank goodness she
had some time to work up the courage to beg off
doing it at all.

"All right," Charles said. "Nancy next."

Anna calmed down as she listened to the other
women sing, and soon she was surrounded by the rest
of the choir as they ran through some hymns. This
was what she loved, the interweaving of the threads
of voices, the way the disparate group—its members
differing in age, appearance, outlook—breathed as
one creature, united in the music. For Anna, it was a
form of prayer.

Sometimes she wished she *could* sing alone. She'd
been told she had a good voice, and at home she sang
her heart out, for happiness or sadness, whatever she
was feeling. It would be a blessing, a witness, to be
able to share it with the congregation; people shared
what talents they had, and though she basked in the

harmony of choral singing, she was saddened by her inability to share her one gift more fully. Almost everyone else alternated solos; for that matter, almost everyone else seemed to have other things to give—administrative ability, stewardship, outreach. . . .

But they did sound awfully good tonight, and she could not be sad for long. They sounded better than they ever had before, in fact; the imminent Christmas season must be motivating everyone to give their fullest voice. The sopranos sounded especially angelic, she thought, and smiled as they approached the end of hymn 94, which had a nice descant in verses two and six. Their voices soared, to high F, high G—

Anna glanced up. Some of the others—a tenor here, a bass there—had stopped singing; their faces were awed and confused. Anna stopped, too, and watched the three sopranos. They sounded much more together than usual, much fuller, not straining for the notes. What was different? As the concluding chords faded away, Anna heard an odd echo, something she'd never noticed in three years of singing with this same group. Something almost like a sigh. . . .

"Wow!" said Mary Ellen, a short, dark-haired soprano. "That was wild."

"Lovely, ladies, lovely," Charles said. "Particularly the descant."

He got them started on the next hymn; they only had an hour or so before people would have to get home for supper. It was Anna's favorite carol, "Angels We Have Heard On High." Partway through the refrain, nearly everyone in the choir stopped singing. Mary Ellen kept going for a few measures, finishing the first half of the refrain, and then her voice, too, dropped away—

Leaving one voice, still singing.

Charles' fingers must have slipped on the keys, for he missed a few notes; his feet dropped completely away from the foot pedals. But he kept playing, and the sweet, heartbreaking, ethereal voice sang the final

"Gloria in excelsis Deo"; then it, too, died away, with the last chord.

For a long moment no one spoke. Some of them stared at each other; some stared at Charles, as if it had been some trick of his instrument. Anna, inexplicably, found her eyes drawn to the rafters; but there was nothing visible in their crisscrossing shadows.

Sam Leeson, a millworker who sang bass, grunted. "Someone's idea of a little Advent humor," he said. But his feet shifted back and forth.

Grace, in a take-charge manner, checked the PA system, which was off; she looked under the lectern, tapped the microphone, went into the crying room and checked the speakers. Alex and Nicholas, brothers who sang tenor, checked the sacristy and the back stairs to the undercroft; other choir members began searching under pews, under the narthex tables, one even shining a flashlight into Father Uher's locked office.

Finally, Charles clapped his hands. "Come on, everyone, this is silly. I have no idea what that was, but we don't have much rehearsal time this season, so we'd better not waste what we have on some practical joke. Let's go. Number 103, in unison."

They gathered reluctantly, sang hesitantly; the sopranos, in particular, looked uneasy. Everyone kept glancing up from the hymnals.

But the eerie, disembodied voice did not sound again.

Anna drove home, past the sparkling Christmas displays of the shops on Main Street, to her lonely two-story house. She kept shivering when she remembered the sound of that voice, but it was more the kind of frisson she got when music deeply affected her, and less the shudder engendered by a spooky book.

It just hadn't felt like a trick, and despite the giggles and head shakes of the choir as they had said good night, she suspected the others felt the same way.

As she hung her coat on the oaken rack, Anna glanced at the pictures of her parents on the sideboard in the front hall.

Loved ones should be remembered with joy, she thought, regarding the freeze-framed smiles of happier times. But the grieving never ends; it just mellows, its sharp peaks weathered down to rounded hills of loss.

She had never married, and held only odd jobs, and Mother and Dad had allowed her to live in this house into her adulthood; when they'd grown elderly and ill, she'd been able to take care of them at home, and the hard work had been well worth it, saving them the indignity of nursing homes and hospitals. But aside from her few hobbies, they had been her life. Now that they were gone, she had only the house they had left her, filled with memories.

I wish this house were haunted, she thought, sliding a frozen dinner into the microwave and wandering back into the living room. Then I could always be with them; I would never be alone at Christmas again. But with that she realized she'd articulated what must have been on everyone's mind: that the voice that had sung with them, adding beauty and clarity to their group without outshining it, had been some kind of haunting.

Anna sat in a faded, floral-patterned wing chair, inhaled the musty scent of the old house, looked at the books and antiques that had been her parents' pride and joy. The only ghosts are the ones in our own hearts, she told herself. She switched on the television set.

At the local library where Anna worked shelving books, the supervisor charged her with putting up the Christmas decorations. It took her a few days, in between her regular assignments, to cart out the boxes of lights and garlands and wreaths, and set up the ladder in various locations to nail them up. But the job cheered her, made her feel Christmassy, and by the time the next rehearsal rolled around, she felt almost too happy to be nervous. It wasn't that bad to be alone during Advent, even if you were as shy and tongue-tied as she was, because there were always people nearby, there was always someone to smile at.

The three altos sang the "Messiah" excerpt together, after the other soloists had run through their own pieces. But even with two voices accompanying her, Anna felt spotlit, scrutinized. She kept losing her place, misreading the words; she flubbed several notes in the faster passages.

It was with a mixture of guilt and hope that she looked up at Charles when they were finished. Maybe he'll let me off the hook, she thought. Maybe I won't have to insult him by bowing out.

But he said, "That's fine, that's coming along nicely. We'll portion out sections next week. Number 109, everyone."

Anna opened her hymnal, feeling numb. Sections? She would have to sing a section alone? What was Charles trying to do to her? Speak up, she told herself; tell him how you feel. But she couldn't do it. She resolved to talk to him after rehearsal, in private. They began "The First Noël."

There was an optional descant, during which everyone but the sopranos sang the refrain in unison. Anna tried and failed to be surprised when the strange extra voice began to sing again, its pure high Gs ringing like chimes, emanating from no pinpointable location. Mary Ellen and the other sopranos dropped out, flustered, but Charles, with an odd look on his face, continued to play. "Keep singing, everyone," he said. "Sopranos, sing melody. That's it!" The choir went through all six verses, with the disembodied voice singing descant on the refrains.

"What on Earth *is* it?" cried Grace, a bit hysterically, when they were through.

"Whatever it is, it's beautiful," said Mary Ellen.

The choir erupted into debate. "It's a ghost!" "That's nuts." "Do you think it will sing with us at

Christmas?" "I'm searching this place top to bottom, right now." "Why bother? It's a ghost, you won't find anything." "That's the most preposterous ..."

Anna could still hear the sweet notes singing in her head. "I think we should call her a her, not an it," she said softly. Then she put a hand to her mouth as everyone turned to her abruptly. She almost never said anything; but in her ghost-induced reverie, she'd forgotten to be shy. "I–I'm sorry," she started, then fell silent.

"That's all right," Charles said gently. "Somehow, Anna, I have a feeling you're right." Before debate could break out again, he added, "Now, I'll talk to Father Uher about this tomorrow, all right? For the moment, let's just rehearse as usual. If it—she—sings, try to ignore it. The show must go on."

And so they sang, and the voice sang with them. They had never sounded so good. It wasn't just the voice; it was the way the voice made them sing their best. Anna felt mesmerized; when you really listened to the voice, got past its silvery beauty and other-worldly reverberation, you could hear a sadness in it, a yearning that made Anna's chest constrict. Her decision to talk to Charles about her solo slipped completely from her mind.

She took the next day off from work and went in to church. Father Uher was out making calls, but Stacy Cox, the church secretary, told Anna that Charles had phoned and that Father Uher had agreed to sit in on their next rehearsal.

"Uh, Stacy, I have a favor to ask you," Anna said, twisting a slim notepad in her hands. "I wonder if you could help me go through the canonical register; I want to try to find—something out."

Stacy cocked an eyebrow. "You want to track down your ghost?"

What makes you think it's *my* ghost? Anna wanted

to ask, but instead she nodded, squirming a little, expecting to be laughed at.

"Sure, come on. Episcopal registers are usually a mess, I should warn you; sometimes I feel like a verger in a Dickens novel, poring over baptismal records to find out who's the heir to some fortune. But I'll point you in the right direction."

It took most of the morning—Stacy left her to it, since the parish newsletter's deadline was the next day—but by noon Anna's notebook contained a list of women who had died in the last few years. She had starred some of the names, meaning that that person had sung in the choir. Not all good singers did, of course; and there was nothing to indicate that the ghost had been a parishioner at all. Anna knew her search was crazy. But something in the memory of that voice compelled her. She tried not to question her own motives.

She spent the afternoon phoning around town, tracking down relatives. She'd crossed off half the names by suppertime, for one reason or another. Just as she was about to give up, she got through to the widower of the least likely name on her list: a woman who'd been baptized and had funeral rites at St. Mark's, but had left the parish forty years before.

"Yeah, Jill loved to sing," Mr. O'Connell said. He'd been suspicious at first, a bit bewildered, but seemed eager to talk about his wife; Anna thought he must miss her terribly. "I'm a Catholic, so she switched over, but she missed St. Mark's something awful. She grew up there, you know. I'll always regret that. . . . Anyways, she came down with cancer, had her larynx removed; had to talk with one of them boxes. Lived a good fifteen years after; died during Advent. Always said she missed the caroling most of all. I had her funeral at St. Mark's, to make up for things, like. Your rector was real nice about it."

Anna listened to him as he went on about Jill; it seemed to make him feel better, and she knew how bereavement felt. "Would you like to come down and hear us rehearse?" she asked, and immediately wondered if she'd made a mistake; then he said yes, if she'd give him a lift, and she didn't know how to retract her impulsive offer.

But when the slight, grizzled man was sitting in a pew, listening to them sing, hearing the ghostly voice, the look of awe and joy on his face convinced Anna that she'd done the right thing. He did break down in tears a few minutes later, so it was fortunate that Father Uher was there; Charles cut the rehearsal short as the priest took Mr. O'Connell into his office to comfort him in private.

"Anna, I remember that funeral," Grace said. "It was three years ago. Assuming that's really her ghost, what made her start singing with us now?"

Anna shook her head; she had no idea. The choir was arguing again, in noisy whispers: "She'll be great PR! We'll have a packed church." "Yeah, and cars all over our lawns and total disruption, like with that statue down in Jersey." "This is a giant hoax; I can't believe you people take it seriously." "What do we tell people at Christmas? 'Our church is haunted.' Yeah, right." "Let's just sing, we'll sound great, nobody has to know why." "That is *so* self-aggrandizing! And I don't know if I want to be shown up by a dead person. . . ." But past the flurries of gesticulation, the faces beaming or frowning or smirking, Anna saw Charles looking at her over the organ's polished surface. When she met his eyes, he just smiled and turned away to gather up his things; but the look had been thoughtful, appraising.

Anna felt suddenly uncomfortable, and went out to get the car so she could pick up Mr. O'Connell at the front door.

"She was shy, you know," said Mr. O'Connell—or Rob, as he had told Anna to call him. "Dunno if she'd like a lot of attention. You know, like the media, all that.''

Anna glanced over at him; he looked tiny, engulfed by the bucket seat of her subcompact, with oncoming headlights deepening the wrinkles in what skin his beard didn't hide. "You know," she said quietly, "I could really use a cup of coffee. How about we stop by the diner on Route 23, and we can talk more about Jill?"

Rob's face opened into a smile. "I'd like that, Anna. I'd like that an awful lot."

The night of the next, and final, rehearsal, Anna went to church an hour early. She lit a votive candle and prayed for a while—for her parents, for Jill, for lonely old Rob, who brightened up so when she visited—then slid a bill into the poor box and went to sit in one of the choir pews.

"Talking to Jill?" It was Charles, standing in the archway of the narthex. She hadn't heard him come in.

She shrugged. "I guess. You'd think her soul would be in Heaven, not down here singing with us. I hope she's okay." She knew she should tell him now, about the trio. It wouldn't be a big deal; Grace and Nancy could split it between them. Instead she said, "Do you think it's really her spirit, or just some kind of—I don't know, psychic echo?"

Charles sat down next to her, elbows propped on knees. "Anna, whatever Jill is, I think she sings because you're afraid to."

Anna paled. How did he know?

"I know you're doing this trio thing for me because I asked you to. I know it scares you. My homespun theory is that the ghost is responding to your emotions somehow. All I know for sure is that if you keep on stifling your own talent, you're going to feel lousy. Will you try the piece one more time, tonight?"

Anna nodded, but what she felt was panic. How could she say no now?

As the choir arrived and rehearsal began, she tried to forget her churning stomach by listening intently to the debate about the ghost; Father Uher had told Charles that he would wait to hear the choir's consensus before doing anything about it. But the arguments themselves were too upsetting; Anna felt they were threatening the poor ghost who, after all, wanted only to sing. Finally, overwhelmed by the whirling viewpoints, she stepped forward and spoke. "Jill's husband said she's shy," she told them. "Really shy. I know how that feels. I think we should just let her sing, and keep it to ourselves. It's the charitable thing to do. In—in my opinion."

Perhaps words from her, being so seldom uttered, carried extra weight.

"All right," someone said; "Okay," said Sam Leeson, "I'm gettin' kinda used to her, wouldn't want to drive her off." One by one, the other choir members agreed.

In her amazement, she sang right through her part in the "Messiah" trio, not brilliantly but clearly, audibly, no quavering, no lack of breath. Jill, she kept thinking, it's okay, no one's going to frighten you away....

Later, during the carols, she thought it might be gratitude that she heard in Jill's ethereal tones.

Christmas Eve. The church was packed, although the town was knee-deep in snow. Pine boughs and garlands festooned the walls, and each pew had a red velvet bow at the end; poinsettias bloomed around the chancel stairs and in every stained-glass window, and every candle was lit. The choir was to sing for half an hour before the service started, alternating performance pieces with carols sung with the congregation. Anna vested in a daze, pulling the cincture too tight around the middle of her white robe before remembering that she would need to breathe. How would

she ever be able to breathe, in front of two hundred
people?

Then the first carol had started, "Joy to the World,"
the altos and sopranos singing in thirds, and Anna
listened for Jill, but with two hundred extra voices it
was hard to tell if she was there or not. And suddenly
it was time: she was stepping forward with Grace and
Nancy, and Charles was playing the introductory measures of their piece. As Grace sang, Anna inhaled
deeply, of pine scent and parishioners' perfume. And
then, miraculously, she was singing—her voice rich,
with a gentle vibrato—and even as she focused intently on the music, she thought: This is for you, Jill,
for the voice that was locked away inside you all those
years, just as mine has been locked inside me. This is
for you, and for me, and for everyone here. This is
my Christmas gift to all of us.

There was no applause at the end; just a pause, and
then the next hymn. But when Anna looked out at
the gathered faces, she saw Rob O'Connell sitting in
the back, and he nodded to her. Then, as "The First
Noël" soared up into the rafters, she heard Jill's voice
clearly, blending into and accentuating the sopranos
on the brilliant descant. It wasn't something anyone
would notice; she could as well have been just another
member of the congregation.

Which, Anna thought, maybe she was. And it was
enough.

At the feast in the undercroft after the service, as
the clock chimed midnight and people wished each
other Merry Christmas, Anna thanked Charles for his
help and encouragement, and accepted a somewhat
startling invitation to dinner; then she turned to Father
Uher, and tried to rally some of her newfound
courage.

"I was wondering," she said; hesitated; then plunged
in. "If you have any openings on the shepherding com-
mittee, maybe I could help visit shut-ins, maybe the

nursing home. I've had a lot of practice with elderly folks, and, well . . ."

Father Uher smiled. "Knowing what you've done for Rob, I'm glad you volunteered before I drafted you."

A talent, to be shared, to be given: fulfilling one had made her recognize that there were others. Ways to come out of her shell, to reach out to people who were even more closed in than she was. Jill had reached out; it could be done.

She went upstairs into the peaceful, darkened church. The only sound was the ticking of snowflakes striking the windows, which glowed softly from the lights outside.

"I don't know if you'll come sing with us again next year," Anna said. "But I thank you, and I wish you well. Merry Christmas, Jill."

Then she turned and went back downstairs, where her family was waiting for her.

GORDIAN ANGEL

by Jack Nimersheim

Jack Nimersheim is the author of more than 20 non-fiction books and a dozen science fictions stories.

"It is required of every man, that the
spirit within him should walk abroad
among his fellowmen, and travel far and
wide; and if that spirit goes not forth
in life, it is condemned to do so after death."

—Jacob Marley's ghost,
A CHRISTMAS CAROL

Jonathan Thackeray is a mystery. He's like some intricate knot that I have to unravel, before I can trace the threads running through his life.

Yeah. That's the perfect description. This job reminds me of a marvelous story about Alexander the Great, the one where he fulfilled the prophecy of the Gordian Knot. Maybe you've heard it.

Seems like an oracle once told the ancient Phrygians, back around 2000 B.C. or so, that their next ruler would arrive riding in a cart. The oracle should have been a little more specific. You see, the next cart that rolled into town was driven by a peasant named Gordius, who, of course, the population immediately elected king; people followed their oracles pretty blindly back then, much like Americans today react to election polls.

It turns out that Gordius was an appreciative kind of guy. In gratitude for this unexpected rise in social

status, he dedicated his cart and yoke to Zeus—
fastened them to a pole, smack dab in the center of
the acropolis of Gordium. In case you haven't noticed,
Gordius was also quite vain. Like most kings, he felt
this overwhelming urge to name all sorts of places and
things in his honor, once he assumed the throne. But
I digress.

Now, Gordius may not have come from royal stock,
but the old geezer sure knew how to tie a knot. The
one he used to secure his yoke to that pole was a
killer. It was so deceptively elaborate, in fact, that
it prompted yet another oracle—soothsaying was big
business in ancient times—to declare that "whosoever
should unloose it would be ruler of all Asia."

By way of job qualifications, this makes about as
much sense as crowning someone king simply because
he knows how to steer a cart. Nevertheless, this second prophesy appears to have discouraged a number
of would-be conquerors from taking over a fairly large
chunk of the world, for a fairly long period of time.
According to the legend, you see, the Gordian Knot
held fast for approximately sixteen centuries, right up
until 334 B.C. That's when Alexander the Great came
along and came up with a creative way to "unloose" it.

Oh, yeah. Alexander went on to conquer Asia, just
like that second oracle foresaw. They didn't call him
Great for nothing, you know.

Anyway, back to Jonathan Thackeray. He reminds
me of that legendary knot. At first glance, Thackeray
doesn't seem all that complicated. Just your run-of-
the-mill serial killer who maimed, murdered, and then
dismembered people. Twelve, in all. Passing judgment
on the soul of a man like that should be a pretty easy
gig, one would think. I certainly did, when they first
handed me the job.

I pictured Thackeray's fate to be a straight line—
one covering the shortest distance between death and
eternal damnation. If ever a post-expiration interview
qualified as a mere formality, this was it. I mean, hey,

the man snuffed out a dozen of his fellow human beings, the souls of whom had already submitted sworn depositions confirming his identity.

The way I saw it, I'd ask a few routine questions, trot out these affidavits, then send Thackeray packing to Perdition City. What could he possibly say or do to diminish his culpability in this matter? Not a darn thing, I figured. (Actually, I would have stated my conviction a little more emphatically, were stronger language permitted here in the afterlife. It's not. So, "not a darn thing" will have to suffice.) Anyway, I expected this job to be the proverbial piece of cake. Wham! Bam! Damnation, man! Then on to my next assignment.

Look. I admit it. I was wrong, okay? So, sue me. When was the last time something *you* planned worked out exactly like you expected it to?

I was waiting for Thackeray as they threw the switch. He looked extremely disoriented, more so than most people when they transcend the physical world and settle into their first few seconds of Eternity. This didn't surprise me. Thackeray's soul literally erupted from his body—forcibly ejected, no doubt, by the 1,500 volts of alternating current flowing between the moistened electrodes attached to his head and right calf. Pretty gruesome stuff. But then, no more hideous than Thackeray's own acts, which procured him a reserved seat in the electric chair to begin with.

Try as I might (although, I must confess, I didn't try *that* hard), I found it difficult to marshal much compassion. Instead, I watched in grim satisfaction as Thackeray's spirit, suspended several feet above a now-charred carcass—medium-rare—*twitched*.

Does that word adequately describe the actions of something so ethereal as a soul? Not really. But in this instance, it works.

I gave my new charge approximately fifteen seconds to adjust to his new surroundings. That's nowhere near enough time, I realize. Tough bananas. Sympathy for the Devil may be a catchy title for a rock-and-roll song, but it's not an emotion I care to cultivate.

"Okay, Thackeray. Intermission's over. Time to move on to the next act."

"Merry Christmas."

This was the only thing Thackeray had said—mumbled, would be a more apt description—since we'd arrived. I asked him if he knew where he was and he answered . . .

"Merry Christmas."

I asked him if he understood why he was booked for a one-way excursion down the River Styx and he responded . . .

"Merry Christmas."

I asked him if there was any explanation, *anything,* he could offer in defense of his indefensible deeds and he replied . . .

"Merry Christmas."

What we had here was your basic failure to communicate. There I was, threatening a crazed psychopath with fire and brimstone, and all he did was keep wishing me a happy holiday. Now I'm no Pythagoras, I'll admit, but either Thackeray was working some totally new angle on me or something about this whole scenario didn't add up to 360°. I had to determine which of the two it was, before passing sentence on this bozo.

You see, our judicial system, for want of a better term, isn't like Earth's. Down on *terra firma,* a legal decision can be rife with ambiguities, leaving a person's final fate somewhat up in the air. Should anything go amiss, there's almost always another court, slightly higher upon the legal ladder, waiting to straighten things out. Since we did away with purgatory a while back, however, all God's children ultimately end up in one of two places: heaven or hell. There ain't no in-between anymore. And there aren't any appeals, once a final verdict is handed down. It would hardly be fair to lock someone away behind the gates of Hades, without first making darn sure this condemnation is justified.

In order to give Thackeray a fair shake, therefore, I had to try to figure out why he was so obsessed with Christmas. I then had to determine what it was about this holiest of holy days that could push a man so far over the edge as to transform him into a savage killer.

A sinking feeling developed where my stomach used to be, back when I had one. My supposed piece of cake was turning into a pan of baklava.

"He's what?"

"According to our research, he's the Ghost of Christmas Present."

That sinking feeling dropped a little lower within the pit of my nonexistent digestive tract. The story of Jonathan Thackeray already had more twists in it than your typical O'Henry plot. This latest, however, was by far the most convoluted of the lot.

"The Ghost of . . . as in Scrooge's second escort from *A Christmas Carol*? C'mon, man. You've got to be yanking my chain!"

"Those of us who work down here in the Bureau of Missing Souls take our responsibilities very seriously, I assure you. We don't yank anyone's chain, as you so flippantly phrased it."

"Sorry, pal. I wasn't trying to insult your precious profession. But the Ghost of Christmas Present? Don't you think you guys might be reaching a bit on this one?

"First of all, *A Christmas Carol* is a piece of fiction. It's a parable, an allegory reflecting the author's belief that everyone has a right to a decent standard of living. Second, Dickens wrote that story in the mid-eighteen hundreds—somewhere around 1840, if I remember correctly. How in the heck does a fictional character from a nineteenth-century fable resurface more than a hundred years later as a very real mass murderer?"

"That's not my problem, is it? You asked us to help you identify a soul you've been assigned to adjudicate. This is precisely what we did.

"The last time this department was evaluated, our performance rating was quite impressive. 99.9997 percent, as I recall. Looking at it another way, there's approximately a .0003 percent possibility that our findings on this matter are in error. I can state with almost absolute certainty, therefore, that your mysterious Mr. Thackeray is, indeed, the Ghost of Christmas Present. A highly unusual revelation, I'll admit. Nevertheless, one can't deny the facts.

"And now, if you'll excuse me, it appears that someone has submitted yet another request for any information we have about Amelia Earhart. That's the second time this shift. The truly great mysteries never lose their appeal."

Talk about a split decision! On the plus side, I finally had an answer to my most critical question: Who was Jonathan Thackeray? Over on the negative side of the scorecard, however, the answer I had only opened the door to more questions.

A few minutes earlier, my only worry was a maniac. Now I found myself dealing with a myth, as well. Some mornings, it just doesn't pay to strap on the old wings and hit the celestial treadmill.

"Merry Christmas."

This riff was beginning to bore me. Since finding out who Thackeray really was, I'd been trying to break through to him for almost two weeks, as mortals measure time. Despite all my efforts, we still hadn't managed to get past the Season's Greetings stage of our relationship.

Once again, I couldn't help thinking about that Gordian Knot. There were secrets bound up inside Thackeray's demented mind that I needed to know. There had to be some way to unravel these memories I just hadn't discovered it yet.

My only solid lead in the mystery surrounding Jonathan Thackeray remained Dickens' popular story. Somehow, I had to get him to remember that time, that place. If I could return Thackeray to the past, maybe we could pick up the trail from there and begin a journey that would lead me, ultimately, to an explanation of his current madness.

That's when inspiration struck. Of course! If *A Christmas Carol* seemed a likely starting point, then why not start there, literally? The idea formulating in my mind was a crazy one, I'll admit. But maybe, just maybe, it would be crazy enough to work.

It took me another week to set up my little experiment. I wanted everything to be just right. It had to be, if this nutty idea was to have even a slim chance of succeeding. I surveyed my handiwork one final time before calling Thackeray into the room.

The walls were covered with all the right foliage—berries, holly, mistletoe, ivy. Laying my mitts on a stand-alone fireplace had been no easy task; the symbolism suggested by fire is anathema to those of us who ended up on—How shall I put this?—the less sweltering side of the Almighty's sunny disposition. But there it was, a mighty blaze roaring on its hearth, flames leaping up the chimney. The *piece de resistance,* however, lay in the great amounts of food heaped upon the floor. Turkeys, geese, game, poultry, brawn, great joints of meat, suckling pigs ... well, you get the picture. And these were just the entrees. I'd also managed to scrape together mince pies, plum puddings, red-hot chestnuts, cherry-cheeked apples, immense twelfth-cakes and assorted other items guaranteed to tempt even the most adamant anorexic. Several seething bowls of punch permeated the air with their delicious steam.

Truth to tell, I felt kind of silly sitting in the middle

of this bounty, clothed as I was in nothing but a green mantle bordered with white fur. The holly wreath bedecked with shining icicles sitting atop my head didn't help matters any. Nor did the rusty scabbard slung around my waist, made all the more ridiculous by the fact that it did not even contain a sword. Oh, yeah. And then there was the torch, a pretty good reproduction of Plenty's horn, if I do say so myself. I seriously debated whether my deception required this last, admittedly melodramatic element. Then I figured, What the heck? I might as well go for broke. It was all for a good cause. Any embarrassment I might be forced to endure would be worth it—provided this crazy scheme worked. Now seemed as good a time as any to find out if it would.

Putting on the most cheery voice I could manage, I exclaimed, "Come in! Come in! and get to know me better, man!"

On cue, someone opened the door and let Thackeray into the room. He entered timidly, his head lowered, and mumbled, "Merry Christmas."

"Look upon me!" I commanded. He did. And when he did, he noticed me. I mean, *truly* noticed me. (Let's face it. I was a little hard to miss, sitting there amidst such grandeur, wearing such an outlandish outfit.) "You have never seen the like of me before!"

"Who? What?" It was the first time Thackeray's eyes had displayed any emotion other than absolute ennui. It was also the first time I'd ever heard anything other than insipid holiday greetings cross his lips. I decided to press on.

"Have you never walked forth with the younger members of my family; meaning (for I am quite young) my elder brothers born in these later years?"

Maybe it was the mention of family that did it; ancestral ties are strong, even in the spirit world. More likely, Thackeray responded to the total tableau. How could he not? So many sights, sounds, and scents—a cornucopia of overlapping stimuli designed to over-

whelm the senses. But would his response be the one
I'd hoped for?

"Don't I know you? I feel as if I should. Wait a
minute. I don't merely know you. I *am* you. Or you
are me. One of the two. I'm not sure which one. But
I do recognize you. I know what you're supposed to
be. I recognize this place also. I've been here before.
This is where I . . . where I . . ." His voice trailed off
into a hollow, haunting silence.

C'mon, man, I found myself mentally prompting
him. *Put it all together. You can do it. I know you can.*

And then, in one terrible instant, he did.

"Oh, my God! This is Scrooge's room. This is where
it all started. The boy, Ignorance. The girl, Want. This
is where they first . . . they first . . ."

The Gordian Knot came unraveled. So, too, did
Jonathan Thackeray.

First, he screamed. Then, he collapsed—curling up
into a fetal position on the floor, there amidst the
turkeys and geese and game and mince pies and plum
puddings and red-hot chestnuts and cherry-cheeked
apples and all the rest.

Except for a table and two chairs, the room was
once again empty. I'd stripped it bare within an hour
of Thackeray's dramatic catharsis. The garish trap-
pings and bountiful feast had served their purpose.
Like Alexander the Great, I'd cleaved the Gordian
Knot. Thackeray's memory had returned.

"Ignorance and Want. They drove me to it, you
realize."

This reference no longer eluded me, not since I'd
managed to dig up an unabridged copy of *A Christmas
Carol*. Not every version of that famous tale includes
a complete account of Scrooge's experiences with his
second guide. More than a few omit the end of this
encounter, segueing immediately from the events at
the home of Scrooge's nephew to the midnight arrival
of the third and final ghost.

The seeds of Thackeray's insanity were planted during those often ignored final moments he spent with Scrooge. That's when, at the old money changer's request, he pulled from his robe two pitiful children, a boy and a girl. They were—well, I'll let Dickens' own words describe them: *"wretched, abject, frightful, hideous, miserable ... yellow, meagre, ragged, scowling, wolfish ... Where graceful youth should have filled their features out, and touched them with its freshest tints, a stale and shriveled hand, like that of age, had pinched, and twisted them, and pulled them into shreds. Where angels might have sat enthroned, devils lurked, and glared out menacing. No change, no degradation, no perversion of humanity, in any grade, through all the mysteries of wonderful creation, has monsters half so horrible and dread."*

Not exactly a family portrait of the Waltons, eh?

The boy, Thackeray had explained to Scrooge in his previous incarnation of Christmas Spirit, was Ignorance. The girl, Want. He also gave a warning to the old man. Once again, I'll step aside, in deference to Dickens' own account: *"Beware them both, and all of their degree, but most of all beware this boy, for on his brow I see that written which is Doom, unless the writing be erased."*

Within a few moments of making this dire prophecy, Thackeray, the Spirit, vanished. For the purposes of Dickens' plot, his story was over. As I now discovered, however, old Charlie had been sorely mistaken.

"You have no idea what it was like, being the custodian of those two. Recall, if you will, how deeply they affected Scrooge, and he only saw them for a few brief moments. I was forced to endure their company for decades.

"It wasn't so bad when they were young, still children in both body and mind. Certainly, they were formidable, even then. But being children, they remained under my control, submissive to my will. During their encounter with Scrooge, for example, as Dickens himself pointed out, they knelt down at my feet, and clung upon the outside of my garment.

"But children do not stay young forever. They age. They grow up. They evolve. And as they evolve, they pass through many phases, one of which is rebellion. In time these two children, which Fate had entrusted to my care, began to defy me.

"At first, their transgressions were minor. A series of innocent pranks. Nothing more. As the years passed, however, they became more and more daring in their deeds, more determined to gain their independence. Finally, they staged the ultimate rebellion. They ran away from home, so to speak, to weave their own designs within the tapestry of Man.

"Imagine Ignorance and Want personified turned loose upon the world, with no restraining hand to guide them. I did. But nothing I could imagine prepared me for the true depth of their malevolence, once they fled my guardianship.

"I watched in despair as the world reflected the delicate influence of these twin scourges. I watched as a pair of primal forces manipulated that world on both a global and personal scale. I watched as ignorance compelled one race or nationality to seek the destruction of another—not once, but time and time again. I watched as want became desire and, ultimately, metamorphosed into greed—stripping people of their innate generosity, their inherent decency, turning them into selfish and self-centered creatures barely deserving of the title humanity.

"For many years I watched. I watched until I could not bear to do so any longer. Then, I acted.

"They're still out there, you know, Ignorance and Want. Roaming a world still unaware of their presence, still falling under their subtle spell.

"I thought I'd found them. At least a dozen times, I thought I'd found them. But each time, I was wrong.

"Mistaken identity. That's all I'm guilty of, you realize. I'd never knowingly harm an innocent. You must believe me."

Strangely, I did. I believed that this sad soul sitting across from me indeed belonged to the Ghost of Christmas Present. I believed he had once been a compassionate and noble Spirit whose only flaw was that he did not possess the strength required to fulfill a destiny thrust upon him by forces beyond his control. I believed that his subsequent actions, reprehensible though they were, were not rooted in evil. I believed that, although responsible for a moral transgression of a nature most vile, he was not himself immoral—by any definition of that word.

I believe all of these things. All of which leaves me . . . where?

The decision I still face is now more difficult than it was before. My convictions, previously black and white, have merged into a murky gray. The nonchalance with which I once approached my responsibility in this matter now seems sorely out of place.

I'd eliminated one Gordian Knot, to be sure. But another had appeared to take its place—this one of my own creation.

THE TIMBREL SOUND
OF DARKNESS

by Kathe Koja and Barry N. Malzberg

*Kathe Koja is a best-selling horror novelist as well
as a science fiction writer; Barry N. Malzberg, winner
of the Campbell Memorial Award, has published more
than 90 books and 300 short stories in his career.*

On November 15, 1900, one week before his death,
Sir Arthur Sullivan is visited for the second and last
time by the specter who had made these last years so
lively for him in retrospect. The first visit came just
after *Ivanhoe* had opened in 1893 and the news had
been astonishingly grim. "Your grand opera will fail,"
the specter had said, through a smile which was in no
way seemly. "Your grand opera will run two hundred
performances and bankrupt Rupert D'Oyly Carte and
will never be performed again in this country in this
century. It will fail as well in Berlin. It will not be
taken up in America. It will be heard of no more. Your
fate is to be remembered as the composer of the operettas. Your name and Gilbert's will be linked through
all of the decades; you will be famous and your tunes
subject for laughter while your cantatas and oratorios
and symphony collapse into the dust. This is the true
and ageless verdict of history and of all forthcoming
prophecy." How distressed Sullivan had been! This
cruel and ungiving news, delivered by a shapeless creature who claimed to be the ghost of the killer in
Whitechapel, the notorious Mystery Jack himself, had

driven Sullivan into a stupor of rage and futility which had not abated in these intervening years even though (or perhaps because) the prediction of the specter more and more seemed to have some basis in fact. The *Golden Legend* sunk, *The Martyr of Antioch* exhumed for the Leeds Festival only because Sullivan had insisted upon conducting it. The disaster of *Ivanhoe* in Berlin. Even the last two operettas with the wretched Gilbert toward which he had been driven only for the cold pounds, and make no mistake of it, had been failures, *Utopia Limited* lasting for only half a year and emptying out at the end (like a slopjar, like a dregged glass), *The Grand Duke* a disastrous one hundred twenty-three performances for the most venomous responses of his career, worse than anything even for the ill-fated *Ivanhoe*. Oh, he was glad to have been out of it then, but the words of the specter had stayed with him for all these years and there was— despite the momentary reassurances, the false gilt of his own devisings—no release, no release. Now in his rooms in London, arched numb against the bed-clothes, feeling the true seediness and devastation of his fifty-eight years and welded to the conviction that his health had collapsed, Sullivan stared at the specter with loathing and attention, the fine features of the ghost hazy and uncertain in the weary off-light of the dawn. He had given up disbelief a long time ago. The night was filled with portents and now all of his friends were dying. Like Sir Ruthven Murgatroyd, descended from the painting on the wall in the second act of *Ruddigore,* the specter seemed very sure of himself, raised a hand in graceful and indolent greeting. "And is it as I predicted?" the ghost asked, with the smile of one who is sure of his answer. "Have you any reason now to doubt what I have said?"

Sullivan looked at the anima, then away, toward the streaks of light. In Whitechapel, prostitutes had been found with their features grazed, then eviscerated; in a dingy room for copulation a prostitute, once as dingy, had been found dismembered in ways so intricate and horrifying that the police would release no details. But nothing done, no violence, no ravages perpetrated on those prostitutes could have been as thorough as what this specter had done to Sullivan's psyche. "Why?" he said, feeling like the hapless Murgatroyd descendant, "why do you haunt me so?"

"Nothing else to be done," the specter said. "Fills in the time, you have no idea whatsoever—but you will, you will—of how eternal eternity can be and I was, I am a man of action after all. Your reputation," and what a twist to the word, must the ghost utilize that particular tone, "is quite secure, you know, you will last through the next century, your works will be played everywhere but will be particularly popular in England and America. Your works with Gilbert, that is to say. The rest of them—well, there's no need to review that depressing business again, is there?"

"William Shwenk Gilbert is a swine," Sullivan said, with what he felt to be a pure dispassion. He pulled the bedclothes toward him, feeling their warmth, their sheer corporeality; surely he was not dreaming this. "He is a cheap hack and a synonym for dishonor. He would have turned me into an accompanist, an organ grinder for his monkey rhymes had I not forced him to be otherwise. And what would you have of that?"

"Very little," the specter said. "Oh, *The Lost Chord* will survive and *Onward Christian Soldiers* ... but they will survive to be mocked, as examples of art gone bad. The *Overture di Ballo* will be played now and then as well. But that's pretty much the certainty of it, Arthur. I wish I could give you better news, I know how ambitious and serious you are, but there's no way I can manipulate the truth. You have advanced kidney failure and your heart—surely you can feel it—is in perilous condition; the extreme hydration has put terrible untoward pressure on the organ. I understand these things, you see, it is part of my insight. All part of the job." The light through his features paler than gaslight, was it light he carried or only the treacherous dawn? "It won't be much longer for you, I am sorry to say, but I won't tell you the exact date or time of your death. That would be, I think—and I think you agree?—much too cruel."

Sullivan feels the arch of his mortality, a cold descending triad, then feels the hammer of that betraying heart as if it were the dead march in *Yeoman of the Guard*. "Oh, it is too cruel," he says, "too, too cruel for you to come and berate me so, to confront me with omens of my impermanence and folly. You, too, are a man, were a man, are you not? I would not do the same to you if our positions were reversed." Killer of prostitutes, he thinks, torturer of women, creature of apostasy and terror in the night, in a hundred nights and a thousand, man of legend free to create his own. What, is this my penance for deferring to Carte's demands, Gilbert's slimy mockery, my own helpless lust for a good tune, and the easy response of fools? I would not have done it so, he thinks. "Begone," Sullivan says, as had Murgatroyd in the second act of *Ruddigore*. "Begone, specter, I will speak with you no more." The hoots of Jack's amusement fill Sullivan's hot and crowded bedroom and he feels a thin and desperate clutching in his throat, some prescience or prestidigitation of doom as the light shifts within the room and he falls back against the sheets, stunned and exhausted, astonished by the force of his grief. He would not have thought of himself as such a simple and vulnerable man.

But there are vulnerabilities and vulnerabilities, simplicities masquerading as cunning complexities as Jack, Mystery Jack, Springheeled Jack himself must masquerade: through dark and light: as toff, as workingman, as doctor, as empty-eyed and smiling drunk: simple as a couplet of Gilbert's base doggerel, come with his hands out to the prostitute herself as simple and base, smiling in the soot and blackness of the alleyways, smiling as he palped and fingered the breast, the belly, her hot and dirty dress rucked up and bare beneath and mumbling about the money first, sir, all the gentlemen must pay first, but for what he seeks no payment is sufficient, no coin can be tendered or accepted; it is a gift, after all, freely given: it is legend in the making; it is art. Imagining him now—as Sullivan lies sleepless in the fretful and unforgiving light, imagining his glide through streets made empty by the rumor of his passing, the surety and elegance of that passing, the shocking shape of the kidney in the box: *kidne,* he had spelled it, a deliberate joke, anything for a laugh. Give the people what they ask for: who, in fact, is subsidizing this performance? The police? The newspapers, panting yellow journalists chasing his exploits with ignorant fervor, keeping score with the dead bodies of women? To whom does he answer, Jack, with his mystery and his smiling knife, to whom must he account? *Has he no partner, no collaborator?* No?—in the huffing dawn, light upon light and the thin wheeze of Sullivan's lungs like the sound of failure itself, no, there is only Jack to come before him, Sullivan in his tormented bed, to bring the news of defeats and disasters and to smile like a gentleman as he does.

Lying with Fanny Ronalds in the rut of the night, attempting to express himself to her as he never has, even in silhouette, been able to open to the common herd, Sullivan in 1884 has a vivid intimation of what Gilbert's death will be like: seventy-five years old in 1911, he will be lying indolently by the lake on his estate, the cries of a woman visitor, some inconsequential friend of Nancy McIntosh in from London will take herself to be in trouble in the water and Gilbert, always a fool and helpless to the distressed sounds of women, will toss aside the newspaper, rush bumbling to the lake and attempt to rescue the young woman, a large and resolute bulk who floundered like a freighter atop the waters, protesting. At that moment Gilbert's heart would give out, Gilbert would feel the empty and suddenly unmotivated coursing of the blood and then Gilbert's ears would fill with the dull and doglike sounds of a man in real distress: that man himself. Terrified all his life by drowning, seized by images and intimations of drowning, Gilbert at last would come to pay to fate what he had so maliciously and gleefully extracted over the decades.

Fanny in his arms, crushed against him in her own swim and pallor, Sullivan refracts the panting and desperate noises of Gilbert's breath with a roaring and coursing of his own, the sound must be so distressing in this isolate bedroom at an inn in Shepperton that Fanny clutches him and cries, "Arthur, Arthur, are you all right?" He does not know if he is all right. Truly, he can make no sense of it. *I have a song to sing-o*. The waters rush in and out of his brain, he is sunk, excavated, drowning, and as he clutches Fanny in the desperate baggage of his own grip he hears the Executioner's lament in *Mikado,* someday a victim must be found and that villain is Shwenk. No, it is Seymour, Arthur Seymour Sullivan. He chokes, trying to drag himself to the surface through the force of his grasp of Fanny. She groans with pain and as Sullivan rises Gilbert sinks into the stinking lake, his emergent, flatulent corpse as helpless and desolate as any Whitechapel victim, riven with bubbles and dust, sea-creatures and foam, and try as he may in that flickering recession of vision, Arthur Sullivan cannot see himself amongst the mourners.

Sullivan conducts *The Martyr of Antioch* in London. The chorus tosses him flowers, Sterndale Bennet pays him compliments, after the performance Parry and Stanford, their virginal faces dolorous with envy pay their abashed regards. Surely his music is of consequence, such triumphs cannot have been contrived—as was perhaps *The Tempest* or *In Memoriam*—upon youth and access, the oratorio is one which Mendelssohn himself would have signed. Over and again Sullivan is assured of this in the haze and glow of the performance and yet somehow he cannot bring himself to sufficient conviction; in the night wind, howling, he hears not benediction but hysterical, harsh laughter. D'Oyly Carte tells him that he is behind on his commitment; what will fill the theatre if *Patience* does not come in? At the reception which should have made his brilliance heat and light for the night wind within, Sullivan finds himself unable to take any comfort whatsoever. Gilbert sends him a polite note the next day congratulating him upon the triumph yet reminding him, like the tolling of a mourning bell made of lead, that rehearsals soon enough must begin. Sullivan stares at the note for a long time, the sound of his brother Fred's voice in *Cox and Box* resonating through the room. Poor Fred, more than a decade passed and never, never to come again. Rataplan, rataplan.

"You see," the specter from Whitechapel says to Sullivan most reasonably, "trying to replicate or relive your life will, in fact, change nothing. All of the choices have been made, they are as irreversible and remorseless as that skein of rope with which I dragged poor Dolly over the edge to her doom. Besides," the specter continues, "it is not a bad fate. It is not nearly the worst fate you could have," with the silent laugh of one to whom fate is a commodity to be delivered, not an appointment to be kept. "Your work will, after all, be remembered after a fashion and who is to contend with the judgment of history? Certainly not those abominable women of the night with whom no man of decency would ever consort, am I right?" Sullivan nods solemnly. The wretchedness from his kidneys and bowels, that new wretchedness which seems to foreshadow his eventual oblivion has coursed through him with the speed of utter conviction. Now and at the end of this, his eyes are fully open to his awful situation. "I mistreated no one," Sullivan says, "I wrote honestly. I missed no effective deadline, not even with *The Grand Duke*. I always produced. Did I want too much? Were my ambitions so unreasonable?"

"You mistreated Fanny," the specter says, as sternly as befits a man who has known and plumbed the secrets of women, who has flexed and griped like a raptor through darkness to ultimate light. "You led her along and gave her only what she needed to continue to bed with you. You lied to other women of affections you could not feel; you never completed your Second Symphony or another major orchestral work; you throttled the Leeds festival when you felt threatened by younger and better composers. Your sins were not great, no," in the musing judgment of a true sinner, a liar, a killer, a spreader of chaos and blood and truly in the face of such disorder, Sullivan thought, his own sins were as nought, depressing as it might be to have them listed this way, "not great but they were recognizable. Gilbert will live only through your music; your music will live only through Gilbert's doggerel. Could one conceive a more fitting fate for either of you, gentlemen of such persuasion and fixity? Come now," the ghost says, "consider the alternatives. You could be one of those women, boxed gizzard, floating intestines, perfect and sacrificial teeth glinting at the horrified constable. Instead, you are going to die in your own bed and make a good job of it, too. You should have no real objection to your fate."

Sullivan does not know what to say to this. Truly, there is nothing to say, he has indeed, as the ghost, as Fanny, as D'Oyly Carte, as Sterndale Bennet had told him, made of his fate what it should be. Victoria had predicted major work from him, had persuaded him to attempt *Ivanhoe*, then had not even had the kindness to attend any of the performances of the opera. There was more to this certainly than simple sloth and indolence. "No more," he says, "I know my health is not good; I can feel that decline within me.

I must rest, I must rest. I tried in life to give no hurt, if I failed it was not from an excess of passion but its deficit, that is all."

Silent in light the ghost regards him; in silence he regards the ghost, smelling in the heat and disorder of the bedroom another smell unpresent, a smell hotter still and not of death; but only the moment that precedes it. And in that moment, itself composed of light, it is again as if he rides in the spectator's seat, with helplessly opened eyes to see the Whitechapel streets, the rowdy shine of the taverns emptying into the larger darknesses: the sallow defeated drunkenness of the prostitute, in her ears one of the tavern songs, on her lips the base quartet of its refrain and: his hand, her breast: his smile, her stare: his motion, her transfixion—like the stare that greets the true emergence of art, the eyes that see clearly, the ears spoiled now and forever for the cheap grind of tavern songs, popular tunes no longer able to enter these ears now ringing to the muffled song of screams: and ripped skirts and spooling guts and that faint whicker of breath as the busy hands stay busy and the night becomes one music in this last and greatest collaboration: she is music and its consummation, it is her song which will live forever: and he her conductor, her accompanist, her instrument as well: and Sullivan behind those eyes sees everything, everything, with the immediacy with which he viewed the death of Gilbert but none of the attending bitterness or satisfaction.

Watching the specter emerge from its portrait, Sullivan had had a sudden, flickering apprehension of his father, the bandmaster, and the professors at the Leipzig Institute, a solemn and portentous bunch like his father, all of them clustered toward him, filled with ideas of what should be done, of what constituted form. He had given them a symphony, then the music for *The Tempest* in response to their urgings and what had he gotten in return? An easy success which went nowhere, then after the travels with Grove, the triumph of the recovered Schubert manuscripts, they had gotten him *Cox and Box* and later *Trial by Jury* and the rest and the—well, then what? What had he become, what had Gilbert been? Dealers in magic and spells and blessings and curses and all kinds of verses, they had lived so that Gilbert—Sullivan had seen with such perfect clarity—would drown and he now would be taunted by the perceived ghost of a madman in Whitechapel who had carved out the bowels of prostitutes in the effort, the solemn and serious effort to produce the light of the world. No less than Sullivan himself, Jack had sought the Light of the World.

Sullivan lay back on the bed, sensing with a sudden and terrible apprehension, the full circularity of his life. So be it then, he said though not aloud. Worthless lover, despoiler of women (but never their eviscerator!), sacker and pillager of his own talent, he lay on the bed, facing the taunting mask of the specter, and said in reply nothing at all, passing at last into some apprehension of a future which neither included nor excluded but simply accommodated him: as Jack was accommodated: as the women in their bloody silence and defeat were accommodated, and preserved.

A week later, Jack, the ghost of past and future as well, came with enormous and clever hands in the early dawn. "Not my kidneys, not that now but my heart!" Sullivan screamed desperately and banged the bell beside him with the heel of his hand, banged and banged the bell, but when his nephew came he could see it was already too late; the dead face of the composer arched against the escaping hands of the assassin seeking the Light of the World, trying to find the Lost Chord while the dusty, unheard choirs urged him indolently to his destiny.

A PROPHET FOR CHANUKAH

by Deborah J. Wunder

This is Deborah Wunder's third science fiction story.

Don't give me any of that Christmas jive! I don't care
that it's almost here, and that people are being wonderful to each other. I don't care that the radio's been
playing carols since the day after Halloween. I don't
even want to know about it. It's not that I don't appreciate the tradition—I grew up, after all, in a working-
class Italian/German/Irish neighborhood; but my holiday—my beloved Chanukah—is treated by most of
you as a poor stepsister to it, and I won't stand for
that any longer!

I sat through it for years, it's true. My kid sister
and I were made to feel we were outcasts because we
couldn't share your big day. When we countered that
our holiday had the obvious (to us, at least) advantage
of eight nights of gift-getting, the other parents com-
plained to ours that we were trying to start trouble.
Of course, Chanukah meant a lot to us as kids: gifts
from relatives, fun things to eat, games, and, of course,
lighting candles each night and saying appropriate
blessings (most of which our parents didn't really
know, so we all faked it a lot).

I officially stopped celebrating Chanukah when I
moved out of my parents' house for the second time,
into a women's hotel in Manhattan, though my observance had been, at best, cursory for years. This particular move was very traumatic, because my parents'
marriage was starting its long, final, downhill slide. My

menorah—a housewarming gift from my best friend, Elizabeth—sat unused on one of the milk crates I used as a bookcase. Why celebrate a family holiday, I reasoned, when I had, in essence, no family to celebrate with? Besides, we had never *really* been very observant; holidays were observed mostly so that the neighbors wouldn't think we were "bad Jews." Anyway, I'd chucked all that standard religious garbage in favor of the "design it yourself" observances of the New Age. What did I need with a religion that was antiquated, created and dominated by men, and impossibly strict? After all, I had learned in college that religions were mainly used by the monied classes to oppress everyone else, and that one of the prime reasons for your Apostle Paul's conversion was the impossibility of successfully following six hundred and thirteen commandments.

All this was running through my mind a few weeks ago, as it often does this time of year, given my curmudgeonly disposition. I was giving my closet its mid-December cleaning when I ran across my mom's memory box—one of those patterned, cardboard boxes you can buy at Woolworth's, assemble, and stick under a bed or stack in a closet. I had inherited the box after Mom died last May, mostly because my sister couldn't handle looking inside. I opened it and started going through the contents. It smelled of Mom; of the Jungle Gardenia that was her signature perfume since before I was born. The contents were all jumbled up—the result of the six moves in two years the box had undergone before landing in my closet. While sorting the various things Mom had considered worthy of keeping, I found a white card envelope under the cowrie-shell turtle that Dad had brought home from the Korean War. The envelope had been addressed to my sister and myself, in a wavering handwriting that I recognized as belonging to my Great-Aunt Rachel. I opened the envelope, and took out the card. It was the "Story of Chanukah" card that Aunt Rachel had given us when I was twelve and Judith was ten. It was a special card to begin with, being the first card that we had ever gotten that was almost a book, but the fact that Aunt Rachel had sent it made it even more special.

Aunt Rachel was my favorite relative on Mom's side of the family. A lifelong spinster, she somehow always knew exactly what to give two children to set their imaginations afire. Further, she was little and delicate, and looked like the engraving of the "Blue Fairy" from the illustrated volume of *Pinocchio* that she had given me shortly after I'd learned to read.

I looked at the card for a few minutes; then opened it slowly, savoring the still-rich corals, sands, and blues of the desert scene on the cover and the gilt lettering, in a style highly reminiscent of Black Chancery, starting, "Many centuries ago ..." I read the text slowly, several times, wondering why I should feel so moved by a piece of paper—a mere "thing"; wondering why Mom had chosen to keep this particular card. Had she meant for it to ambush me, after she was gone, with feelings I'd long forgotten? I had no idea but, believing heavily in what the New Agers termed "synchronicity," I decided to ponder my find over a cup of tea.

As I waited for the water to boil, I read the card again. Although I had always been a bit vague on the details, the story of Chanukah, and of the reclamation of the Second Temple, had always been one of my favorites. I knew that the Second Temple had been defiled by one of the many groups that had persecuted the Jews, and that when Judah ha-Maccabee and his men reclaimed the Temple, they only found enough consecrated oil to last for one day. I also knew that the oil lasted long enough (eight days) for more oil to be produced, but that was about it. You don't learn all that much in one year of Hebrew school—just the basics. I let myself get lost among the colors swirling across the cover. When I looked up, I was no longer alone. I wondered if I was daydreaming, but the lady seated across from me looked to be as real as I was.

"Who are you?" I asked. She was dressed in robes similar to the people on the card—plain cloth of a neutral color, woven of rough-spun thread.

"I am Deborah, whose name you bear. Since there are no men here, may I remove my veil?" As she unfastened the material, I wondered how we communicated, since she couldn't possibly know English, and I know neither Hebrew nor Aramaic.

"Would you like something cold or hot to drink?" I covered my confusion with the good manners Mom had drilled into me.

"Thank you, no. I cannot."

"You said, 'Deborah,' like in the Prophetess and Judge of Israel?"

"Exactly."

"How is it, may I ask, that we can understand each other? I wasn't aware that we had any common language."

"Are you not the person who believes that God appears to each group of people as they can best perceive Him?"

"Yes. It seems the only logical explanation."

"Well, that is how we are communicating. I am what you are capable of perceiving me as."

"Dare I ask why you're here?"

"Your attitude has drawn me. You, among many of today's nonobservant Jews, retain some curiosity about your heritage. If you throw that heritage away, you lose much of what you are."

"But how can I not reject it? It's cruel, man-made, demeaning to my whole gender."

"So you would throw the baby out with the bathwater? Come with me. If you observe one holiday thoroughly, you might get a better idea of the riches you are rejecting."

"One holiday?"

"Yes. Chanukah. It is the season, after all."

"Do you really believe that looking at one holiday can change how I feel?"

"I do not know. All I can do is present the facts of history. You will be free to draw your own conclusions from them."

"Where will we be looking?"

"Various places. I think about 165 B.C.E. might be a good place to start."

"165 B.C.E.?" This was beginning to take on the flavor of a bad Dickens novel, although I was curious as to how she planned to show me anything. Still, I had been cleaning for at least four hours. It was definitely time for a break.

"Jerusalem during Kislev should be a good time. When the Maccabees and their men entered the Temple, after the Syrian Greeks had defiled it, all was confusion. Look for yourself."

A tableau opened before me, along the eastern wall of my apartment—the one with no hangings or paintings. I could see the courtyard and main area of the Second Temple as clearly as if I were viewing them through my dormer window. A number of men were going through the remains, making disgusted grimaces. The apparent leader called the others to order and started organizing tasks. I could see them building a fire outside the Temple, to purify the implements used during services. I could see several of the men weeping openly, as they handled each piece with the same reverence they would normally reserve for handling the Torah. Others were wiping blood and entrails from the altar, and removing idols that had been placed there. One group was sent out to find Torah scrolls that had not been burned by the Syrian Greeks. At some point, the people trying to purify the altar realized that the job was impossible and, with much mourning, rending of clothing, and covering of their heads with ashes, they made a new altar and utensils and buried the old ones. During the search, one uncontaminated flask of oil was found—sealed with the high priest's own seal. It was used to light the lamps for the next morning's services, including the Eternal Light in front of the Ark of the Covenant. This was the famous vial of oil that we were taught in school had lasted eight days, until more consecrated oil could be prepared.

"This is the miracle we commemorate by celebrating Chanukah," Deborah noted. "Not only were we able to reclaim the Temple; we were able to complete our observances despite great obstacles thanks to God's intercession. Because we Jews are a stubborn people, this has been true many times throughout history."

"How do you figure that?"

"Did you not learn that, no matter what the risk to themselves is, there have been Jews celebrating the holidays and practicing the strictest forms of Judaism for almost 3,700 years?"

"I was taught that in Hebrew school when I was a kid, but sometimes it doesn't seem to make much sense. Anyway, I assume you have more than that to show me."

"Why don't we look at England in the late twelfth century; shortly before Richard Lionheart massacred the Jews of York."

"Richard Lionheart did what?" I had learned in school, if I remembered correctly, that Richard had spent the majority of his reign outside of England, either on Crusade in the Holy Land or as a prisoner of the German Emperor.

"His archbishops waged war on the Jews of York, with his knowledge and compliance, shortly after his marriage to Berengaria. The Jews of York were forced to lock themselves into one area where they starved to death, as at Masada, rather than submit to forced conversion."

"Definitely not what they taught us in school."

"Perhaps they have learned shame for their past misdeeds."

"Nah. More likely, it's just another case of history being written by the winners." The wall again went screenlike, showing a fortressed area that even I could tell was England in the late 1100's.

The focus was a small family, not too shabbily dressed. They were gathered around a simple wooden table with a cloth of homemade lace, and a crudely fashioned menorah, with small cups for oil. I figured that it was the first night, because only the cup at the far right had a wick in it. I could hear as well as see this time, and the words of the blessings rang out clearly, as the mother steadied the shammes light in the hand of one of her daughters.

"Boruch atah Adonai Elohenu Melech ha'olom, Shehekianu v'kiymonu v'higi-onu lazman hazeh." They finished the first night's blessings, and proceeded to light the wick.

"Papa, what does that mean?" the youngest, a boy dressed in green, tugged at his father's waistcoat hem.

"It says, in Hebrew, 'Blessed art Thou, O Lord, our God, King of the Universe, who has kept us alive and sustained us and enabled us to reach this season.'"

"But what does it mean?"

"That God has kept the Jews alive through centuries to bear witness to His Greatness and Generosity. We must always remember that God has set us up to be an example of the goodness that comes from keeping His ways, regardless of any danger to our persons. Further, it is a law that during times of religious persecution, such as now, one must be even more stringent in his practice. One of the ways we can best do this is to raise our voices in blessing and song, so let us sing 'Ma'oz Tsor.'" All joined in the traditional song, singing with gusto.

"Come, let us eat while the food is still warm." The lights had burned down, and the mother and daughters started carrying in platters from the cooking area. There was meat of some kind, various side dishes, and a large platter of what looked like potato latkes.

Deborah assured me that they were not latkes, since potatoes had not been brought to England yet, but were fried dough, sweetened by dripping honey over them. A blessing was said over the various foods, which were consumed with a liberal amount of wine.

"Fried dough?" I blanched at the thought. That could do a hatchet job on anyone's cholesterol, and mine was none too good the last time I'd had it checked.

"Yes. We eat foods on Chanukah that have been fried in oil to remind us of that one small flask of oil which proved so important. Also, did you observe that the women did no work from the time the candles were lit until they burned down? Although this is not law, it is our custom, in honor of the women whose sons were martyred, or who played a significant role, in the Maccabeean revolt." Slowly, the scene faded out. I wondered why Deborah was so intent in impressing on me the one thing I already knew about the day. Having recently spoken to an Orthodox friend, I knew that the holiday was more about the reclamation of the Temple than about the miracle of the oil, but to many people the oil and the lights seemed to be the whole focus. I found the dichotomy confusing.

"Where to next?" I tried the old trick of covering my discomfiture with a question. In spite of my apprehensions, this was starting to get interesting. After all, how many people got their own personal, guided tour of the past?

"How about your own area? Let's look at, say, Oceanside, New York."

"Oceanside?"

"Why not? Surely you can identify with the assimilated Jews who live there?"

"I suppose. I mean, I never had much in common with the Long Island kids, in general. . . ." We zoomed in on a typical Long Island family; they could have stepped from the pages of a fashion magazine. Their home was impeccably decorated, and spotlessly clean.

It was obvious, even to me, that they had gone beyond the "upwardly-mobile" stage of existence several generations back. Their menorah was stylish; clear lucite, shaped like a Star of David. Holders for eight candles were spaced equally along the top bar, and one for the shammes was at the upper point of the star. I silently gave thanks that it wasn't one of those tacky electric menorahs that you see more and more of these days. The candles were brightly colored; obtained, no doubt, from one of those boxes that various yeshivas and Jewish welfare organizations send out as fundraisers. I noted that I had at least three boxes of them somewhere. Guilt had impelled me to return the envelopes they came with, enclosing small donations— five, maybe ten, dollars.

The father and his young son were placing the candles in the menorah, which was then placed on a clear plate. "Miriam, call the kids. It's time." After the entire family assembled, the shammes was lit and given to the eldest child to hold. Their blessing rang out, "Blessed art Thou, O Lord, our God, King of the Universe, Who has sanctified us with His Commandments and has commanded us to kindle the Chanukah light." The eldest lit the first candle, then passed to shammes to his sister. She lit the next light, then passed the shammes to the youngest child. The fourth and fifth candles were lit by the parents. Dreidels (tops) were brought out and spun by the children, in a traditional game that I'd never quite learned the rules of, and Chanukah songs were sung. Even if it wasn't the most religious of observances, it was clear that the family was enjoying itself immensely, and had a strong sense of their identity as Jews.

"Do you remember what the Hebrew letters symbolize?"

"Hebrew letters?"

"On the dreidel. Do you know what they mean?"

"No."

"They are an acronym for 'A great miracle happened there.' They were used also used as a means of teaching. When questioned by an oppressing force's soldiers, men spinning dreidels would simply state that a gambling game was being played and, no, the carved letters didn't have any meaning beyond that of counting devices.

"The ceremony hasn't changed very much, has it?"

"No, but that works to the good. You cannot surpass the feeling of being a vital link in a chain spanning centuries, can you?"

"I guess not. But it sure differs from what and how I was taught."

"How so?"

"For one thing, observance always seemed to be something imposed on us, rather than actions based on belief or feelings. For another, it always seemed to me that the emphasis was more on avoiding contact with modern American customs, rather than learning the meaning behind the prayers and rituals. I was never taught how to make it work in context with the life I lead here in twentieth century New York. Besides, if Jews are not going to emigrate en masse to Israel before the Messiah arrives, then isn't it logical for those who don't to try to assume parts of the culture they are living in?"

"It would seem logical, except that such acculturation is often little more than an excuse to become lazy about observance of HaShem's Commandments. As for not learning the meanings behind things: Can you make a dress without knowing how to sew?"

"No, but you can see the result of putting stitches in the cloth. Just memorizing a prayer doesn't tell you why we pray for a thing in that specific manner, or give you a feeling of tradition and continuity."

"True enough, but you need to master each step in its own time. Still, if tradition and continuity are what you feel is missing, why don't we look at a more traditional celebration?"

"I think that some sort of roots are more what I'm

missing, but I'm not really sure. What do you have in mind this time?" I could feel her subtly pressuring me to accept the religion I'd rejected wholesale so long ago, and I resented it. The decision to become observant or not was mine, after all, wasn't it?

"I thought we might look at a more Orthodox family; perhaps in Brooklyn."

"Do I have a choice?"

"In what we observe? Not really. My task is to show you what Chanukah is about. It is not for the student to pick which lessons to study."

"Then I guess we're going to look at Brooklyn," I sighed. "Let's get on with it." I waited as the wall again became a translucent, glowing screen. I was interested in what Deborah was showing me, and in obtaining some of the "connectedness" she was so sure I would find, but I was not, by any means, convinced that it would be the road for me. I was also beginning to resent, very strongly, her pushiness.

The focus cleared on my friend Fran's apartment. It had clearly been freshly cleaned, because it lacked the usual clutter of books, yarns, and computer disks and manuals. She placed candles in her small silver menorah, and placed the whole on a silver tray. She then covered her head with a lace shawl. She and her husband, David, recited the blessings, then lit the candles—Fran holding the shammes; David's hand covering Fran's. They placed the Menorah on the living room windowsill, and sat down at their small table in front of the window to the dinner Fran had prepared. They seemed so close and so happy that for a brief moment, I was touched by envy. I wondered if lighting candles with Eddie would feel at all like what Fran and David shared, even though I doubted such a thing would occur, since Eddie is neither Jewish nor religious. I wanted what they obviously had, even though I knew that, if asked, Fran would deny having anything special.

"They look so happy together." Even if it was a cliché, it was the only thing I could think to say.

"Yes. They know how observing the holidays can bring a couple close together. They have a good marriage, and it is strengthened because it is built on the foundation of sharing their religion."

"I can see how having the same views on major issues could strengthen a marriage, but I don't see how this fits with what you've shown me so far."

"Family has always been one of the most important aspects of Judaism. Our religion provides a code of ethics which, if observed, almost guarantees that many of the abuses in family relationships will not occur."

"That sounds good in theory, anyway." I was less than convinced, having been the person that most of my Dad's abuse had been aimed at and, in fact, having the scar up one leg to remind me—as if I could ever forget. Deborah seemed to realize that this particular example had not scored whatever points she was aiming for, and seemed rather anxious to get on.

"Let us now observe someone celebrating the holiday secretly."

"Why would anyone do that, outside of Russia?"

"Sometimes, when a person first begins to return to Judaism, he or she is embarrassed to celebrate in front of family. Perhaps the family is already too assimilated; perhaps they will ridicule the child of return."

"Seems silly to me, but I guess it could happen. Still, I can't imagine observing a holiday that way." The wall turned again. This was becoming so familiar that I wondered if it would continue to do so after Deborah left, and if I would miss it much if it did not. This time, the screen showed my old room. I was about thirty-two, and was on my knees lighting candles in the menorah my friend had given me. I had moved back into my parents' house after my Dad had a stroke, and was making one of a number of periodic, abortive attempts to explore my roots. Many of my friends had attempted these explorations but, other than my cousin Michael, and my friend Fran, none of us had stuck with it. My parents had, in fact, ridiculed these attempts, so I had confined my observances to my room, cherishing the roots I thought I had found, and feeling vaguely superior for having found them.

"I guess I'd forgotten about that." I felt pretty sheepish. I tried to remember why that particular attempt had failed, and couldn't. I wondered whether it had been lack of community—lack of someone to share the rituals with—or just the effort of trying to make extremely large-scale changes in a relatively short time, but couldn't, for the life of me, remember.

I briefly wondered if I could fit such celebrations into my life now. After all, one of the things I'd kind of lost while assuming New Age practices was holiday observances of any kind. Was it possible to really celebrate a holiday, even while having largely rejected the tenets of the religion that the holiday was part of? And, if I wanted to pursue this, what kind of place would it have in my life? The few religious friends I had, no matter which religion they followed, often seemed to have to pass things by because of one religious stricture or another. Would I be able to do that?

Why, I wondered, am I asking myself these things? I wasn't sure, suddenly, if these were my own thoughts, or a result of Deborah's subtle pressure. My resentment bubbled to the fore, finally, and I wondered, "Why Deborah? Why not, say, Ruth—who was, after all, the first noted convert to Judaism—or Judah ha-Maccabee?" Deborah was at least as pushy as I am, and I didn't feel completely comfortable with her in my kitchen. I decided to handle the situation more or less the way I handle most things: direct confrontation.

"Why are you here?"

"I told you. Your attitude has drawn me."

"But why you? Why not Ruth or Judah ha-Maccabee? Either would seem a more logical choice."

"Why do you feel they would be more logical?"

"Judah ha-Maccabee is already strongly associated with the holiday, and Ruth was, we were taught, the first major convert, and would have had to learn all the rituals and their meanings as an adult."

"For one thing, Chanukah didn't exist in Ruth's time. And Judah ha-Maccabee was no prophet; merely a righteous man. Besides, they're busy plaguing Saddam Hussein with nightmares these days. Although my era was closer to Ruth's than to the Maccabees, I took this on because, as a prophetess, my calling is to educate Jews and encourage a return to observance."

Her idea of encouragement felt more like a lesson in Applied Jewish Guilt #101, but I held my tongue and thought over all we had looked at so far. The richness of the celebration was not lost on me; neither was the closeness among the celebrants, regardless of the setting. If I was less than thrilled with my guide, well, that was my own problem, I guessed.

"What would happen if there was no Chanukah?" I mused.

"If things keep going as they have been, this will occur several centuries in the future."

"You can't possibly mean that?" I was thoroughly taken aback by the prospect. I could see choosing not to observe the holiday, but not having it around to observe was another thing entirely.

"Oh, but I do. According to some British calculations, there will be one year on your calendar in which Chanukah is not celebrated."

"Not celebrated at all?"

"Unless the Messiah arrives, the Third Temple is built and dedicated in Jerusalem and the Sanhedrin is reconvened, it will come to pass that the year 3316 will have no Chanukah. The Chanukah that you would expect to have that year will not begin until sundown of 1 January, 3317. It will, however, be celebrated in the Hebrew calendar, in the year 7077, so it will not be lost to those who are observant."

"I still don't understand this. How can a year not have Chanukah?"

"The Hebrew calendar has been calculated correctly until the year 6,000. After that, we are lost unless the Messiah arrives. When the Sanhedrin is reconvened after the Third Temple has been rebuilt and dedicated, they will examine witnesses to determine when the new moon falls, and will recalculate the calendar from that point." I was still a bit perplexed. I'd had no idea that the Hebrew calendar had, in effect, a termination date. I'd just assumed that it went on indefinitely, much the way our Gregorian calendar does. I had a lot to digest, just from this question.

I'm not exactly sure when Deborah left my kitchen, or how. At some point, I realized I was alone again. I went over all I had seen with her, then double-checked my apartment wall to make sure that it had not been rigged with some sort of projection device.

I returned to cleaning my closet, mostly repacking all the stuff that I had gotten out earlier. I made sure Mom's box was on top, so that I could go through it at my leisure, to see what other curves I'd be thrown.

I had learned a lot about Chanukah, and about myself. Although I was beginning to accept that, for many people Judaism is not only alive, it is thriving, I wasn't sure I'd seen enough to make me change my beliefs about it in general. My curiosity had been whetted, even though I still felt that Judaism was, at best, antiquated. I also had a lot of questions about the way I'd learned to look at Judaism—the whole bit about very publicly observing some holidays while ignoring others, and ignoring the meanings behind them. I saw the dichotomy in my own militancy about Chanukah being "better" than Christmas, and how I had mindlessly adapted the very attitudes I condemned most in my parents. It seemed to me that, at the very least, a few trips to the library were in order, and I vowed to do some serious rethinking and reeval-

uating of things that I had taken for granted, and attitudes that I had held, for most of my life.

Meanwhile, it wouldn't hurt if I got my menorah
down from the top of the refrigerator, where I'd kept
it since moving into my current home, and cleaned it,
and if I found at least one of those boxes of candles.
They'd make a lovely light in my front window.

DUMB FEAST

Mercedes Lackey

Mercedes Lackey is a best-selling science fiction and fantasy novelist.

Aaron Brubaker considered himself a rational man, a logical man, a modern man of the enlightened nineteenth century. He was a prosperous lawyer in the City, he had a new house in the suburbs, and he cultivated other men like himself, including a few friends in Parliament. He believed in the modern; he had gas laid on in his house, had indoor bathrooms with the best flushing toilets (not that a polite man would discuss such things in polite company), and had a library filled with the writings of the best minds of his time. Superstition and old wives' tales had no place in his cosmos. So what he was about to do was all the more extraordinary.

If his friends could see him, he would have died of shame. And yet—and yet he would have gone right on with his plans. Nevertheless, he had made certain that there was no chance he might be seen; the servants had been dismissed after dinner, and would not return until tomorrow after church services. They were grateful for the half-day off, to spend Christmas Eve and morning with their own families, and as a consequence had not questioned their employer's generosity. Aaron's daughter, Rebecca, was at a properly chaperoned party for young people which would end in midnight services at the Presbyterian Church, and she would not return home until well after one in the morning. And by then, Aaron's work would be done, whether it bore fruit or not.

The oak-paneled dining room with its ornately carved table and chairs was strangely silent, without the sounds of servants or conversation. And he had not lit the gaslights of which he was so proud; there must only be two candles tonight to light the proceedings, one for him, one for Elizabeth. Carefully, he laid out the plates, the silver; arranged Elizabeth's favorite winter flowers in the centerpiece. One setting for himself, one for his wife. His dear, and very dead, wife.

His marriage had not precisely been an *arranged* affair, but it had been made in accordance with Aaron's nature. He had met Elizabeth in church; had approved of what he saw. He had courted her, in proper fashion; gained consent of her parents, and married her. He had seen to it that she made the proper friends for his position; had joined the appropriate societies, supported the correct charities. She had cared for his home, entertained his friends in the expected manner, and produced his child. In that, she had been something of a disappointment, since it should have been "children," including at least one son. There was only Rebecca, a daughter rather than a son, but he had forgiven her for her inability to do better. Romance did not precisely enter into the equation. He had expected to feel a certain amount of modest grief when Elizabeth died—

But not the depth of loss he had uncovered. He had mourned unceasingly, confounding himself as well as his friends. There simply was no way of replacing her, the little things she did. There had been an artistry about the house that was gone now; a life that was no longer there. His house was a home no longer, and his life a barren, empty thing.

In the months since her death, the need to see her again became an obsession. Visits to the cemetery were not satisfactory, and his desultory attempt to interest himself in the young widows of the parish came to nothing. And that was when the old tales from his childhood, and the stories his grandmother told, came back to—literally—haunt him.

He surveyed the table; everything was precisely in place, just as it had been when he and Elizabeth dined alone together. The two candles flickered in a draft; they were in no way as satisfactory as the gaslights, but his grandmother, and the old lady he had consulted from the Spiritualist Society, had been adamant about that—there must be two candles, and only two. No gaslights, no candelabra.

From a chafing dish on the sideboard he took the first course; Elizabeth's favorite soup. Tomato. A pedestrian dish, almost lower-class, and not the clear consommes or lobster bisques that one would serve to impress—but he was not impressing anyone tonight. These must be *Elizabeth's* favorites, and not his own choices. A row of chafing dishes held his choices ready; tomato soup, spinach salad, green peas, mashed potatoes, fried chicken, apple cobbler. No wine, only coffee. All depressingly middle-class. . . .

That was not the point. The point was that they were the bait that would bring Elizabeth back to him, for an hour, at least.

He tossed the packet of herbs and what-not on the fire, a packet that the old woman from the Spiritualists had given him for just that purpose. He was not certain what was in it; only that she had asked for some of Elizabeth's hair. He'd had to abstract it from the lock Rebecca kept, along with the picture of her mother, in a little shrinelike arrangement on her dresser. When Rebecca had first created it, he had been tempted to order her to put it all away, for the display seemed very pagan. Now, however, he thought he understood her motivations.

This little drama he was creating was something that his grandmother—who had been born in Devonshire—called a "dumb feast." By creating a setting in which all of the deceased's favorite foods and drink were presented, and a place laid for her—by the burning of certain substances—and by doing all this at a certain time of the year—the spirit of the loved one could be lured back for an hour or two.

The times this might be accomplished were four. May Eve, Midsummer, Halloween, and Christmas Eve.

By the time his need for Elizabeth had become an obsession, the Spring Equinox and Midsummer had already passed. Halloween seemed far too pagan for Aaron's taste—and besides, he had not yet screwed his courage up to the point where he was willing to deal with his own embarrassment that he was resorting to such humbug.

What did all four of these nights have in common? According to the Spiritualist woman, it was that they were nights when the "vibrations of the earth-plane were in harmony with the Higher Planes." According to his grandmother, those were the nights when the boundary between the spirit world and this world thinned, and many kinds of creatures, both good and evil, could manifest. According to her, that was why Jesus had been born on that night—

Well, that was superstitious drivel. But the Spiritualist had an explanation that made sense at the time; something about vibrations and currents, magnetic attractions. Setting up the meal, with himself, and all of Elizabeth's favorite things, was supposed to set up a magnetic attraction between him and her. The packet she had given him to burn was supposed to increase that magnetic attraction, and set up an electrical current that would strengthen the spirit. Then, because of the alignment of the planets on this evening, the two Planes came into close contact, or conjunction, or—something.

It didn't matter. All that mattered was that he see Elizabeth again. It had become a hunger that nothing else could satisfy. No one he knew could ever understand such a hunger, such an overpowering desire.

The hunger carried him through the otherwise un-palatable meal, a meal he had timed carefully to end at the stroke of midnight, a meal that must be carried out in absolute silence. There must be no conversa-tion, no clinking of silverware. Then, at midnight, it must end. There again, both the Spiritualist and his grandmother had agreed. The "dumb feast" should end at midnight, and then the spirit would appear.

He spooned up the last bite of too-sweet, sticky cobbler just as the bells from every church in town rang out, calling the faithful to Christmas services. Perhaps he would have taken time to feel gratitude for the Nickleson's party, and the fact that Rebecca was well out of the way—

Except that, as the last bell ceased to peal, *she* appeared.

There was no fanfare, no clamoring chorus of ecto-plasmic trumpets—one moment there was no one in the room except himself, and the next, Elizabeth sat across from him in her accustomed chair. She looked exactly as she had when they had laid her to rest; every auburn hair in place in a neat and modest French Braid, her body swathed from chin to toe in an exquisite lace gown.

A wild exultation filled his heart. He leapt to his feet, words of welcome on his lips—

Tried to, rather. But he found himself bound to his chair, his voice, his lips paralyzed, unable to move or to speak.

The same paralysis did not hold Elizabeth, however. She smiled, but not the smile he loved, the polite, welcoming smile—no, it was another smile altogether, one he did not recognize, and did not understand.

"So, Aaron," she said, her voice no more than a whisper. "At last our positions are reversed. You, si-lent and submissive; and myself the master of the table."

He almost did not understand the words, so bizarre

were they. Was this Elizabeth, his dear wife? Had he somehow conjured a vindictive demon in her place?

She seemed to read his thoughts and laughed. Wildly, he thought. She reached behind her neck and let down her hair; brushed her hand over her gown and it turned to some kind of medievalist costume, such as the artists wore. The ones calling themselves "Pre-Raphaelites," or some such idiocy. He gaped to see her attired so, or would have, if he had been in control of his body.

"I am no demon, Aaron," she replied, narrowing her green eyes. "I am still Elizabeth. But I am no longer 'your' Elizabeth, you see. Death freed me from you, from the narrow constraints you placed on me. If I had known this was what would happen, I would have died years ago!"

He stared, his mind reeled. What did she mean? How could she say those things?

"Easily, Aaron," Elizabeth replied, reclining a little in the chair, one elbow on the armrest, hand supporting her chin. "I can say them very, very easily. Or don't you remember all those broken promises?"

Broken—

"Broken promises, Aaron," she continued, her tone even, but filled with bitterness. "They began when you courted me. You promised me that you did not want me to change—yet the moment the ring was on my finger, you broke that promise, and began forcing me into the mold *you* chose. You promised me that I could continue my art—but you gave me no place to work, no money for materials, and no time to paint or draw."

But that was simply a childish fancy—

"It was my *life*, Aaron!" she cried passionately. "It was my live, and you took it from me! And I believed all those promises, that in a year you would give me time and space—after the child was born—after she began school. I believed it right up until the moment when the promise was 'after she finishes school.' Then

I knew that it would become 'after she is married,' and then there would be some other, distant time—" Again she laughed, a wild peal of laughter that held no humor at all. "Cakes yesterday, cakes tomorrow, but never cakes today! Did you think I would never see through that?"

But why did she have to paint? Why could she not have turned her artistic sensibilities to a proper lady's—

"What? Embroidery? Knitting? Lace-making? I was a *painter*, Aaron, and I was a good one! Burne-Jones himself said so! Do you know how rare that is, that someone would tell a girl that she must paint, must be an artist?" She tossed her head, and her wild mane of red hair—now as bright as it had been when he had first met her—flew over her shoulder in a tumbled tangle. And now he remembered where he had seen that dress before. She had been wearing it as she painted, for she had been—

"Painting a self-portrait of myself as the Lady of Shallot," she said, with an expression that he could not read. "Both you and my father conspired together to break me of my nasty artistic habits. 'Take me out of my dream-world,' I believe he said. Oh, I can hear you both—" her voice took on a pompous tone, and it took him a moment to realize that she was imitating him, " 'don't worry, sir, once she has a child she'll have no time for that nonsense—' And you saw to it that I had no time for it, didn't you? Scheduling ladies' teas and endless dinner parties, with women who bored me to death and men who wouldn't know a Rembrandt from an El Greco! Enrolling me without my knowledge or consent in group after group of other useless women, doing utterly useless things! And when I *wanted* to do something—anything!—that might serve a useful purpose, you forbade it! Forbade me to work with the Salvation Army, forbade me to help with the Wayward Girls—oh, no, *your* wife couldn't do that, it wasn't *suitable*! Do you know how much I came to hate that word, 'suitable'? Almost as much as the words 'my good wife.' "

But I gave you everything—

"You gave me nothing!" she cried, rising now to her feet. "You gave me jewelry, gowns ordered by *you* to *your* specifications, furniture, useless trinkets! You gave me nothing that mattered! No freedom, no authority, no responsibility!"

Authority? He flushed with guilt when he recalled how he had forbidden the servants to obey her orders without first asking him—how he had ordered her maid to report any out-of-the-ordinary thing she might do. How he had given the cook the monthly budget money, so that she could not buy a cheaper cut of roast and use the savings to buy paint and brushes.

"Did you think I didn't know?" she snarled, her eyes ablaze with anger as she leaned over the table. "Did you think I wasn't aware that I was a prisoner in my own home? And the law supported *you,* Aaron! I was well aware of that, thanks to the little amount of work I did before you forbade it on the grounds of 'suitability.' One woman told me I should be grateful that you didn't beat me, for the law permits that as well!"

He was only doing it for her own good. . . .

"You were only doing it to be the master, Aaron," she spat. "What I wanted did not matter. You proved that by your lovemaking, such as it was."

Now he flushed so fiercely that he felt as if he had just stuck his head in a fire. How could she be so—

"Indelicate? Oh, I was more than indelicate, Aaron, I was passionate! And you killed that passion, just as you broke my spirit, with your cruelty, your indifference to me. What should have been joyful was shameful, and you made it that way. You hurt me, constantly, and never once apologized. Sometimes I wondered if you made me wear those damned gowns just to hide the bruises from the world!"

All at once, her fury ran out, and she sagged back

down into her chair. She pulled the hair back from her temples with both hands, and gathered it in a thick bunch behind her head for a moment. Aaron was still flushing from the last onslaught. He hadn't known—

"You didn't care," she said, bluntly. "You knew; you knew it every time you saw my face fall when you broke another promise, every time you forbade me to dispose my leisure time where it would do some good. You knew. But all of that, I could have forgiven, if you had simply let Rebecca alone."

This time, indignation overcame every other feeling. How could she say something like that? When he had given the child everything a girl could want?

"Because you gave her nothing that *she* wanted, Aaron. You never forgave her for not being a boy. Every time she brought something to you—a good grade, a school prize, a picture she had done—you belittled her instead of giving her the praise her soul thirsted for!" Elizabeth's eyes darkened, and the expression on her face was positively demonic. "Nothing she did was good enough—or was as good as a boy would have done."

But children needed correction—

"Children need *direction*. But that wasn't all—oh, no. You played the same trick on her that you did on me. She wanted a pony, and riding lessons. But that wasn't suitable; she got a piano and piano lessons. Then, when her teacher told you she had real talent, and could become a concert artist, you took both away, and substituted *French* lessons!" Again, she stood up, her magnificent hair flowing free, looking like some kind of ancient Celtic goddess from one of her old paintings, paintings that had been filled with such pagan images that he had been proud to have weaned her away from art and back to the path for a true Christian woman. She stood over him with the firelight gleaming on her face, and her lips twisted with disgust. "You still don't see, do you? Or rather, you are so *sure*, so *certain* that you could know better than any foolish woman what is best for her, that you still think you were right in crushing my soul, and trying to do the same to my daughter!"

He expected her to launch into another diatribe, but instead, she smiled. And for some reason, that smile sent cold chills down his back.

"You didn't even guess that all this was my idea, did you?" she asked silkily. "You had no idea that I had been touching your mind, prodding you toward this moment. You forgot what your grandmother told you, because I made you forget—that the dumb feast puts the living in the power of the dead."

She moved around the end of the table, and stood beside him. He would have shrunk away from her if he could have—but he still could not move a single muscle. "There is a gas leak in this room, Aaron," she said, in the sweet, conversational tone he remembered so well. "You never could smell it, because you have no sense of smell. What those awful cigars of yours didn't ruin, the port you drank after dinner killed. I must have told you about the leak a hundred times, but you never listened. I was only a woman, how could I know about such things?"

But why hadn't someone else noticed it?

"It was right at the lamp, so it never mattered as long as you kept the gaslights lit; since you wouldn't believe me and I didn't want the house to explode, I kept them lit day and night, all winter long. Remember? I told you I was afraid of the dark, and you laughed, and permitted my little indulgence. And of course, in the summer, the windows were open. But you turned the lights off for this dumb feast, didn't you, Aaron. You sealed the room, just as the old woman told you. And the room has been filling with gas, slowly, all night."

Was she joking? No, one look into her eyes convinced him that she was not. Frantic now, he tried to break the hold she had over his body, and found that he still could not move.

"In a few minutes, there will be enough gas in this room for the candles to set it off—or perhaps the chafing dish—or even the fire. There will be a terrible explosion. And Rebecca will be free—free to follow her dream and become a concert pianist. Oh, Aaron, I managed to thwart you in that much. The French teacher and the piano teacher are very dear friends. The lessons continued, even though you tried to stop them. And you never guessed." She looked up, as if at an unseen signal, and smiled.

And now he smelled the gas.

"It will be a terrible tragedy—but I expect Rebecca will get over her grief in a remarkably short time. The young are so resilient."

The smell of gas was stronger now.

She wiggled her fingers at him, like a child. "Goodbye, Aaron," she said cheerfully. "Merry Christmas. See you soon—"

SHADES OF LIGHT AND DARKNESS

by Josepha Sherman

Josepha Sherman is a fantasy and science fiction novelist who is also an editor for one of the major sf publishers.

It wasn't fair! It simply wasn't fair!

Natasha Piotrovna just barely stopped herself from stamping her foot in frustration, pretending to busy herself instead with straightening a fold of her wide skirts, and told herself sharply, *Don't be foolish!*

No, being stuck here in the middle of—of nowhere wasn't fair, particularly now, with Christmas so near, but she wasn't going to help Pappa or poor *Maman* and her headache by acting like a baby! She was a young lady, after all, a woman almost, of nearly seventeen.

Besides, Natasha told herself resolutely, if Pappa had decided they would spend Christmas with his brother out here in the country instead of back in Moscow (oh, Moscow, with all its wonderful, glittery parties, and maybe even an invitation to one of the Tzar's own holiday galas ...) well, that was his right. It certainly wasn't Pappa's fault that the runner had snapped right off the family sleigh with only this small peasant village nearby to serve as refuge. Nor could he be blamed for the snowstorm that had trapped them all here behind the village's old-fashioned wooden palisade.

The peasants had been very kind. (Or, a dry little part of Natasha's mind murmured, very much afraid of *not* being kind to the nobility.) These rooms in the village's one inn were plainly furnished but scrupulously clean.

But these rooms were also so *small*! Now that all their belongings had been transferred to here from the sleigh, Natasha thought, there was barely enough space left in which to turn! If she had to stay cooped up here much longer ...

What else could she do? Stifling a sigh of sheer impatience, Natasha pulled open a wooden shutter a crack so she could stare out at the village. Ach, bright! The sun was out at last, dazzling on the snow, turning the icicles hanging from every eave to sparkling crystal, and the sky was the clear, flat blue of fine enamel. Her father was off with the village smith, going over what could be done to mend the damaged sleigh, but her mother remained here, shut in this tiny, stuffy room—

"*Maman* ... ?" Natasha asked tentatively.

"Close the shutters, there's a dear." The woman lay with her eyes covered by a damp, perfumed cloth, maid-servants fussing over her.

"I'm sorry, *Maman*. There, is that better?"

"Much." She spoke in French, of course; their native Russian, those who set the fashions had decreed, was only for peasants. Natasha thought wryly that even with an aching head, her mother wasn't going to be anything but fashionably correct.

"*Maman*, I'm sorry your head hurts. But I only wanted to ask if—"

"Ah, darling, not now."

"But I—"

"Darling, please. Don't be so tiresome." The woman broke off with a faint moan, and her servants hurried to bring her a newly soaked cloth for her head. "Let me be," she told Natasha with a languid wave of her hand. "Go and—and *do* something."

"Yes, *Maman.*"

Natasha curtseyed properly and left with equally proper obedience. But she was fuming. Maman *acts as though I'm still a little girl! What does she expect me to do? Go play with* dolls?

Enough of this. "Misha," she called to her own maid-servant, "come help me into my greatcoat." The fur of that coat was warm, but it was heavy. "Oh, and get your own coat."

Misha was a pretty, cheerful girl Natasha's own age, with blonde braids fairer even than Natasha's own, but she wasn't always too clever. "Mistress? Are we going somewhere?"

"The air is stuffy in here. We're going out to see whatever sights this village possesses."

There weren't many. Every house was of wood—not surprising, with the forest all around—mostly of logs left with the bark on them for added warmth, and the sharply sloping roofs warned of long, snowy winters. All the door frames and window shutters were intricately carved and brightly painted. And for a time, Natasha and Misha enjoyed looking at them, giggling together, their breath pluming in the cold, clear air, ignoring the occasional curious stare from this villager or that. But all too soon, the girls had made a circuit of the whole village.

Natasha's laughter faded. Now what were they to do with themselves?

"Mistress?" Misha asked suddenly. "Look, up there on that hill, there. What do you suppose *that* is? A—a ruin?"

Natasha blinked, stared, stared again. "A mansion!" she gasped. "Misha, that has to be some rich man's mansion!" She glared accusingly at the watching peasants. "Why weren't we directed up there?"

Ach, no, of course the peasants wouldn't understand French. Natasha caught the glance of a solid, rosy-cheeked woman, stocky form nearly hidden beneath countless layers of skirts and shawls, and asked in Russian, "Who lives up there?"

"No one, lady."

"But—"

"The old Duke is long dead, lady. And his son . . ." The woman crossed herself. "No one has lived there for ages."

"How sad."

"Ah . . . yes, lady. Very sad."

But something odd glinted in the peasant's eyes, something secret, and Natasha inexplicably felt a little shiver race up her spine. She glanced at Misha, who was licking her lips nervously, then straightened indignantly. It was fine for a maid servant to be superstitious, but a lady was supposed to be above such things. Besides, what secrets could a simple peasant woman possibly possess?

"It's such a beautiful day," Natasha decided aloud, "I think I'll take a little stroll outside the village gates. Misha, come."

"Be careful, lady!" the peasant woman called.

"Of what? We won't go too far. There aren't going to be any bears about in the middle of winter. And surely no wolf is going to come so close to a village!"

Again, that eerie hint of a secret flickered in the peasant's eyes. "Just do not stay out too long, lady," she said evasively. "The days are short, as you know. Come back before the sunlight fails. *He* can only do so much."

"*He?*"

But the woman had already scurried away.

"How strange!"

"Mistress, maybe we shouldn't . . ."

"Nonsense. The woman was only trying to frighten us. Everyone knows these country folk are full of weird old beliefs." Closely followed by Misha, Natasha stepped through the open gate in the palisade out into the surrounding forest. "Oh, lovely!"

Every branch seemed to be outlined in sparkling

white, diamonds against the dark green velvet of the larches, and snow lay in smooth folds, like so much ermine, on every side.

For a time the two girls walked silently together. They broke into laughter when a crow shook snow down on them, then fell quiet once more under the weight of the forest's peace.

But the unmarked mounds of white were just too tempting. Natasha forgot all about being a young lady, almost a woman, and grabbed a handful of snow, flinging it at Misha. The servant shrieked as flakes wormed down her neck, and daringly snatched up a handful of her own

"Now, Misha, you wouldn't—"

Natasha gasped as snow hit her right in the face.

"All right, that does it!"

Rank and dignity were shed. Squealing and giggling and scurrying this way and that, the two girls started a small snowstorm of their own. But suddenly Natasha froze. It was difficult to see the sun under the canopy of larches as they were, but surely the brightness was turning more and more swiftly to the soft blue of twilight.

"Ah well, Misha, I suppose we'd best be getting back. Besides, think of how nice a good, hot cup of *chai* will taste! Misha? Come on, girl, don't dawdle. Misha!"

Suddenly Misha was virtually in Natasha's arms. "M–mistress, Mistress, there's something out there, something t–terrible!"

"What nonsense—Stop pulling at me!"

"We have to get away! We have to—"

"Misha! Stop it!" Natasha gripped the girl firmly by the shoulders, resisting the urge to shake her. "Now. What did you see?"

"A . . . darkness . . ."

"Ach, Misha! Since when are you afraid of shadows?"

"It wasn't—Mistress, hurry, it—it's coming!"

Natasha whirled, staring, thinking wildly, *A bear? What's a bear doing out of hibernation?*

But it wasn't a bear, it was a—a darkness, and with it a chill, dank sense of such evil her blood seemed to freeze in her veins.

"Hurry, Mistress! *Run!*"

Misha scurried off without a backward glance. But running, Natasha knew with a quiet, dreadful certainty, wasn't going to do any good. The darkness, she was sure, could move more swiftly than anything mortal. Heart pounding painfully, she closed a trembling hand on the tiny golden crucifix on its chain about her neck, praying its power would be enough, and waited. . . .

Without warning, the darkness swirled back on itself. Without warning, it was gone completely, leaving Natasha gasping in relief.

"Go back, lady," a man's voice said softly in Russian. "Go back to the village."

Natasha gave a startled yelp. Who—what—

He was young, this sudden apparition, tall and lithe, his face finely drawn, his hair so pale it seemed to glow with its own light. His eyes, a fierce, clear gray that revealed nothing of his thoughts, seemed to glow, too, and the jewels in his elegant, old-fashioned caftan glinted without sunlight to spark them.

Oh, nonsense. They're probably reflecting off the snow or something. And as for him, he's some local nobleman trying to play a prank on me, he—he has to be. Of course! The whole thing has to be only a prank!

"Who are you?" Natasha snapped. "And what was all that about?"

The steady gaze never flickered. "Nothing to concern you, lady." The young man bowed gracefully. "Call me Stefan if you must have a name for me." He straightened, still staring at her. "The *kudlak* had no chance to form itself; you are quite safe. But now, back to the village before full night is here."

That piercing, unreadable gray stare was starting to

frighten her. Hardly knowing what she did, Natasha turned and hurried back to safety. Misha, shamefaced, was waiting for her in the gateway.

"Mistress, forgive me, I didn't mean to—"

"Hush." Natasha squeezed the girl's cold hand in her own. "It's all right. I was frightened, too." She glanced back over her shoulder, but the villagers had already shut the gates behind them for the night. "I wonder who he was. Really was, I mean."

Misha shivered. "No one for us to know, Mistress. A devil, perhaps or something out of the old, evil days."

She hastily crossed herself. But Natasha, remembering the steadiness of that gray stare, shook her head. "A devil . . . ? No . . . I don't think so. But just what this—this Stefan might be . . ."

There wasn't an answer for that. Natasha shuddered suddenly with a perfectly prosaic chill. "Ach, hurry, Misha," she said, pushing thoughts of mystery from her mind, "let's get back inside where it's warm! But you are *not* to say anything of this to Pappa or *Maman*. Is that understood?"

"Yes, Mistress," Misha murmured, and seemed all too glad to drop the whole subject.

But that night, the tall, elegant figure wandered Natasha's dreams till she woke, staring blankly up at the gaily painted ceiling.

Who *was* Stefan? When she'd asked that peasant woman about the mansion on the hill, the woman had as good as said the whole noble line was extinct. Yet Stefan was so blatantly noble, even with his unfashionable clothing and choice of language! From where else in this backcountry place could he have come? And what in Heaven's name had he been doing out there in the forest all by himself?

Come morning, Natasha decided firmly, *I will learn the truth.*

But all the next day, frustratingly, no matter what

villager she managed to corner, the result was the same: he or she would murmur something about *krsnik*—whatever *that* might be—then hurry off.

"Natasha, dear," her mother scolded her mildly at dinner, "you've been vague all day. Whatever is the matter with you?"

How could she answer? How admit that the fierce-eyed, noble figure who called himself Stefan was haunting her mind? "I . . . was just daydreaming a bit. Forgive me, *Maman*, Pappa."

"Mm." Pappa wasn't really listening. As soon as Natasha finished, he began explaining to *Maman*, "My dear, I'm afraid we aren't going to reach my brother's estate in time for Christmas."

"Oh, dear, why not?"

"When the runner tore free, it did a fair amount of damage to the underside of the sleigh, more than can be repaired in just a day."

"But to spend Christmas *here!* These folks have been very kind to us, surely, but . . . well . . . to spend a holiday *here!*"

"There really isn't much of a choice. We can hardly set out in some ox-drawn cart!"

"Oh, but *here!*"

As her parents argued, Natasha let her mind wander. She was sorry for poor, disappointed *Maman*, but what difference did it make where they celebrated (since they couldn't be in Moscow), as long as they were alive and well? As long as they weren't alone.

Alone like Stefan. *Who* are *you?* Natasha wondered, and then, rather to her surprise, found herself adding, What *are* you?

This is ridiculous, Natasha scolded herself. *This is worse than ridiculous, this is madness!*

And yet, her feet continued to move her toward the palisade gate almost of their own will, her hands continued to pull it open just enough to let her slip through into the cold, cold night. For a long moment,

Natasha stood shivering in her warm furs, staring into blackness, telling herself that now she would give up, now she would go back to her bed and forget there ever had been anyone named Stefan and—

"My lady."

He was there in the darkness, fair hair glowing, fierce eyes blazing. Heart racing, Natasha did the only thing she could think to do and swept down in a proper curtsey. "My lord Stefan."

His bow was curt. "You should not have come." Stefan's voice was strangely distracted, his gaze continually raking the forest. "It is nearly time."

"Time? Time for what? For the—the *kudlak* to appear?"

The steady gray glance flicked to her, then away. "For what must be."

"Stop that!" Natasha snapped, and Stefan turned to look at her fully, one fair brow raised in surprise. Odd, how she could see him so clearly even in the darkness, almost as though he bore his own inner light. Which was nonsense, of course; his pale hair and face must be reflecting . . . what? Starlight? Feeling her own face starting to redden, she hurried on, "I didn't come out here to listen to—to mysticism."

"Why did you come?"

Oh Heavens, she was blushing worse than before. But Stefan, mercifully, didn't seem to notice. "I . . . I don't know," Natasha stammered. "Curiosity. Confusion. What was that thing last night, that . . . *kudlak?* How did you frighten it away?"

"I didn't frighten it. The time had not yet come, that's all."

"There you go again! *What* time? Why are you out here every night?"

The fierce eyes all at once, startlingly, glinted ever so slightly with amusement. "The night is my friend. I don't fear it."

A sudden gust of wind made Natasha shiver and

hug her coat about herself. "What, or—or feel the cold, either?"

"No."

Something in the simple way he said that sent a new shiver prickling up her spine. But the odd little hint of amusement still flickered in his eyes, and Natasha thought sharply, *He's teasing me! He has to be.* "I came out here," she said daringly, "because I was worried. About you."

"Ah. Thank you, but you need not worry. And, as I've said, you shouldn't have come at all." He stirred restlessly, almost as though embarrassed. "Ach, enough of this! I am long past silly flirtations. Go away, Natasha."

She stiffened. "How d–did you know my name?"

Now he definitely was embarrassed. "You must have told me."

"I didn't! How did you know? Who *are* you, Stefan?"

His sigh barely troubled the night air. "Has no one told you?" he murmured. "*Krsnik*, Natasha. I am *krsnik*."

"That doesn't tell me anything! What does—"

"Hush." Stefan came suddenly tautly alert, alert as some fierce predator, staring into the forest. "Go back, Natasha," he said shortly, and now there wasn't the slightest trace of amusement to him. "*Go back!*"

And Natasha found herself at the village palisade without the faintest idea of how she'd gotten there. Back pressed against the sturdy logs, she stared into the night. Stefan was a barely seen glow against the darkness. . . .

The darkness that was suddenly more terrible than anything natural. The darkness that . . . hungered. *Kudlak.* Whatever *kudlak* might be. Hand at mouth, Natasha watched—

Watched *what*? Suddenly light and darkness rushed together like so much swirling mist, and she could see nothing.

Oh God, oh God, Stefan . . .

Then, as suddenly as before, the darkness was gone, leaving only normal night behind it. Natasha cried out in fright as Stefan staggered, then crumpled to one knee, and rushed to his side.

"Stefan! Are you hurt? Let me—"

"No!" he gasped, struggling to his feet, gray eyes wild. "Do not touch me. You must not touch me."

"That's the most ridiculous—" To her horror, Natasha realized she was close to tears. "What's going on? Oh, please, Stefan, you have to tell me! That—that *kudlak*. Is that . . . thing a devil? Why are you fighting it? Are—are you a sorcerer?"

"Ach, Natasha . . ." Stefan started to raise a hand, almost as though he meant to stroke her hair, then froze. Letting his hand fall again, he gave her the faintest ghost of a smile. "Why couldn't I have met you . . . earlier?"

"What do you—"

"No. I am not a sorcerer. I am *krsnik*. And what that is . . ." Gray eyes looked into hers, and just then they were so sad she wanted to weep all over again. "I shall not tell you."

"But—"

"No. Go back, Natasha."

"But I can't just leave you here!"

"You can. And you will. Go."

The power in his stare was beyond bearing. With a strangled little sob, Natasha went. Hurrying all the way back into the inn, she threw herself down on her bed and wept fiercely, not at all sure why. At last, exhausted, she wiped her eyes and curled up like a child.

But her thoughts were anything but childish.

It's not settled between us, Stefan. Not at all.

Tomorrow, Natasha realized with a sudden shock, was Christmas eve. Nothing evil would be abroad then, surely, not if the tales were true.

But . . . what if Stefan disappeared as well?

Oh, nonsense! That was saying there was something supernatural about him!

And wasn't there? Hadn't she seen him vanquish the darkness? Hadn't she—

"No!" Natasha snapped, then echoed herself, more softly, almost wistfully, "no."

The village priest, Father Gleb, was a stocky, round-cheeked little man, rather flattered that a daughter of nobility (and all the way from Moscow, too) should come to him, but far too busy with the coming celebration to spare her too much time. As he bustled about overseeing the scrubbing and dusting of his tiny wooden church, Natasha followed him around, asking him bits and pieces of questions, innocent things about village life and customs. And then, heart racing, she added, as casually as she could:

"I've heard some odd snips of local tales since my family's been staying here. But I don't really understand all of them. What, for instance, is a *kudlak*? Oh, and *krsnik*?"

Father Gleb froze in dismay. "Those are pagan things, my child. You shouldn't even know the words."

"But—but what do they *mean*?"

The priest sighed and took her gently by the arm. "Come with me, child. Away from prying ears. Yes. This will do." He hesitated an awkward moment, then began carefully, "You must remember these are only stories from the old, ignorant days. But a *kudlak* is said to be a creature of darkness, a foul, evil thing that preys on beasts and men alike. When it finds a whole village on which to prey, no one is safe." Father Gleb crossed himself. "Stories, as I say."

"Of—of course. And . . ." Natasha swallowed dryly, then choked out, "What of the *krsnik*? Is . . . that an evil creature, too?"

"Oh, no, my child! The old stories say that a *krsnik* is a magical being, a village's protector, the only being capable of banishing the *kudlak*."

"Then he's a . . . sorcerer?"

"Nothing so mortal. A *krsnik,* the old tales say, is no longer a living man at all. And—why, child, what's wrong? Wait, where are you going?"

But Natasha, fighting back tears, had already raced from the church. *It can't be true, it can't, not Stefan, he's so—so alive, so real!*

There wasn't anything she could do about it, not until night fell. All that long, endless day, Natasha endured, not daring to think about what Father Gleb had told her, not daring to think about what sorrows might yet be to come.

Much to *Maman*'s distress, the village was too small to have anything as grand as a midnight service. Instead, she and Pappa and Natasha celebrated Christmas Eve with what seemed like everyone else in the village crowded into that tiny wooden church, listening to rosy-cheeked, stocky little Father Gleb. *Maman* sniffed something in French about him being only a peasant, but Natasha knew he was devout enough. And if he wondered about her sudden rush from the church that afternoon, he didn't seem to mind.

Not that Natasha truly heard what was being said. She wandered through the service like someone in a dream, and endured yet more seemingly endless hours till at last her family was back in the inn and safely asleep. At last she was able to slip from the village out once more into the forest, looking wildly about.

"Natasha," said a quiet voice, and she turned to see Stefan watching her somberly.

"He told me," she blurted out. "Father Gleb told me all about the *kudlak.* and the *krsnik.*"

"I see." Stefan sighed almost soundlessly. "And you're terrified his stories might be true."

"Are they?"

"They are. I am no living man."

"But— No— You can't be—"

"Dead?" he finished gently. "I'm sorry, Natasha.

The last thing I wanted was for you to learn the truth."

"But you look so *real*!"

"I *am* real. In a fashion." His voice just a touch too casual, Stefan continued, "I was mortal, once, truly, and of noble stock, for what that's worth now. That ugly old ruin of a mansion up there on the hill was my rightful estate."

"Oh. Y–you're the son that peasant woman mentioned." *I can't believe I'm saying this, I can't believe I'm accepting that—that he ...*

"I was," Stefan corrected softly. "We never really appreciate what we have, do we? Here I was, well-to-do, young, and healthy, but ... well, I wasn't exactly evil, but I admit I wasn't exactly good, either. Too much temptation, perhaps." His smile was rueful. "I've had plenty of time to regret that. But I did have one virtue: I cared about the welfare of these my tenants." His sweep of arm took in the whole village. "I still do."

"How did you ..."

"Die? One day I didn't make it back from my hunting trip." Stefan shrugged. "Accidents happen, and boars do sometimes win. My servants did what they could, but I was dead before they'd reached my estate. Ach, no, don't pity me, Natasha. That happened long before your birth."

"And you've been *here* ever since?"

"Indeed. The combination of my less-than-spotless life on one hand and my love for these folk on the other hand has left me here as their protector. Waiting."

"Forever?"

"Ach, no. They'd hardly need one such as me against mundane problems! No, a *krsnik* can only fight against supernatural ills. I have certain ... abilities now no mortal man possesses. If I can defeat and banish the hunting *kudlak* that's discovered this village before it gathers all its strength to it, then I need not remain *krsnik,* but can go on to . . . whatever one goes on to. And," he added, his voice losing its too-casual lightness, "that final battle will be this night."

"*Now?* Stefan, this is Christmas Eve!"

"Even so. It will be the last chance of the *kudlak* to get past me and drink all those nice, warm human lives before human joy in the holy day drives it back. So I really do think you should return to the village, now."

"I can't just abandon you!"

"I'm *dead,* Natasha! You can't do anything for me." The steady grey gaze studied her, then flicked uneasily away. "And you can't possibly love me."

"I don't," Natasha insisted, and told herself it was the truth.

"Ach, Natasha . . . Go. Please."

"No! First tell me what happens if you . . . lose."

"Ah well, I'm not sure. If the *kudlak* doesn't devour my soul, I suspect I'll be trapped here, *between,* forever. But," he added sharply, "I have no intention of losing. Or of keeping you out here in peril! Get back to the village before—"

"Too late . . ."

The voice was deep, rough, chill, the words barely understandable, so full of inhuman hunger, inhuman hate, Natasha knew even as she turned what she'd see.

The *kudlak.* The *kudlak* fully formed, a great, vague manshape to which darkness still clung and swirled. Natasha heard Stefan draw in his breath in a quick, fierce hiss, and hastily scrambled back out of the way to give him room to do . . . whatever it was a *krsnik* did.

"I shall pass . . ."

"I think not." Stefan's voice rang out cold and hard as steel, never a mortal man's voice.

The *kudlak* rushed forward. Stefan rushed to meet it. Natasha's merely human eyes lost track of what happened: flashes of light, swirls of darkness. Now it was two men who grappled, now two stallions beating at each other with deadly hoofs, now two terrible winged things, one light, one dark, that screamed and tore at each other with blazing talons.

And just as suddenly, *kudlak* and *krsnik* broke away, the *kudlak* back into the darkness, Stefan stumbling and falling to one knee almost at Natasha's feet, shaking in every limb.

"So strong . . ." He glanced up at her, gray eyes wild with strain. "I never thought it would be so strong."

"You can't give up!"

"I'm not."

Stefan struggled back to his feet as the *kudlak* charged. With a fierce shout, he leapt back into battle. Again light and dark swirled together, again *kudlak* and *krsnik* whirled through a dozen deadly shapes. And again they were hurled apart. But this time Stefan fell flat and did not move.

"Stefan!"

"I'm afraid . . . there's still too much of . . . human in me." His voice was the barest wry whisper. "Not enough *krsnik.*"

"No, that's not—you—"

The *kudlak* laughed, very softly and terribly. Natasha straightened with a gasp and found herself staring right into the empty blackness of its eyes. And that was so very terrible her mind quite simply refused to accept her fear. Almost calmly, she moved to stand between the *kudlak* and Stefan's crumpled form.

"Go away." Was that her own voice, so small yet sure of itself? "You ugly creature, go away."

The *kudlak* stiffened in surprise, almost, Natasha thought, as though a rabbit had dared defy a hawk. Plainly no human had ever dared speak to it. *"You shall be the first,"* the creature promised her. *"The first on which I feed."*

"So you say. But I don't see you doing more than talking." *What do you think you're* doing? part of her mind gibbered. *Don't* bait *the thing!* Yet Natasha heard herself continue, quite rationally, "In fact, I don't think you *can* do anything else. Not while I refuse to be afraid of you." *Not afraid!* the inner voice shrieked. *Have you gone mad?*

Behind her, Natasha heard the faintest of rustlings. Stefan was regaining his strength. *Keep talking,* she told herself, *just keep talking.* "As a matter of fact, I don't think you're half as powerful as you pretend. I mean, just look at you! Not even a decent, solid shape to you: all that silly swirling darkness, like tattered old rags."

The *kudlak* hissed, stirring restlessly. *"Small thing, foolish thing, you shall die forever . . ."*

"Nonsense. We humans have been promised eternal life in Heaven—but you wouldn't understand about Heaven, would you, or salvation or—"

It understood. It knew and ached for what it would never have. A furious blow hurled Natasha aside as though she were a child's toy. Mercifully she landed more on snow than frozen ground, but even so, she couldn't seem to catch her breath, and the *kudlak* was looming over her—

"No!" Stefan roared. "You shall not have her! You shall not have any of these my people!"

He hurled himself at the *kudlak.* And this time Stefan blazed with all the pure, bright, avenging fury of the *krsnik,* so bright Natasha couldn't bear to look. But she didn't dare *not* look. Glancing from behind shielding fingers, she saw the *krsnik* drive the *kudlak* back, saw Stefan tear darkness from it shred by shred, tear shape from it, tear the very existence from it. With one great, terrifying rush of light and wind it was gone, and only Stefan remained.

"Stefan!" Natasha struggled to her feet, ignoring her aching muscles. "Are you all right?"

The blazing light was slowly ebbing from him, leaving behind only one tall, slender young man, weary and disheveled and looking so very human, so merely human she ached to weep in despair. "Yes," he said breathlessly. "And you?"

"Bruises, that's all," she gasped, "nothing worse."

"You saved us both. Gave me a chance to catch my
... ah ... breath. Gave me a prod to my pride, too!"

"Stefan ..."

"The *kudlak* isn't coming back. No other is likely
to come in its place. I can leave now."

"No."

"Yes." He paused, studying her. "Come now, you
knew it would come to this."

"Yes, but ..."

All about them, the forest was slowly turning from
black to twilight grey. Stefan glanced up and smiled,
his face suddenly radiant with joy. "Look, the dawn
is nearly here. Happy Christmas, my dear."

But Natasha couldn't answer.

"Oh, don't be ridiculous, Natasha! We'll most probably meet again, somewhere, somewhen else. Now do
wish me a Happy Christmas, and let me go."

His eyes were so very gentle and amused that all at
once Natasha, to her amazement, felt joyous laughter
bubbling up within her. "Yes, oh yes, be free! Happy
Christmas, Stefan! Happy Christmas, my love!"

Even as she spoke, he began to fade, as softly as
mist. Natasha caught one last glimpse of his amused,
tender gaze.

Then Stefan was gone as the sun rose and the village bells chimed out the coming of Christmas Day.

THE RIVER LETHE
IS MADE OF TEARS

by John Gregory Betancourt

John Betancourt is a successful science fiction writer and anthologist, and is the editor/publisher of Wildside Press.

Keith was playing sad, half-familiar little riffs on his guitar when I walked into his room at the Radisson New York. The melody was soft and simple and rather haunting, which wasn't like him. Soft and simple and rather haunting doesn't crack *Billboard*'s Top Ten these days unless it's by Paul Simon, and Keith De-Vito—lead guitarist for Diabolique—was none of those things in real life.

But then it hadn't seemed like real life in a long time.

Keith put a hand over the strings before I could identify the song, and the sound quieted. "Hey, Jamie-boy," he said. His voice was hoarse, little more than a whisper. "You feeling okay?"

"Not too bad," I lied. "How about you?"

"Hey, this is me we're talking about. What do you think?" He managed a lopsided grin. It wouldn't have fooled anybody, but I let it pass without comment. Everyone copes with death differently. With Keith it was denial. If you didn't say it, if you didn't *believe* it, if you pretended you'd never known David Keyes, then it wouldn't matter if he was dead and buried the day before Christmas. I understood that. I wished I could be that way, too, sometimes. But David had been my brother, and we'd been through too much together for me to ever push him away like that.

We'd been to David's funeral that afternoon. Seeing David in that casket with too much makeup on his face and too much lipstick on his lips, with his mouth twisted into that slight beatific smile, had been one of the worst experiences of my life. That *thing* in the casket wasn't him, I wanted to say. It was some sick practical joke.

But I knew inside that it really was David. The morticians had done the best they could; he'd been a real mess when he died. At least our parents weren't alive to see it.

Just thinking about the funeral got me all choked up. It couldn't have happened, I kept thinking. But it was real, it *had* happened, David *was* dead and he *wasn't* coming back, and there wasn't a thing I could do about it. The truth was like a sledgehammer blow to my chest. If not for Keith and Demi and Mary, I might have cried for the first time in twenty years, it hurt so much.

That morning, before the funeral, I thought the worst had been over. It had been *three days* since the accident, for crying out loud. Three days of nothing but Keith and Demi and Mary sobbing on my shoulder, while I had to be strong enough for all of us. David had been *my brother* and I couldn't even weep for him, since the others needed me strong.

That afternoon Keith, Demi, Mary, and me—the four remaining members of Diabolique—had stood around the open grave while that damned Catholic priest droned on and on. They all started to break down again, the chinks in their mental armor opening wider than ever. It was *me* who held their hands during the service, wiped their tears away, kept them all going while my own horror built and built inside me till I thought I'd explode.

Please, David, I remembered thinking. *Just get up.*

It's all a joke, right? Please, God, please get up. I'd do anything for another chance. Oh, God, please—

It wasn't like Dave had AIDS or cancer or some slow wasting disease. He was clean, didn't drink, didn't sleep around, loved his girlfriend Mary. Everyone figured he'd live forever. He and Mary were planning to get married and settle down in June—no more touring, just studio albums for a few years while they raised a bunch of happy, squealing kids.

Where did all that goodness get him? Smeared across the pavement four days before Christmas by a hit-and-run gypsy cab on 44th Street. The police caught the driver a few blocks away when he crashed into a vegetable stand. Drugged-out Cuban trash, it turned out; didn't even know he'd hit David. His public defender was already pleading insanity, and I had a feeling in my gut he'd walk away from murder with a slap on the wrist, some time in a rehab clinic, and a few hours of public service. There's no goddamn justice.

Demi, Keith's wife, was sitting against the king-sized bed's headboard with a pillow clenched between her knees. There were tears on her cheeks and her eyes were closed. She was rocking back and forth, but she'd stopped sobbing out loud. Thank God for that. I don't think I could've handled any more tears, not hers, not anybody's. David had been her lover briefly, about five years ago, when we first put Diabolique together, but since then they'd been more like brother and sister, or very close friends. I knew his loss left her feeling all chopped up inside ... maybe not as bad as David's fiancée or me, but still plenty bad.

"Mary finally settled down," I said to break the tension in the air. "She's talking about going home to her parents in Nebraska."

"Ah," Keith said distantly. He didn't sound surprised.

"I think she'll stay, though," I said.

After holding her hand and letting her cry on my

shoulder for the last four hours, I'd finally gotten her to take a sedative. Twenty minutes later she'd been out cold. On my own way to bed I'd stopped in to see Keith and Demi one last time. No more eulogies, no more words of wisdom, no more shoulder to cry on—I felt like an empty bottle, all gone, all used up. Diabolique was my family now that David was gone, and I had to support them, comfort them, keep them going somehow, no matter what it cost.

"Ah," Keith said again. He hit a chord, then let it die unfinished.

I sighed. "She said she's not sure she can ever play again. Like that's what David would've wanted."

Keith looked pained, and for a second I thought he was going to say something, but he didn't. He just turned his face away. I shouldn't have mentioned David's name, I realized. It was all too soon, his hurt too raw for that.

The awkwardness grew.

"I think I'll turn in," I said after a moment. "Call me if you need to talk. Room 1412. I'm always there for you. You know that."

"Yeah," Keith said. He strummed his guitar, then started to pick out that haunting little tune again. "Thanks, Jamie-boy," he whispered, more to himself than to me.

"Good night, " Demi said. "Sleep tight. Don't let the bedbugs bite."

Each to his own therapy, I thought. Keith by denying it and retreating into his music, Demi with her clichés, Mary with her parents and religion. Perhaps it would work out for them. Perhaps.

I eased my way out the door, not at all comforted myself, and went back to my room. Inside, I discovered that the maid had turned down the bed and left a little chocolate on the pillow. I stared at it. It seemed surreal, somehow, but I couldn't manage a laugh. What a way to spend Christmas Eve.

I flopped down on the bed and stared up at the

ceiling. The white tiles seemed to swirl ever so faintly. I pressed my eyes shut and felt like throwing up.

Far off, a clock chimed midnight. In the next room, someone was watching television. I could hear CNN droning about revolutions overseas, Christmas coups, bloody executions, and purges.

There's nothing in this world a bullet can't fix, I thought. I almost wished I had one myself; too bad I'd never believed in guns. Today, though, I would have welcomed the release. I wanted to curl up into myself and die. There was a darkness at the edge of my vision, like the world closing in on me. There's nothing left here, I thought. Nothing at all.

"Jamie . . ."

I came awake with a start. A voice like velvet and gravel—David's voice. I could have sworn I heard it—

I sank back. Of course the room was empty. I felt cold, suddenly, and shivered. I'm really cracking up this time, I thought. It's only the television next door.

"Jamie . . ." that same voice whispered, stronger now, almost by my ear. *"Listen . . ."*

The hairs on the back of my neck stood on end. There was an almost electrical charge to the air, and a smell like ozone after a lightning storm, only more so, a thousand times more. I sat up slowly, my heart pounding, a lump the size of a baseball in my throat.

"David?" I said.

I turned, slowly, so slowly, and it *was* him. He floated two feet off the floor, his body stretched out behind him like a swimmer in a pool, pale as milk, gauzy and indistinct. He even had his trademark diamond-stud earring in his left ear.

When he whispered, *"Jamie . . ."* again, the breath caught in my throat. Then he smiled, so perfect, so beautiful, like the angel from God he'd been in life, and reached for me.

I buried my face in the pillow, knowing he wasn't there. This couldn't be happening, couldn't be real.

I felt a sudden weight shift the bed, and then he

was sitting beside me, as solid as ever, like he'd never been away. His fingers radiated cold, though, when he took my arm and pulled me up beside him.

My fear must have been obvious. But he was the one crying, not me. I could only stare in bewilderment and ask, "Why?"

"Shh, Jamie, shh," he said gently. "I'm here for you. That's all you need to know. Trust me, Jamie."

"But why?" I insisted.

He sighed and brushed at his own tears. "You were always the strong one, Jamie. Do you remember? You kept us together when we were children and they wanted to split us up. You made me laugh whenever I hurt inside. You did without so I could have everything I needed. Do you remember, Jamie?"

I thought the world was falling out from under me. I closed my eyes, willed myself awake, willed myself away from here, away from the nightmare. David was dead. *David was dead!*

"You weren't born to suffer," he said. "Don't take the whole world's grief onto your shoulders. My passing was meant to be. Just as you were meant to carry on with life."

I looked at him. "Is that why you're here? To lecture me?"

He said nothing, but held out his arms like a mother to a child. "Please," he said.

I bit my lip and felt tears start to well up inside. Instinctively I pushed them down.

"Please," he said again. "For me, Jamie."

David could have gone to anyone, I realized. He could have gone to Mary or Keith or Demi, but he'd chosen *me*. I moved closer, and then he put his arms around me and held me like I used to hold him, back when he was a frightened little boy with no mother or father in the world.

"You'll never be alone, Jamie," he whispered.

He rocked me gently, not saying anything, speaking more with that silence that we'd ever said to each other as adults, and somehow that was enough. I clung to him. The cold left his body and I could hear a heartbeat in his chest, warm and strong and reassuring. He was there when I needed him, as strong as I'd always been, and I knew deep inside that I wasn't alone anymore.

"Thank you," I whispered.

Then the floodgates opened and my tears began to flow. I wept into his chest, all the sorrow, all the hurt, all the pain I'd been keeping inside suddenly pouring out for the first time since childhood. I thought of our parents, dead in a plane crash when I was ten and David was six. I'd sworn I'd never cry again after they died. Perhaps it was the greatest mistake I'd ever made.

David held me and let me cry for what seemed hours. When at last my shaking quieted to little sobs, then little shivers, he rose and began to drift away like a balloon in a wind.

"David—" I called, reaching for him. *"David—!"*

And then he was gone like a bubble bursting. I blinked and the room seemed to slide back into focus. Far off, a clock was chiming one o'clock.

I rose, hugging myself, and went to the window. Carolers were passing in the street below. Their words seemed to float up to me alone. *"God rest ye merry gentlemen,"* they sang, *"let nothing ye dismay. Remember . . ."*

That was the song Keith had been picking out on his guitar in his room, I realized. *Remember, remember, remember.* Like a ghost of an echo, David's words came back to me. . . . *You'll never be alone.*

"Thank you, David," I whispered, staring up at the cloudless night sky. The stars glittered, cool and distant, the milky way a pale river in the heavens. There was a lump in my throat, but all the pain inside was gone, washed away. "I'll never forget again."

ABSENT FRIENDS

by Martha Soukup

Martha Soukup is a Hugo and Nebula nominee.

It was a mistake getting the tree. Douglas' hands were scraped and sore, and his joints ached from spending too much time wrestling with the thing in the damp, steady wind. Ten minutes just to get it up the stairs to his second-floor apartment.

Ah, well, but an Iowa winter would surely kill him. That, or his parents' cutting concern. Better to take his chances with San Francisco, and loneliness, and Mrs. Aguilar downstairs.

On cue, she started with the broomstick, banging it on her ceiling. *Bang, bang. Bang, bang.* Douglas had expected it. He had provoked her by dragging a heavy Christmas tree up past her door at nine at night. He had provoked her with the noise of his grunts as he wrestled it up the stairs, and with the scattered pine needles he was too exhausted to sweep off the stairs. He always provoked her, with his friends, his hours, his clothes, his inability to understand Spanish, his pallor and thinness. His existence.

The first hadn't troubled her for some time, and the last shouldn't trouble her much longer.

He sat very still, waiting. If she didn't use the broomstick for more than a few seconds, she usually didn't go on to call the cops. The tree lay on its side across from his worn sofa, filling a third of the space in his living room. Bedroom. Room. He couldn't put it up tonight, or she would call the cops. By tomorrow it would be half-dead. "Sorry," he told it.

The tree was silent. It was a good neighbor.

Douglas risked getting up and going to the kitchen for a hit of oxygen. He walked carefully in stocking feet, but he could hear the floor creak. Damn. He put the mask over his nose and mouth, turned the valve, took a few deep breaths. He felt a little less dizzy. Had he eaten today? His volunteer would be pissed at him if he hadn't made a dent in his larder next time she came by. Tough love, that's what she was into. Douglas had liked his previous volunteer better, but Ray had got sick, and had to quit. Maybe now Douglas' new volunteer was visiting Ray's house, too. Douglas didn't want to call him. He might call and find out—he might get bad news.

He couldn't put up the tree now, and he couldn't fall asleep for hours, probably not before three or four. He took a jar of crunchy peanut butter and a half-full bag of pretzel sticks and went back into the main room, pushing his feet along without lifting them. The floor creaked.

"Damn it!" Douglas said. He was just sure tonight she'd call the cops.

It was Christmas Eve.

The cops were always nice; they always seemed to guess about his illness; they always left again after talking to Mrs. Aguilar for a time and him for a time, not saying they thought she was crazy, but showing it in their eyes. And pity for him. But it was embarrassing, it rattled him, and he had enough trouble sleeping at night. She'd call tonight, of course she would, because it was just his damn luck.

Don't think about it. He'd worry himself sick. Couldn't afford to. Wouldn't. He sat and unscrewed the jar, the lid rasping hollowly, and jammed a pretzel stick in the peanut butter. The pretzel, when he bit into it, was stale. He'd left the bag open. His feeble excuse for an appetite left him, but he finished the pretzel. There, Margaret, I've eaten, are you happy? he thought. There's half an ounce less I'll have lost at my next checkup.

Oh, hell, even Margaret with all her stubborn volunteer concern wouldn't be thinking about him tonight, wrapped in the bosom of her family in Christmas bliss.

Fine. Enough. He leaned forward in his unfolded futon sofabed, one of two pieces of furniture in this room, to the coffee table. He felt a little dizzy as he reached for the lower shelf. The scent of dying pine in the room was too strong. He grasped for his photo album, found it, and opened it in his lap.

There was a file label stuck to the first page: "Christmas—1958-1981." The page was empty. The next ten pages were empty, front and back. The film over each page showed marks where it had once held down snapshots. Douglas could remember a few. There was a picture of him at two in his grandmother's lap; she had died when he was four. There was one of him at twelve with a blue, adult-size bike. One of him at five in a cowboy suit. Now he knew friends of friends who decked out in cowboy paraphernalia every night they went out, but he didn't think his parents would think that cute. It made him think of himself as a little kid at Christmas, playing with his new plastic six-shooters: not his idea of sexy.

Those photos were gone. He'd ripped them up and thrown them out last year, when his sister said she couldn't possibly come visit. She had to worry about her small children, and whatever the doctors said, how could you be sure? And his parents had supported her. So much for Christmases past. They didn't want him now, he didn't need them then.

Past the blank pages was the label "Auld Lang Syne." These pictures were still there. He wasn't related to anyone in them. They were in no good order: faded pictures of grade-school friends lay side by side with photographs taken only a few years before. There was Jerry. He was dead. There was Patrick.

He was dead. There was Rob. Douglas pursed his lips, considering. He didn't know if Rob was dead. He hadn't seen him in three or four years. Safest to assume he was. There were George and Carlos. Carlos was dead and George had gone home to Mississippi to die. Mississippi had to be a worse place to die than Iowa. Douglas was lucky.

Except he wouldn't go home to Iowa.

"Home? Screw it," Patrick had said. What was it, six years ago? He'd had an enormous party, tinsel and presents and mistletoe, in his flat on Noe, the place that was the envy of most of them, right near the heart of the Castro. Douglas had been living in the Sunset district then. He liked going home to a quiet neighborhood. "This is home and this is family. We can make our own traditions and screw anyone who doesn't want us in theirs." Patrick had had a few.

Who else was at that party? He couldn't remember. That was before any of the gang was sick. A life away. Many lives. All his old Christmases were gone. New Christmases might never come. This could be it. The ultimate, final extent of his Christmas cheer.

Suddenly furious, he threw the album against the wall. Pages came loose and scattered on the floor. Pounding started up beneath his feet.

Douglas sat breathing hard, fists clenched. He wanted to go down and confront the woman. Shout at her. Give her what for. Who was he kidding, though? She could knock him over with one blow, overweight woman of fifty that she was. Pathetic.

There was a rap on the door. Douglas started. Mrs. Aguilar? She preferred to act as though he didn't exist, assaulting his floor or calling the police without ever speaking to him. He stayed still. The pounding had stopped downstairs. The rapping came again from the door.

She had to have run up the stairs. Did she think yelling at him in Spanish would do any good? Maybe she was going to hit him with that broom.

He got uncomfortably to his feet and went to he door. He would speak slowly and maybe she would understand. "Ma'am," he said, opening the door, "please, it's Christmas Eve."

"Ma'am?" said the man at his door. Douglas blinked at him. "Excuse me, but I think I'm as macho as anyone you know, fella."

"Rob?" Carrying a bottle of burgundy. "You're not dead."

Rob gave him an incredulous look. "Well, thanks, Dougy. You're looking good, too. Are you going to let me in?"

Embarrassment fought with old irritation at the unwanted nickname, with nervous relief at seeing an old friend alive, with the knowledge he was *not* looking good. Douglas gave up on trying to make his mouth work and stepped back from the doorway.

"Hey, a picture show," said Rob. He walked over to the wreckage of the photo album, bootheels clicking on the wooden floor.

"Um," said Douglas. Rob took off his heavy leather jacket and tossed it at the coffee table. It skidded off and thumped on the floor, zippers jingling. "You have to be careful here. About noise."

"Pal," said Rob, "you don't have to tell me what I have to do."

"It's the downstairs neighbor, she's sort of sensitive and she gets upset. She can't sleep. If there's any noise."

"There's traffic and people playing their radios out there, Dougy, she's going to get upset because someone walks on your floor? Not on Christmas Eve, pal. This is a party."

Douglas sat carefully on the futon bed, hoping Rob would follow his lead and stop pacing the floor. "What are you doing here, Rob? Where have you been? It's been years."

Rob shrugged. "Hanging out with people." He circled the room, examining the old posters taped to the walls, glancing at the prostrate tree.

"Not anyone I've been hanging out with."

"The looks of things, you haven't been hanging with anyone, Dougy. Hot parties in clubs all over the city, and you sit at home Christmas Eve. Is the dust half an inch thick in here or is it just your mood rubbing off on everything?"

He went past Douglas into the kitchen. The click of his boots on the linoleum was high and sharp. Douglas winced. Rob came back into the living room with two glasses filled with wine. "Good god, man, you've got no two clean glasses the same. Is this why you never invited any of the gang over to your old place? I always thought it was because you were afraid of what your nice straight neighbors would think."

"Jesus, Rob, did you look me up to insult me?"

"Not me, Doug." Rob's voice softened. "I'm just here to spend Christmas Eve." He handed Douglas a root-beer mug. "Look, some wine for you. A toast."

Douglas' wrists ached, holding up the heavy mug nearly topped off with dark red wine. He raised it silently in both hands and let Rob clink his juice glass against it.

"To friends," Rob said.

"Absent friends," Douglas said.

"Absent, hell, what good is that?" Rob said. He took a big gulp from the juice glass. "Let's invite 'em over."

"Rob—"

"How long has it been since we all got together? I ain't seen *you* in ages, just for one."

Didn't he know they were all dead? "Rob, you can't."

"Can and did," Rob said. "Ran into an old high-school buddy of yours. It's what made me think of coming over to start out with, when we found out we knew you in common. He's on his way. Had further to come."

"Who?"

"Billy McElroy." Douglas vaguely remembered a skinny blond kid he thought was Billy. "You know he told me he never knew you were gay? What a missed opportunity."

"What, you mean?"

"You didn't know either?" Rob shook his head. "Typical. Well, here's your big chance. So romantic, reunited across the years—"

Douglas was losing patience. "You never change."

Rob stopped and looked at him. "Not anymore," he said. He looked like he would say something else. "Wait, there's the door." He trotted across the room, his steps echoing like gunshots from the walls. This time maybe it *was* Mrs. Aguilar, and Rob would talk to her and make things so much worse. Douglas drank several long swallows of wine.

"Billy, man, glad you could make it!"

"I wasn't doing anything else. I'm glad to be here. That is, if Doug even remembers who I am—"

"You bet he does. The one that got away. All he can talk about, poor sap. Come in, come in!"

Rob escorted the newcomer inside, arm around his shoulder. Billy looked much as Douglas would have expected him to, thicker around the middle and thinner on the top. A little uncomfortable. He was shy, back in school. Billy shook free of Rob's arm, removed his jacket, and draped it quietly across the coffee table.

"Let me get you a drink, Billy," Rob said. "I'm sure I can find a Flintstone glass or something."

Douglas put his mug down and stood up to shake hands. "Um, hi, Billy. Long time."

"Yeah," said Billy. He looked around, and finally sat awkwardly on the coffee table. "Nice tree."

"I should have picked a smaller one." Douglas shrugged, self-conscious. "It's too big for me."

"Thought you liked 'em that way, Dougy boy!" Rob shouted from the kitchen.

"Are you just going to leave it lying there?" Billy asked.

"I have this downstairs neighbor," he said. "If there's any noise at night she goes ballistic." It sounded stupider every time he explained it. It was better than saying he was too weak and tired to put up a damn Christmas tree, though. He took up his mug and drank half the remaining wine.

"Yeah, okay," said Billy.

"So, um, what have you been doing the last— eighteen years? Jeez, is it eighteen years?"

"I guess it is. Well, I went to college in Illinois. Northwestern. Studied engineering."

"And since then, what, you've been an engineer? What have you been up to?"

"Nothing, really." Billy looked like he didn't want to talk about it. That was all right. Douglas knew very well about not wanting to be pushed.

Rob came back from the kitchen and handed Billy a tall iced-tea glass. "Cheers," he said. He poured more wine into Douglas' mug.

"To friends less absent than before," said Rob. He and Billy clinked glasses and smiled at each other. Douglas wondered just how good friends the two were. "It's too damn quiet in here," Rob said. "Could drive a man crazy. Let's have some music, for god's sake!"

"Wait, Rob, come on—"

"You got any Christmas music?" Rob was squatting down by the short piles of CDs stacked in the corner behind the boombox Douglas used for his stereo. "No, no, no, no—your taste in music is still boring, pal, by the way—nothing Christmasy here at all. Where's your spirit, Dougy?"

"*Gee,* I'm sorry, Robby," Douglas said. "I didn't prepare properly for this party. Thoughtless of me."

"You ought to put this tree up," Billy said. He sounded worried. He rustled its branches, examining it. "It's getting dry already. Dying. And it's a fire hazard."

"No problem," said Rob. His bootheels made war on the floor as he went over to where his jacket lay on the floor. He pulled a blank-labeled cassette out of the inside breast pocket. "You wouldn't have seen this. It's the Christmas compilation album I waited all my life for. Sisters of Mercy doing 'Silver Bells'— really, I'm doing you such a favor." Three strides and the cassette was in the boombox. The first bars of "White Christmas" floated glumly across the room. It sounded like Lou Reed. Then it sounded very loudly like Lou Reed, as Rob cranked the volume all the way. "There's Christmas for you!"

"Let's put the tree up, okay?" said Billy. "Really, okay?"

"Dance first," said Rob. He grabbed Billy by the hand and swung him into the small clear space in the middle of the room. The creaking of the floor was just audible over the music booming through the apartment.

"Guys—"

"Okay, it's not the most danceable tune on the album," Rob shouted. "Next one works a lot better. Come on, we don't need to divide by partners for this, Dougy, get off your butt and enjoy yourself a little!"

Billy was dancing with his eyes shut, brow furrowed in concentration, head thrown forward, back. He was completely off the beat. His sneakers thudded more quietly than Rob's boots, but the floor was groaning.

"Great tune, but you really can't dance to it," Rob shouted. "Just a second!" He bent over the boombox. The music shut off as he hit Fast-Forward. Billy's solo shuffling was still loud, unaccompanied. There was no broomstick against his floor. She must have called the cops. Probably half the cops in the precinct were bearing down on him, pissed at having their Christmas disturbed.

Rob hit Play with a loud click and the boombox

screamed with electric guitar. Douglas couldn't recognize the tune over the distortion and the riffs. "All *right*!" Rob shouted. He leapt into the air and crashed to the floor doing air-guitar. Billy increased his pace to a near-flamenco.

"Stop it!" Nothing changed. Douglas screamed, "*Stop* it!"

Rob stopped. Billy stopped. The music stopped.

"What the hell are you *doing* here? Are you just here to make what's left of my life hell?"

"Not us," said Rob.

"My neighbor hates me, you're going to get the cops called on me, maybe I'll be evicted, this could be my last goddamn Christmas and what are you *doing* to me?"

"Spending Christmas," Rob said.

"Jesus, don't you see it? I'm dying, you moron. You're spending your goddamn Christmas with a goddamn dead man."

"You?" Rob sounded amused.

"Did you ever hear of rest in peace? Would you get the hell out of here?"

"Everyone isn't here yet."

"You should put the tree up," Billy said. "You've got to trim off the bottom so it doesn't die so soon. I don't think you should wait any more."

"I don't give a damn about the tree. I hurt. I have nausea and I can't breathe right sometimes and you are pissing the hell out of me. Go away. Go away!"

"We have no place else, Douglas," said Rob. "For a so-called dead man you're not so swift on the uptake. You should at least give everyone else a chance to come by and have Christmas."

Billy went to the door and opened it. "I don't know these guys," he said.

"Jerry," said Rob. "Patrick. Carlos. George here?"

"Not yet," Carlos said. "He's a tough one."

"How are you doing, Douglas?" Jerry asked. The last time Douglas had seen him, he was skeletal, enmeshed in tubing, blotched with K/S. Five years ago. Now Jerry's thick hair was beginning to gray and there were more wrinkles around his eyes. He looked older.

Rob smirked. "Oh, he thinks he's dead already."

"There's a difference, Douglas. Trust me, you can tell," said Jerry.

"Do you have any of that wine?" Patrick asked Rob.

"In the kitchen," Rob said. "Help yourself. I'm turning the music back on." Electric guitar filled the room again, somewhat less deafeningly. Rob hadn't touched the boombox.

"Go away," Douglas said. "You're not real. Leave me alone. All of you." He sat heavily on his futon. It came to him that, beneath the wild improvisation, the tune was "I'll Be Home for Christmas." "Who the hell is playing that?"

"Hendrix," said Rob. He shrugged. "I waited all my life to hear Hendrix do Christmas. Had to wait for your life."

"Never understood why you were so into that guy," Jerry said.

"You're dead? Billy, *you're* dead?" Billy smiled faintly. "It?"

"Oh, no, that's the part I hate," Billy said. "I was a virgin. Wiped out by a semi truck. I was nineteen. I barely knew who I was yet; I was just figuring myself out. You're a lucky guy, Doug."

"Is that what this delirium is about?" He was furious. "My subconscious telling me where there's life, there's hope? Buck up, take your AZT, tomorrow there's a cure and true love is around the corner? Well, screw that. Tomorrow I could be in intensive care, and I never found true love, and I don't need a bunch of party animals from beyond the veil telling me pie in the sky!"

"Screw you," said Patrick, coming from the kitchen with a coffee mug of wine. "Who said this is anything about you, Douglas? What about us? Where the hell do we exist except in you? Our loving families? Give me a break. *You* go gentle, but if you're taking me with you, I'm gonna fight, man."

Douglas blinked. His anger had spooled itself out in one burst and now he didn't know what to say.

"Hey," said Carlos. "We're the guests here, guys, be nice. Come on, Douglas, sit back down." His hand on Douglas' arm felt strong and real.

"If this is really your last Christmas, Douglas, how are you gonna spend it?" said Jerry. "Pretending for your neighbor's sake you're already dead?"

"Can we put the tree up?" Billy asked. "Let's put the tree up."

Douglas looked around at all of them. Hendrix faded into Sisters of Mercy. "It's really drying out, isn't it?" he said.

"Yeah, but it'll last a while longer if you get the bottom sawed off. You have a saw?"

"In the kitchen," Douglas said. "Bottom drawer next to the stove." Billy turned to get it. "Hey, Billy?"

"Yeah?"

"If—it happened—when you were nineteen, how come you look like my age?"

"It's 1993, Doug," Billy said. "How old should I get to be? I didn't come here to be nineteen forever."

Douglas nodded. "Righthand side of the stove."

Officer Yi sighed as he climbed the stairs of the old Mission district building. He was too damn old to still be working Christmas Eves. His partner, Kelley, behind him, had heard about this building. "This dizzy old woman calls on this poor asshole all the time, Jim," he'd told Yi in the car. "Claims he's, I dunno, bowling with elephants up there. Every one noted as unsubstantiated when the cops got there. One night she called three times. I think she just hates his ass." Better than a domestic dispute, though. You never knew who might wave a gun in your face when you went to one of those.

He knocked loudly on the door. Get it over with and find out what the next call was. Finish the shift, then get about two hours of sleep before his kids woke him so they could tear into their stockings.

"George?" said a voice on the other side of the door. It opened. A very thin man in pajamas stood looking at him. He was pale, though there was color high in his cheeks. Another poor jerk with AIDS, for sure.

The man smiled crookedly and held up a teacup filled with wine. Behind him, in the corner of a small studio room, a scraggly, undecorated Christmas tree tilted at a precarious angle in its stand. A boombox hissed white noise.

"Oh. You're alive." He handed Yi the cup of wine. "Come in and help me get this tree straight, would you?"

Yi looked at his partner. *Looney-tunes,* Kelly mouthed.

Yi smiled. "What the hey, it's Christmas." It seemed like something to do. The three of them went into the apartment to fix the tree.

PRESENTES

Nicholas A. DiChario

Nicholas A. DiChario is a relatively new writer; this is his eighth professional sale.

Frankie nudged his way through Sears and headed north, more or less, toward the center of jam-packed Blossom County Shopping Mall.

Before the breakup of Frankie's live-in relationship with Gina, he could never have imagined the trauma involved in shopping the weekend before Christmas. Teen-aged girls traveled in packs like wolves, hunting for mates in varsity football jackets. Women dressed like snow-bunnies, wearing tight white ski jackets, hopped past him as if he were standing still, making him dizzy and snow-blind. Salespeople in elf hats handed him coupons and flyers. Inept dads bruised his ankles with baby strollers at every turn.

Frankie squeezed through to the food court where he waited for a seat to free up, then out-sprinted a mother of three for it. The woman sneered at him. He had problems of his own: A Christmas list as long as his leg and only one box under his arm—a Liz Claiborne blouse too small for his mother and too large for his sister, but the blouse had been the only thing left on the rack with a "recognizable name," and the singular piece of advice he remembered from his boyhood days of shopping with Mama was to buy brand-name merchandise or don't buy at all.

Frankie sagged in his seat. Sweat ran down his ribs, beneath the parka and sweatshirt only an idiot would

have worn to a packed mall. He closed his eyes against
the deafening noise (as if that would help), and for a
moment he couldn't decide whether he was in a shopping mall, an airport, or Hell.

Frankie's belly grumbled and his legs felt like egg
nog. He needed food, but if he got up to get something to eat he'd lose his seat. Which did he need
more, energy or rest? He was too damned tired to
decide. Could the holiday season have taken such a
toll, or was it really the absence of Gina dragging
him down?

Smells—oh, God—pizza, cheeseburgers, pastries,
hot pretzels—

"Mary *Madre*," said an old lady who had snuck up
beside him while his eyes were closed. "What a bunch
of crazies these people before Christmas, no?" She
glanced heavenward. Her Sicilian accent reminded
Frankie of his late grandmother's.

"No," he said. "I mean yes."

She smiled at him. "Mind if I sit?" She held a half
dozen bags in each hand, squeezed several boxes
under her arms, and a black-leather purse hung over
her shoulder. She deposited her packages on the floor,
deftly edged past the table next to Frankie's, grabbed
a chair out from under a teen-aged girl who had just
stood to leave, and slid easily into the empty seat—all
in one remarkably graceful motion.

She reached into one of her bags and dropped a
huge piece of hot pizza on the table in front of
Frankie, and the smell shot straight up his nostrils.
He salivated.

"Go ahead," she said, "eat."

"No, I couldn't."

"Eat, eat."

"You mean it?"

"*Si!*"

"Thanks," he said, deciding not to wait for the old
lady to change her mind. He took a huge bite and
chewed open-mouthed to cool his palate. He thought

the old girl reminded him a bit of his late Aunt Rosa, the way she sat cockeyed with a crooked smile, the way she held her thumbs and forefingers slightly parted, as if poised to pinch his cheeks, and that fleshy neck, about the same circumference as her thigh. "What do I owe you?" He put down the pizza and reached for his wallet.

"Never mind the money," she said. "You look like you're starving. All ribs, you young people today. You call that healthy? In my day that was sickly."

Frankie chewed and swallowed and chewed, deciding he'd pay her as soon as he finished making a pig of himself.

"It doesn't look like you have much shopping done," she said.

Frankie shook his head. " 'Fraid not."

The old lady placed a paper cup and a straw in front of him. "Large Coke," she said, winking and nodding. "Had it stuffed in one of my bags. A real shopper finds a way to carry everything she needs with no being clumsy—Drink, drink!"

"You sure?"

"Please. Looks like you have rough morning."

"Amen," Frankie said to that, sipping at the soda.

"Rough year, probably, too, no?"

Frankie glanced up at her. She was still smiling innocently, with a vacant look in her eyes, a look he was sure he'd seen somewhere before, maybe his own baby pictures.

"Don't look so surprised," she said. "It's written all over your face. You young people today and your crazy relationships. You don't know what you want, and you all hurt each other."

Frankie nodded. That was certainly true. He still remembered the day Gina announced she no longer loved him. Eight months ago. And twenty-one days. Almost to the hour.

"So she said she didn't love you anymore." The old lady shrugged. "Is that the end of the world?"

"We'd been living together for three years. We shared everything. At least I thought we did. I had no idea anything was wrong." Frankie tore off a piece of crust and stuffed it in his mouth. Apparently a lot of things had been wrong, mostly with him: the way he dressed too casually for every occasion, the way he didn't mingle enough with her crowd and his inappropriate comments when he did, the way he always used her toothbrush, his softball league in the summer and his bowling in the winter, his love of cheesy made-for-television movies. . . .

"How did you know she said she didn't love me?"

"It's written all over your face," the old lady said. "Let me tell you what else I read there. This Christmas you wanted to show everybody in your family you're okay, you're surviving and moving on with your life and everybody can see how strong you are. No? And what happens? You get busy at work and you're not so good at taking care of yourself and you get behind in your shopping . . . and here you are, three days before Christmas and you got one blouse that doesn't fit anybody."

The Oswego County Choir blared "The Twelve Days of Christmas" remarkably off-key. A kid in Santa's lap shrieked like a trapped hyena. A man dressed in a white-chocolate Fanny Farmer santa-suit flipped off his manager and stomped away, cheeks as red as a bowl full of cherries. At the Hickory Farms, Mrs. Claus beat one of Santa's elves over the noggin with a huge beef-stick. His mother had always warned him Christmas brought out the worst in people.

Frankie pushed aside the pizza. "How did you know about the blouse?"

"Call it intuition."

"No, it's more than that. C'mon. What is this? *Candid Camera* or *America's Funniest Home Videos* or something? Who told you so much about me?"

"Let's just say I'm good friends with the Ghost of

Christmas Past. He'll tell me anything I want to know for a plate of *calamari* and tomato sauce."

Frankie sighed. It's not worth an argument, he thought. The old lady had been nice to him and he was grateful for that, but he had a lot to do today. His stomach churned thinking about his Christmas list. "Thanks for the pizza and Coke." He stood up and pulled out his wallet.

"What about your nephew?" she said.

"What about him?"

"Little Joey worships the ground you walk on and you don't even put him on your list."

Frankie thought about it. How could he forget Joey?

"Here, take this." The old lady reached into one of her bags and pulled out a bright, lime-green box. "It's one of those crazy Pong Blasters. He'll love it."

"Pong Blaster?"

"*Si,* look, you load it up with a dozen Ping-pong balls, and then you just pull the trigger—*bang, bang, bang*—like a real *carabina*—it's got a range of up to twenty feet. He asked Santa for it." She smiled and wrinkled her nose, reminding Frankie of his late Grandpa Mario.

Frankie sat down. "You're related to me. You have to be. You know too much about me and my family, and you look—I mean you remind me of all my dead relatives. Who are you?"

"I took this form because I knew you would be comfortable with me like this."

"Took what form? What are you talking about?"

"Look at this," she said. She pulled out another bag. "This would be perfect for your sister. She needs a new purse and she won't buy herself a good leather one. Too much money." She dropped the purse on the table in front of him.

She opened another bag and placed a small box in the palm of her hand. "And how about this for your mama? Your sister's getting her a pair of slippers and a bathrobe. That's nice. She needs those things. But I bet you don't know how much your mama adores turquoise."

"Does she really?"

She opened the box. "A turquoise-and-silver pin. It will go beautifully with that lovely black dress she wears to funerals and baptisms."

"How do you know about Ma's birth-and-death dress?"

"And how about this?" she said.

A tin of butter-cookies for his Aunt and Uncle Molanaro. A cuticle set and a lint brush for his corporate executive brother, Pauly. A collection of silk kerchiefs (hand-woven, made in Italy) for his Aunt Teresa. Cherry cordials spiked with rum for his second-cousin's grandmother who used to drive him home from high school when he missed the bus after baseball practice. . . .

And on and on.

"This stuff is perfect!" said Frankie. "What do you want for it all?—name your price—I'll write you a check—anything you want—"

"Please, enough already about the money. I don't expect any money from you. You're going through a difficult time and I'm here to help. Just remember this: *E meglio piegarsi che scavezzarsi*. It means, *'Tis better to bend than to be broken*. What I'm saying is that it's okay to be a human being, it's okay to have faults and weaknesses, people won't love you any less—"

She waved her arms at Blossom County Shopping Mall, at the throngs of people, as if she were giving her blessing to the chaos of a holly-jolly Christmas. "This is a special time of year, you know, a time to celebrate life, not failure; a time of hope, not despair; a time to renew and step forward."

The mall seemed to spin, as if Frankie were riding the merry-go-round a few hundred feet away in Little-Kiddie Land. Jesus, his nerves were shot. He sucked in a deep breath and tried to remember the last time he'd seen life as something to appreciate, not fear. What the hell was hope, anyway? What did it feel like? He couldn't even remember. There were times, like now, here with this old lady, when he feared the loss of his sanity. How much of himself had he invested in Gina?—so blindly, so naively—and among all the gifts the old lady had purchased for his family, was there something there for him? Something that could cure a maimed ego, a broken heart? Something that could make this Christmas, just this one, here and now, worth living?

"Yes," she said, "there is something here for you, too. You have only to find it. It will not be wrapped in a little box with a bow, it will be out in the open, in the air, it will be free, and it will be inside, too." She tapped her fist over her heart. "*Capisci*?"

Frankie nodded. Yes, that made sense, in a strange sort of way.

"You're going to be all right, you know," she said. "I have it on good authority. The Ghost of Christmas Yet To Come is a friend of mine. He'll tell me anything I want to know for a plate of linguine and shrimp marinara."

"Who are you?" asked Frankie.

"You don't know yet who I am? No?" She stood, placed all of the packages, all of the wonderfully perfect gifts she'd bought for his family's Christmas, in a tidy stack on the chair she'd just vacated.

"I am the Ghost of Christmas Presents."

PETER'S GHOST
by Marie A. Parsons

Marie A. Parsons is a new writer in the field; this is her third published story.

Torin walked the New York streets, searching every doorway, peeking into restaurant windows and ignoring the holographic carolers and the actual tourists gaping at the virtual image of the Millennium Center Christmas tree. The old man had to be somewhere; he couldn't just vanish, unless he was a hologram, or a ghost.

The December night was warm and breezy, like past Christmas Eves had been. The L5 habitats and comm satellites lit up the sky with their red and green colors.

The holidays had always given Torin moderate pleasure in the past, and he had always taken notice of the wreaths and lights and the singing. Now all he could think of was doing away with the old stranger who had watched Torin take Peter's throat between his hands and squeeze the last breath from his body.

Peter was a stupid fool. He could just have ignored Torin's smuggling operation from the Martian mines. Torin hadn't wanted to kill him.

"But you did kill me, Torey. True, I would have died in a month anyway. The doctors said I had let things wait too long. I had briefly considered suicide, did you know that? But along you came, and sped my demise quite considerably and probably less painfully too, although I wouldn't have chosen asphyxiation as

a form of mercy killing. I suppose I should be a bit grateful. Then again . . ."

Torin shook his head. It sounded like Peter's voice at his elbow, but that was impossible.

Peter Selayo had been the controlling partner in their mining firm, but Torin had recently begun smuggling some of the Martian minerals to some proscribed governments. These governments were willing to pay handsomely, and Torin had discovered he had some rather exotic needs and expensive tastes.

Unfortunately for them both, Peter had scruples. Last week, when Peter stumbled upon Torin's long-running black market operation, Torin had offered to cut Peter in for a reasonable percentage.

"No, Torin, I just can't do this. *We* can't do this. This business has a reputation to uphold."

Of course, Peter had immediately threatened to call the police, the sanctimonious bastard. Then, claiming he was remembering their boyhood friendship, Peter changed his mind and had offered to forget the whole thing if Torin would quit the smuggling and make some restitution, giving Torin one week to think things over. Torin had considered the offer but had decided that he liked the intrigue and the adventure of being part of a smuggling racket. Besides, the money was top-notch.

"But simply smuggling wasn't enough for you, was it, my friend? You had to become a murderer as well."

As he passed the glass-sided Merchant Center building, Torin thought for a moment that Peter had been walking beside him, whispering in his ear. This was crazy. Peter was dead. DEAD.

"You know, if you would agree to run the business as I always have," the ghostly voice continued, *"close down your smuggling operation, everything we were talking about last week, it's not too late to fix things. We could arrange my body to look like a suicide and get you off the hook for good. I know you aren't a bad man at heart, Torey. Just in too deep right now."*

Torin flinched as something cold touched him on his shoulder. He turned, and there was Peter, or at least Peter's ghost, staring at him with deep sunken eyes. Torin gasped. The ghost cackled with glee.

"Oh, come on, Torey. You can't tell me you don't retain a few old superstitions, can you? I've seen your lucky Gold Spaceship piece. So what's a ghost between old friends?"

The ghost leaned in, and Torin got a whiff of decay from Peter's breath. *"Now, about my offer. You going to take it?"*

"Still trying to make me do things your way, eh, Peter? Even after you have become disembodied?"

As the ghost chuckled, Torin realized he had suddenly decided to accept this apparition as a genuine ghost. Well, stranger things could happen. It might even turn out to be amusing, something Torin could share with his smuggler buddies at a future date.

Torin thought about what the ghost had said. That suicide thing wasn't a bad idea. But no, Torin had paid too high a price to gain sole control of the company, and he planned to run things just as he pleased. Peter couldn't control what he did now, that was for sure.

Torin stopped at a chestnut stand to buy something for munching. As he paid the man his credits, Torin looked at his hands. Both were curled into the same position in which they had been when wrapped around Peter's throat. Torin hurriedly grabbed the bag of chestnuts and turned away, sticking one hand in his pocket.

"Didn't you know that murder marks a man?" the ghost moaned in its best moaning voice.

"If you're trying to scare me with a trick of muscular control, forget it. We aren't children any more, Peter."

Good thing there were mostly holographic people out tonight. Torin didn't know how he would explain his behavior, talking to the empty air.

"You still plan on finding this man and killing him? Maybe by then you really will *bear a mark."*

"Still playing the big brother, Peter? Why can't you play DEAD like you really are and go away?"

Peter had brought Torin into the firm more as a favor for their past childhood friendship than because Torin had any real business acumen, but Torin knew Peter had never quite trusted him. Torin had never been afraid to dirty his hands and deal with the slightly less savory characters in the Moon and asteroid mines to keep operations going when there was trouble, all the things that Peter had scorned doing. If Peter had thought Torin would ever change and become like him, he had learned too late that he had been mistaken.

Peter had called Torin earlier this evening to come to the office for a drink and to discuss Torin's future. Peter had poured them each a glass of non-alcol sherry to celebrate the holiday season. As he turned to put the bottle back on the shelf, Torin had struck him with a paperweight. Torin thought he had killed him then since he could see blood on Peter's dark curls, but as he searched the desk for the partnership agreement Peter had groaned and stirred. Torin went over and knelt by his body. Peter began to open his eyes. Without stopping to consider, Torin reached down and choked Peter to death.

That should have been the end of things, and it would have been too, except for the old man outside the office door. As Peter gasped his last breath there was a sound from the hallway. Torin whirled around and caught a glimpse of snow-white beard and something red. He quickly looked around the office to ensure he had left no trace of his visit behind and then hurried out to catch the old man.

But other than a faint jingle of bells which must have drifted up from the street, Torin could find no sign of the stranger.

One old man couldn't be that hard to track down

in a city of bioengineered youth and beauty. Torin had to be patient, but time was growing short. Soon the Eve would be over, and the actual residents of New York would begin to pour into the streets to frolic, making his task much harder. Avoiding holograms was easy, but Torin didn't relish dealing with crowds.

"What will you do when you find him, Torey? Kill him to keep him quiet? Suppose someone sees you do that? Will you kill a third time?"

Just as Torin ate the last chestnut, he caught the faint jingle of bells again. He looked up at the glass elevators of the Marriott hotel, and there inside stood an old white-haired man wearing a red suit. Torin chuckled. Soon all his worries would be over and he could lay Peter to rest once and for all. He entered the hotel and bought a bunch of newspapers. It wouldn't hurt to pretend to be a deliveryman. Torin walked over to the elevator bank. He'd take a chance that the old man went up to the penthouse. When the doors opened Torin entered the elevator and said "P, please." The voice-activated elevator doors closed and the car began to climb.

"Nice view from here, isn't it, Torey?"

This time when Torin glanced over, he noticed that Peter's ghost bore the imprints of Torin's hands around its neck. It occurred to Torin that he had never considered the logical reasons behind the appearances of ghosts to the living. Torin couldn't believe *he* was manifesting signs of insanity.

"It's not as crazy as you think. People whose lives have been cut dramatically short have always been able to return and put things right if need be."

Torin suddenly realized how close the ghost was to him, and moved away with a shudder.

"What's the matter, Torey? Don't you like sharing an elevator with a ghost?" The ghost chuckled. *"Have you asked yourself yet, Why has Peter returned from beyond?"* It grew serious and looked Torin squarely

in the eyes. *"You intend committing another murder and, quite frankly, I intend to prevent it."*

Now Torin had to laugh. This had to be his imagination. He always did have a vivid one, but this was beyond compare.

"And just how do you plan on preventing me, Peter?"

Torin reached out to touch the ghost, but his hand passed right through it.

"Just as I thought, Peter. You have no substance. So what can you possibly do to me, eh? Perhaps you should leave now before you embarrass yourself further."

The ghost sighed. *"Torey, you always did have to be shown things before you understood."* The ghost reached out with his finger and touched Torin's chest. An icy chill spread through Torin from the place where the finger had met his skin. With that, the ghost raised his hand and vanished. The elevator doors opened onto the penthouse.

Torin shook himself and walked out into a plush living room area. Wrapping paper lay everywhere, as did trinkets, toys, and gifts of every size and shape.

There was a voice coming from the side bedroom. Torin crept over as quietly as he could and stood listening.

"No, no, Harry, that just won't do. We need the extra bags immediately to take over to those kids at Children's Hospital. Give Prancer the package."

Torin nearly collapsed with laughter. Fine, just what he needed, some crazy old idiot who had a Santa obsession. Looking around at the furnishings, Torin knew this was a mighty rich old idiot. Good; when the police found his body they'd suspect robbery.

"You are really quite cool about this, aren't you, Torey? Almost as if you plan murders every day."

The voice from the bedroom stopped, and footsteps began coming in Torin's direction. Torin ignored Peter and quickly hid behind the sofa. He peeked out and

watched as the old man sat at the table and began to
wrap some presents.

Torin looked around the room for a weapon or
something heavy. The old man didn't look very frail,
but he shouldn't be much of a problem.

"Oh, no? Let's just see about that, shall we?"

Suddenly a breeze erupted from nowhere and began
to blow the paper and ribbons all around. The old
man looked up in confusion, stood up, and walked
over to the patio doors. As he was checking them,
Torin quickly moved to the fireplace and grabbed a
statue from the mantel.

"I really can't let you do this, you know."

As Torin was creeping quietly toward the old man,
he suddenly tripped over a spool of ribbon which had
appeared in front of his feet. The statue dropped to
the floor. The old man turned at the sound and sighed,
"Oh, hello, I didn't know I had company."

Torin cursed.

"I'm sorry! Are you hurt?" The old man helped
Torin to stand. "I don't know how all this stuff got
all over the floor. I was trying to keep things neat and
tidy so that the owner wouldn't find anything amiss
when she returned."

A squatter? So much the better. Nobody would care
if a crazy lunatic were to be found dead in someone
else's apartment.

The old man kept babbling on. "You see, I only
have this one day to get everything wrapped. The boys
will be coming by solarcar later to hitch up the reindeer and . . . what was that you said?"

Torin had burst out laughing. This guy really must
believe he was Santa Claus. Well, no matter. Nothing
was altered by Torin seeing what a nice harmless old
man this "Santa" was. Torin still had to kill him before he remembered seeing Torin commit murder and
tried to call the police.

Santa continued on. "Anyway, whenever I come to
this city I try to stay in penthouses. They usually have

enough room for my reindeer and the owners are rarely home and . . . am I boring you, young man?"

Torin had been looking around for a rope or something. He couldn't stay here all night and it could only be a matter of minutes before "Santa" recognized him.

"Uh, sorry, what were you saying?"

Santa looked at him closely. "You know, I feel I have seen you somewhere before." Torin tensed, preparing to spring on the old man before he could cry out and alert the AI security system. "But then, I have met so many people in my travels it's hard to remember them all." Torin relaxed for the moment.

"Oh, that's all right. People tell me I have a rather familiar face."

"Yes, that must be it. Forgive me if I seem a bit muddled, but the day hasn't been going well. One of our biggest contributors, Mr. Peter Selayo, seems to have vanished. He and I had an appointment for earlier this evening, but just as I reached his office I was called away to an emergency." The old man sighed. "I probably wouldn't have met with Peter anyway. I am sure I heard someone with him as I was leaving. He must have gotten involved in some business."

Santa or no "Santa," this lunatic was playing him for a fool. he must know that Torin was at Peter's office and he must have seen him choking Peter. Any minute now the old man would probably try to blackmail him.

Torin could wait no longer. He picked up a length of ribbon and twirled it in his hands.

"Excuse me, but I think I hear the boys now. I must go out to the patio."

Torin followed "Santa" through the outside doors. He looked up, but couldn't see any solarcar or other vehicle. The old man was definitely crazy.

Santa moved over to the railing and stood looking up at the sky. "They should be here any time. We have a schedule to keep, you know."

Torin dropped the ribbon. All he had to do was give one good push and ... he grabbed the old man around the throat in a half-Nelson and began to push him forward over the railing.

Suddenly Peter was standing there, looking just as he had in the elevator, though his face and body had begun to lose their shape. He shook his finger in Torin's face.

"This is really quite naughty of you, Torin. And after I gave you every opportunity to reconsider."

Peter blew a cold fetid breath into Torin's face, forcing him to release Santa, who collapsed unconscious onto the tiled floor.

"What are you going to do, Peter? Make me repent? Turn myself in? Ghosts can't really do that, you know, no matter what that old story said."

"Torey, do you know you were about to murder Santa Claus, just because you are terrified he might turn you in? Santa Claus, for pity's sake."

Torin studied the old man at his feet. White curly hair, long bushy white beard, rosy-red cheeks. He wore a white thermal shirt tucked into a pair of bright red trousers, and had shiny black boots on his feet.

Okay, so the guy *looked* like Santa Claus, or at least like the old pictures in the books Torin read as a kid. Costumes were cheap these days with the new disposable materials.

Torin looked at Peter's ghost. "Sorry, he's just a crazy old man. What do you think you can do about it?" He began to bend over the old man and take his throat in his hands.

"No, Torey, it's me who is sorry. You get one last chance. Then we'll see."

With that, the ghost waved a hand, and the patio and penthouse, in fact the entire city, began to fade into mist. Torin's spine felt icy needles. Maybe there had been some hallucinogen in the chestnuts. That sort of thing went on all the time.

When Torin could see clearly around him again, he

was in the living room of a large country house. A genuine pine tree cut from the nearby woods adorned one corner of the room, and it was covered from head to foot in garlands, lights, glitter, and color. Presents covered every inch of floor under the tree.

A small reddish-brown puppy ran into the living room and began sniffing the presents.

"No, Jasper, don't you rip any presents. Santa left them for us. They aren't yours!"

Torin froze at the sound of the laughing young voice. It was soon followed by the appearance of a small dark-haired boy accompanied by a slightly taller red-haired boy. The two boys stopped and stared at all the gifts, then turned to each other.

"Pete, did you ever see so many presents?" The young Torin could not believe his eyes. This was his first Christmas since leaving the orphanage to visit with Peter and his parents, who served on the orphanage board of trustees.

"My dad says that Santa Claus flies his reindeer sleigh late on Christmas Eve to arrive in plenty of time to drop presents at every house where children live."

Torin was young, but he had already learned not to believe everything he heard. "You don't really buy into that garbage, do you?"

Peter smiled and shook his head. "Does it matter? The presents are here. And I can promise, most of them have our names on them. They won't all be toys, mind you but they'll definitely belong to us."

The boys proceeded to open the presents, and sure enough, after every piece of wrapping paper had been ripped apart and every box and bag had been opened, nearly every gift had been for Peter and Torin.

Looking back in later years to that time, the happiest in his life, Torin had remembered having been astonished that people would do something so nice for someone they barely knew, just because they wanted to do so.

Right now though, Torin found himself reliving that

first Christmas of his friendship with Peter. Watching Peter help him put his first bicycle together. Teaching Peter how to use his anti-grav boots. Laughing together as they teased Jasper with virtual paddleball.

Peter's ghost waved his hand again, and Torin saw himself and Peter one year later on Christmas Eve, plotting to keep each other awake so they could spy on Santa or his emissaries. The two boys laughed uproariously the next morning after they each discovered the other had fallen asleep.

With a final wave of his hand, Peter's ghost brought Peter four Christmases forward. That was the day the two boys swore eternal friendship, no matter what the world would throw at them.

Torin felt the tears well up in his eyes, and angrily pawed at them. "All right, Peter, get me away from here," he snarled.

Peter's ghost waved both hands, and back they were on the penthouse patio. "Santa" lay on the ground, still unconscious.

"See what you have given up, my friend?" The ghost spoke softly, watching Torin sniff and wipe his eyes. *"There is still time to arrange things. I don't require seeing you suffer on the penal asteroid for doing to me what nature would have accomplished eventually."*

Torin walked to the railing and looked out over the city. He thought about the past he had just revisited, about the boy he had once been, the childish dreams and ideals he had once shared with a friend. He thought about the excitement and the fun he had been having in the present, the freedom to do exactly what he wanted, and the price which he had paid and been willing to keep paying to preserve that lifestyle and that freedom. Torin then thought about the kind of life he would have if he chose Peter's alternative. No fear of retribution, certainly. He'd be free as if Peter had never died. But with Peter being in fact dead, Torin would become full owner of the firm. As such,

Torin would have respect, even honor, from every corner of the globe.

Torin looked at Peter's ghost, but could find no help in its decaying features. He found himself wondering if Peter had found a new kind of freedom in the afterlife. No responsibilities, no anxieties, no partners to share profits or losses. Torin sighed. No nothing, most likely. He looked down at the old "Santa" and then up over the city.

Torin looked back over his life, reflecting on what he had accomplished and still could. The possibilities were endless and all led in one direction. Suddenly it all seemed very clear. Torin realized there was really only one decision he could possibly make. It wasn't so very hard after all.

He climbed over the railing and stood on the outside rim of the building. Torin turned to the ghost and said, "You know, Peter, in life, you were always a dull sort. I don't think I could comfortably be like you were. Nor do I relish the thought of serving out my days on a penal colony."

Torin looked again at the old man. "Bring him around as soon as possible. He has a schedule to keep."

With that, Torin turned away, walked forward and stepped out into oblivion. Peter's ghost stepped to the railing and looked down. "Strange. I never once considered *that* to be an option." The ghost snapped its fingers and Santa awoke. Looking up, the two saw a sleigh circling to land on the balcony.

"Merry Christmas, Santa." Peter's ghost disappeared into the darkness as Santa and his elves began to load the sleigh.

THE CASE OF THE SKINFLINT'S SPECTERS

by Brian M. Thomsen

Brian Thomsen is a full-time science fiction editor and has recently become a prolific writer as well.

Marley was dead, to begin with. There is no doubt whatever about that. The register of his burial was signed by the clergyman, the clerk, the undertaker, and the chief mourner. Scrooge signed it.

Old Marley was as dead as a doornail ... but that was seven years ago, and besides, I hadn't been hired to investigate Marley. Scrooge was the subject of my investigation, and after a month of tracking down lost leads, ancient archives, and absentminded former acquaintances, I now had a dossier in front of me that could have been called "Everything you always wanted to know about Ebenezer Scrooge but couldn't care less about."

I was waiting for my mysterious unnamed client to come by, "he" who had earned my loyalty by paying in advance provided that no questions were asked, and that the information could be picked up no later than early Christmas Eve morn.

It was just past dawn on December twenty-fourth, and I was waiting to fill my half of the bargain so that I could go off on my usual holiday bender down in the sin dens of Whitechapel.

My name is Malcolm Chandler, Mouse to my friends, and I'm your typical down on my luck Victorian gumshoe, who'd probably be spending Christmas in the poorhouse if my client hadn't come through with enough of an advance to settle a few way over-due debts to some reputable establishments who had in the past shown a certain willingness to donate the services of some of their less fortunate debtors to the local treadmill (as well as a few other creditors who enjoyed the sound of kneecaps shattering). Money is good, honestly earned or otherwise, and quite neces-sary for one's general well being since London had become so tough on its debtors.

I sipped from my mug of early morning grog, and hoped that my client arrived shortly. It wasn't as if I had any Christmas shopping to do or anything. It's just that I enjoyed the concept of a case closed, and as soon as I had handed over this file that was the concept to be imprinted.

The warmth of my draught awakened the slumber-ing little gray cells that had been dormant since I closed the file the night before. They had the uncanny knack of asking my senses the most awkward ques-tions at the most awkward times.

"Mouse," said the gray cells. "Mr. Scrooge is a sin-gularly uninteresting character. Why would anyone need to know his life story?"

"Shut up," I said.

"Why would the selfsame person be willing to pay so much for the aforementioned information, particu-larly from a down on his luck gumshoe like you?"

"Because I'm good, and you get what you pay for," I replied.

"The gentleman on Baker's Street with his physi-cian companion is better."

"Shut up!" I insisted, just managing to stifle my outburst before my client entered the office.

Regaining my composure, I quickly jumped to my feet, and offered my hand to help my benefactor off with his cloak. He quickly denied the offer, saying, "The file. Do you have it?"

"Right here, my lord," I offered in my classiest tone, pointing to the sheaf of pages on my desk.

The client picked up the folder, and quickly began skimming through the material. As he skimmed, I scanned. I couldn't help noticing that he was dressed almost purposely to disguise his build and obscure his face. His cloak was long and drawn across the bottom half of his face like some sort of Rumanian count out for a good evening. A gentleman's silk topper covered his crown, and a muffler succeeded in obscuring the territory between his cloak and the hat. Even while he was rifling through the pages, he managed to carefully balance his masks like a sheik in a sandstorm.

He must have sensed my eyes boring into him, because he quickly looked up and said, "Fine. Your services are appreciated and no longer necessary" and then reaching into his pocket, he extracted a coinpurse, and lobbed it onto the desk, saying, "consider this an added bonus. Now forget everything you've learned over the past few weeks. Forget Scrooge, forget me. In fact, you and I have never met."

"I don't even know your name," I added.

"Exactly, and let's keep it that way," and with that he was gone.

Any other day of the year, I would probably have just left the office at that point and headed off to the sin pits, but since I probably would not be making it back before the New Year given my current state of flush, and wishing to avoid the unnecessary difficulties that ensue when one trips over debris, I decided to give my office a slight once-over before leaving (my underpaid secretary, Victoria of the elegant legs, had gone home to Wales for the holidays).

After removing and disposing of several left-behind corset stays from some former business acquaintances, a few tobacco stained IOUs, and a Hogarth pin-up, I came across a business card of a certain F.S. Rogers, Esquire.

Since I didn't know anyone called F.S. Rogers, Esquire or otherwise. I was fairly certain that he must have been my mysterious employer.

Rogers ... the name rang a bell, but I couldn't figure out why ... in fact this further tickled my curiosity to the point where I quickly found myself muffled and mittened against the cold, and off down the street to the address on the card.

No sooner did I arrive within half a block of my destination, did I recognize my former employer heading off in the opposite direction. Doing a quick 180, I took off in hot pursuit at a discreet distance.

I soon found myself in the theatrical lowlife section of town where the division between actresses and harlots, and actors and conmen depended on one's income for a given week.

My quarry ran into a rundown tavern called The Charley D, where he quickly joined three equally bundled and obscured figures, at a table.

I took a seat at the bar, yet well within earshot, being careful not to remove my muffler or turn down my collar so as to give my presence away.

"Mighty cold out," said Bumble the bartender.

"Sure, guvner," I replied, watching the four figures remove their long coats.

"What'll it be," he asked, not having time for deadbeats.

"A spot of brandy, and an extra shilling if you can tell me who that gentleman is with that motley trio."

"Sure. That's Mr. Rogers, a regular patron of the arts he is."

Bumble fetched my brandy and returned to serving the rest of the bar while I set my efforts to spying.

The three figures my former employer was conversing with were an odd lot. On his left was a strangely androgynous, almost childlike, albino who was no taller than five one. Next to him, or her (or whatever, it took all types in the theater world) was a burly bear of a fellow who could have just as easily made a living on the loading dock or in the wrestling arena. Every few minutes the tavern's conversation would be interrupted by his boisterous laugh that threatened to shake the bottles down off the shelves and the inebriated off their perches. The third was a tall yet somewhat emaciated fellow who could have won the best-looking cadaver contest at any local poorhouse. All three listened to my former employer intently.

"All of the information is in these notes," he said and then focusing on the wan one continued. "Remember, you are the past. Bring up all about that horrible Christmas season he had at boarding school, adding details like how he loved the Arabian Nights, and such. Then move into his apprenticeship under Fezziwig. Dick Wilkins was his old crony, and Belle was the girl that got away."

"Yessir," the wan one replied in an asexual lilt.

"And you," he continued, moving on to the bearish fellow, "remember to cover his current life. All of the facts on that guy Cratchit's family will do the trick. Play up that brat Tim, the one with the gimp. The old buzzard has to wallow in guilt, and regret."

"What about the nephew?" the bear asked. "This guy named Fred."

"Oh, yeah," my former employer agreed. "Cover him, too."

Turning to the walking corpse, he finished with, "You don't say anything. Just show him those pictures, and try to look creepy . . . like death warmed over."

"Is that all?" the cadaver inquired.

"That's it. You already have your cloaks. White for past, green for present, and black for . . ."

"Yet to come," the cadaver interrupted.

"Whatever. Just remember to show up starting at twelve, one of you on each hour. No later than that or the drug that will be mixed in his dinner will have worn off. By morning, he'll be a raving lunatic, and by New Year's Bedlam's latest inmate."

"And bonuses all around," added the bear.

"Here, here!" the group replied.

From my tavern stool observation post I was horrified. It was clear that they were using the research I had carefully gathered to drive an admittedly unlikable yet innocent man insane.

The question was why, but it quickly all clicked in place.

The nephew Fred, the son of Scrooge's sister Fantine.

Fantine's married name was Rogers.

How could I have been so blind? Fred Rogers, Scrooge's nephew, was my former employer.

I was so busy flagellating my stupidity, that I didn't even hear the bear come up behind me and put me in a choke hold.

I passed out as the weight of a thousand curses of stupidity came crashing down.

I came to, what must have been hours later.

I was trussed up like a holiday goose, in the back area of some storeroom. Above I heard the voices of a crowd at play, a Christmas party of some sort. My head hurt, and the more I struggled the more exhausted I became.

After an infinite amount of effort I finally managed to work the trusses off my ankles, freeing my legs from their bondage of unending bending.

I passed out again, the stupid singsong of a holiday round beating through my skull.

My rest was disturbed by a lantern bearer, who doused my face with a glass of holiday cheer.

"Stupid detective," a voice behind the light scolded. "All of the party guests have gone home, and now I must deal with you."

"I guess so, Fred," I said, and then added in false bravado. "And, by the way, seasons' greetings."

"I was afraid you had put it all together, Mr. Chandler. That's why I had Barnaby escort you here. You may not remember. You were quite unconscious at the time."

"Barnaby the bear," I offered.

"You could have been enjoying the holiday right now, but no. You had to be nosy," he accused.

"And you had to be greedy," I countered "You're Scrooge's only heir. God knows he's not going to give it to charity. Couldn't you just wait? His days are obviously numbered at this point."

"With any luck, tonight's little dramatic recital will have taken care of that already. The best case is his ticker gives out, at which point I inherit the firm. The worst case is he goes crazy, at which point, I take control of the firm and he goes to the loony bin. I win either way."

Somewhere in the distance the bells of Christmas dawn tolled.

"There! A new day is dawning. Scrooge & Marley will now be Fred Rogers and Company," he laughed, and then added, taking a gun from out of his pocket, "And you are the only flaw in a perfect plan. A flaw that will be taken care of now."

The gun was trained on me, and I was about to kiss my arse good-bye, when a ghostly bellow shook the cellar.

"I don't think so," the unearthly voice cried, accompanied by shaking chains, and the sounds of ledgers and coin boxes dropping. "It's still my business."

Taking advantage of this otherworldly occurrence that had temporarily distracted my former employer, I barreled forward into Fred's midsection, knocking him down, and beat a hasty escape up the cellar stairs and out a nearby servant's exit.

I heard a scream that sounded like Fred's, but kept on running.

I finally reached my office, where I eventually worked my hands loose from their bonds.

Exhausted, I locked the door and passed out from fatigue, exhaustion, and the beatings my body had taken.

*   *   *

The rest of the facts of the case are rather sketchy. Scrooge got up Christmas morning, and was a changed man ... maybe crazy mind you, but at least for the better, and not in a way that he could be committed. He became a regular humanitarian, helped out his clerk, and signed over all of his estate to charity.

Fred Rogers was found cringing in his cellar, claiming that a dead man was trying to kill him.

He was Bedlam's newest inmate of the New Year.

What can I say—poetic justice.

Nosing around, I later heard that the word on the street was that Scrooge had joked about being visited by four spirits on Christmas Eve.

Four, I thought, but Fred had only hired three stooges to be ghosts. Who could the fourth have been?

The following year on Christmas Eve, I had once again managed to drink myself into a stupor and wound up sleeping it off in the office.

When I came to, I felt strange ... as if I had been visited by someone the night before.

On the floor leading to my desk were scratches as if left by some chains that had been dragged across it bit by bit.

On top of my desk was an envelope with a fifty pound note.

There was also a short note attached.

It read: "For your trouble of last holiday season—JM"

JM, I thought, who could it be?

Then it dawned on me.

... but Jacob Marley was dead, and there is still no doubt about that.

I decided not to think about it, put the fifty pound note in my pocket, and made the New Year's resolution to cut back on my drinking.

CHRISTMAS PRESENCE

by Kate Daniel

Kate Daniel is a full-time young adult novelist; this is her third short story.

Ding dong merrily on high,
  In heav'n the bells are ringing . . .

The clang of the hand bell fought with the recorded carol blaring from the loudspeaker across the street. Allan Mann scowled as he pulled the scarf closer around his neck and pushed past the Salvation Army kettle. The woman swinging the bell faltered for a moment as he passed, then regained her rhythm, an odd counterpoint to the song. Carefully ignoring her, he stepped to the curb to flag a cab. Behind him, he thought she raised her voice to carry, as some sucker dropped his pocket change into little red pot.

"God bless you, sir. Merry Christmas!"

Yeah, right, Allan thought. Like shedding a couple of quarters is really going to gain you points with the Big Boy upstairs. Or Santa, take your pick. He stepped back as a car cut too close to the curb and sent up an icy spray of slush, soaking his pants leg. But he didn't underestimate how many of those quarters fell into those little pots all over the country. The woman, face red and nose watery from the cold, had a lot of company swinging those bells, and the take added up, even if they did blow it all on winos. It wasn't as much as the company would make from Twinkle-Tunes, though, not if he was lucky. And that should help him get something better next year.

228

Maybe if he played his cards right, he could get a piece of the Live-Action Dragon Dudes. That is, assuming those were still big by then. You never could tell, with toys.

But in the meantime, those damned bell ringers were a public nuisance. A cab cut across and pulled up alongside Allan, adding a fresh spray of slush to his pants. Allan swore as he climbed into the welcome warmth of the interior. *Jerk can forget about tips till he learns to drive better.* The cabby added insult by beeping the horn a couple of times at the kettle lady. She waved back with the bell, sending Allan off with clangs. The war of nerves had been going on for over a week now, ever since he'd signed the petition to ban the bell ringers in the Loop during rush hour. He'd made the mistake of telling her one evening when she'd given him that Merry Christmas routine. He'd had a headache that night, which the bell hadn't helped. She hadn't said another word to him. But ever since, the way she swung that bell when he walked by her felt like a personal attack.

His sour mood lasted all the way to the apartment. Twinkle-Tunes were doing all right, although sales were a little slower than the forecast, but they were a seasonal item only. Toy companies made most of their sales around Christmas, sure, but there was no real future in something like toy Christmas lights. Maybe they could spin off a line with computerized chips that tinkled out *Happy Birthday* or something, not just those damned carols ... Nah. They still looked like miniature Christmas tree lights. Dumb idea, but people were buying the things for their kids. Allan didn't care if the kids hung them from their noses, as long as all the mommies and daddies paid for them.

He paid the cabby the exact meter fair, enjoying the sullen thanks he got in response. The satisfaction from the minor win faded before the elevator arrived, and the problem reoccupied his mind. All the real work on Twinkle-Tunes had been done months before; this was pay-off time. But the pay-off wasn't as big as he'd expected. He needed a lever, something new to move him up in the company.

Drink in hand, he sank onto the couch and picked up the TV remote, at loose ends for once. Simes had canceled dinner, pleading the flu that had half the city sneezing on each other, and in fact he hadn't been able to get through the conversation without two sneezes and a coughing fit. So far Allan hadn't come down with it, and he was just as happy to avoid contagion. But it left an empty evening. He played channel-changer roulette for a while, his mind still wrestling with the problem of a new product. He'd have to go visit his brother again and see what the kids thought. Allan's nephews, ages eight and eleven, were an asset in a way; unmarried himself, the boys were his only direct contact with the potential market. But he couldn't stand them. Rowdy, noisy, rude, endlessly destructive—fear of getting stuck with something like them was as good a reason as any not to get married.

He flipped into the middle of a commercial for a new doll that burped real spit-up. God, it wouldn't stop till they had real babies on the market, or clones, or some sort of robot. He took another drink, eyes staring without focus at the screen. That was a thought, some sort of a robot doll, something with a chip that could do more than wave arms and make faces and say stupid cutsie-poo babybabble. But he wasn't sure the state of the art in artificial intelligence was up to what he needed yet. . . .

The commercial ended and the program resumed, but Allan didn't see it. His mind was still juggling the costs of special R&D, potential payback, possible short cuts. He didn't really notice what was on the oversized screen until a voice behind him drew his attention to it.

"Wonderful costume. The holly wreath is a classy touch."

For just a moment, Allan stared at the television,

where Francis DeWolff chuckled heartily at something Alastair Sim had just said. Dickens. It was the old movie version of *A Christmas Carol*. Then his ears replayed the sound of a voice here in the room with him. He hadn't let anyone in. He dropped his glass and twisted around, ready to run or yell for the cops if it was a junkie looking for cash. The voice went on.

"It's better than I've got, I'm afraid." The voice was a warm, educated baritone, and the speaker was a complete stranger to Allan. The guy didn't *sound* like a junkie, but he looked like a refugee from an adman's nightmare. Big frame, full curly brown beard streaked with white, long hair—that part was all right, just an aging hippy, but the clothes! The guy was wearing some sort of bathrobe in Day-Glo red and green, trimmed with tinsel straight off a streetlight. A pin covered with blinking lights spelled out *Merry Christmas*. The most bizarre touch was the guy's hat, or whatever the hell it was; a ring of plastic greenery dripping with tin-foil icicles and set with tiny winking lights. There was a thread of overly-familiar sound coming from them: Twinkle-Tunes Toy Christmas Lights, playing a dozen of Your Christmas Favorites, just like the ads said.

Allan became aware that he was staring at the guy like an idiot. With those Twinkle-Tune lights—who the hell in advertising had come up with *this* bright idea? It had to be a setup for an ad campaign, and they were trying it out on him as a gag. Only that didn't make any sense; with Christmas in three days, there wasn't time for that. Maybe the gag was all there was.

Well, Allan wasn't laughing. The costume was garish, not funny, and there wasn't anything amusing about breaking into his apartment. He'd see if the guy kept laughing when the cops arrived.

But for some reason, he couldn't stretch his hand out for the portable phone on the end of the couch. The man laughed and pointed to the TV. Unwillingly,

Allan looked back. Francis DeWolff was saying something. DeWolff's costume as the Ghost of Christmas Present caught his eye. An open, fur-trimmed robe, a holly wreath set with icicles and candles as a crown—Alan looked back at his self-invited visitor and took in the man's outlandish outfit again.

"It's not a joke, Allan. I'm the Ghost of Christmas Present. The costume's been updated. Unfortunately I don't think most of it's an improvement, but ..." The extremely substantial ghost shrugged shoulders that looked like they belonged on a Bears' fullback. There was nothing in the least specterlike about Allan's visitor.

"And I'm Scrooge? Yeah, right, give me a break. I'm the toymaker, man, I give the kiddies the goodies they want. Besides, aren't there supposed to be three of you? Or are you trying harder because you're number two?" Allan scowled, trying to ignore his hand's refusal to pick up the goddamned phone. It had to be some sort of a gag. "Now why don't you cut the crap and tell me who set this up? Joe Murray over in Sales? Simes, is *that* why he canceled out tonight? Or ..."

"Stand up, Allan." The visitor was no longer smiling. "It's not a joke, and there isn't much time. We have far to travel tonight."

Allan screamed at his muscles not to move, not to *twitch*, but he stood up anyway. He was starting to feel scared, the way he had back when he'd been a little jerk kid and the only way he could keep the bigger boys from ganging up on him was to give them his toys. The toys he built for himself, the toys he'd grown up to design and sell.

"Touch my robe."

Allan's hand didn't even feel like a part of him. He watched it reach for the tinsel trim on the red sleeve. As his fingers brushed the shiny metal, the room about them flickered, like the lights were going off. For a moment, it was dark, no light at all, and Allan heard himself whimper. Then the lights came back. Only they weren't in Allan's living room any longer.

They were standing in front of the Picasso sculpture downtown, and it was broad daylight. From the clouds of frozen breath surrounding everyone, it was well below freezing, and the big bird-shaped hunk of metal had a white frosting of snow. But Allan's feet, still in the slippers he'd replaced his muddy shoes with, were warm. The stranger stood beside him, smiling around at the crowd. It wasn't a normal crowd; this collection was too mixed, and smiling too much as they listened to a group of kids singing. The carol was a familiar one, something about bells, and the kids sounded better than any of the recordings Allan had heard lately. He didn't care about the song, though.

"The booze," he said, mumbling to himself. "Maybe someday spiked the booze with something. God, what have I taken?"

"Now *these* are people who know me!" Allan's visitor waved an arm, encompassing the crowd, the choir, even the bird. His voice boomed, loud enough to compete with the singing, But no one glanced around. Allan moved aside as a woman almost walked into him. It wasn't rudeness; she was smiling at someone behind Allan. Behind him. Him, with his slippered feet and shirt sleeves, she didn't even see.

"Or maybe it's a nightmare. And everybody will laugh, because I don't have any pants on—" Allan looked down. His pants legs, still damp from their earlier slush-bath, brushed the tops of his slippers. He'd never believed people really had dreams like that anyway.

"Allan." The—Ghost?—shook his head, with a look of patience that immediately got Allan's back up. Dammit, no one was going to treat him like a kid too stupid to know what was going on. "It's not a dream. Or alcohol."

"Yeah? Then what is it?"

"Why, it's Christmas!" On the last word, he touched

Allan's hand, and the lights did their flickering routine again. Since there were no man-made lights, just that from the sun, the effect was interesting. When the light steadied, this time they stood in a crowded department store, filled with hurried last-minute shoppers. Most of the faces here had expressions opposite those in the plaza. Good will was at a low ebb.

Allan thought he recognized the store, but he wasn't going to let himself be distracted this time. "All right, you're the Ghost of Christmas Present. Great. It's crazy, but all right, I'll go along for now. So why me? And why are we here?"

"So you can see Christmas, Allan. And we're here so you can see—*that*!"

The Ghost pointed to a display Allan knew all too well. He could have sketched it blind drunk; he'd been living with it for months. Tinkle-Tunes. Damn, he hated those things. The endlessly repeated snatches of songs, played by the slightly off-key microchip, had ruined what never was a good season for Allan.

"They get on my nerves as well," the Ghost said. His voice was lowered, even though once more no one seemed to notice them. "Why you couldn't have used a decent recording—but that's not important. *There* is why we are here, why *you* are here."

A little girl was staring at the display of tiny colored lights, her eyes opened wide enough to rival her mouth. Allan was hazy on the ages of actual children, although he was an expert at assigning age groupings to toys. He thought she might be about five, but it was possible she was younger. She was cute enough to be in commercials, though.

"No, not a commercial," the Ghost said. Allan jumped slightly; was the guy reading his mind now? "To us, these toys are junk. And they're off-key. But to her, the lights are a glimpse of Magic. I wear them for her, not you."

She did look like she saw more in the stuff than he did, Allan thought. His memory flashed to the moment of sparkle that had accompanied the original idea for Tinkle-Tunes, the moment that marked all of his best ideas. That one split second when he still believed in magic. Then the memory faded, as the moments always did. Before he could say anything, the store lights faded as well. He recognized where they were when the light came back, and shuddered. They were in the family room of his brother's house out in Schaumburg. His nephews were fighting over the Nintendo.

"Here?" His voice cracked on the single word. Neither boy looked around, which wasn't a surprise. The boys weren't too big on Miss Manners stuff. But when his sister-in-law passed through the room with a distracted, "Boys, settle down!" and complete indifference to Allan and the Ghost, he relaxed. They were apparently still invisible, which meant this time, at least, he wouldn't have to put up with his brother's interminable stories about his job.

By this time the boys had switched their fight to another toy. With a jolt, Allan realized the Christmas tree in the corner no longer had the piles of professionally wrapped packages under it that had nudged the lower branches the last time he'd been over. Instead, there were drifts of wadded-up colored paper in one corner, an overflowing trash basket with more paper in another and several of the toys he'd gotten wholesale for the brats were lying around, abandoned. The blue Dragon Dude had already lost his lance.

"Hey, today's just December 22!"

"We are here so you may see the present Christmas," the Ghost said. He winced slightly as Joey, the younger boy, set up a wail of "I'm telling!"

"Why me? I'm no Scrooge." Allan pushed back the memory of the petition to get rid of the bell-ringers. That *did* sound a little bit like bah-humbug, when he stopped to think about it. "And what happened to the Past Ghost?"

"Have you memories of past Christmases you cherish?"

Allan didn't answer that one. He and his younger brother had grown up in a house that was always freezing, no matter what the temperature. Plenty of everything but life.

The non-answer was answer enough. The Ghost nodded and said, "These two are noisy, but if my colleague ever needs to visit them, he'll find material to work with. These won't be bad memories in twenty years."

"That?" John was making faces at Joey now.

The Ghost shuddered again, but he also smiled. "Obnoxious twerps, aren't they? But they're normal, Allan. Loud, and not the best behaved kids I've seen, but—normal. They'll have decent memories." He touched Allan's hand. This time his voice continued as the lights started changing again. "None of the toys you've given them are part of those future memories, though."

"They never say anything besides, 'Is that *all* there is?' " Allan whined the last words out, his voice jumping two octaves.

"Possibly they don't mean toys," the Ghost said. "You could be part of their memories, if you—do you recognize this place?"

For the first time since they left his living room, Allan didn't have any idea of where they were. It was a big step down the social ladder from the places they'd been. Many of the people in this crowd were wearing clothes that looked as tired and old as they did. The large room was warm, too warm in fact, but the constantly opening door sent icy breezes along the floor. It was some sort of charity meals organization, he supposed, since all the long tables were filled with people eating. A number of them were shoveling the food in with a lack of manners equal to his nephews, but not all of them. And while he spotted quite a few obvious winos, there were a number of family groups as well. The more he looked at the crowd, the more it looked like a cross-section, like the people in the plaza or the department store. Except these people were eating a charity meal.

"I get it," he said. "The whole thing's about those damned kettles, right? That's why I'm getting the cut-rate Ghost business, isn't it? I'm not a full Scrooge, so I don't get the full act, I just get one of the three stooges. . . ."

"What kettles?"

The whole story came tumbling out of Allan's mouth before he knew he was telling it. The self-justification he heard in his own voice made him wince, but he couldn't stop. Finally he ran out of words and excuses.

"So, what's next?" he finished bitterly. "A Christmas Future that looks like the Grim Reaper, to tell me I'll croak before next year if I don't give all my money away and save Tiny Tim?"

"As you said, Allan, you only got one of the three—stooges, I think you called us." At that, Allan took a closer look at the Ghost. The bastard was *laughing* at him. If you could call a ghost that. Funny, this guy really didn't sound much like the ones Dickens had written about.

"Master Dickens wrote for a different world. And he dressed it up a bit, to suit the style of the times." He'd read Allan's mind again. "But for what it's worth, I'm not here because you're scheduled to die. You might be, but I wouldn't know about that. No, this is just a small reminder."

"Because of the kettles. I knew it," Allan said.

"As a matter of fact, this isn't the Salvation Army. It's the Community Home Soup Kitchen. Different outfit. They do a lot of the same sort of thing, though. No, we came here to see one of my people, one you know." The Ghost pointed to the serving line.

Allan looked at the short stocky man behind the counter scooping up mashed potatoes and swore. "Damn it, what's he doing here? And what do you

mean, one of *your* people? Jake doesn't even celebrate Christmas!''

"I know. He has his own traditions.'' The Ghost
smiled broadly toward Jake, who was joking around
with the people in line, chatting with them, as though
he did this every day. Like he worked here instead of
being the vice prez of an up-and-coming toy company.
"It counts, it all counts. For Jake, this is a mitzvah.
December 25, he comes and helps out down here, lets
some of the Christian volunteers have the day off.
Twelve years now he's been doing it. A tradition. Like
I said, he's one of mine.'' Allan could have sworn the
Ghost whispered *mazel tov* to Jake.

And without any lightshows, Allan was back in his
living room.

"Jesus, don't *do* that!'' he gasped. "I was just getting to know how to tell we were going to jump, and
you change things. Is the tour over?''

No answer.

Allan looked around. No Ghost. No trace of anyone
else. It was night again; there was the semi-dark of a
city night sky beyond the drawn curtains. The film
credits were rolling on the TV.

He collapsed onto the couch, breathing hard. There
was his glass, still on its side, a darkish stain on the
cream carpet where a small amount of liquid had
spilled onto the rug. He picked it up and sniffed it
suspiciously. It smelled of expensive booze and nothing else, but would he be able to tell if there were
anything else there?

After a while he got up and fixed himself another
drink, opening a fresh bottle just to be on the safe
side. Allan didn't think he'd lost his grip on reality,
which meant that either someone had slipped him
some chemical dreams, or he'd been asleep, or it had
happened. All right, suppose it really *had* happened?

He tried to remember the ending of the movie. He'd
seen it before, even if he hadn't really watched it tonight, and years before that he'd read the story. The

last Ghost had been the one for the future, and Scrooge hadn't had much to look forward to. But Scrooge had been a hard case. He wasn't. This was just a little warning, the Ghost had said so. Allan was relieved, since he didn't even *have* any bed curtains to be stolen from his corpse, rings and all, and he didn't like to think what the 1990s equivalent would be. DOA in an alley and nobody identifying the body, maybe. Something grim.

On the other hand, the Ghost had said he didn't know. Not that Allan wouldn't die, but that the ghost didn't *know*. And death wasn't the only possibility. That soup kitchen—it would be a hell of a note if the next holiday saw him across from Jake, getting a free meal, one of those people. For a moment, Allan had a chilling vision of standing there, his feet colder than they'd been while he'd stood in the snow in his slippers alongside the Ghost. He could feel the holes in the bottom of his expensive shoes, the ache in his bones from sleeping beneath a bridge. Then it faded. The Ghost of Christmas Yet to Come hadn't really visited him. Just Christmas Present.

Jake. There was a possible reality check. If Jake really *did* volunteer at that place every Christmas— but that was no good either. Allan realized glumly that was the sort of thing that he could have heard without listening to, fuel for his subconscious. If it was a dream. Or a hallucination.

Allan had several more drinks, considering it. After a while, he realized he wasn't making any progress, he was just getting drunk. He finally said to hell with it and went to bed.

The dream or whatever it had been was fogged in his memory the next morning by a hangover of classic proportions. He considered calling in sick, but it was the last day before the holiday, and it wouldn't look good. He finally made it in to the office, feeling like his complexion was a nice seasonal green.

But the hangover, or nightmare or whatever, paid off. Halfway through the morning, Allan came up with what he thought was his best idea yet. The Ghost Gang! Maybe he'd be able to find some sort of thermo-sensitive plastic, so the ghosts could turn invisible in the kids' hands. He'd try the idea out on the brats when he spent Christmas out at his brother's, the way he always did. And he'd spend his week off outlining the proposal, so he could turn it in as soon as he got back to work in January.

By the time he left that afternoon, Allan's briefcase held sketches and an outline for a possible cartoon tie-in show. On impulse, he stopped as he left the building, right in front of the woman swinging her bell. Ignoring the startled look on her face, he mumbled "Merry Christmas" as he fished in his pocket for change. He dropped the dime in the kettle, then hurried to the curb to hail a cab. Behind him, the woman called out a startled thanks.

Ghosts, huh. Nothing had happened the night before; he'd just had too much to drink while watching an old movie. Nothing more than that. He could *use* it, and he would. For the Ghost Gang.

But a little insurance never hurt.

THE GHOST OF CHRISTMAS SCAMS

by Lea Hernandez

Lea Hernandez is a successful comic book artist and writer; this is her third science fiction story.

Snow, falling in sticky clumps, patted the windows of Detective Pere Sampson's office on the second floor of the downtown station of the Police Department. She looked past the white blobs suiciding, then melting, against the glass to the department store across the street. It was festooned with the tackiest holiday frippery money could buy: giant evergreen wreaths on the marble facade, wicker reindeer anchored by their festive crotches with theft-deterring chains to planters on the sidewalk.

The front doors were flanked by a toy-collecting Marine on one side, and a Salvation Army bellringer on the other. The constant *tink-a-tink-a-tink* was driving her crazy. Pere thought again about wearing ear plugs until Christmas was over. Only one week to go, and it would be.

"Hey, it's Rudolph the Red-Nosed Rein-Pere! How's my favorite holiday empath?" The door to Pere's office banged open, and Cholly King bounded in, waving a file. Cholly was almost always happy and noisy, and was, with Christmas coming, even happier and noisier. He smiled often, which made his eyes scrunch up. Pere fixed him with a hard look over the top of her glasses, deciding that she didn't care for scrunched-up eyes, especially *cheerful* scrunched-up eyes.

Cholly stopped smiling, and looked around her office. "Woah. Maybe it's Pere *Scrooge*. Where are your decorations? Didn't Kelly at least bring you a wreath?"

"Isn't my cheerful holiday demeanor enough? Don't you feel the love in this room? I told Kelly I'd put him out with the reindeer across the street if he tried to hang even one pine needle in here. Gimme that." Pere snatched the file from Cholly as he went to the window.

"Ouch!" said Cholly as he looked at the hapless deer. "Say, you reconsidered that Christmas Eve din—"

"What is this, Cholly? Little old men and ladies giving away lots of money to perfectly good charities? So what?"

"Well . . ." Cholly began.

"Are their kids afraid they won't get any inheritance? If there's a problem, this one's for fraud."

"I—"

"You know I only deal with ghosts and hauntings."

"That's the thing, Pere. All of these folks say that they were *told* to give the money away."

"By ghosts?"

"By the Ghost of Christmas Past."

"Oh, yes. Just like in the story. A pretty child with a bowl on her head, and when she lifted it off, there was a light. Are you sure you don't want a cookie?"

"No, thank you." Pere waved the plate of sugared Santa faces away. The woman she was questioning was tiny, with snowy hair and pink skin. She looked . . . elfin. Pere winced inwardly. Christmas was following her everywhere.

"So, the first night the ghost showed you . . ." Pere hesitated. "Christmases past?"

"Yes! I've always loved Christmas. The ghost showed me my childhood again. It was lovely. I was married on—"

"When did the ghost tell you to give away your money?"

"When it came back."

"Came back?"

"Oh, yes. The ghost came back the next night and told me where to send my money."

"And where was that?"

"To children's charities. You know: shelters, hospitals. She said I mustn't forget that Christmas was for the children."

"Has the ghost visited since?"

"No."

"Mind if I look around?"

"Not at all."

The woman lived in what was obviously a comfortable retirement. The two-bedroom house was furnished with antiques, but a minimum of kitsch. A large Christmas tree twinkled in the front window, the angel on top blowing a kiss. Pere could sense none of the usual resonances of a haunting, but she thought she felt something else.

"Do you think the ghost will be back?" asked the woman.

"I don't think so."

"Oh, that's too bad. She was so pretty."

"So what we got is older folks, all of them look like they've got some money, all of them visited two, three times. Not much of a haunting." Cholly tapped his pen against his chin.

"If it *is* a haunting, it's not a very accurate one. How many visited so far?" asked Pere.

Cholly flipped through his notebook. "Five."

"Consecutive nights?"

"Yeah."

"How big an area?"

"All over. But only in pretty nice, but not *too* nice, neighborhoods."

"Have we gotten any calls from anyone who's been visited once?"

"Yeah. A fellow named Michael Weeks."

"This in the papers yet?"

"Nope. About that dinner . . ."

"Good. Keep it out. I'm going to spend the night with Mr. Weeks. You have pen marks on your chin."

Mr. Weeks, to Pere's chagrin, looked like Santa. He was roly-poly, and more appallingly cheerful than Cholly. He welcomed her into his comfortable house with a laugh suspiciously like a ho-ho-ho.

"You're the investigator from the station? The empath? You read minds?"

Ho-ho-ho. "No, Mr. Weeks, I don't read minds. I read feelings. My specialty is in reading resonances from hauntings and communicating with the ghosts that make or leave them."

"The feelings of dead people?"

How could anyone talk about ghosts and look so damned *cheerful*? Pere wondered.

"Most ghosts are only one strong feeling: anger, hurt, confusion. . . ."

"This ghost wasn't like any of those. It looked and acted like a nice kid. I *know* kids."

"You don't play Santa at the mall, do you?"

"No."

Thank goodness.

"They overcharge folks for crummy Polaroids, and pay the Santas nothing. . . ."

Pere was almost beginning to like Mr. Weeks.

"I play Santa at the children's hospitals."

Pere suddenly felt like the star in a demented play: "Christmas in Your FACE!" There really was no escape this year. She made an effort not to look at Mr. Weeks' tree, the one he was telling her his children and grandchildren had helped him decorate.

"That's very nice, Mr. Weeks. Let's get started."

*   *   *

Pere sat cross-legged on a cushion in the closet of Mr. Weeks' bedroom, where she quietly sipped coffee to stay awake. The door, when open slightly, showed her all of the room except the window. A two-way radio, its twin on Weeks' nightstand, carried the sound of his deep breathing to her hideout.

Pere's plan was to observe the ghost for one night, then try to get it to leave or catch it the next. She didn't have to try hard to convince Mr. Weeks to feign enough uncertainty to insure that the ghost would return a third time; he had a hammy side almost as expansive as his cheery one. Pere hoped he wouldn't overdo things.

It was nearly one o'clock when Pere heard a soft whooshing over the monitor, closely followed by a whiff of cold, snowy air. She could hear Mr. Weeks' whispered "Who's there?" followed by a soft response over the radio. Pere leaned carefully toward the door to get a look.

There *was* someone at the foot of Weeks' bed. She was pretty, and dressed in a white gown, but she looked more like a teenager than a child. Her hair looked blonde—no. Pere blinked, hard. Her hair had looked decidedly dark for an instant. Her lips were moving, forming words, but Pere could only make out Weeks' side of the exchange.

"—back, just like you promised. What do you want, Ghost?"

Pere rolled her eyes. This was exactly what she didn't want.

"I do many good works already. Are you sure you want me to give money?"

Don't lose her!

"I don't know. If you come back tomorrow, I'll believe you're for real. You can tell me where to send money then."

A last whisper from the ghost, and she faded out of sight.

Pere waited until Weeks called her over the monitor.

"Did you see her?"

Pere stepped out of the closet, stretching and rubbing her legs. "Yes." She went to the spot where the ghost had stood. The resonances were fresh, and nothing like the psychic echoes of a restless spirit. Pere went to the window. There were small puddles of snow melting on the sill. A flicker of movement caught her eye. Disappearing over Mr. Weeks' backyard fence was a figure dressed in white.

"So what did you think of the ghost? Wasn't she something?"

"Mr. Weeks, whatever that just was, it wasn't any ghost."

"Cholly, did any of the hauntings take place on the same night?"

"Nope." Cholly was tapping a pen on his chin again. It was capped. "What do you make of this?"

"Like I told Mr. Weeks, it's definitely not a ghost. The feelings are all wrong."

"Well, what is it?"

"I checked the yard, which is something no one bothered to do at any of the other hauntings, because everyone was so sure it *was* a ghost. Our spirit took a trail where the snow was shallow, and swept her tracks on the way out. I've never met a ghost that had to cover a trail."

"So why do people think they're seeing a ghost?"

"I'm going to find out tonight. And before you ask, you know I don't do Christmas, and that includes dinner."

Pere was hiding in Mr. Weeks' bed, pillows stuffed around her to approximate his shape. Mr. Weeks was spending the night with his wonderful daughter. She tugged the covers over her head, and waited for one o'clock.

*   *   *

Pere was awakened by the sound of many tiny bells ringing. A soft voice was sighing, calling. "Michael, Miiichael ..." Pere peeled back one corner of the covers. The bedroom window was open, a cold, snow-carrying wind blowing in. Had she fallen asleep?

"Miiichaellll ... Miiichaellll ..."

Pere threw back the covers, kicking pillows out of the way. The ghost was there, robed in white, her bright blonde hair curling around her rosy-cheeked face. The ghost might have been smiling until Pere popped out from under the blankets. Now she looked extremely surprised. She faltered, and for an instant Pere glimpsed the dark-haired teenager that she had seen the night before.

"You're not—" she sputtered, all ghostly composure gone. She moved quickly for the window. Pere sprang out of the bed and caught her in a flying tackle. When they stopped rolling, Pere could see that she was holding a dark-skinned, dark-haired girl in a white dress.

"What do you think you're doing?" Pere demanded. The girl smiled benignly, and the room disappeared.

... Walking past store after store decorated with toys and Christmas trees straight out of a child's dreams ... December after December, where every kid talked about what Santa was bringing, or even of Chanukah ... every kid but Pere Sampson ... year after year where the countdown to the twelfth month was a countdown to misery, then numbness, until twelve-twenty-five was just another square on another calendar that would be thrown out in less than a week ... Stop! ... gifts of clothing and toys from friend's parents returned ... Stop it! ... parents too broke, too proud, too angry ... Get out! ... to afford Christmas ... Get out of ... to accept help ... Pere Sampson doesn't do Christmas ... Get out of my head! ... "About that dinner ..."

"Get out of my head! It won't work! I didn't *have* Christmas!"

The visions and illusions were gone, and Pere was angrily shaking someone by the shoulders. She almost couldn't feel the funny way her eyes were stinging.

"Hey lady! Lady! Stop! I give up! Lady, you're hurting me!"

Pere opened her hands abruptly, and the girl staggered away, rubbing her shoulders.

"Don't even think about going for the window, kid."

"I won't." The girl turned to look at Pere. "Jesus, lady, at least me and my folks *believe*. Christmas hasn't been good to you at *all*."

Cholly came into Pere's office with a subdued bound, remembering the reindeer. Pere was finishing her report.

"Nice work, Pere, but you knew it wasn't a ghost right away. Why didn't you just let someone else take over?"

"Because I figured if it wasn't a ghost, it had to be an empath. I wanted to know."

"How'd she get in and out without being seen?"

"By being careful. Not hearing a window open was part of the whole act. It was a good act, too. She'd case the houses, looking for people who put up trees, who had grandchildren visit, that kind of stuff. She never visited more than one person a night. She's good, but she'd wear herself out. It didn't always work, either. When she could tell someone wasn't buying the act, she'd fade and not go back."

"Why'd she do it?"

"Because her family's broke, and her little sister is sick. She knew she'd get nailed if money went straight to her family, so she was convincing people to donate to charities that would help her sister and her folks. Imagine that—a *helpful* scam!"

"So what happens to her now?"

"School. She's too good to run around loose. She's perfect for some talented-and-gifted program."

"What about the old folks?"

"Nobody's pressing charges. Nobody wants their money back. Because she's a nice kid who was trying to get help. Because . . ." Pere frowned.

"Because it's *Christmas*?"

"I suppose so."

"That bother you, Pere?" Cholly suddenly glanced past her shoulder to the windowsill. "Say, what's *that*?"

Pere whirled and snatched something from the window before Cholly reached it.

"I saw that, Pere. It's a Christmas tree."

"It is not." Pere reluctantly placed a tiny potted evergreen on the desk. Cholly bent to look at it.

"You still haven't gotten this Christmas thing down yet, Pere. Where are the ornaments? Where's the star?"

"It's not a Christmas tree. It's a Solstice tree. My pagan cousin sent it."

"It's a start." Cholly beamed at her, his eyes scrunching up. "Okay, if you don't do Christmas Eve dinner, would you do Solstice dinner?"

Maybe scrunched-up eyes weren't *that* bad, Pere thought. If Cholly could just take the edge off his cheerfulness. . . .

"You're on."

WISHBOOK DAYS

by Janni Lee Simner

Janni Simner is a full-time editor who recently started writing science fiction; this is her sixth sale.

"Hey, hey, hey, it's the Ghost of Christmas Future, coming straight at you from KHSN, *your* home shopping network!"

Gary groaned and opened his eyes. A tall, thin figure stood at the foot of his bed. It wore a red robe, loosely belted, and its white beard fell to its waist. The air around it shimmered, and static crackled as it spoke. "It's already July, and you know what that means. Only 175 days left until the big gift-giving day!"

Gary buried his face in his pillow. If he ignored it, maybe it would go away.

"But for a limited time only, I'm prepared to offer you a special deal!"

"I'm sure you are," Gary grumbled. He threw the pillow across the room. It flew straight through the man, hitting the floor behind him with a soft thud.

Damn holograms.

Gary sighed. He swung his legs over the edge of the bed and stood, pushing his stringy hair out of his face. "I disconnected my video, you know. That's supposed to take care of hologeeks like you."

The hologram continued, undaunted. "That's right—it's wishbook time at KHSN! Just like the wishbooks of the paper age, only better." It nodded enthusiastically, beard swaying from side to side.

Gary fumbled through the dirty clothes on the floor, pulling up a blue terrycloth robe. He belted it tightly around himself and stumbled out of the bedroom. The hologram followed. Bits of robe trailed behind it like confetti, flickering once or twice before dissolving into the air.

The living room was a mess. To the right, beer cans and takeout cartons were strewn across a faded blue couch. To the left, a small television was crammed between a grime-coated window and the outside door. By the far wall, a stain had spread across the brown carpet, stretching from the closed office door to the kitchen entryway. Gary kicked aside a pizza box and walked across the room. The carpet felt warm and sticky beneath his feet.

The kitchen floor was sticky, too, damp with summer heat. The microwave door had swung open, revealing a half-full bowl of oatmeal. Dishes were piled high in the sink. Gary opened the back door, letting in a hot breeze. He had turned off the central air a month ago, after he'd lost his job. What choice did he have? Not much work for an unemployed print journalist, not with St. Louis' last hardcopy paper out of business and the national papers close behind.

Gary reached for the phone—a small, handheld unit, with illuminated buttons and a long antenna—and dialed.

"Yes," he told the operator who answered, "I'd like the number for KHSN."

The hologram stepped in front of Gary, throwing its arms open wide. "No longer are you limited by the handful of items mere paper can hold! The Ghost of Christmas Future will deliver any product to your door—any product at all!"

Gary couldn't hear the operator speak. He slammed the phone down on the counter.

"But this special offer won't last forever—only until Christmas! So order now, and make all your loved ones' dreams come true."

Gary buried his head in his hands. A headache was beginning behind his eyes. "Just get lost, will you?"

The hologram froze for a moment. Then it flickered, once, and continued.

"Would you like a KHSN estimate before I proceed?"

"Just go away," Gary said.

"KHSN thanks you for your patronage. Remember—if we don't deliver to your specifications, your account will not be charged."

"What account?" Gary looked up, but the hologram was gone.

"Thank God," he muttered. The privacy act of '23 was supposed to take care of unwanted holograms, but sometimes something slipped through. He lifted the phone again and dialed. This time, no one interrupted, and he quickly reached a KHSN receptionist.

"Yes," Gary told the man on the other end of the line, "this is Gary Carpenter in St. Louis. I'd like to report an unauthorized video intrusion. . . ."

Gary pounded a fist against his computer. The hard drive groaned, then went silent. He pounded it again. Nothing. Damn.

After two months of job hunting, he'd finally landed a freelance assignment, writing for one of the electronic tabloids. It wasn't hardcopy, but at least it wasn't one of the video rags, where you had to stand in front of a camera and deliver the story yourself. Gary was a writer, not an actor—though fewer and fewer people understood the difference.

Of course, if he didn't get the computer running again soon, it wouldn't matter if he danced and played the saxophone, too—he'd miss his deadline. He sighed, looking about the room. It was an overgrown closet, really; the computer and printer took up most of the space. Beneath the room's only window he'd managed to squeeze in a rickety bookcase. A few dozen mass market paperbacks, from the days when paper books were still printed, lay piled on the shelves.

Gary stared out the window. The leaves were just beginning to turn from yellow to red, and the air smelled faintly of winter. He breathed deeply. Maybe he should do something else for a while. There were bills to deal with, after all, though that was a juggling act of its own. He'd have to pay his ex-wife, if nothing else, or Claire's lawyer would get on his case again. Claire had a job that paid well enough, and their son had left for college in Vermont a year ago, but Claire still insisted on receiving support.

There was a sound like static, and Gary turned hopefully back to the computer.

"Hey, hey, hey—it's the Ghost of Christmas Future!"

The hologram stood there, shimmering brightly. "I have granted your wishbook request!" it said. Its head bobbed up and down, like an overeager puppy.

Not again, Gary thought. He stood.

"I didn't make a wishbook request," he said, struggling to keep his voice low. "I spoke to KHSN two months ago, after the last time you crashed through my apartment. So if you don't get lost—fast—your sponsors are going to have a lawsuit on their hands."

"You asked me to get lost last July," the hologram said. A big, stiff grin spread across its face. "I have just returned from a full thirty-four days, eight hours, three minutes, and seven one-thousandths of a second being lost! Would you like a summary of your bill?"

First it invaded his home, and now it wanted him to pay for the privilege. Great. "What bill?" Gary demanded.

The hologram made a clicking sound, as if it were pushing its tongue against the roof of its mouth—or, more likely, accessing memory. Gary had never understood how a hologram could be operated by a computer thousands of miles away. Never cared, either.

When the hologram spoke again, its voice seemed

stiffer, somehow, less human. "Expenses," it began. "One hour writing 'get lost' program. Eighteen hours circumventing safeguards that prevent holograms from leaving the system. Thirty-five minutes writing 'get found' program. Thirty-four days, eight hours, three minutes, and seven one-thousandths of a second being lost. Total cost: $29,892.64."

"Nice try," Gary said. "Listen, I never asked for any of this—"

Another click. "In a transaction dated 8:39 a.m. on July 3, 2031, you instructed the KHSN Christmas Ghost to 'just get lost.' Would you like an audio playback of the exchange?"

"No thanks," Gary said. Then he laughed. "It doesn't matter, anyway. I don't have that kind of cash."

"KHSN also accepts check, charge, and electronic transfer from savings. Which would you prefer?"

"I don't owe you," Gary said. Couldn't this thing take a hint?

"Are you refusing to pay your bill?" the hologram asked.

"Damn right I am."

The hologram froze. "Accessing client information—"

"I'm not a—"

"Name: Gary Carpenter. Assets: checking, $2.93; savings, $30,097." There was a moment's silence. "Total bill, $29,892.64, has been deducted from savings."

"Hey!" Gary said. "That was my rent money. And Claire—"

"Yes, it's another fine product, brought to you by KHSN, *your* home shopping network!" The hologram nodded cheerfully. "Our wishbook promotion is still going strong. Is there something else the Christmas Ghost can bring you?"

This wasn't funny anymore. "I want my money back," Gary said.

"Perhaps a gift for the special someone in your

life—a personal trinket that says 'I love you' better than words.''

A rueful grin crossed Gary's face at that; he couldn't help it. "You think there's a special someone in my life, do you?"

"Now, thanks to KHSN, you have the power to make your loved ones' wishes come true!"

Gary laughed bitterly. "You show me that special someone, and then we can talk about gifts."

The hologram froze again. "Would you like a KHSN estimate before I proceed?"

"Oh, no, you don't. Not again." Gary took an angry step forward, then stopped. What was he going to do—attack the thing? He'd seen people try to attack holograms before. It looked damn silly.

"KHSN thanks you for your patronage. Remember—if we don't deliver to your specifications, your account will not be charged." The hologram flickered and disappeared. Gary glared at the spot where it had been.

He stormed out of the office, through the living room and into the kitchen. He grabbed the phone, stabbing at the buttons. His voice, when he reached the receptionist, was loud and angry. Yes, Gary explained, he'd called before. Yes, they'd said they would take care of it. The receptionist transferred him to customer service.

He was transferred twice more before someone could help him. The woman he finally reached asked more questions. Name. Address. The amount of money in dispute. She pulled up his records as she spoke.

"Oh," she said, sounding startled, "it seems you already had an order in the last time you called. We can't cancel accounts with requests still pending."

"What do you mean, I had an order in?"

The woman's voice was so polite Gary wanted to scream. "Something about getting lost." She hesitated. "They're not supposed to be able to do that," she said.

"Damn right—that thing wiped out my savings!"

"Well, I'm sorry you've had such problems," the woman said. "Why don't we start by canceling your account again?"

"Why don't you?" Gary said.

The receptionist was silent, the only sound her fingers against the keypad. "Oh, my," she said at last.

"What now?"

"It seems you have another request pending. You've ordered a—a special someone, our records say. That sure sounds strange, doesn't it?"

"You're asking me? Listen, just unorder it and cancel my account, okay? According to the privacy act—"

"You'll have to speak to a manager," the woman said. She sounded relieved. "I'll have someone return your call, if that's all right with you."

"No, it's not all right," Gary began, but then he heard a dial tone. The woman had already hung up. He slammed the phone back down on the counter. Damn computers. More trouble than they were worth.

He sighed and returned to his office, to see if he could get his own machine running again.

Gary couldn't restart the computer on his own, and the repair person couldn't come until three days later. He missed his deadline, and a month later, he still hadn't found more work. KHSN hadn't fixed his account, either, though they insisted they were working on it. That meant Gary couldn't visit his son, up at college, for Thanksgiving.

"Yeah, John, I'm sorry, too." Gary stood in the kitchen, holding the phone tightly in one hand. With the other, he rummaged through the refrigerator for a beer. The room was chilly, but he was trying not to start the heat yet. "Airfare's just too high right now. Maybe when your Mom flies you in for Christmas—"

John's voice sounded thin through the phone. "There's always the teleport, Dad."

"You know how I feel about those things." Gary

wasn't about to let someone break him into tiny pieces, send him over the radio waves, and reassemble him on the other end, no matter how cheap it was. He'd remained in one piece for over forty years. He intended to stay that way.

"Come on, Dad. It's safer than driving, you know."

The argument was an old one, and Gary wasn't in the mood to repeat it. "I have to go, John. You have a good holiday, okay?"

"Yeah, Dad. Sure." Gary couldn't tell whether his son was angry or disappointed, but John hung up without saying anything else.

Gary'd make it up to John in December. What else could he do? Right now, he couldn't even pay the rent, and the last of his credit cards had reached its limit. He sighed, taking a sip from his beer.

Static crackled. Gary wondered if he'd left the phone on, but then he heard a loud voice behind him.

"Hey, hey, hey, it's the Ghost of Christmas Future!"

Gary didn't even turn around. "What are you doing here?" he asked through clenched teeth.

"I have granted your wishbook request! A 'special someone' is waiting for you, just beyond your door!"

Gary whirled about. The hologram stood there, a broad grin plastered to its face.

"This I've got to see." Gary set the beer down and strode past the hologram, through the living room and to the front door. He reached for the doorknob, then stopped. The hologram couldn't really have found him someone, could it? Of course not, he decided, but his hands started shaking. He threw the door open.

His ex-wife stood there, with a frown on her face and a suitcase in each hand.

As always, her brown hair was short and neat, her suit perfectly tailored. Her black pumps were newly polished. In jeans and a torn T-shirt, Gary felt suddenly shabby. He wasn't even wearing shoes.

"Claire," Gary said. "What an unexpected—" He

hesitated, fumbling for words. "What an unexpected surprise."

"Don't fool yourself," Claire said. She stepped inside, setting the suitcases down by the television. "I'm only here for the money."

Of course she was. "I just put in for transfer of this month's payment," Gary lied. "You should have it by morning."

Claire smoothed an invisible wrinkle from her skirt. "Not your money," she said. She walked over to the couch, where the hologram stood watching them. Pizza boxes were piled on the cushions; Claire picked one up and sniffed it. "This place is a disaster. If I'm going to live here, you'll have to clean it up." She glanced at a cluster of beer cans on the floor. "And no drinking, not in my home."

"Since when is this your home?" Gary reached for a beer can, gulping the contents defiantly. The liquid tasted warm, like acid. Gary spit it back into the can.

Claire rolled her eyes. "Don't be gross, Gary." She gestured toward the hologram. "This thing promised me a million dollars to live with you. That's the only reason I'm here."

"That's right!" the hologram said. "This special gift is yours, courtesy of KHSN and the Christmas Ghost! And because our wishbook days are still going strong, we're charging only 20 percent above cost—a mere $1,200,000!"

"Get out," Gary said.

"Are you refusing to pay your bill?" the hologram asked.

"Not you," Gary said, looking into Claire's brown eyes. "Her. Get out."

"Not until it pays me," Claire said.

"Will that be check, cash, charge, or electronic transfer from savings?" the hologram asked helpfully.

"She's not staying here. I'm . . ." Gary smiled. "I'm sending her back. Returning the purchase."

"Who are you calling a purchase?" Claire's eyes flashed with anger, and she pursed her lips together.

"KHSN does offer a money back guarantee. Does this product somehow not meet your specifications? If so, please explain. Speak slowly and distinctly, and tell us how this special someone . . ."

"She's not my fucking special someone! She's my ex-wife, and she's leaving. Now!" Gary stormed over to the door and flung it open. "Get out!"

Claire followed, but did not leave. "Not until I get paid," she said.

The hologram appeared beside them, so suddenly they both jumped.

"KHSN is sorry you are not completely satisfied," it said. "You are under no obligation to keep this special someone. Would you like another?"

"Hell, no."

Claire stared at the hologram for a moment, then turned and glared at Gary. "Whether I get my million or not," she said slowly, "you still owe me two months' support. It had better be waiting in my account by morning, or my lawyer's going to pull the rug out from under you so fast you won't know what hit you." She smiled sweetly and walked out the door.

Gary slammed it shut behind her.

"KHSN apologizes for not meeting your expectations. Is there something else we could get you instead?"

"You can get—" Gary cut off the sentence. He wasn't telling it to get lost, not again. He took a deep breath.

"No," he said, "there's nothing you can bring me. Not unless you can find me some quick cash. Can you do that, Mr. Ghost-from-KHSN? You seem so good at everything else."

"KHSN can make all your Christmas wishes come true," the hologram said simply.

"Yeah?" Gary laughed. "Get me my job back, then."

"Would you like a KHSN cost—"

"I'll tell you what I'd like. I want my job. On the old, hardcopy *Post,* the one that existed before all this computer stuff began. You do that, and I'll pay it off for the rest of my life if I have to."

"KHSN thanks you for your patronage," the hologram said. "As always, if we don't meet your expectations, your account will not be charged." It flickered and was gone.

Gary laughed again, a high, wild sound. For a long time he just stared at the spot where the hologram had been. Then he walked to the kitchen and reached for the phone, gearing up for another fight with KHSN. After a moment he sighed, setting the phone back down.

"Screw it," Gary said. He opened the fridge and reached for another beer instead.

By Christmas Eve, even Gary's beer money had run out. He turned instead to a bottle of old vodka, purchased a decade before to celebrate his fifteenth anniversary. His marriage hadn't lasted that long, and now seemed as good a time to drink it as any. He sat on the couch, with the bottle to one side and a stack of papers to the other.

On top of the stack was a single sheet with the words "Eviction Notice" printed in red across the top. The fact that the landlord had used paper, and not computer mail, meant he was serious this time. Gary had until January 1 to vacate the premises. That gave him eight days.

Beneath the eviction notice was a short note from John, saying he wouldn't have time to visit before going back to school. In the note John said he was sorry, but not as if he really meant it.

The rest of the stack contained a series of letters, each longer than the one before, from Claire's lawyer. The last letter said that they were going to take him to court, even if it meant driving him bankrupt. Gary laughed. There was nothing left to take. He reached for the bottle.

"Hey, hey, hey, it's the Ghost of Christmas Future!" The hologram flickered into place in front of him.

Gary lifted the bottle into the air. "Merry Christmas," he said. "You want some money, too?"

"I have granted your wishbook request! A job on the old, hardcopy *Post* is waiting, just beyond your door."

"Sure it is. It's Christmas, right? Anything can happen." Gary took a gulp of vodka. "Let me guess—how much do you want to charge for this privilege?"

"Costs," the hologram began, "Development of time travel technology, twenty three billion, nine hundred thirty million and—"

There was a knock on the door. "Want to take bets on whether that's the landlord or the lawyer?" Gary asked. He stood and stumbled toward the door.

Behind him, the hologram continued its list. "Bribery of Van Neumann, $1,004; destruction of ENIAC, $21,083; delay of second world war—"

Gary opened the door. It was dark outside, and snowing; the streetlights looked funny through the thick white flakes.

A man stood in the doorway, not the landlord or the lawyer, but someone Gary had never met before. He wore a hat and strange suit, with a bow tie fastened around his neck. Behind him, an old car was parked by the curb—an antique, by the looks of it, dating well before the turn of the century.

"Can I help you?" Gary asked.

"Sure can, Gary." The man stepped inside, brushing the snow from his shoulders. Gary shut the door behind him. "There's been a burglary, down by the river, and I need someone to cover it for me. I know it's Christmas, but I was hoping that you could help me out. The reporter on duty is already busy."

Gary stared at the stranger. "Do I know you?" he asked.

The man seemed startled for a moment. Then he sniffed the air. "I should have guessed," he said. "It is Christmas Eve, after all. Think you can sober up fast enough to get to the river?"

"We've never met," Gary said. Was he drunker than he realized?

The man laughed uneasily. "It's Ed Mathers, your editor on the *Post.*"

Gary's editor had been a woman named Shawna McCullen.

"That's right!" the hologram said. Gary and the stranger both turned at the sound. "This special gift is yours, courtesy of KHSN and the Christmas Ghost!"

Special gift? What special gift?

The stranger looked from Gary to the shimmering hologram. "Oh, I get it," he said. "It's a costume party, isn't it? I thought you were dressed kind of strange. Well, I'm sorry to interrupt, but I really do need a reporter."

Gary glanced at his T-shirt and jeans, then back to the man. "Why don't you have a seat, Mr. Mathers? I have a hologram to get rid of, but I'll be right with you, okay?"

"Mr. Mathers? Gary, you've called me Ed for years."

Gary turned to the hologram. "We need to talk," he said.

The hologram followed him into the kitchen. "This Mathers guy—he has something to do with you, doesn't he?" Gary kept his voice low so the stranger couldn't hear.

"The KHSN Ghost has delivered, just in time for Christmas!"

"What is he? An actor?"

"You asked for a job on the old, hardcopy *Post*—"

"It was a joke. There is no hardcopy *Post.*"

"Would you like a summary of your bill? Development of time travel technology—"

Gary sighed. "I'd better deal with Mr. Mathers first,

and you later." He stepped back into the living room, then stopped. Something was wrong. He looked about the room.

The couch was smaller, somehow, and the cushioned back looked stiff and uncomfortable. The carpeting was gone; a rug covered half the hardwood floor. There was a fireplace where the television and window used to be. A log burned brightly, and the entire room smelled of burnt wood.

No way, Gary thought.

The bills had disappeared as well. So had the vodka, unfortunately; Gary could have used a drink. He felt horribly sober, with a sick feeling in his stomach that was worse than any hangover.

"I'll be right back," he told Mathers, and started walking through the apartment. The hologram followed.

The kitchen had also changed, though Gary had been there just a moment before. The microwave was gone, and the refrigerator looked small and dingy. He almost didn't recognize the telephone. It was made of some sort of black metal, with a dial on the base and an earpiece connected by a cord.

At least there weren't any dishes in the sink.

Gary took a deep breath and started toward his office. Then, with one foot in the doorway, he stopped cold.

There was no computer. Just a small, ancient-looking typewriter on a wooden table, with a sheet of white paper threaded through the carriage. The keys were all round, raised up off the base. The table was propped against one wall. The other walls were lined with bookshelves, filled to overflowing with hardcopy books.

"You really did this, didn't you?" Gary whispered. "Sent me back in time." He stared at the hologram. "That's impossible. That's goddamn impossible."

"Nothing is impossible during wishbook days at KHSN."

Gary walked slowly to one of the shelves and picked up a book. It had a thick cover, and the binding was edged with red and gold. He flipped to the copyright page. "Printed in 2021," he read aloud. "Ninety-eighth printing."

He let out a breath. It was a trick, that was all, an actor and some new furniture. "You blew it," he told the hologram. He laughed, but there was an edge of hysteria to it. "You forgot to change the dates on the books. Damn near fooled me, though. How'd you do it?"

"After an extensive analysis, it was determined that the best way to grant your wish was to retard technological development."

"You mean time kept going, but nothing changed?"

"That is correct."

"No way," Gary said. His voice rose. "You can't do this. You have to change it back. Christ, I have bills to pay. And my landlord to deal with. And Claire's lawyer. I have to—"

Gary stopped mid-sentence. He had plenty to do—none of it pleasant.

"Would you like to return your gift?" the hologram asked.

Gary walked around the room, looking at the bookshelves. It'd been years since he'd seen this many books in one place. He stopped at the desk, and gazed at the typewriter. He hit a key. It made a satisfying metallic clack, and the letter "e" appeared on the paper. Real. Solid. The letter wouldn't disappear when he pulled out the plug.

Gary thought about his landlord, about Claire. He thought about his son. Did John still exist in this unchanged world? He almost felt regret, but not quite.

Gary walked past the hologram and back into the living room. Mathers was standing, pacing in front of the couch. "Well?" he demanded. "Are you going to write this story or not?"

Mathers wanted him to write. Not to act, not to run a computer—to write.

"Would you like to return your gift?" the hologram demanded.

"No," Gary said slowly, hardly believing his words. "No, I don't."

"Hey," Mathers said, "tell your friend I'm sorry to break up the party, but you really have to get going."

"It's not my friend," Gary said. "It's just a hologram." He turned to face it. If there weren't computers, he realized, there shouldn't be holograms, either. Yet it still stood there.

"Will that be cash, check, charge, or electronic transfer from savings?" When Gary didn't answer, the hologram continued. "Accessing savings." It was silent for several seconds. "Unable to access savings. Unable to access KHSN mainframe. Awaiting further instructions." The hologram froze, then flickered and disappeared.

Mathers' jaw fell. "What the hell—"

"It's—" Gary hesitated. "It's just a ghost," he said. "A ghost of a time that never quite was."

Gary stared for a moment at the spot the ghost had been. Then he turned to face his editor. "So," he said, "tell me about this story you want me to write."

HOLIDAY STATION

by Judith Tarr

Judith Tarr is a best-selling fantasy author.

Prologue: Happy Holidays

If the Stationmaster hadn't got pregnant when he did, the rest of it would never have happened. It was his turn, it being baby number three and he being number three in the group-marriage rota, and the Stationmaster did take his duty seriously. The trouble was, he had to get pregnant just when Elthree was about to become Holiday Station.

All the El-stations were having to decide whether to go commercial or obsolesce. Elwun had folded outright; Asia Major shot it down for target practice. Elfive was an orbital pleasure palace—all right, not to be too finicky about it, a brothel. Eltwo and Elfour were still trying to hang on and keep the ships coming through, even with the big lunar stations for competition. Which left Elthree, and Holidays Incorporated, and a desperate grab for the tourist trade.

Which would have been a very good thing, except that this was Elthree. Trojan Point Tertius. Last and best enclave of Jehovah's Scientists since they got run off Earth.

It's not that Jehovah's Scientists don't believe in holidays. Or even that they think a man taking his turn having a baby is an abomination in the face of the Lord. It's that Holiday Station had to open on Harmony Day, and the Stationmaster was the most convenient scapegoat, and—

But that's getting ahead of the story, isn't it?

266

Scene One: What Child Is This?

Stationmaster was pregnant, and he was at the miserable stage. Nothing fit, including the station-issue coverall, size extra-large, paternity cut. Here he was, bulging like Mother Earth in a convex viewplate, trying to maneuver through the jungle of cables and scaffolding that would, eventually, be Independence Era Module. Tech was running holos in the middle of the construction. George M. Cohan was dancing "Spacer Doodle Dandy" with Judy Garland in a very abbreviated Auntie Sam tutu, while the band played "The Stars and Planets Forever."

On the other side of the production number, just as Mr. Cohan started to melt and ooze down the side of the bandstand, Stationmaster ran full tilt into a delegation from the Jehovah's Scientists in Kingdom Module. Elder Mobius got the worst of it, seventy-five kilos of hurtling Stationmaster with baby on board; fortunately this was some ways out from spin center, and they bounced when they landed, with Stationmaster rotundly on top.

The delegation hadn't been in a wonderful mood to begin with. When Elthree voted to go public and incorporate, they voted resoundingly against, but they were too small a minority. Now, not only was their station invaded by the forces of Babylon, the very Whore herself had struck down Elder Mobius. Which he made clear at top volume, in phrases that blistered the paint off bulkheads as far down as Maintenance Six.

Stationmaster was normally a patient man. He had to be, to keep his job. But he was pregnant, he'd just been derailed on his way to welcome the first shipload of VIPs to Holiday Station, and the one and only coverall that still fit was split at the seams. He let go with a blast of his own.

There was bare metal on the bulkheads in Mainte-

nance Six. The delegation was so shocked it actually
retreated, dragging a frothing Elder Mobius. Stationmaster stopped in the middle of a word. He looked
around. The holos were all frozen, even the puddle
that had been George M. Cohan. Tech was carefully
looking elsewhere.

"Damn," said Stationmaster. "Double and triple
damn."

Over in the corner, a holo started to whistle
"Dixie."

Scene Two: Maiden Mother Mild

"This," Aunt Margaret said, "I don't like at all."

We were hiding out in Old Module, the one that's
supposed to be shut down but somebody forgot to
turn off life support, so there we were, and there was
the terminal with its antique keyboard and broken
voder and 2-D screen that at least still worked. I was
supposed to be at my school terminal in Kingdom
Module, but with Daddy out being an Elder I could
plug in the Yes-Daddy-I'm-Here macro and go somewhere interesting. Aunt Margaret was supposed to be
in a module with holo capability.

Aunt Margaret's a ghost. A holo, I mean, but Old
Module isn't supposed to support full-service holoimaging, and she was right next to me, as big as life
and only about half blurry around the edges. I couldn't
feel her or anything, no cold chills. She was just there.
She was leaning over my shoulder, frowning at the
screen, which she'd made me split. One half showed
Stationmaster, bulging out of a fresh shipsuit, welcoming a gaggle of VIPs to Harmony Day Module. The
other half showed Elder Mobius and the other Elders,
which included Daddy, sitting around a table and not
saying much, except for Elder Mobius, who was in a
rant. There wasn't anything to hear, with the voder
broken, but Aunt Margaret didn't need a voder.

"Violence is never a useful solution," Aunt Margaret said to the screen. She always looks severe, she can't help it. Her face was her fortune as she likes to say, but it wasn't your usual kind of fortune. First time she showed up she gave me nightmares for a week. She was in persona then, green skin, black pointy hat, broom and all. Except she talked like a nice maiden lady, and I knew inside of a millisecond that she wasn't any kind of wicked witch. My subconscious needed a week to be convinced, but that's a subconscious for you.

Anyway, she can't help but look severe, with her big hooked nose and her thin mouth, but right now she looked downright grim. "What are they going to do?" I asked her.

She looked at me. I thought for a minute she looked just a little greener and wickeder than she usually does, with a shadow doing duty for a pointy hat. Then she was Aunt Margaret again in her nice silk dress and Early Hollywood 'do, and she said, "I never did believe in the sins of the fathers, least of all with you. Still, I wonder. . . ."

I love Aunt Margaret even if she is a ghost, but sometimes she's just too adult for words. "They're going to blow up a module, aren't they? They've been talking about it ever since they lost the vote on Holiday Station. Which one are they going to try for?"

"Harmony Day Module, of course," Aunt Margaret said. That's one thing about her being a ghost. She can change gears in a nanosecond, and she doesn't natter on or act silly about what children know. Not that I *am* a child, mind you, I'll be thirteen Standard in Threemonth, but you know what I mean.

And of course it would be Harmony Day Module, seeing as to how the opening was supposed to be on Harmony Day and in the Module. "That's so painfully obvious," I said. "Security will stop them before they ever get that far."

"I'm not sure of that," Aunt Margaret said. "Security has enough to do with the mobs of visitors coming in; it's grievously understaffed. And to be quite blunt, my dear, your father and the rest of the Elders are not the most highly respected men in the station."

I knew that. I'd heard people say so, and not just when I was trolling through the net. "Oh," they'd say, trying to be charitable and broad-minded and religiously correct, "Jehovah's Scientists. Yes. Fascinating sect, just fascinating. But a little . . . odd, don't you agree? All that insistence on only the most primitive of technology—holograms as tools of the devil, if you'll believe it—why, they barely educate their children." Which last part wasn't true, I had a teaching terminal just like anybody else in Elthree, it just didn't have holoimaging, that was all.

No, Daddy didn't know about Aunt Margaret. In case you're wondering.

And now I suppose you see what the problem was with Holiday Station. It was supposed to be one huge complex of holoimages, with realmeat staff in costume to do the work, and some of the most complex programming in the System. The ads were making it out to be a triumph of technology, which it was.

And here was Kingdom Module right in the middle, full of people with a religious objection to holoimaging. Normally the Religious Autonomy Act would apply, but you couldn't expand it to a whole station when only one module was affected. There were no holos in Kingdom Module. Kingdom Module had shuttle bays and exit ports of its own, as well as bypass corridors for outsiders, so nobody in it had to go through other modules to get in or out or to receive supplies. That did it for the RAA. Kingdom Module was autonomous, technically, and that was it. No way around it. No appeal.

So the Elders were taking the only really spectacular way out. "Nobody believes they'll do it," I said. "They're just those funny little men in the funny little module, aren't they?"

I must have sounded more upset than I was, because

Aunt Margaret tried to pat my shoulder. I didn't feel any touch, but I felt better somehow, a little. Even when she said, "They won't listen if you try to warn them."

"But—" I started to say, then I stopped. I'm really not a child. I can see what's in front of me, which was, in that case, that I was twelve years old, still a minor under any code, and my father was an Elder of the Jehovah's Scientists. They might pat me on the head and offer sanctuary, seeing as to how I was obviously unhappy with my parental allotment, but they wouldn't listen to what I had to say. Children exaggerate, right? They blow things out of proportion. And Security was drastically understaffed, and Stationmaster wasn't in a mood to listen to anyone, let alone me.

Still, I thought. There had to be something I could do. Something spectacular enough to get everybody's attention, but not so spectacular it backfired.

"Aunt Margaret," I said, "they're not really going to do it, are they?"

Aunt Margaret says it's not polite to point, but this once she pointed at the screen. I don't know what she did. The voices didn't come through the broken voder, but there were words under the screen with the Elders in it. Elder Mobius' mouth was moving. The words said, *You all appreciate, I'm sure, the symbolism of a sequence of detonations in the shape of the carbon molecule. We stand for life under universal law—not for the life of artificial constructs.*

The second half of it was straight out of his favorite sermon. The first half was enough to tell what I wanted to know.

I felt cold. It wasn't as if it was any surprise. Violent solutions are allowed in the Book of Albert, if nothing else will work. I just hadn't expected them to go that far.

"They can't be that stupid," I said. "They'll all go into permanent detention, and everybody will know how retro they are."

"But Holiday Station will be crippled," said Aunt Margaret. "It operates on the edge now. It has to open successfully, or it goes under. It can't afford even a small disruption, let alone one of this magnitude."

I didn't want to say it, but I had to. "They'll close the station?"

"They'll have to," she said.

What she wasn't saying was if the station closed, we all had to leave. I'd go into an orphanage or whatever they did to the children of criminals down on Earth. But she couldn't leave. She was part of the system. When it was shut down, she went with it.

Not that I really needed encouragement. I just had to be sure there wasn't any other way out.

"All right," I said, and took a deep breath. "How far down can you go in the programming?"

Aunt Margaret didn't answer for a bit. Let's say she was processing data. It looked as if she was figuring out what I meant, and making a decision.

Then she said, "How far do you need to go?"

Scene Three: Prince of Peace

Harmony Module was up and running at full capacity. There was real snow on the ground, and more falling at just the right speed. The big old Inn was lit up everywhere, and people kept pouring in, past the doorposts wrapped with fir and holly, into the foyer with its tree that went up all the way to the ceiling, and on to the ballroom where the music was the very best Irving Berlin, live or holoimaged. Bing was playing host to the hilt. Fred, minus Ginger, was being just the right kind of cad. All the men were sleek and sophisticated, and all the women were blonde and beautiful.

The VIPs were like kids on Harmony morning, all wide eyes and ohs and ahs. "Is this *real*?" one of them squealed, grabbing at a glass of champagne. He squealed again when he found out it wasn't a holo. I

saw the waiter stop to breathe after his crosscourt
sprint. The other realmeat staff got the point: they
started being a little more careful about staying
around the VIPs.

Aunt Margaret was at her own screen, another one
in the bay that she'd powered up. She didn't need it
and she couldn't use the keyboard, but it did help
to have two full screens. When I looked, hers had a
schematic, blue dots flagged in red.

"Holoimages," she said, pointing to the blue. "Live
action," tapping one of the red with a finger that
didn't quite touch the screen. I could see that it was
a diagram of the module, with enlarged detail of the
Inn, where everybody was.

"Are these what I'm afraid they are?" I asked.
Some of the red dots had yellow ones attached.

On my screen there wasn't anything to see. Just
people milling in a ballroom.

"Oh, they *are* clever," said Aunt Margaret.
"They've subroutined the security programming. It
doesn't see anything they're bringing in."

My screen certainly didn't. I'd have recognized faces
if there really were people from Kingdom Module im-
personating holoimages. All I saw was a blur, and a
lot of blondes in slinky dresses.

"However," said Aunt Margaret in her crisp last-
century voice, "they seem to have reckoned without
me." She allowed herself a bit of a cackle, just enough
to make my backbone shiver.

I didn't have very much to do once I keyed in the
lines of code Aunt Margaret gave me. Nobody knew
about these terminals, you see. If they had, they'd
have shut them down. But they were old and obsolete,
and they needed somebody who could use a keyboard,
which was basically me, because Aunt Margaret
showed me how.

The code opened a very particular line of access.
Aunt Margaret was running down it, or the AI that
was Aunt Margaret was. She'd warned me that she

couldn't keep her holoimage going past a certain level, so when she started to flicker, I didn't get too terribly alarmed.

By that time the red-and-yellow dots on her screen were starting to move. They were supposed to be casual, stroll along, drop their devices in planters and under mistletoe and even in a tuba. Then they'd get out as fast as they could, and their timed bombs would detonate Harmony Module in the name of the Lord.

The party was in full swing, or whatever they used to say. The VIPs were swimming in champagne. It was getting easier to tell real from holo. Real was red in the face and starting to stagger.

I hadn't seen Stationmaster anywhere in the crowd. He had to be there or be impolite, but he must have had some trouble thinking of a way to look authentic. I could see the rest of his connubial group, looking a little more sober but not much less happy than the VIPs.

And then in he came, ho-ho-ho-ing and scattering gift-wrapped cheer. The red suit didn't need much padding. The white beard almost hid his titchy expression. His party was a roaring success, but he looked too pregnant to care.

One of the svelte blondes tripped over his sack and went flying. Half a dozen people scrambled to rescue her. Five of them grabbed air. The sixth mutated.

Aunt Margaret was in full persona. She picked up the blonde in a hand like a claw, and the blonde shriveled into a broomstick that she brandished while she wailed her lines. "Beware! Beware the tides of treachery!"

Wrong script, I thought. Not that it mattered what she said, as long as the diversion worked.

Every blonde in the room changed at once. A crowd of winged monkeys flapped toward the chandeliers. The suave men in black and white swelled into green-faced soldiers with pikes, stabbing at anyone who hadn't changed.

The VIPs were in a huddle. Some of them were laughing. "Jolly good show!" one kept whinnying. "*Jolly* good!"

Stationmaster was hemmed in by soldiers. I'd have thought it would dawn on him of all people that they weren't real, but he stayed where he was.

Unfortunately, other people didn't stay put. They'd been Aunt Margaret's red-and-yellow dots: men in tuxedos on my screen, with anonymous faces, thanks to some clever reprogramming. They still had tuxedos, but I knew who they were. One of them was Daddy. Daddy's wrongheaded about some things, like holo-imaging, but I'd have thought he was too old for this, or at least too smart.

I thought as fast as I've ever thought in my life. I didn't know if I could do what I had to do—Aunt Margaret had made some major changes in the routines—but I tapped out the codes anyway. And the system hung on me.

I hit the screen so hard I almost broke my hand. Then I got up to start running. Harmony Module was clear at the other end of the station. I'd never get there in time to do anything, but I couldn't sit there and watch Daddy get caught.

Something happened on the screen. I had to blink to see. My eyes were leaking like a baby's. Cool, calm, save-the-station me, right. That was Daddy out there. He was bone stupid and dead ignorant, but he was still Daddy.

Maybe he was there. I couldn't see. A whole troop of soldiers closed in where he'd been standing. If he tried to walk through them, he didn't have any luck. They just kept surrounding him in a sort of infinite loop.

The others were running to drop their cargo. The more they ran, the more the holos ran with them. They must have been dizzy, but they were strong in the armor of the Lord. They kept on coming.

I started praying. "Please. Please let Security catch on. Please."

If that was sinful, then it was sinful. I can't believe any self-respecting, scientific deity would let people blow up a module. Even if they did say they did it in his name.

Security wasn't doing a thing. Aunt Margaret's soldiers were herding giggling VIPs toward the doors. "Is there another show outside?" one of them asked. Somebody else was being sour. "Eclectic. Much too eclectic. An extravaganza needs *some* dramatic unity."

"All right," I said, not to the critic. "Aunt Margaret, I know you said not to, but I have to." I hit the macro I'd been saving.

Sirens went off all over Harmony Module. I'd stolen the voice from Aunt Margaret's best film. Maybe I should have gone with Charlton Heston, but the Wizard sounded more like it to me. *"Stop in the name of the Lord! Drop your weapons, swear peace, or be damned to everlasting."*

Not much for script, but the volume flattened everybody with functional ears. Including most of the Elders' agents.

One still wouldn't drop. He wasn't old enough to know any better. I turned the volume up another notch. *"Jonathan Save-the-Faith Mercer-Meyers, you put that bomb down now!"*

I'll say one thing for the training we get. It gives us incredible guilt reflexes. Jonathan dropped the thing he'd been carrying. It hit the floor with a clatter. He, being only about half stupid, bolted straight for the door.

And there we were with a dilemma. The VIPs were outside in the snow, being wrapped in synthfurs by staff who still didn't seem to have caught on. Every soldier in the ballroom had dropped his pike when I let go with my Wrath-of-Jehovah speech. Jonathan had gotten away. Daddy was trying to find his way blind through a constantly repeating sequence of soldiers. The rest of the Lord's assassins were flat on their faces.

Aunt Margaret saw the problem about as soon as I did. She stopped whirling and walked up to the Stationmaster, who hadn't moved a muscle—maybe he couldn't. "Really," she said in her normal voice, "I think you'd better summon Security. Your module is about to be blasted out of orbit."

Stationmaster might be titchy, but he wasn't a splutterer. He took one look where Aunt Margaret's broomstick was aiming, saw the lump of metal and coils that Jonathan had dropped before he ran, and said perfectly calmly, "Security. Priority One alert. Instanter."

Epilogue: Harmony Day

So that's how Aunt Margaret and I saved Holiday Station from the wrath of Jehovah's Scientists. Not that anybody knows about us. As soon as Security showed up, Aunt Margaret's program went back to default, blondes and men in tuxedos. Debugging didn't come up with anything. It wouldn't, with Aunt Margaret doing the programming. They just decided that it was an encrypted Security subroutine, which actually it was, and closed the file on it.

As for Elder Mobius and the rest, Stationmaster had his own way of dealing with them. Security took them all into custody, there wasn't any getting around that, but they had to wait a while. Stationmaster had his baby on Harmony night, and they named her Harmony, what else?

When Stationmaster was up and tending to the station again, he had the prisoners brought in. They weren't exactly repentant, though some of them looked embarrassed.

"So," he said, looking as severe as Aunt Margaret, which took doing: Stationmaster is a round man even when he's not pregnant, and the most he can usually do is look titchy. "You know that your offense, under station law, could earn you the capital penalty."

"We die in the name of the Lord," said Elder Mobius.

"I don't think so," said Stationmaster. Elder Mobius opened his mouth to start thundering. Stationmaster cut him off. "No, I won't make martyrs here. You did a very foolish and potentially murderous thing in a fairly reasonable cause. I can take you to trial, knowing that you would very likely be condemned. Or I can offer you an alternative."

"What alternative is there but death?" Elder Mobius asked, putting on his most annoyingly smarmy expression.

"Why, several," said Stationmaster. "You can be accorded the status of an isolationist state. Once your module is sealed, no one will enter your module and no one will leave it, and supply runs will be performed solely by machines. Or you can be deported either to Earth or to one of the lunar colonies. Or, as I said, you can stand trial for crimes against the station."

"We choose trial," Elder Mobius said promptly.

Daddy wasn't supposed to be there, but somehow he'd gotten in. He clapped a hand over Elder Mobius' mouth and looked Stationmaster in the eye. "Is that all you can offer us?"

"It's all you're entitled to," Stationmaster said.

"Maybe," said Daddy, "but then again, maybe you're sitting on something else. Maybe there's restitution to be made on both sides. You robbed us of access to the station under our laws. We might have blown up the station, but we didn't. What if we take care of this old blowhard, and you shift Kingdom Module out past South Pole, where we can carry on our lives in some sort of peace?"

"That's the isolationist option," Stationmaster pointed out.

"No, it's not," said Daddy. I was proud of him right then, even if he had carried a bomb in the name of the Lord. Probably he felt he had to. Daddy's like that. "We'll keep our jobs, those of us who can do it without sinning. You'll assess us a good, fair fine for our transgression against your people, which we'll pay in wages and goods. And we won't try any further sabotage, on pain of isolation, exile, or death."

It went back and forth for a while, but in the end they went with Daddy's solution. It took a lot of swallowing all around, which Aunt Margaret says is the way of the world. She doesn't just mean Earth.

We've still got the terminals set up in Old Module. There's been some talk of making it over into another part of Holiday Station, but so far none of it's come to anything. Maybe we help that along a bit. Aunt Margaret's been teaching me about holoimaging, damning me hopelessly, of course, but I can't help it, can I? Not all witches are bad witches, and not all holos are empty constructs.

Someday we'll rebuild Old Module our way. I know just where I'd put the Emerald City, and just what I'd do with those unbearably silly Munchkins.

"Do be kind, Dorothy," Aunt Margaret says to me, "and do be accurate. Even the wickedest witch of them all never dined on Munchkin á la Queen."

"There's always a first time," I say as darkly as I can. Aunt Margaret always looks severe, and her nose gets just a little sharper, and her chin just a little pointier, and she goes just slightly green; but she never stays irked with me for long.

"The Munchkins I can bear," she says. "Just. That simpering idiot Glinda, however, that miserable excuse for a self-respecting witch. . . ."

She's too polite to spit, but not to put on her most spectacular persona. She mounts her broomstick in a swirl of black skirts and pointy hat and flies cackling down through the long empty module, trailing blood-red smoke. It's spectacular. It's shivery-making. It's Aunt Margaret all through. And maybe as she flies, just for a second, I feel a touch of ghostly cold.

STATE ROAD

by Alan Dormire and
Robin J. Nakkula

Alan Dormire and Robin Nakkula have both sold poetry; this collaboration marks their first science fiction sale.

We'd been on the road about six hours, having left Columbus before noon. "Do you want to take a short break, Jan? We're about a half hour out from my brother's, but I doubt they plan on eating until all the other kids are there. A couple of them had to work today."

"Okay," she replied, "I have to use the necessary, anyway." We pulled off the expressway, looking for a restaurant. Only the Burger King seemed open this late on Christmas Eve. Fortunately, the manager hadn't decided to close as early as most of the other restaurants nearby. The restaurant's dining room held about a half-dozen people, none of whom I knew.

After hurried stops at the restrooms, Jan and I met back at the counter. Two double cheeseburgers, fries, and soft drinks later, we found ourselves a table. Five minutes into our meal, Jan tapped my wrist. "You know, Mark, that guy over there bears a surprising resemblance to your dad. Is he some sort of relative of yours? I know this part of the state's just lousy with them. . . ."

I gave her a dirty look. While I had grown up around here, most of my relatives lived farther north.

I was about to reply when I noticed that the guy did look like my father.

The last time I saw my father alive was two or three days after Christmas two years ago, just before we had moved. He had driven over to Lansing to look at my old Mazda. We had just bought a new car, and somehow, my sixteen-year-old brother had gotten it into his head that he could have the Mazda. I had told him if Dad said it was okay, he could have it, but that I really planned to junk it. After looking at the car, Dad had agreed with me and left for home. After he left, Jan and I went over to the Burger King nearby in Frandor Shopping Center for a quick lunch, where we found my father having his midday meal as well. We joined him, and we talked for close to an hour, just the three of us, something we had never done before.

We hadn't gone home to Michigan for Christmas last year, and had missed not being there. We had just spent our first year in Ohio, and didn't have the money to spare to make the trip. Then my father had died this past spring. While unloading bricks at a construction site, he hit a power line with the boom on his truck. At the funeral, my sister-in-law told me that on both Christmas and Christmas Eve, Dad had sat by the window, watching for us to show up at his trailer.

The man at the other table dressed like my father: baseball hat with a seed company logo, cowboy boots, bib overalls, a white tee shirt, and a red plaid flannel shirt on the outside of the bibs. We had even buried my father in that outfit, minus the hat. And from what I could see, the fellow at the other table kept his head shaved as well. I went back to eating my cheeseburger. A lot of farmers, truckers, and construction workers dressed that way. I still did myself, even after years of living in town, though I wore blue jeans instead of the bibs, and I'd kept my hair. I thought about telling my brothers and sisters about this guy, and Jan's comments. They'd probably get a good laugh.

I started thinking about the funeral last May. A lot

of people loved my father, which became obvious
from the attendance at both the visitation and the funeral. We kids had spent the visitation laughing and
telling our favorite stories about Dad, as did his
friends and coworkers. The funeral had been packed,
not only with family and his friends, but with a lot of
my siblings' childhood companions as well. He had
been one of the few adults that they could come to
when they needed someone to talk with while growing
up. (Sometimes, it seemed like I was the only kid he
didn't understand.) The funeral director said it had
been one of the best funerals he had held. Everyone
had reminisced about the man with no one turning
maudlin.

"Mark." I looked up from my memories. My father
stood there next to me. I didn't know what to do.
"How have you been?"

"Okay, I guess," I started. I had a knot in my stomach, and it got worse when I saw the burn marks on
his hands where the electricity had entered his body
from the boom controls. "I'm working for a small seed
corn company now."

"That's good," he said as he sat down with us at
the table. Jan turned pale, not at all sure how to handle this. "How do you like it?"

"Good company, family owned, and I'm doing okay.
I have a good sized territory around Columbus. Some
large grain farms, quite a few dairies, and a lot of hogs
in the area. A lot of good land down there. But like
up here, people seem to think houses and golf courses
are worth more than corn fields and pastures." I
talked more about my job, telling him about the hy-
brids I sold and arranging field trials. I had done all
sorts of odd jobs since I had finished my degree, and
this was my first professional job.

We spent a lot of time talking about the farms I
visited on the job. Dad's first love was always farming,
and he had passed that love on to me. I had majored
in agriculture because of him, even though he didn't

understand why I wanted an education. To be honest, I would have rather talked farming with him than anything else. He also loved driving trucks, thankfully, which gave him a career after losing his farm.

What do you talk to a dead man about? I wasn't sure. Hell, I didn't understand why he was here talking to me in the first place. I knew that he had delivered both the blocks and bricks used to build this restaurant. (I had driven through town several years back and had watched him unloading the bricks from his truck, operating the hydraulic boom from the back of the truck.) For that matter, he had delivered the blocks for a lot of the buildings in this stretch of town near the highway, with the exception of the stores built during the couple of years he had tried to make it farming full time.

"Dad, remember we thought we were having a battery problem with that car we had bought just before the move?" He nodded his head. "It wasn't the battery, it was the alternator. The dealer wanted three hundred for a new one, and the parts stores wanted two. I finally found one for fifty dollars at a junk yard."

Car repairs, I figured, were another safe topic. We both hated working on equipment. I remembered a conversation we had when I was in high school, over a decade ago. A day or two before Christmas, the pump on the well had gone down. We had worked in the cold December wind, half in, half out of the small plywood wellhouse surrounded with straw bales to protect it from the cold wind. "I know you hate working on this stuff," he had said. "So do I. Your grandpa made me do it when I lived at home, and I've always been grateful to him for it." Years later, the skills I learned working with my father had kept us in groceries more than once. Maybe my having told him about the car was my way of letting him know I appreciated his making me do the work.

He looked over to Jan. "So how are you doing in

graduate school?" I became real nervous. Jan freaked when she heard that someone had a minor accident, and never accepted a death well. I could see she was having a difficult time of it. However, she managed to explain everything that had happened to her since starting graduate school, including her research. Once she started, though, she fell into explaining things in much the same way she did to her freshman biology students. She loved her work, and while Dad didn't understand most of what she told him, he had always appreciated folks who loved their work.

"Are you still playing the guitar and singing?" he asked when she finished explaining a titration procedure that even I had a hard time following.

"Not as much as I did up here. Graduate school doesn't leave me a lot of time to practice. We brought the instruments along with us, though."

"Good," he replied. "We missed both of you last year. Why didn't you come up last year?"

"Money was tight last year, Dad," I replied. "Besides, Jan spent both Christmas Eve and the day after Christmas working in the lab."

"Excuse me," Dad said as he got up. "I'm going to fill up my pop."

He walked over to the fountain area. Jan looked at me. "Why is he here?"

"You know as much as I do. I'm sure we will find out somehow."

"Are you going to ask him anything about why he's here, or what he's been doing since . . . ?"

I sighed. "Jan, I'm not sure I want to know how it is that he's here, or what he's been doing, or if he's been doing anything. He may not know. Maybe he doesn't know he's dead. Hell, maybe he's hanging out at Burger King because he heard Elvis did it when he was dead and figured it was the thing to do. Never mind that we're two and a half hours from K'zoo." She gave me a dirty look. Her curiosity had just kicked into gear, and I could see she wanted answers. Possibly, she wanted the answers as much as I didn't.

"Jan, just don't ask. Please, don't ask him."

"Okay, but . . ."

"Please?"

Dad had returned to the table about that point with a full cup of cola. I began telling him about Farm Science Review, the big ag show in Ohio, about the state fair, the Beef Expo, and the horse shows that the state fairgrounds hosted year round. I tried to stick to what I figured were safe topics. We never talked about the other kids, for example. I stayed mostly to what Jan and I had been doing.

"Your sister visited us this summer, Dad." My aunt lived on the West Coast, and we saw little of her. "She and her girlfriend traveled the country on motorcycles this summer. They took Jan and me out to a seafood restaurant to eat. When they returned home, they mailed us a map of the rest of the trip with some pictures. I guess she changed jobs and now works with troubled kids instead of straight teaching. We had a good time."

Dad looked at me. "I need to get going soon, and there is something I want you to know. Mark, you've always been different. Since you were a kid, you've always had your nose in a book. I never could do that. I could never read for more than about a half hour to a time, and then my head would hurt so bad I couldn't stand it. I never understand how you could sit there and read for hours on end.

"That's always been one of your strong points, your reading. You understood things I never did. It allowed you to get into college, and even though you screwed around some, you kept at it and finished. Mark, I'm proud of you. I'm proud of both of you." He got up. "Well, I'll see you both later. Merry Christmas." He headed for the door.

He had never told me he was proud of me when he was alive. I know he had told neighbors, friends, his coworkers, even the DeLaval dealer, but never me. I'd heard from others about how proud he was, but I had a hard time believing it. I had spent my whole life trying to please the man.

My eyes followed him out the door. He got into his red pickup, the Chevy with the stock racks he had had on the farm, not the Ford he had owned when he died. I always pictured him driving the red Chevy whenever I thought of him anyway. It could have been either of two identical trucks, bought three years apart, the only new vehicles he had ever owned. He pulled onto the road and headed north, though if he was heading to the farm he no longer owned, the trailer he had lived in when he died, or the block plant where he had worked most of his adult life, I couldn't tell you. All three were in that direction, as was the farm where he had been born and had grown up. We had to pass each on the way to my brother's place. The truck faded from our view into the descending December twilight.

Jan looked at me. "Are you going to tell your brothers and sisters?"

"I don't think so. I doubt that they would believe us if we told them. And somehow, I think this was meant for just you and me. One last Christmas gift, maybe, to make up for us not being able to see him last year.

"Well, we'd better get going as well. All of a sudden, I want to make another stop before we get there."

We returned to the car, and then we, too, turned north. As we passed the various places, I looked for his truck, even though I knew it wouldn't be there. Both his farm and the grandfolks' had changed a lot over the years though the block plant hadn't. I drove by the turnoff to my brother's place, and instead drove up to the cemetery. Jan gave me a questioning look. "I've got to do this." I pulled into the cemetery and parked in the back close to his grave.

I sat in the car for a few minutes. The snow had started to fall into the dark December night and for a moment I wasn't sure if I could find the grave. Yet I intuitively knew where he lay and finally had to leave the car. "C'mon Jan," and she walked with me to the stoneless grave. "Dad, I'm glad you decided to visit with me this evening, I've missed you. Why couldn't you have told me when you were alive that you were proud of me. It was the only thing I ever really wanted from you, Old Man, to hear those words directly from you."

I turned to Jan. "I'll be right back." Jan started talking to him as I went over to the car. Opening the trunk, I quickly found one of my company's baseball-style hats and their seed corn brochure. Jan was still whispering quietly as I returned to the grave. "Merry Christmas, Dad," I said as I placed the hat and the brochure over the snow covered grave. "I hope you rest now in peace."

I waited a minute. "Are you ready to leave, Jan?"

She had tears in her eyes. I probably did, too. "I think so."

"It's time to leave. If we don't arrive soon, we'll worry the other kids. Dinner will be ready by the time we get there and then it will be time to get ready for the Christmas Eve service." I turned back toward the car. "Good-bye, Dad." The wind picked up slightly as we returned to the car, swirling the snow. Yet neither the hat nor the brochure moved from where I had set them on his grave.

THE GHOSTS OF CHRISTMAS FUTURE

by Dean Wesley Smith

Dean Wesley Smith is not only a successful author, but also the editor and publisher of Pulphouse.

Come on in. I'm open on Christmas Eve. Ghost hunting with a time machine. That's right. That's my business.

Okay, okay. So my time machine isn't really that special. Not once will it squeak or rattle or blow out noxious clouds of burnt rubber smoke. It won't go "pop" and disappear out of the middle of the room. It won't explode and send you spinning. It won't even send you into a black void of weightlessness that signals movement like white space between paragraphs of a novel.

No, with my time machine you have to move yourself. You can drive. You can walk, fast or slow. The only thing that matters with my time machine is sight. You must be able to see. And maybe to think. But with ghost hunting, seeing comes before thinking.

Now, if you want to search for ghosts of Christmas futures, follow me into my not-so-special time machine. We'll go down the road a bit and see what we can find.

The smell of sweat, rotted food and years and years of living fills the small, dark two-room apartment. A small, half-dead house plant occupies the center of a scarred old end table beside the television.

A young girl, six years old, dressed in a tattered, dirty skirt and a baggy sweater, stands in front of the plant draping tinsel and Christmas decorations over the drooping leaves. She had found the decorations behind a department store that afternoon. The plant she had gotten out of the dumpster behind a florist. She hadn't been this excited all year.

Her mother lies on the old couch, watching television, sipping on her third glass of Jack Daniels. Every so often she shakes her head at the girl and mutters under her breath. In an hour she will be drunk enough to pass out and forget this Christmas Eve. Forget everything for a short time.

But her daughter won't. Her mom had hit her two weeks before for making a wish list for Santa. The bruise still showed on her arm when she took a bath. Her mom said there was no Santa, that there never had been for her and there never would be for her daughter.

But the little girl had secretly made the list and mailed it without a stamp, hoping that Santa would get it somehow. Now, on Christmas Eve, she hopes that tomorrow morning there will be just one little present under the make-believe tree.

You want me to fill you in on what happens?

Tomorrow morning, real early, the little girl will climb out of bed and discover that Santa didn't come. There will be no present and she knows there never will be. She will look at her mother, asleep on the couch, smelling of bourbon and sweat, and the little girl will think that maybe her mother was right. There really is no Santa. At least not for the poor like her.

So the little girl will take down the decorations and the plant and throw them into the garbage. Then, on her way back to bed, she will stop beside her sleeping mother and pick up the half-filled glass. The sip of bourbon will make her gag and the brown liquid will burn her throat, but she will force herself to finish what is left before going back to bed.

Well, did you see the ghost of Christmas future there? Nice time travel, huh? Simple, cheap, and no chance of getting lost in space and time somewhere.

Oh, you don't think that counts. You want to visit your own ghost of Christmas future. And you bet my machine can't do that for you.

Wrong, I'm afraid. Follow me if you really want to see.

Faint Christmas music fills the background of the empty, urine and antiseptic-smelling halls. A huge Christmas tree occupies the front foyer and a nurse in a white uniform sits behind the counter.

The special Christmas Eve dinner of turkey, mashed potatoes, and cooked carrots is over and all the residents of the home have been taken back to their rooms. Eighty-seven of the one hundred and twenty-six residents are still here this evening. Eighty-seven do not have families or live too far away from their families to spend Christmas Eve away.

Go ahead. Pick a door and we'll visit one. Any one.

Fifth door down on the right past the nurse's station. Good choice. That's Mrs. Gantz. She's eighty-three. Her husband died about five years ago. She has three children and seven grandchildren. Shall we find out why she's alone tonight?

Mrs. Gantz sits hunched over in her wheelchair in front of her television, the blue light from the picture flickering in her dull eyes. She wears a stained pink sweater, a brown skirt bunched up because of the diaper under it, and black shoes. She smells of urine because her diaper needs to be changed and the nurses are short-handed because it's Christmas Eve.

In the last five years Mrs. Gantz has suffered five strokes and no longer recognizes any of her family. They will visit her for a few minutes on Christmas day, but for the time being they do not think of her because there is nothing they can do.

Drool runs off her chin as Bing Crosby sings of a white Christmas.

See the ghost of your Christmas future now?

No. This won't happen to you? Of course it won't. And you're right. My time machine really isn't much of a machine. All it shows is ghosts.

Ghosts in the present that warn of the future.

Don't be angry. You're the one that wanted to see.

THREE WISHES
BEFORE A FIRE

by Kristine Kathryn Rusch

Kristine Kathryn Rusch is a Campbell Award winner, a Hugo and Nebula nominee, and the editor of The Magazine of Fantasy and Science Fiction.

He didn't know the guard at the gate, but the guard knew him. The guard leaned out of the small booth and smiled.

"Merry Christmas, Mr. Gells. Forget something this morning?"

"No," Rob said and drove on in. The lights illuminating the drive made it almost seem like day. Off to the left, the standing outdoor scene looked like the New York he had flown out of two weeks before. Farther along, the square sound stages reminded him of warehouses, and the bungalows of outmoded campus housing.

He wasn't used to the place being so quiet. And empty.

He had come here for a bit of life, but he should have realized that all life changed on Christmas Eve.

To think he could have been with Janine: *All wrapped up in a bow for you, honey. Nothing but champagne and me. Doesn't that sound like fun?*

Fun, yes. Christmas, no. He hadn't ever had a proper Christmas, at least not the kind his characters had. The warm mom-and-pop scene. The touch of magic, the touch of love.

Never. Not once in 40 years.

He pulled his car into its space in front of the two-story Spanish style building the series' producers used as their headquarters. He always could tell which series led the Nielsons by the size of the building its producers had. The lights were dark.

He got out of his car and stepped into the sixty degree air. He expected to be cold in December. At least New York had given him that. When he had presided over the lighting of the Christmas tree at Rockefellar Center, he had worn a leather coat and matching leather gloves. And even then, he had been cold. Not this cloying almost warmth that made him think of late springtime in the Midwest.

He shoved his hands in his pockets and walked to his trailer. It was parked near their soundstage, where he had finished his last scene in Episode 12 just that morning. The crew hadn't wanted to work on Christmas Eve Day. He had. And the studio had agreed.

The trailer was dark, like the rest of the lot. He pulled out his keys, opened the door, and flicked on the light. Just as he had left it. The pathetic little Christmas tree the girl in makeup had given him stood near his leather sofa. Two glasses waited for a wash beside the tiny sink. Magazines spread across the coffee table, and working scripts for Episodes 13, 14, and 15 piled on the end table. His costume from that morning, ripped and covered with fake bloodstains, tossed carelessly over a straight backed chair.

Nothing here. Not that he knew what he was looking for.

He turned off the light and closed the door, locking it behind him. Then he continued walking to the soundstage.

Janine had finally gone to see her family in San Diego. The household staff had the evening off, leaving him with a cold salmon dinner, a bottle of California white, and good wishes. He had three parties he could have gone to, or he could have sat in front of

his own fire, looking at the tree lights, listening to
some soft Christmas music, and reading as he had
done in years past. Instead, something inside told him
to return to the studio.

He stopped in front of the soundstage and glanced
around. He had a key, and he knew the security code.
Back when the producers thought the series wouldn't
last six episodes, they had entrusted him with the ability to go anywhere on the lot. The theory was that
the series was short-handed, and rather than go
through the usual channels, the actors would share a
degree of the responsibility.

After five years, Rob was the only responsible actor
left, the only member of the original cast to still spend
his twelve-hour days on the Fox lot. The others had
gone on to sink into the oblivion of actors who believed they were the reason for their series' success.

He let himself in. Half lighting was on, giving the
entire open room a dusky appearance. His footsteps
were the only sounds in the building. He remembered
the first time he had walked into a soundstage, his
heart stuck in his throat, watching the actors perform
in front of a dozen people, all paying more attention
to the equipment than the dialogue.

Ten years ago, and he could still taste the disappointment. No magic. No glamour. Trailers, smog-
filled L.A., and warehouses set up to look like the
real world. When he went to his twentieth high school
reunion, people kept asking him what's it like? what's
it like? He had lied to everyone, told them the glamour stories that he did know, lied to everyone except
the school nerd, the guy who could outthink the entire
class and whom everyone, including Rob, had put
down. Rob had looked at the nerd, who was a nerd
no longer, who, instead, had become one of the most
powerful attorneys in the state of Minnesota. Rob had
looked at him, after too many drinks and too many
questions, and said, "What's it like? It's the silliest
goddamn thing a human being could ever do. They

pay me too fucking much money to stand in front of a camera and pretend I'm you."

The former nerd had stalked away, insulted, when Rob hadn't meant it that way. There was a man who had done something with his life, who had used his brains and his fire to create more than a name. He defended people, he saved them, he *thought* his way through his life, while Rob let others write his words, tell him where to stand, and how to behave, and then let people he didn't know pretend he was the characters he played. He didn't think his way through his life. He waited for someone to give him a cue and then he performed, all mirrors and tricks and fabrications.

"Mister?"

Rob jumped, heart pounding in his chest. He was supposed to be alone here. He turned and saw a too-thin boy of maybe ten years. Some unthinking parent had given the kid a crew-cut so short that it made him look as if he were bald. He wore a brown and white striped shirt, and new jeans that had to be rolled into three inch cuffs above his scuffed, dark blue Keds.

"You an actor?" The kid's voice held wonder.

Rob glanced around for someone else—the kid's parent, a security guard, anyone. "Yes," Rob said. "I'm an actor."

"And this is where they make movies?"

"T.V.," Rob said.

"Oh, wow!" The kid stepped into the light and rubbed his hand gingerly along the side of a camera. The fluorescent beams fell on him like a halo, illuminating his too pale skin and the ugly purplish bruise marking his chin and cheek. "Can you show me around?"

"Where's your mom?" Rob asked.

The kid stepped back and all the enthusiasm drained from him. He brought one small hand up to his cheek and stroked the bruise. "Is she here?"

"That's what I'm asking you," Rob said.

"I didn't want her to be here," the kid said. "Dougie said that if you closed your eyes and wished three times on a Christmas Eve fire, you got your wish. But I didn't include her! I didn't! I don't want her here!"

Rob crouched down and held out his hands, trying to make himself as nonthreatening as possible. The building was soundproofed, but still he didn't want to take any chances that security would hear the kid screaming.

"She's not here if you didn't bring her," Rob said.

The kid's lower lip was trembling. Tears filled his eyes, but didn't fall. "I don't want her here," he said again.

Rob stood up. He hated that kind of ugliness. It made his skin crawl. "Well, let me show you around," he said.

He led the kid through the permanent sets, showed him the mat paintings and the elevators that went nowhere. He explained the cameras and the boom mikes, smiling at the kid's fascination with the thick cables and movable walls. Rob showed him the klieg lights and a shooting script, which the boy studied with the intensity of a straight-A student before a test.

Then the kid looked up, eyes shining. "You're really an actor?"

"I'm really an actor."

"I want to be an actor," the kid said. He sat on a stool near the makeshift wall of the circuit court set. "I sit there sometimes after—" he glanced at Rob "—you know, after things get bad, and I stare at the set and I know I can just go inside and be someone else. I could ride a horse, or solve a mystery, or eat dinner with a real family—"

The kid stopped as if he had said too much. Rob resisted an urge to put his hand on the kid's shoulder. "It's not real," he said.

"Oh, yes it is," the kid said. "I mean, I know that it's all make-believe. But I figure that for a few minutes, when you're pretending it's real, it really is real.

THE GHOST OF CHRISTMAS SIDEWAYS

by David Gerrold

David Gerrold is a best-selling novelist, as well as a successful television writer, and the creator of Star Trek's "tribbles."

When the ghost appeared, Kris Kringle was humping an elf.

The centuries-old oak bed was creaking loudly and groaning like a whale with indigestion, as Kringle pounded furiously away. The headboard banged against the paneled wall with every thrust. Kringle's red pants were down around his ankles, so were his silk boxers. The flabby pink mounds of flesh that were his buttocks shook like two great bags of jelly; they looked like Christmas puddings, all blotchy and purple with veins.

"Kriiiinnngllllle. . . ." the sepulchral voice repeated ominously, this time accompanied by the rattle of rusty old chains.

The fat man didn't hear it—or maybe he didn't want to hear it. He kept grunting with lust, again and again, while beneath him, the elf—almost smothered by his weight—shrieked in ecstasy or discomfort. It was impossible to tell.

"Kringle! Goddammit! Stop that now!" demanded the voice.

Kris Kringle rolled over abruptly, rising up on one elbow, his tumescence shrinking and disappearing into the folds of flesh at his groin. "Ho ho ho!" he boomed jovially. "Mmmmeeeeerrrrrrryyyyy CCChhhhrrriiisssstttmmmaaaaassss!! And what would you like Santa to bring you, little boy?" Beside him, the elf lowered its knees from where they had been pressed against his chest. He wore an annoyed expression as he struggled to sit up, straightening his long blonde wig, and at the same time trying to pull down the nearly-transparent nightie to cover his childish modesty. His lipstick was badly smeared.

"Kringle. . . !" The apparition's words came from the darkest depths of the grave; they were hollow and raspy and carried the weight of years. *"I have come for you!"* Again, there came the hopeful rattle of moldering chains.

"Ho ho ho—"

"Wait a minute, goddammit!" squeaked the elf. It reached up onto the headboard behind itself, fumbling for the remote control. At last, it found the clicker and hastily punched the pause button. Santa stopped booming in the middle of a loud enthusiastic "Ho—!" His deep voice trailed off slowly, the bright twinkle faded from his eyes, and some of the redness faded from his bulbous nose. The machinery whirred softly to a halt and Santa sat silently waiting, his naked lap open.

"Odds bodkins!" squeaked the elf. "What is it *this* time?"

In response, the tall gray specter elongated itself, stretching out one bony arm to reach across the intervening distance. It plucked the elf up out of the cushiony feather bed and held it aloft. "Do you recognize me, Brucie Kringle? *Ho ho ho. . . !*" it moaned.

The elf's eyes widened in sudden horror. "Ye gods and little fishes!" He chittered like a cockroach with a thyroid problem. "I thought we *killed* you!"

"You did!" rasped the wraith. *"Ho ho ho—!"* It rattled its long popcorn chains and leered malevolently. Its eyes burned like ornaments.

The ghost made a mysterious gesture and—

Suddenly, the two of them were standing out in a frozen cold wilderness, the blue sun was a bitter pill on the horizon. A furious wind whipped at the elf's nightgown. Nearby, a red and white striped pole stood next to a tiny cottage. *"Look!"* pointed the ghost, stabbing with a bony finger at the tiny house. A yellow window glowed with beckoning warmth. Framed by red and white curtains, Santa's body, stuffed to an ample girth with styrofoam peanuts, rocked steadily back and forth in a motorized chair. It puffed merrily at its pipe. Periodically it lifted its hand and waved out the window, while a synchronized recording repeated Santa's infectious laughter against a background of Jingle Bells.

"A very good job you did, little sprite! You left no detail unattended to."

"Thanks," blushed the elf, forgetting for the moment its precarious predicament.

The ghost made another mysterious gesture and—

Suddenly, the two of them were standing in a cold gray field—no horizon, only gray mist and cruel grass. Nearby, stood three men clad in hunters' garb and carrying rifles. Suddenly, one pointed upward. The other two raised their rifles, took careful aim, and fired off three quick shots each. The reports of their weapons sounded small and flat against the silent tundra— but far in the distance, a dark object plummeted heavily to the ground, smacking into it with a terrible wet impact.

"You sold my reindeer to a hunting farm!" the apparition accused.

The elf squirmed in the bony grip. "Hey! That wasn't my idea. The lawyers ordered it. They said we should downsize the operation. We needed to invest in new transportation. And we got a terrific deal from the Airbus Consortium. The goddamn elk were too old and too slow anyway—and you never paid any attention to how much those hayburners ate, did you? The upkeep was horrendous! If we didn't act when we did, the whole thing would have gone into Chapter 11. Down the tubes without a flush. At least this way, we have a chance to compete against the Japanese—"

"Always with the excuses, Bruce! Remember, an excuse only satisfies the person who makes it."

"Yeah, yeah, yeah—the old-fashioned ways are always the best. The time-honored tradition of the Christmas spirit—and all that jazz. But have you seen how Christmas is celebrated lately?" This time the elf made a mysterious gesture. "Look at this, you fat old fart—"

This time, the haunt and the elf found themselves in a gaily-lit concourse, a suburban mall filled with joyous music, dazzling decorations, towering displays, spotless storefronts, and crowds of anxious looking people milling from one ramp to the next with desperate expressions on their faces. Many of them were parents, escorting small children.

The children wore costumes of all kinds. The girls were mostly dressed as glittery princesses, ballerinas, winged fairies with plastic wands, mermaids, cowgirls, and witches—a lot of little witches. The costumes of the boys reeked of violence—there were killers of all kinds: gunslingers, terminators, ninja, turtles, batmen, supermen, vampires, and pirates. Many of the costumes seemed to be generic, probably purchased from the Disney outlet in the mall. At each store, tired-looking employees in gay apparel smiled wanly and passed out generic candies.

"*This* is Christmas now!" declared Bruce Kringle, pointing at a shop window showing Santa waving from a pumpkin patch, another shop window showing Santa riding on the back of a witch's broom, a third display showing the gay old saint passing out candy to costumed children at the front door of his north pole workshop, and a fourth one showing Santa sitting in the command seat of the starship Enterprise while a dozen little Vulcans in green uniforms smiled and waved.

"But this is not Christmas—" the spook whispered. *"It's only Halloween."*

"Yeah, that's another thing. We had to merge the holidays. Greater profit potential. Longer selling season. We had to drop the Christ angle, of course. Too tricky. But now, we get into high gear the first weekend before Halloween and we go straight through until the middle of January."

"What have you done?" The ghost demanded cavernously.

"Hey—this was all your idea," the elf replied strongly. "We pick up another five percent just with the post-season white sales. We've got a Japanese conglomerate funding the expansion, and we're looking at an eventual extension of the selling season all the way into Valentine's Day. Of course, the long-term goal is to make Christmas a year-round festival. You always said, you wanted people to have the spirit of Christmas all year round. Well, this is the first step—merchandising."

Brucie Kringle was about to explain about cost-leveraging and swing-markets, when suddenly a blood-curdling shriek of terror came from nearby.

"What's that?" asked the ghost.

"Uh—it's just a little extra innovation. Something to shake them up a bit. An idea we got from the amusement parks."

"Tell me!" demanded the wraith.

"Um—better yet, I'll show you." Shaking free from the bony grasp of the specter, the elf jumped down to the tiled floor, grabbed the haunt by its cobwebby robe, and dragged it toward a ramshackle-looking structure; it seemed to have been dropped in a heap in front of the entrance to the J. C. Penney's. A short line of people waited to enter. Periodically, a hunch-back would stagger out of the entrance, grinning and drooling, to wave another small group of people inside. As they watched, another terrifying scream came floating over the top of the walls.

"What's happening in there?" said the spook.

"It's called a haunted house. We're scaring the bejesus out of them. It helps to put them in a buying mood—"

The ghost and the elf joined the line—nobody paid them any undue attention. Shortly, the hunchback guided them into the interior of the fabricated structure, where they were treated to a series of tableaus portraying the worst excesses of vampires, chain-saw murderers, and back-alley abortionists. The rooms were decorated with coffins, skeletons, and big glass jars with strange-looking creatures floating in amber alcohol. They saw corpses, dismembered body-parts, and all manner of hairy little bugs and slimy snakes and worms. Deformed mutants leapt out of the walls at them. All around them, the costumed children laughed and shrieked in delight. Flashes of lightning and crashes of thunder punctuated the screams of the banshees and the moans of the zombies.

"See!" said the elf, when they found themselves out in the crush of the mall again. "It's all in fun. Nobody gets hurt. Okay, yeah—so it's not dancing sugarplums. But you were out of touch with all that sugary crap. Don't you know that sugar is bad for kids. This is more realistic—more educational. It's more in tune with the times. I mean, just look at yourself! Do you think you really represent the spirit of Christmas?"

The ghost was sorely offended. It stiffened to its full height. *"I am the spirit of Christmas!"*

"Right, sure," said the elf. "And just how jolly do you think you're going to make people feel, looking like that? At least we've got them laughing at their fears."

"Laugh at this!" said the spook, grabbing the elf by the arm and dragging him into a kitchen appliance store. He seized a cordless electric knife from the wall display—"No More Hassles Carving Your Christmas Turkey!"—and began hacking off the elf's arms and legs. With each cut, the ghost reminded the screaming elf who it had been when it was still alive. *"I used to*

*bust my ass all year long just for the privilege of work-
ing like a frenzied demon racing the dawn on what was
supposed to be the holiest night of the year. I had a
spastic colon, two crushed vertebrae, a double hernia,
hemorrhoids, varicose veins, swollen ankles, colitis,
phlebitis, an ulcerated bowel, psychosomatic impotency,
and chest pains strong enough to fell a horse. But I did
it for the children—and you've turned it into a
mockery!"*

By this time, the elf had been sliced into seven or
eight different-sized pieces, all of them wriggling excit-
edly on the floor, reforming and growing even as the
undead spirit watched. Each piece of the elf was becoming a whole new elf. Almost immediately, they were
leaping to their feet, chittering and squeaking in their
little high voices. "Now, there are eight of us! Eight little
Brucies! H'ray! We can have a daisy-chain!"

The ghost began grabbing them one by one, cackling hideously as it shoved them all into an industrial
size food processor. The elves screamed in agony as
the ghost punched up the *puree* setting. The many
shrieks of "I'm melting—" died away quickly, smothered by the sounds of tiny bones crunching into soup.

Before the fragments could reform into a Brucie-
blob, the ghost slid the whole pitcher into a brand-
new Radar-Range Microwave oven (with carousel and
browning circuits), and programmed it for popcorn.
Almost instantly, myriads of little gremlinlike creatures began spurting out of the pitcher, yelping and
sparking as the microwaves sleeted angrily through
their bodies. They cursed and swore, but their voices
were way too thin to be audible. Instead, they sounded
like the angry buzz of summer cicadas. Soon, they
began smoking and popping, vaporizing painfully
into nothingness.

Brucie Kringle, the elf, woke up in a cold sweat.
"Oh, my goodness—what a nightmare," he piped. Beside him, the naked Santa-droid rested heavily in the

feathery mattress. Bruce leaned over and mopped the cold sweat from his face with Santa's beard. "Whoa," he said to himself. "That was scary. I just gotta watch what I eat before going to bed. I think there was more gravy than grave in that one." And then his words stuck in his mouth. Fear grabbed his throat with icy claws.

Standing at the foot of the bed was a tall dark wraith; its ample girth and jolly posture revealed its nature even before it spoke. *"He he he!"* it cackled. *"Thank you, Bruce, thank you! You have taught me a very valuable lesson. The time is right for a whole new spirit of Christmas—you will get the Christmas that you deserve. And this time, my little sugar-plum, no one will ever be able to kill the Christmas spirit! Ho ho ho!"*

THE BEAR WHO FOUND CHRISTMAS

by Alan Rodgers

Alan Rodgers is a best-selling horror novelist.

Joey Robins' Dad got transferred that December from Newport News to San Diego.

Christmastime.

Transferred at Christmastime.

It was the worst news Joey had gotten in a year full of bad news: in a life full of rotten holidays and empty Christmases, moving cross-country at Christmas promised to make for the very worst Christmas of all.

Because Joey hated moving.

Hated it!

Hated it three days before Christmas when the green-and-white Bekins van rumbled up to the old house with the front porch and the window frames made out of wood. Hated it as the movers loaded all their stuff in their big truck for hours in the bright Virginia cold. Hated it as they closed up the back of the moving van and drove away with everything but the car and Joey and a couple days' worth of clothes.

And his parents.

And Bear.

They sure couldn't take Bear. Joey wouldn't let them—wouldn't no matter what.

Because the stuffed toy bear was his only friend, when you got down to it. They were constant companions, or as constant as circumstances allowed. Joey had

307

no other friends to speak of, partly because the Robinses never stayed anywhere long enough for Joey to get to know anyone. But partly, too, Joey's best friend was a stuffed toy bear because something in the boy was broken, busted good a good long time ago, and the plain fact was that Joey wasn't made right inside for getting on with people made of flesh and blood.

Maybe it was moving that broke him.

The Robinses moved at least three times every year, and sometimes more. That didn't make having friends impossible—not quite.

There were the kids back in Raleigh—after he'd been there six weeks they'd elected him president of his third-grade class for the month of March. But before April was over they'd moved again, to Boston. What good were friends like that when you could only have them for three months? And besides, the teacher really goaded the class into electing him. That wasn't fair, and when Joey was being honest with himself he knew it wasn't real.

Mom and Dad weren't much for company.

Dad was always working—till nine, ten, eleven o'clock at night. Even later sometimes.

Mom was even worse. Not because she wasn't home for him—she was *always* home—but because she liked to drink.

Mom got mean when she drank. When she was drinking Joey did everything he could to avoid her.

It isn't right—isn't *healthy*—for an eight-year-old (going on nine!) boy to love a Teddy Bear more than anything else in the world.

When his Dad had time to worry over Joey, he worried about the bear especially.

But it isn't right for anyone to be as alone as Joey Robins was, either, and loving a Teddy Bear like it was your Dad, your Mom, and all your friends is a lot better than not having anyone to love at all. Or so his father tried to reassure himself.

And maybe he was right.

Because Joey loved the bear so hard and long and pure, so deeply and so truly and so powerfully that the bear began to grow a heart.

Not that you could touch or feel or notice it. It was a spirit heart, made of ghost instead of flesh and blood. It didn't make him speak or sing or move or grant miracles. The only difference it made was that as Joey loved the bear, the bear began to love him, too.

It happens to toys sometimes. No one ever notices.

The first night on the road they stayed in a Ramada Inn in West Virginia. Joey slept badly that night—holding Bear tight beneath the strange musty sheets. And he dreamed. He dreamed that he could hear Bear's heart beating inside his soft felt chest.

They spent the second night in a motel at the near edge of East St. Louis, just a few miles from the Mississippi River.

Not just any hotel, in fact, but the Holiday Inn at the edge of what was once the Terrible Swamp—a haunted bog where all the best and worst things in the world used to wait hiding, gathering manna for the day of Armageddon.

Absolute truth: the Terrible Swamp was once a frightful place. But even the wonders of the world are nothing beside three crews of men with dozers, backhoes, and tractors; and now for years the Terrible Swamp has been no swamp at all but drained bottom land. The best and worst things are blown away on the dust. All that remain of them are ghosts and vapors.

It's been years, now, since anything unnatural wandered out from the swamp's east edge. Years since developers came in to build their shopping mall with its adjoining office complex. The hotel, the shopping mall, the offices—all of them share a peculiar reputation among those who travel often in the region—but they do a crisp and mundane business, and they serve their customers well enough.

As certainly they served the Robinses.

Joey was already asleep when his Mom shut off the television at ten o'clock. Riding in the car all day always made him tense and miserable, and when he finally got to bed he slept hard and deep from exhaustion.

Ghosts and vapors above what was once the Terrible Swamp.

Ineffectual ghosts; ephemeral vapors. Nothing that even a child might have reason to fear.

And still.

The holidays are special in their way, and there are plenty enough reasons why. And during the holidays (and especially on Christmas and Christmas Eve) the best and worst things are alive again, and they haunt the swamp that is no longer any swamp.

And they *do* things.

It was Christmas Eve when Joey's father woke at six fifteen in the morning, took his shower, loaded up the car. Which didn't wake Joey, though noises in the morning almost always did. By seven both his father and his mother were packed and ready to go and Joey still wasn't awake. And his father didn't have the heart to wake him.

So he carried Joey to the car, set him carefully on the back seat, and let him sleep.

He drove west into the morning, leaving Bear behind at the edge of what was once the Terrible Swamp.

Where the ghosts and vapors found Bear, lonely and abandoned.

And they touched him.

Even before they touched him, Bear could tell he was alone. He could feel it: as the Robinses drove west his tiny, ghostly heart felt Joey getting farther away. Bear pined for him, missed him more from three hours' absence than ever after an entire day at school.

At eight o'clock Bear felt the maid come into the room; felt her straighten things up and toss him onto her cleaning cart. He knew—dimly, vaguely—where he was.

And he knew where he was at eight-thirty when she took him off the cart and threw him into the garbage dumpster with the other trash. Bear landed in the dumpster and Joey woke to find him missing at almost the same instant; Bear heard Joey's screaming, somehow, a hundred and fifty miles away.

He knew from the sound of the scream that he was lost, and that Joey would never find him.

The knowledge and the hurtfulness of that burned at his ghostly heart, tickled it with tongues of fire, until finally it burst aflame.

The best and worst things, vapors that they were, could see Bear's heart afire. How could they not? It burned bright ethereal fire any ghost could see miles away.

And there in the hotel dumpster on Christmas Eve, the vapors *touched* Bear. And in a moment miracle light danced around his tiny mattress-fluff-and-cloth body, consuming and disgorging him—

—and a foul wind blew into the dumpster from the west—

—and there, at the edge of what was once the terrible magical swamp, Bear came to life.

Cloth eyelids he never had except in Joey's dream pulled closed then open, back and forth over his beautifully boöpic black plastic eyes. And his eyes somehow focused and brought him vision, even though they had no mechanism for sight inside them.

Bear flexed his arms, craned his head, marveled at the miracle of movement. Wondered at the sight of the sky above the dumpster. Stood up clumsily (for his legs, like his arms, ended in stumpy cylinders instead of paws), and peered over the rim of the dumpster.

And saw the mall.

The moment he saw the mall Bear knew that was where he had to go. It was a magical place, that mall, a place full of haunts and vapors and destiny—and besides, when he looked at the mall Bear's heart told him that Joey lay in that direction. If Joey was thataway, that was where Bear was going, no two ways about it.

There was a wide soggy field between the Holiday Inn and the shopping mall. Drained land that never drained completely, or someone would've built something big and expensive astride it—that land had *location,* and in real estate it's location location location, right? Except where it comes to building permits. Even in a county like this one, where folks cared so little about swamps that they let a developer come along and drain the Terrible Swamp which everybody knew was haunted—even here no architect or geologist would sign off on a permit to build on that field. Lots of developers tried, lots of times, but no one had managed it.

Anyway, because that field had never drained, the haunts and vapors never left it. Oh, they didn't thrive there the way they'd thrived in their salad days when the swamp was greenery moldering everywhere. After all, vapors despise the unimpeded light of day, and haunts abhor publicity (a thing no haunt who lived in plain view of a shopping mall could avoid). But they did well enough living deep down in the murky muck—and that was where they were when they first caught sight of Bear.

They would have followed him if they could. But it wasn't quite that simple: where in high summer that field was sopping wet and squishy, this cold December (meanest the state had seen in generations) the squishy field was frozen hard as stone.

If it were summer, Bear surely would have sunk

right through the muck and down to where the vapors lived. And if he hadn't, they'd've followed him easily enough. But it wasn't high summer, and Bear tromped right on across the frosty muck, slipping and sliding a little over the icy parts. Stumbled a couple times over knots of brittle grass. Across the field to the drainage barrier that separated the field from the mall's parking lot. Over the barrier, through the lot, right up to the entrance of the mall.

And the vapors—well, they could have busted the frozen mud above them and grabbed Bear fast enough. But that would have made the kind of broad-daylight spectacle no vapor ever wants to make. So instead they cut a slow and careful hole up through the icy crust, turned themselves invisible, and followed Bear as discreetly as they could.

It took some doing, but it wasn't any special effort. They would have risen out of the dirty ice soon enough regardless: the vapors always haunt that mall at Christmastide. They just love the decorations.

Rightly so. When the seasonal and promotional people decorate that mall, they spare no spectacle. Certainly the sight gave Bear pause.

Such decorations! he thought. Like a revelation to his Teddy Bear heart!

Bear recognized them right away, even though he'd never till that moment seen them. He knew just what they were, was all. Of course he did! He was a toy, and every toy God ever made knows Christmas.

It's Christmas! Bear thought, looking at the particolored ribbons, bows, tassels, bells, and foofaraws that hung above the mall entrance. *Joey's having Christmas!* He rubbed his chin. *If I could only find Christmas,* he thought, *I'm sure I'd find Joey there.*

That decided Bear, as much as he hadn't decided already: it was into the mall for him, and if he just looked around there long enough he knew he'd find Christmas.

Soon as he found Christmas, he'd find Joey right there.

But what he found inside the mall wasn't Christmas or Joey or anything of the sort.

What he found was looters.

It was looters that got Bear in, in a way: they were the ones who broke open the big locked doors that kept the mall closed. They broke right through them— busted the glass and walked on in, and never mind about the keys. Night watchman (sleeping not far from the broken doors) didn't even notice. Maybe his hearing aid was off?

Bear got to those busted doors, and for the longest time he stood trying to decide what to do. Shuffling his stumpy little legs back and forth through the shards of glass all over everywhere.

It's a robbery, Bear thought. *Somebody is stealing Christmas.*

When he thought of it that way, Bear knew he had to do something. Why, he couldn't let them get away with Christmas! If he did, he might never see Joey again!

So Bear charged in through the busted door, and straightaway he confronted the looters. It wasn't hard to find them; they clustered around the nifty toy store with the wide glass display window. Which kind of figured, since it was the only store in this wing of the mall that didn't have a chain-steel security door to protect it during the off hours.

That was one of the things about looters, and nobody had to tell Bear: they only went for the shops that made easy targets. Unless they had a lot of time, which they sure didn't right now, even if the night watchman was still snoring asleep by the broken door.

"You there!" Bear shouted as he approached the looters. "I say! Stop that this very moment!" Later he wondered where he got the nerve to say such a thing, but just then in the heat of the moment it was easy.

"Put those toys back where you got them or I'll be having words with your parents!"

Two or three of the looters looked up from their spoils to face Bear's harangue. "What the hell is that?" one of them asked in no particular direction, "some kind of a robot toy?"

And they all laughed and laughed, but Bear didn't see what was so funny.

"I'll have you know I'm an officer of the law," Bear said. This was a bluff, but it was the only bluff he could think of on short notice.

One of the looters cocked an eyebrow, snickered, " 'Zat so?" And they all started laughing all over again.

Bear harrumphed. This wasn't going right—not at all. "You're under arrest. All of you! Up against the wall!"

It was the wrong thing to say. Absolutely! It made the looters laugh harder than ever. And worse yet it inspired the biggest of them to grab Bear by the ear and lift him way up into the air!

"Put me down this moment!" Bear shouted. But nobody listened.

"You know," the big looter said, "I think this is one of them robot-things. I bet it's worth some money."

Several of the looters murmured in agreement.

"We get enough, we can have us an outrageous Christmas. Have a party for everybody in the building. Toys for all my little cousins!"

"Yeah, Wild Man. You get us a Christmas!"

"Let me see him, Wild Man. Careful with his ear—you don't want to rip it off! I bet I could fence him today if I hurry. One of them rich people would pay right out the nose for a robot toy like that one."

"Christmas!" one of the looters shouted, and they all shouted back at him: *"Christmas!"*

Shouted loud, too.

So loud they woke up the old man security guard,

who till that moment had slouched napping not far from the broken door.

"Oh hey-zoo, man," Wild Man said, "now look what you gone and done. Somebody ice that fogey before he gets us into trouble."

It was already too late: the security guard blinked, saw the broken glass scattered all sparkly across the polished terrazzo. Looked up to see the looters as he took a cell phone off his belt and started screaming bloody murder.

Wild Man screeched in frustration. Yanked Bear out of the hands of the fencer-looter, pulled him way up into the air, and threw him against a wall.

"You *broke* him!"

Bear bounced off the wall in time to see one of the looters lift a gun, aim at the security guard—

And saw Wild Man slap the gun from his hands. "It's too late, you moron. He already made the call. Shoot him now and we all go away for murder. You want to go away for murder?"

The looter looked—angry. *Really* angry. "Hey, Wild *Man*—you think I care? You tell me. You tell me what the hell I got to lose for murder! I ain't got nothing but what I steal! I don't got nothing to care about, and I don't care! That old man wants to try and take what I got away from me, I ain't going to let him—I swear I ain't!"

And before anyone could stop him, the looter shoved Wild Man away with his left hand as he lifted the gun with his right.

Took aim and fired, all in one continuous motion.

The bullet caught the security guard square in the neck, and blood went everywhere bright red all over everything already red from Christmas.

Before any of them could so much as say *Oh, no!*, there were cops all over everywhere. Sirens and flashing lights all over everywhere, the whole parking lot out there a big sea of splashing blue and red lights.

The looters took off into the mall, all of them but the crazy one with the gun who stood wild-eyed and stupid looking, staring at the broken security guard and talking to himself, talking to himself over and over again he said *I did it just did it I did it* and Bear wasn't sure what he meant.

Bear just didn't know what to do. But he was worried for the security guard, who was dead or dying or maybe he just needed help? Bear didn't know, so he went to the man's side and rested his head against the man's hand to comfort him.

The security guard was alive, the way it happened. He patted Bear on the head. "Sons of britches," he said. "Those stupid sons of britches what the heck kind of Christmas they think they're going to get trying to steal it like that? What the heck? Lootering like a bunch of wild men. You know that, Teddy Bear? I tell you that? I was like them once. I knew them. I was a boy and I wanted to steal because I didn't have no chance to get for myself." Two policemen and a medic knelt beside the guard and began examining his wounds, but the guard didn't pay them any mind—he kept right on talking, patting Bear on the head. "They wrong, Bear. I learned that in this life: you make it for yourself, or you don't, any way you go. I lived a life to learn that. All you ever do by stealing is make decent folks run away from you. Ain't no Christmas in that, huh, Bear?"

Bear shook his head, and the old man laughed.

"Don't you worry, old fella," the medic said "you're going to be just fine. You're a lucky man! Bullet missed your spine, your arteries. Didn't go anywhere near your throat."

And they lifted him onto a stretcher and carried him away before Bear so much as had a chance to say good-bye.

Joey woke just past Independence, Missouri, and right away he reached out to give Bear a hug.

He did that every morning.

Only this time Bear wasn't where Joey expected him to be. So Joey groped around and around, opened his eyes to see where he was in the moving car on the Interstate highway and how did he get there and where were they and he remembered they were moving again. And remembered going to be in the Holiday Inn last night, remembered checking into the hotel. As they pulled into the lot he'd looked at the empty field beside the hotel, looked at the mall beyond it, and he couldn't stop shivering no matter how he tried.

It was so cold. That's all it was; he couldn't help but shiver in this cold.

Bear was somewhere around here. Had to be! Joey rubbed his eyes, looked on the floor, looked on the seat, looked everywhere. . . .

Bear was gone.

Joey felt like a hand gripped his stomach and pulled it inside out—like someone pushed him off the world to send tumbling through hell.

"Bear!"

Joey screamed and screamed.

His mother—half asleep and half awake trying to wear away a hangover in the front passenger seat—woke startled and angry. She released the latch on her safety belt and came at Joey looking like a madwoman. Turned around, reached over the back of the seat, and just kept coming—grabbed Joey by the collar and shook him over and over as he screamed.

"What's your problem, you little wretch? What? *What?*"

And Joey screamed.

Till his father pulled the car off onto the shoulder of the road, put his hand on Mom's back and said, "No, no, you're hurting him. Can't you see that? Don't hurt the boy," and Mom let him loose a little.

"Bear," Joey said. "I can't find Bear anywhere we left him, I know." And then he started crying again.

He loved Bear so much.

Bear was the only friend he always had, and he wanted to start crying but he couldn't because he already was crying.

"It's all right, son," Dad said. He didn't miss a beat. "We'll go back and get him."

Mom didn't like that at all, but she didn't argue about it.

The mall opened twenty minutes after the ambulance took the security guard away. Rich people began to stream in right away. That was one of the things about rich people, Bear thought: they never missed a beat.

Mom said she needed coffee, so Dad pulled through the Dunkin Donuts drive through while they were off the highway turning back toward St. Louis.

Joey was relieved when he saw they were going through the drive through. Dad usually went in by himself, which left Mom and Joey alone in the car together—and Mom had it bad this morning. Scary-bad.

She got that way sometimes after she was drinking. Mornings especially—mornings after she drank too much were the very worst of all, but there were other bad times, too, bad times so bad Joey didn't like to think about them.

But no matter how bad it got, Dad never seemed to notice. Joey didn't understand why, but it had to do with the way Dad was always working to support them. Maybe he worked so hard his eyes got too tired to see, or maybe she was careful around him.

Or maybe he *couldn't* didn't see.

"Joey? Are you awake, son? Do you want a doughnut?"

"Oh," Joey said. "Sorry, Dad. Yes please."

All the way back to East St. Louis.

All the way back across the Mississippi.

The way Joey's father saw it, there wasn't a whole lot of choice. Even if it was unhealthy for the boy to get his love from a stuffed toy bear, it was better he got it there than no place at all.

He sighed, pushed the accelerator as he merged back onto I-80—eastbound, this time.

It wasn't good, working all these hours. Moving all this often. No matter how much they needed the money, no matter how much it mattered to his career, it just wasn't good. Never mind Belinda's drinking; the boy was strangling for want of attention, and that was Sam Robins' own fault as much as it was anybody's.

Something somewhere had to give—and soon. It just had to.

Rich people.

Rich people were a revelation to Bear. So many of them dressed so fancy rushing into the mall like a swarm of hornets. And every single one of them so—*rich*.

Those rich people are awful! Bear thought as he watched them. *They get their Christmas and they don't share it with no one.*

And wouldn't you know it? That was just when he began to notice how they really weren't miserly after all.

Joey went straight for the dumpster when they got to the Bottomland Holiday Inn.

Watching him, Sam Robins thought it was almost as though the boy had a homing instinct. How could he know just where to look? Wouldn't it be more sensible to start searching in the hotel room? Sam wanted to go to the manager, to ask the maid if she'd found Bear when she'd cleaned their room.

But Joey shouted, "C'mon, Dad. This way!" and how could anyone argue with that? It was Christmas Eve. This was no time for arguing with little boys.

The dumpster was empty, of course.

Joey climbed up the side of it, peered over the top, looked in—and the air seemed to rush out of him all at once.

"Gone."

Sam Robins bit his lip.

"We'll find him, son. Don't worry. I'll find the hauling company, see where the truck is headed—"

Joey shook his head. Turned, let go of the edge of the dumpster. Fell so limp to the ground that Sam was sure the boy would hurt himself—but he didn't. He landed on his feet, just fine, the boy was fine there wasn't anything to worry about.

"Bear isn't in any old garbage truck," Joey said. "I'd know if he was."

Sam shrugged. "If you say so, Joey."

But Joey didn't even hear; he was already moving. Around the dumpster. Up to the edge of the field that glistened with patches of ice. . . .

"Bear went to the mall," Joey said, pointing at the brightly-decorated cluster of buildings and towers that gleamed like some mercantile Camelot in the near distance. "We have to go to the mall."

Sam wanted to argue with the boy. He wanted to tell him that there was no way in hell they were going to tromp across all hell and creation looking for—what? A Teddy Bear that'd got up and walked away from the trash?

Bizarre, that's what it was. *Bizarre.*

"Joey—"

But when it came to it, he just didn't have the heart.

"What, Dad?" The boy stopped a dozen paces into the field, looked back over his shoulder and darn near broke his fool neck when his feet started to slip out from under him.

"Careful, son. That field is a mess."

Joey nodded. He looked resolute. "Bear's in trouble, Dad. We have to save him."

There wasn't any way to argue with him; the way the boy spoke, Sam Robins half believed what he said himself. He shook his head. Reached into the car, took the now-cold coffee from the holder in the arm-rest—he'd put it there after they'd stopped at the Dunkin Donuts back in Independence.

Closed his door and started after his son.

Trouble was Belinda didn't see things quite so straightforwardly.

"Where do you think you're going?"

She didn't ask the question so much as she growled it. She was hung over again—Sam could smell last night's liquor when she spoke.

"Going to the mall, Bel. With Joey."

Bel hissed. "Still looking for his *toy*?" Sam felt like an idiot when she asked the question that way. "He's eight years old, Sam. Let him grow up."

Sam Robins didn't know what to say. No—he didn't want to say it. Any of it. All the words that came to him were fighting words, and he hated fighting with his wife more than anything else in the world. "It's Christmas, Bel. The bear's important to him."

She made a sound like a sigh, but louder and meaner—all anger and frustration. "*I'll* take care of this." She got out of the car and stomped to the edge of the field. *"Joey!"*

The boy was already halfway across. He didn't look back when she called; maybe he didn't hear her.

"JOEY!"

Joey didn't hesitate, not for an instant. After his mother had screamed at him so loud—no way he didn't hear it. Was he ignoring her on purpose?

His mother must've thought so. Because she screamed in fury and took off running after him across the icy field. When she was close to him, she started shouting. "Urchin!" she shouted, "you little *urchin*!"

Joey didn't seem to realize she was after him until she was almost on top of him. He turned to glance back at them with a look on his face that said *What's keeping you?*—and saw his mother. His eyes bugged

THE BEAR WHO FOUND CHRISTMAS 323

open, and he made a startled sound, and he started to run like he was scared for his life.

Maybe he was right to be afraid for his life, Sam Robins thought. Belinda was a terror when she was angry.

Maybe I ought to do something.

He started after them even though he wasn't sure what kind of *something* the situation called for. It was a good thing he did. Because Bel caught Joey by his collar just as they reached a long slick patch of ice. Caught him and tried to haul him up off his feet—only the ice underneath her was too slippery. When she tried to haul him up, her own legs went flying out from under her.

And they both went sliding, rear-ends-first, across the icy field.

"Mom—"

"You miserable, miserable, *miserable* little brat . . . !"

Sam was only a few yards behind them, now—running along the edge of the ice as his wife and son slid across it. And there ahead of all of them—oh, Lord, look at it.

Enormous.

An enormous hole at the far end of the ice.

Four, five feet across and so deep Sam couldn't see the bottom standing damn near the edge of it.

How . . . ? What on earth would make a hole like that?

As his screaming wife and son slid over the edge, into the pit forever.

No. No no no no.

It didn't happen like that; Joey, Bear, Joey's Mom—any of you could have told you. The only one who saw Joey and his Mom go over the edge to meet their fate was Joey's Dad. And the only reason he saw it that way was dread: dread as he stretched himself to reach across the ice to catch his wife by the shoulder, to brace himself to brace them and hold them and love them and God, God, look, they were poised at the edge balanced on the edge and suddenly still, stock still on this side of eternity. . . .

Even from there—even standing holding Bel and Joey balanced at the edge of the pit—even from there Sam couldn't see the bottom.

Maybe that was a trick of the light.

Joey and his Mom didn't realize how they drifted right up to the edge of oblivion. She was too busy trying to get her hands around him to see where she was; Joey, confused and scared out of his mind, was trying like hell to get *away*.

"I've got you, got you now, you little wretch. And *I'm* going to teach *you* a lesson!" She was up on her knees, trying to get to her feet. She held the boy by the back of his collar and she shook him back and forth, side to side, shook him over the pit and twice she nearly dropped him.

Sam Robins couldn't take it any more. He didn't dare! What if she dropped the boy? What if she hurt him, shaking him back and forth like that?

He patted her shoulder with the same hand he'd used to stop them. Got her attention as firmly and quietly as he could.

"Bel," he said. And stopped. He had to stop; he didn't know what else to say. *Don't hurt my boy, Bel.* Was that what he had to say? She turned to face him, and when he looked at her—when he looked at his wife that moment it seemed to Sam Robins that he saw her as though looking through some vast ocean, murky in its deeps.

He took the boy from her, cradled him in his arms. All the while he kept looking into his wife's eyes. She was down there, wasn't she? Swimming through her life in a sea of alcohol so deep it clouded her judgment.

Sam winced at the image.

"Think about what you're doing, Bel. You don't want to hurt the boy, do you?"

Bel shivered.

"No, Sam," she said. "I don't want to hurt him."

When they got to the mall, they found the entrance cordoned off, surrounded by policemen.

Bear's in there, Joey thought. *I know he is. He came this way.* He tried to peer through the broken doors, the police crowding everywhere around the entrance—if he looked hard enough, he thought, he'd see Bear, and they'd find each other, and everything would be great!

Would be . . . no, not great. Not even fine. But at least he'd have Bear back, anyway, and that was important.

If Bear was in there someplace beyond the crowd, Joey couldn't see him. So he shrugged and went over to the bench where Dad sat sipping his coffee. There wasn't much of it left—he'd spilled half of it on his trousers running across the ice field.

After a while Mom came out of the Mexican restaurant where she'd gone, the moment that they got here. When she came out she carried a tall Styrofoam cup with a straw poking out the top. She laughed a little funny when Dad asked what was inside.

"Hair of the dog that bit me," she said. And laughed again.

Dad wasn't smiling. He looked worried.

Rich people embarrassed Bear in no time at all.

There he was, following them around and thinking how awful they were (being so *rich* and all) and two of them go into this little side-door cul-de-sac that turned out to be an obscure entrance to the mall. And wouldn't you know it? There was a derelict lying on the floor not far from the door.

A derelict! A wino! A vagabond!

Bear watched the rich people step gingerly around

the dirty gross stinky old man. He cursed them as they passed, and demanded that they give him money—

—and they opened their wallets right up and gave him some.

Can you beat that? They gave him money!

Rich people, giving away money!

You can't get rich giving away money!

The wino grumbled and cursed some more, but he took their money all the same.

Bear was so astonished he forgot all about the rich people. Walked right up to the derelict and asked, "Did they really give you money?"

The derelict rolled his eyes. Shook his head, blinked, looked Bear up and down four times.

Shrugged.

"What do you expect? They're rich. They can afford it." He sat up, shifted partly out from under his filthy coarse-wool blanket.

Bear didn't understand. "But why?"

The derelict was staring at him again—trying to figure Bear out. Maybe he thought Bear was a robot, the way the looters did?

"What the hell are you, anyway?"

Bear sighed. "I'm a Teddy Bear." Of course he was a Teddy Bear! What did the derelict think?

Just then two rich people wandered by, staring at them.

"Look at that!" one of them said to the other. "He has a Teddy Bear!"

"Awwwww...."

They both dropped wads of bills onto the derelict's blanket.

The derelict snatched up the money, counted it, and squirreled it away beneath his blanket. When he had it hid real good, he started swearing. "Tightwads!" he shouted. "Is that all Christmas means to you?"

The rich people scurried away from them.

"Tightwads ...?"

The derelict didn't answer. "You know, you're good

for business, Teddy Bear," he said. He snatched Bear off his feet, tucked him under his arm. "I like you." And he laughed, kind of quiet and greedy sounding.

Then a whole bunch of rich people came by, and another bunch right behind them, and more, and more, and all of them gave the derelict money. He cursed each and every one of them—though he was careful not to let anyone hear him curse before they'd given.

When the last of them were gone, Bear finally managed to get out from under the derelict's smelly armpit.

"I don't understand, mister," Bear said. "How come you say such awful things about them when they're all sharing with you?"

The derelict took a flask from his pocket. Opened it, took a good long drink, put it away.

He sat there for a long time—not talking, not moving. Staring away at the distance like he was trying to find words for an answer he knew but didn't understand.

"They never share the important parts," he said at last.

It made no sense to Bear at all. "What parts? What do you mean?"

The vagabond shook his head. "It's like—Christmas," he said. "Christmas is when you got all these people around who you've known and loved all your life. They never share that with nobody, no matter what. You ever notice that, Teddy Bear?"

Bear kept getting more and more confused. "But you don't know them," he said. "How could you share that if you never knew them?"

The derelict sighed. "That's the whole point, Teddy Bear. You can't give nobody Christmas if you don't know them well enough to love them. Those ol' rich people just don't know how to share."

"They don't?" Bear kept thinking about the money falling and falling out of rich people's wallets.

"I hate them, Teddy Bear. I do. Rich people never made a Christmas for nobody but them and theirs, even when they try. They owe me, Teddy Bear! They do! You know they do."

But all Bear could think was that there wasn't nothing rich people could do to make Christmas for anybody else. No matter even if they tried. And he thought: *The derelict knows that, too. And he hates that most of all.*

A few minutes after eleven o'clock the police finally took down their saw-horse barricades and cleared themselves from the mall entrance.

When they were gone, the Robinses went in hunting for Bear.

They didn't have much luck. No matter how they searched Bear was always just around the next corner, in the next store over, just out of sight behind the parti-bright Christmas decorations.

Joey!
Bear could feel him—closer. So much closer now! He was somewhere here inside the mall, wasn't he?
I've got to find him.
"I'm sorry," Bear said to the derelict. "I'm sorry, but my little boy has come to find me and I've got to meet him now."

The derelict coughed all long and phlegmy. When his throat was clear, he growled, "Sure you do, Teddy Bear. Heh heh heh heh." And he grabbed Bear all over again, tried to tuck him back under that stinky old armpit.

Which was exactly when the cavalry came over the hill. Thank goodness! Six, seven, maybe eight tall men with uniforms marked BOTTOMLAND MALL— SECURITY on the shoulder patches.

They went right up to the derelict and Bear. Stood over them patiently, like they were waiting for the derelict to realize something he ought to know already. Whatever it was, the derelict either didn't know it or didn't let on that he did—he just sat there huddled meek beneath his blanket, staring up at the security police.

"Time to move along," the tallest of them said.

The derelict ignored him.

This is going to come to trouble, I just know it, know it, Bear thought.

And sure enough, it did. The big guard said, "If we have to move you, we will."

The derelict ignored that, too.

The tall guard pointed toward the derelict, toward the door, toward three of the tallest guards.

As the derelict sighed and shook his head—

—as the guards bent to lift him—

—as the derelict turned into a vapor and vanished into the air.

Vagabond, blanket, stinkiness and all: the only things that didn't disappear were Bear and a big green pile of rich-people money.

Bear wandered out of the cul-de-sac as the security guards stood staring at the mound of money where the derelict used to be.

It *was* a mound of money, too. Money in a big old pile like rich people have. Only the derelict wasn't rich, was he? He was a derelict.

No, he wasn't even a derelict—just a ghost out of the swamp that wasn't here any more. Bear knew that.

Or at least he thought he did.

Anyway, none of the guards noticed when Bear wandered away. Even if they had noticed, it wouldn't have made any difference. No one trains mall security guards to cope with Real Live Teddy Bears walking around their malls; it just isn't in the manual.

Most people think that's for the best. Bear sure thought so.

By and large folks in the mall weren't much different from the security guards: they saw Bear and as-

sumed he was an animatron or a child in a costume
or—who knew what? And they'd point, and they'd
smile, and most of them let him be.

Oh, a couple of children followed him, or maybe
more than a couple. But soon enough their mothers
called them back to shopping, and Bear wandered free
to look for Joey.

But free or not, he couldn't find him. Because now
it was like—like Joey wasn't there, almost. Bear could
feel the boy in his heart, but here in the glitter and
the glamour that was Christmas, it was hard to tell
just exactly which direction Bear had to go in.

Partly that was because the mall was twisted and
partitioned and segmented in such a way that straight
lines hardly ever crossed the distance between people.
But partly, too, Bear was confused: the looters, the
vagabond, Christmas—there was something he had to
make sense of and it made no sense at all.

Whatever it was.

All the way up one long arm of the mall. Past the
Food Court. Down an escalator to the big rotunda at
the mall's center.

All the time he walked, Bear kept scanning the
crowd. Looking each and every little boy in the eye.
So many of them! Bear didn't know there were that
many boys in the whole world!

But no matter how many there were, none of them
was Joey.

There was a great big Christmas display in the rotunda. Santa Claus in a homey house, taking Christmas wishes; a big tin shack that said TOY FACTORY,
and inside there were Santa's animatronic puppet
elves, building toys—only Bear knew better, Bear
knew that they weren't *all* robots because a couple of
them waved and winked when they saw him coming—

Haunts and vapors! Oh, my!

—winked when they saw Bear coming.

Lots of kids and elves and Santas and haunts and
vapors everywhere. But no Joey.

No Joey noplace.

A *papier mâché* mountain towered above the toy factory and Santa's homey house. At its summit there was a sign:

ALL YOUR HEARTS DESIRE

And when he saw that, Bear knew it must be the most wonderful place in the world. *Joey!* He thought—*Joey's up there!*

Bear looked the mountain up and down, gauging the distance to the top. Wondering how he could ever climb so much *papier mâché*.

So tall, that mountain. Bear couldn't imagine how a Teddy Bear could ever climb such a thing.

It doesn't matter how tall it is. I've got to climb it. No matter what.

Bear didn't even stop to think about it: he tromped off the escalator, ducked under the wood-rail fence, and went straightaway to the mountain.

Climbed right up the base of it, tromp tromp tromp, till it got so steep he had to hold on with his arms and climb with his legs, hold and climb, hold and climb, almost like he was an inchworm pulling himself up the face of the mountain—

He almost made it.

Almost! He got so close to the summit he almost could have reached out and touched the word DESIRE.

And then something went wrong.

So wrong!

Bear pressed his left leg into the rough lump left and below the summit. Sidled over, reached up as he lifted his right leg—and lost his grip.

Just like that.

Bear lost his grip and went tumbling head over heels over head over heels right back to where he started, boombadoomba*thump*thump all the way back to where he started at the bottom of the hill.

Three times Bear climbed that hill, and three times

he came tumbling down on his cloth-and-fluff noggin.
If he'd been a real bear or a little boy the mountain
called ALL YOUR HEARTS DESIRE surely would have
been the end of him.

But he wasn't a real bear, and he wasn't a boy, and
he was *determined*! And a good thing, too, or he'd
never have made it to the top.

The fourth time he thought ahead. Looked the
mountain up and down until he figured it out: went
to the edge where the slope met the rotunda's back
wall. And bracing himself between the two he pressed
like a wedge—all the way to the top.

After the third time up and down the mall, Dad
decided it was time to try some phone calls. Joey knew
that was a waste of time, but he also knew there
wasn't any use arguing about it: Dad had that look in
his eye, and when Dad got that look there wasn't any
stopping him.

That meant Joey was alone with Mom. He wasn't
real comfortable about Mom—no way he could be
after what happened in the iced-over field. But here
in the mall she wasn't all that bad. Especially after
she stopped at the Mexican restaurant and had the
cup of dog hair.

Dog hair always made Mom all relaxed and happy.

It was better when Mom was happy, even if being
happy did make her weird some times.

Three, four times while they were in the mall she
stopped at restaurants to refill her cup. As the day
wore on, Mom got happier and happier.

Happy and weird, too.

"I want to go to the center again, Mom," Joey said.
"Is that okay? Going to where Santa is again?"

Mom smiled.

"Of course it is, Joey. Christmas Eve—wherever
you want to go, we'll go there."

But they didn't get there as directly as Joey would
have liked. Because halfway to the center they looked

up to see a store window Joey hadn't noticed before, and there was an amazing display in that window. Animatronics! Pirates so real you wanted to shout at them—a dozen, maybe two dozen pirates invading a quiet New Englandish town, chasing the people who lived there—rich people, from the way they were dressed—all over hell and creation.

In the center of the display there was a pirate queen all hungry and triumphant. In her left hand she held a boy by the scruff of his neck; in her right she held a bottle of rum, three quarters empty.

The boy twisted and struggled, scared out of his mind, but it didn't do him any good.

Joey gasped. He wanted to run. Wanted to hide! Wanted to run deep down into the center of the earth and hide buried there forever—

Mom didn't understand. She heard Joey gasp. She saw how he was shaking. And she said, "Joey, Joey what's the matter?" which Joey couldn't answer, of course. She looked back and forth and back from the display to Joey and back again, and even scared as he was, Joey could tell she was confused.

And then it sank through to her.

"Oh, Joey," she said, and Joey looked up to see her turning pale pale white as bed linen. *"Joey."* And she hugged him, and she started to cry.

In a moment they were both crying.

The way it turned out, ALL YOUR HEARTS DESIRE didn't lead to Joey at all.

Not directly, anyway.

It led up into some sort of maintenance access corridor for the mall. Bear didn't know whether to be confused or disappointed or just plain depressed: he felt like he was farther away from Joey than he had been in a long time.

I've got to keep searching, Bear thought. *I can't afford to let myself start meeping.* But he meeped anyway, meep meep meep meep, and if there'd been anybody there to see they surely would have said *Aw, look at the poor little Teddy Bear, isn't he* so *sad!* And the last thing Bear wanted was for people to feel sorry for him like that. After all, he had his pride.

Anyway, Bear kept searching, even if he did meep. Down this hall and around the next; out this ramp and along the access way. . . .

And by and by he wasn't in the mall anymore.

Oh, it wasn't that he'd left it, or fallen through creation into the primordial salad days of the Terrible Swamp or anything like that. He just wandered into the next building over—the office tower and hotel complex attached to the mall.

And the more he wandered, the deeper and deeper he got into government territory.

Government territory! Some of the most dangerous places known to man and beast are run by the government—and they're dangerous to Teddy Bears, too. Oh, it wasn't like anyone had ever *meant* that tower to become infested with government. But the office tower never managed to attract much in the way of real paying tenants, and the government—which had underwritten the tower's construction with a triple-rated bond issue—ended up owning the damnable place by default.

Government didn't mind that at all, the way it worked out: there were always more programs to house, and that meant new offices to house them.

Like these offices that lined the corridor where Bear stepped through a maintenance door into a carpeted hall. Some of the most diabolically insidious government offices ever to house a program: the East St. Louis Official Government Christmas Office—an enterprise intended to see to it that each and every one of the county's thousands of residents *got theirs* at Christmas time.

Bear got his, all right. They gave it to him at the office.

*   *   *

The door said OFFICIAL GOVERNMENT BUSINESS, and it looked like it meant it.

Bear saw those words and felt afraid. He was in the wrong place, somehow. Joey wasn't in any government program! He didn't have any government business!

And he knew right from the start that he wasn't going to find any Christmas behind a door marked OFFICIAL GOVERNMENT BUSINESS.

It was time to turn around and go back, Bear thought. Time to admit he'd made a wrong turn someplace and retrace his steps. . . .

Which was when Bear stumbled into the door, of course. One minute he was turning around on his stumpy little legs; the next he was going down *crash* face first into the door.

And wouldn't you know it? The door fell open.

The first thing he saw was the big green Christmas tree and all those blinky lights. So beautiful! So scintillant! Then he saw the signs: CHRISTMAS FOR EVERYONE! UNCLE SAM LOVES YOU! A YEAR WITHOUT CHRISTMAS IS LIKE A YEAR WITHOUT BASEBALL! As soon as he saw them, Bear knew he must've died and gone to heaven.

The tree was artificial, but never mind that. Offices have safety regulations, many of them justified.

Bear heard someone clear his throat, and turned left to see an aging man dressed in a limp gray suit. "May I help you?" the man asked. He didn't look very happy.

"I'm here for Christmas," Bear said. "Do you really have Christmas here?"

"We certainly do," the man said. He nodded toward a sign on his desk: EAST ST. LOUIS OFFICIAL GOVERNMENT CHRISTMAS DESK. He bent down, took papers from a drawer, stood, and offered them to Bear. "Fill out these forms and it's yours."

Bear looked at the forms. Oh but there seemed to be so many of them! "But I can't," Bear said, clapping his stumpy arms against one another. "I don't have no hands, no toes, no pencil, no way." He hung his head. He felt so ashamed. "I'm sorry."

"Ah-hah! A challenged client!" The government Christmas administrator clapped his hands. "We know just how to meet your challenge, little bear. Heh heh heh."

Before Bear could ask him what the heck he meant by that, a young woman materialized (out of nowhere, it seemed, but Bear knew that couldn't be) just a little to the right of the gray man. She smiled and wrinkled her nose when she saw Bear. He liked her right away.

"Miss Simmons here will fill out your forms," the gray man said. "If you have any questions, she can answer them."

Miss Simmons smiled again. "Pleased to meet you, Teddy Bear."

The gray man opened a filing cabinet and began sorting papers. After a moment it was like he wasn't even there.

Bear didn't know what to think. Something—just wasn't right. There was something strange about the way things were going, even if he did like Miss Simmons.

"First," she said, "I need to know your name."

"Bear."

She frowned. "Is that your first name or your last name?"

"It's the only name I've ever had."

Miss Simmons shook her head. "You've got to have two names," she said. "They won't know how to file you if you don't."

"But—"

"I'll just call you Theodore—Theodore Bear. Teddy, get it?" Miss Simmons giggled. "That's a good name for a Teddy Bear."

"But—"

"Occupation?"

Bear blinked. "Ock what?"

"Your *job*. What do you do for a living?"

Bear shook his head. "I've never had a job. And I don't know much about living."

Miss Simmons *hmmmm*ed. "I'll list you *unemployed,*" she said.

Bear didn't like the sound of that at all.

"Residence?"

"I live with Joey," Bear said. "We're in the middle of moving."

"Just like I thought," Miss Simmons said. "You're homeless!"

"*I am not!*" Bear was flabbergasted. "Where do you get off saying such a thing . . . ?"

Miss Simmons rolled her eyes toward the heavens. Shook her head. "Don't worry about me, Theodore," she said. "I'm *simpatico*! I *want* to make sure you get a Christmas!"

Bear didn't like it at all. Not one bit! But he didn't know how to fight it. So he went along as best he could. In a moment they were finished with the form, and Miss Simmons took it to the Christmas Administrator, who still stood peering into his files. They whispered to one another, and whispered some more, and in a moment Bear could hear them giggling delightedly.

"You qualify, Teddy Bear! You qualify for Christmas!"

Bear didn't know what to say. "Gee, really?" He tried to smile. "Gosh."

Whistles sounded, bells clanged. The lights on the Christmas tree went flash flash flash, bright as the sun. Miss Simmons looked so happy. Even the gray Christmas administrator seemed to beam as he handed Bear his Christmas.

"You're so lucky, Theodore. It's official! You've got an Official Government Christmas!" She stepped around the counter carrying a pale brown bundle. Stooped and handed it to Bear.

Bear knew it was wrong.

The moment he saw it he knew it was wrong. No—

he'd known since he'd first seen the office. It wasn't right. It wasn't even possible!

Official Government Christmas came in a carefully wrapped box that didn't look like Christmas at all. No bows or bangles or decorations; just a drab brown box with drab brown wrapping. And even more than it didn't look right, the box didn't ... *feel* right. Never mind the way it felt in his hands—never mind how it was a skimpy little box that didn't weigh much and looked kind of cheesy—when Bear took that box it made his heart feel *wrong*.

Wrong wrong wrong.

Just plain wrong.

There was a label square on top, right in the middle, but it didn't say FOR BEAR, like he expected. It said DO NOT OPEN UNTIL CHRISTMAS.

Bear tried to hold his tongue. He really did. After all, the government Christmas people meant well— Bear knew they did. And it wasn't right to say mean things to people trying to do you a favor.

But it finally got to be too much for him.

"This isn't Christmas," he said. "It isn't right."

The gray man was aghast. "It certainly is," he said. "Open it for yourself and see."

"But it says not to open it till Christmas!"

"Never mind that," the administrator said. "You go ahead and open your Christmas. You're entitled."

It wasn't easy for Bear to open the package. It was thoroughly, carefully wrapped, and all Bear had for hands were the stumpy ends of his paws. But he finally managed to do it—and when he did he surely wished he hadn't bothered. Because the *Christmas* there inside that box was even worse than he imagined: a dried out ham sandwich and a couple of cut-along-the-dotted-lines paper dolls.

It wasn't much as Christmas presents went. And it didn't make him *feel* like Christmas, either—things with real Christmas in them helped him see the way toward Joey, and nothing in that box made Bear think of Joey at all.

Bear found himself talking before he could stop himself again. "Not much of a Christmas," he said. And right away he felt so lousy!

Felt like an ingrate.

"Well!" the gray man said, "I never!"

Bear brightened. "Exactly!" he said. "I don't know where you people get these weird ideas! You can't get Christmas from nobody you don't know! Not if you don't love them, at least a little! Haven't you figured that out by now?"

The gray man scowled.

"I'll have you know we give a very fine Christmas around here!"

Bear shook his head. "Christmas is about love," he said. "Official government programs don't love nobody."

Bear turned and marched out the door without looking back. Didn't even take his Christmas with him!

And maybe he should have turned a moment to look over his shoulder. For as he left, the gray man and Miss Simmons and the Christmas tree and the holiday slogans pasted to the walls and everything— every single solitary trace of Christmas inside the office turned to vapor and vanished in the air.

When they got to the center of the mall, Mom said she needed a rest. Joey didn't object; now that he was back in the middle of things he didn't know which way to go any more.

Mom got herself another drink—something with a little kick this time, she said—and they sat in the padded seats by the Christmas fountain where water misted on them every time the heater vents kicked in.

Mom didn't say much. She looked so sad ... Joey felt bad for her. He wondered if he ought to comfort her. Was there something he had to say? Something he

had to do? *You need to stop drinking, Mom.* But he
knew that if he said that she wouldn't hear. Joey told
her lots of times. She never heard. She couldn't see;
she didn't know what it was like to be with her when
she was hung over. Sometimes, late at night when Dad
was sound asleep and Mom was drinking all night
long—sometimes she got mean when she was drinking,
and she'd wake Joey up. . . . Those were the worst
of all.

She never remembered those times. She never listened when he tried to tell her what was wrong.

Scary.

So scary.

Joey didn't think his Mom would ever hear.

He looked out across the fountain pool at Santa's
homey house with all the kids inside saying what they
wanted for Christmas. Looked at the Toy Factory and
all the merry elves building all that cool cool stuff.

Bear was somewhere—not far from here. Joey had
a feeling that he'd come this way—maybe not too long
ago. But where was he? Which way had he gone?

"Mom? Mom, I want to go look for Bear. Okay?"
But Mom was passed out and snoring, sound asleep
with her mouth wide open.

Poor Mom. She looked so sick when she slept that
way. It always worried Joey.

She'll be okay, Joey thought. *I'll go look for Bear.
She'll be better when I get back.*

But he didn't know if she would be.

Bear was so depressed. Everything he did to look
for Joey only seemed to lead him farther and farther
away! He didn't know what he had to do. Didn't know
anything but how rotten he felt.

So rotten. Rotten rotten.

He leaned against a wall. Slumped down to the
ground limp like a rag doll—so depressed he almost
was a rag doll.

Sat against the wall meeping like a Simpery Sally

doll, meeping right out loud, *meep meep meep meep* so sad little fluff tears rolling down his cheeks.

"Joey," Bear said, and he meeped some more. "Joey Joey Joey Joey."

But there wasn't any way Joey could hear him.

Joey went to Santa's homey house to look for Bear. No Bear there, of course. Just a long long line of Christmas kids waiting to sit on Santa's lap and tell him what they wanted.

"Santa," Joey called out from the far side of the velvet rope, "have you seen my Bear? My Teddy Bear? He's just called Bear, is all. You'd know him if you saw him."

Santa laughed, ho ho ho, all false cheeriness and cigarette breath Joey could smell from here. "Can't say I have, little boy. Should I bring you a new bear for Christmas?"

Joey wanted to hit him! How dare that old Santa Claus act like Bear was just some throw-it-away-and-get-another-one toy? Bear was *special*. Joey loved his Bear. "No, Santa. I don't want any old bear. I want *my* Bear."

Santa went ho ho ho again and waved. Joey turned and walked away.

Wasn't any way that old Santa was ever going to understand anyhow.

Belinda Robins stirred in her sleep. Somewhere way back in the back of her head she had a notion something was wrong. That something was missing. But in her daze she couldn't think what it might be, and anyhow she felt too sleepy to wake up.

The elves weren't even people, weren't alive, weren't nothing but mechanical toys. And even so they were more help than cigarette-breath Santa was.

Joey stood by the fence-rail at the edge of the elf display, not far from the base of the mountain ALL

YOUR HEARTS DESIRE. He watched the big toy elves tapping away in their factory. What was it like, he wondered, to be a toy elf like that, tap tap tap all your life away only coming out for Christmas ... so boring almost all the time but think what it must be like at Christmas, all the time you were out in the world and working it was Christmas and you worked on toys, no one ever screamed at you or hurt you. Everybody always paid attention to you. The only bad part was Bear—elves don't have anybody like Bear.

God knew Joey needed Bear.

Bear.

Joey sure missed Bear. He loved his Bear.

"Elves," Joey said—not even thinking how they were toys and how it didn't make sense to talk to toys who couldn't hear—"Elves, have you seen my Bear? I sure do miss my Bear."

And the tallest elf looked up from his work, smiled, and winked.

"Up the mountain," the elf said. He pointed at the sign up top of the hill that read ALL YOUR HEARTS DESIRE. "But be careful! He had a heck of a time getting up there."

Sam Robins wasn't getting anywhere.

Half an hour, forty minutes' worth of phone calls—tracking down the number for the Holiday Inn East St. Louis, Bottomland. Then back and forth through the switchboard, switching from line to line to line—first the hotel manager, then the head of housekeeping, who passed him to that morning's housekeeper. Who didn't remember seeing any Teddy Bear—didn't even remember cleaning out the room they'd stayed in.

Sam got sarcastic after a few minutes. "What do you think I am, crazy? You think I imagined staying at your hotel?"

The housekeeper didn't say a word. She just transferred him to another extension. Three rings and a young man answered the phone: "Front desk. Can I help you?"

"My name is Sam Robins. We stayed at your hotel last night. My son left behind his Teddy Bear—it's very important to him. Can you tell me if you've seen it?"

"Just a minute, Mr. Robins, while I look up your room number...." And the young man coughed. He sounded surprised. "Mr. Robins, we don't have a record of your staying here last night. Are you sure you have the right hotel?"

Sam Robins screamed.

He knew damned well he had the right hotel.

Joey should have thought a little before he started up the mountain ALL YOUR HEARTS DESIRE. He should have looked how it got *so* steep up there at the top. He should have listened to the haunted elf who told him to be careful. He should have used some common sense!

But he was a boy, and that's the trouble. Boys don't have much common sense where it comes to acts of bravery and daring. Some say they have none at all— and it's hard to argue otherwise.

Joey went straight up the face of ALL YOUR HEARTS DESIRE, but he never made the summit.

Sam Robins was at his wits' end with the runaround from the staff of the Bottomland Holiday Inn. It was no use talking to those people—they were off in a little world of their own someplace, completely out of touch with reality.

So he called the hauling company, to find out where they'd taken the hotel's trash that morning.

No runaround there. The dispatcher at the hauling company knew exactly the hotel, exactly the driver, exactly the destination of the hotel's trash.

Trouble was when the trash dispatcher looked up

the schedule and found that they'd picked up the Holiday Inn's trash two days before.

They weren't coming back till after Christmas.

No way the haulers got Bear.

Joey got almost all the way to the top before he lost his nerve.

I haven't got a grip, he thought as he tried to reach out to touch the word DESIRE. *If I move another inch, I'm going to fall.*

And he hugged the wall for all he was worth. And he bit his lip.

But he didn't cry. Joey never cried, not even at the very end.

The whole world was beginning to seem confused and unreal to Sam Robins. He wanted—to get back to work.

Christmas, and he wanted to get back to work. That was the trouble, wasn't it? Work was sane; it was predictable; it was a place where you saw something wrong and you applied yourself and it began to *work.* That was why Sam Robins worked so hard, so long: because he liked it. Because it made sense.

Because it worked.

The mall made no sense at all. Nothing made any sense since—since. . . .

Nothing made any sense at all since that truck had nearly run them down on the road through Kentucky.

The missing Teddy Bear, his son starving for time and attention, his wife gradually metamorphosing into an alcoholic—what the hell could Sam Robins do about problems like those?

Not a damned thing, he thought. His life was a wreck and he was sure he couldn't do a solitary thing about it.

And wouldn't you know it? That was exactly the moment his beeper went off.

*   *   *

Joey thought about trying to ease himself back down the mountain. Twice he even tried to do it—and nearly killed himself.

He was stuck, no two ways about it.

I've got to call for help, that's all. Hold tight and shout Help! *and someone will hear. And when they do, they'll get a ladder up here to me.* Joey knew about malls. He knew they had to be able to cope with kids getting in the wrong places, people having accidents, problems like that.

They had to have a ladder.

"Help!" he shouted. "Help help!"

And he waited and waited for someone to reply, but he didn't hear a solitary sound.

The vapors touched Belinda Robins' heart as she sat snoring on the padded bench.

She woke sudden and sober not long afterward. More sober than she'd been ... she couldn't remember when she'd felt so clear, so awake and aware.

And she woke knowing something was wrong, too.

At first the clarity and the sense of wrongness confused her, and she tried to remember the touch and what had touched her—but those things were gone like haunts in a dream. There wasn't any finding them, and as the moment passed, the vestigial memory of *touch* faded, too.

And it finally came to her what really was wrong.

"My little boy! Oh, dear God I've lost my little boy—"

And then she saw her son hanging in the air precarious as a doomed cartoon. She didn't think how she might distract him if she wasn't careful. Didn't think about the crowd, the scene, didn't think about anything but her son. And she screamed: *"Joey!"*

But the boy didn't even seem to hear her.

Bear curled up into a ball so no one could see him meeping—not that there was anyone in the maintenance corridor to see.

Curled up so tight his face pointed right into his own chest.

Which meant he was looking at his heart.

And when Bear looked into his heart he saw all sorts of things—sadness, happiness, love, fear . . . and Christmas.

And Joey.

Bear saw Joey in high panic clinging to the mountain ALL YOUR HEARTS DESIRE.

"Joey! Oh, no!" Bear shouted, "No, look, look he's going to fall!"

And he took off running like a bear out of hell.

Sam Robins turned off the beeper, ignored it. There wasn't time for a long harangue right now—it was too late. And whoever the hell it was who wanted to talk to him this late on Christmas Eve wouldn't have the courtesy to be brief—no more than whoever it was had the courtesy to let business wait till the holiday was over.

Or maybe he'd answer after he checked in with Joey and Bel.

Maybe not.

Maybe whoever it was with the wonderful manners ought to take the beeper and the job and bury the both of them in a deep dark hole.

Joey kept shouting, but nobody heard.

"Help!" he shouted again and again. "Help, help!"

Only silence answered.

Deep dark shadowy silence like a sound absorbed by ceiling tile, never to reverberate.

So hot and sweaty up there by the vents. And Joey even hotter because he was scared out of his mind. Shouting and shouting at the top of his lungs and nobody heard and the effort and the fear and the heat all combined made him flush and sweat.

And the sweat made it harder and harder to hold on.

*   *   *

Sam Robins rounded the corner by the benches and saw his wife standing at the base of the artificial mountain, screaming hysterically. Screaming and terrified and for the first time in God knew how long she looked sober. Sam looked up to see what she was screaming at—

And saw Joey.

Joey clinging for dear life to the *papier mâché* mountainside. Clinging and slipping, bit by bit—

—as the insistent beeper began bleating again, shrill and insistent—

—the boy slowly falling—

Sam Robins didn't look; didn't think, didn't hesitate: he panicked.

Threw the beeper into the fountain, and ran to catch his son because it was the only hope he had—

Joey still clung to the mountain when Bear got to him.

Just barely.

"Joey," Bear said, "Joey, take my hand."

And somehow Joey heard him, despite the way he was so obviously too scared to hear anything but anything at all.

"Bear."

And Joey reached up to take Bear's stumpy handless arm as Bear reached out over the edge to help him. . . .

Only the thing neither one of them thought about was gravity. And physics.

And the way a five-pound plush-toy-bear doesn't weight enough to anchor and lift a sixty-pound boy over the summit of a *papier mâché* mountain.

The way Joey took Bear's arm and instead of Bear lifting him up, the effort yanked Bear right over the edge and sent him tumbling to the ground.

And without two arms to cling to the face of the mountain, Joey lost what little grip he had.

And fell splat to the ground and broke his neck and died.

Sam Robins saw his son's life pass before his eyes in a flash: that fast, quick as a flash and the boy hit ground in the tiny bit of empty floor between Sam and Belinda Robins. Hit ground *whump!* like a rock padded with flesh, and Sam looked down to see his son pale and still and bleeding bubbly blood from the mouth and nose. . . .

No no no no. . . .

No!

No no no no it didn't happen like that.

Oh, Sam Robins saw what he saw. Joey fell, but he bounded three times against the mountainside as he dropped. That slowed him down a lot. And when he finally did hit bottom, he landed on top of Bear.

Bear probably saved his life, the way he cushioned Joey's landing.

Or maybe something else saved Joey's life.

Maybe . . . maybe it was the haunts. The vapors! Haunts and vapors everywhere all around them in the mall, Joey could see them now opening his eyes to see his Mom, his Dad both hysterical and terrified; see the mall around them haunted—

No.

The mall wasn't haunted.

The mall was a haunting. Look, look now at the shops, the decorations, the customers all dissolving like mist on a sunny morning, and all there was anywhere around them was Mom and Dad and him and Bear and the abandoned half-built skeleton of a shopping mall.

Not a shopping mall at all, in fact: a construction project abandoned years ago because everything that ever could have sabotaged its completion came to pass.

Not a mall, not a swamp, nothing at all but a relic

haunted by all the best and worst things, waiting for the second coming.

And all of that evaporating now, sifting half a world away to that place not here nor there—the place where haunts and vapors wait to watch our world most all the year but Christmas.

Nothing in the abandoned shopping mall. Nothing but Joey and Mom and Dad and Bear as Mom and Dad both stooped to lift him, to hold him—

Joey tried to say, *It's okay, really, really it's okay. I only bit my tongue, I'm fine,* but no one heard him.

They took him to the hospital emergency room that night. Joey tried to talk them out of it, but no way they would listen.

Mom and Dad, neither one of them ever had much inside for listening.

But at least they were there—really there and paying attention.

And they kept paying attention, too, no matter how they didn't listen. The fall, the mall, the Christmas—it was a wake up call for Mom and Dad. After that night they couldn't ever blind themselves to Joey. Not completely.

Oh, they didn't suddenly turn perfect or anything like that. Dad still worked too late more often than he didn't, and even after Mom quit drinking she still went to extremes.

But there's a distance between indulgence and addiction, between abandonment and inattention—and in that space there's room for common sense. And so long as common sense holds sway, human nature rarely boils toward abuse.

Bear and Joey got along famously for years. They had all kinds of tumults and adventures, and all of them had happy endings.

Mom and Dad never did see how Bear was alive. Joey never tried to tell them. Sometimes he couldn't believe it himself. Worse, as he got older he stopped seeing it himself—and the day came, when Joey was seventeen, when he began to think that maybe he was mistaken, and Bear was nothing but a toy after all.

Maybe those adventures were nothing but his dreams.

And maybe they were. Does it really matter? The important thing isn't believing or not believing. The important part was how he loved Bear and Bear loved him back.

Nothing ever changed that.